SETTING ACCOUNTS

Madelyn
Who knew that buying
the first novel would
lead to this.
Hope you enjoy it.

M° Ga
11/200

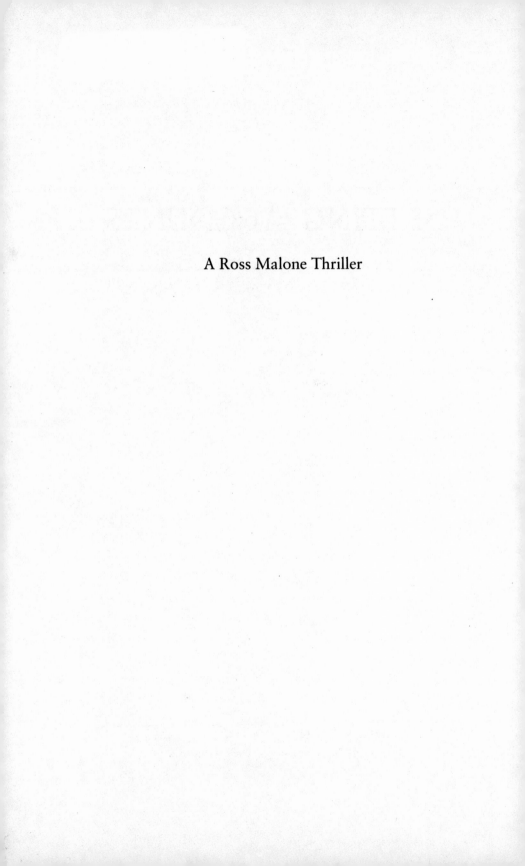

A Ross Malone Thriller

SETTING ACCOUNTS

A Ross Malone Thriller

Jeffrey McGraw

Writers Club Press
San Jose New York Lincoln Shanghai

Setting Accounts
A Ross Malone Thriller

All Rights Reserved © 2000 by Jeffrey McGraw

No part of this book may be reproduced or transmitted in any form or by any means, graphic, electronic, or mechanical, including photocopying, recording, taping, or by any information storage retrieval system, without the permission in writing from the publisher.

Writers Club Press
an imprint of iUniverse.com, Inc.

For information address:
iUniverse.com, Inc.
5220 S 16th, Ste. 200
Lincoln, NE 68512
www.iuniverse.com

This is a work entirely of fiction. Any similarity to actual events or persons living or dead is purely coincidental.

ISBN: 0-595-12951-X

Printed in the United States of America

For John who gives me another reason to be proud
every day of his life

"When in doubt, have two guys come through the door with guns."

Raymond Chandler

Acknowledgements

To Mom and Dad, Dan and Andrea, Tom, and Marianne and Tom for their support. To my best friend, Robert Barrow for helping me to learn that edit really is a four-letter word. To Linda Fullan for her tireless reading and rereading of this manuscript, always to the right, never to the left. To Rebecca Fullan for helping me to see that dreams are for those that dare. To Casey Jessup, a jewel if there ever was one. To my favorite WeeBoniLas who pointed out the obvious in the book which I was too myopic to see. And as always, to Rosemary, forever and then some.

-I-

"Haven't you left for the airport yet?" Her voice was a delicate blend of sweetness, light and insistence.

"Sue, how can I get to the airport when I am spending most of my time answering the telephone?" I said.

Demur arrived with an audible sigh. "I'm sorry Ross. I haven't really called that much, have I?"

"Six times since eight o'clock this morning," I said.

"And it's now 8:15," said Sue Abilene.

"Exactly," I said.

"I'll see you when you get to D.C." Twelve hundred miles away the phone line went dead. Quickly, I snatched up both of my soft-sided suitcases made of recycled parachute silk, dyed steel Grey. When I had purchased them, I wondered why this fabric was no longer good for parachute duty. The answer didn't comfort me. The white frosted glass insert in my office door proclaiming it the domicile of Ross Malone, private investigator, rattled mightily as I kicked it shut. Next stop was my Jeep Cherokee, then off to the airport to see my sweetie before the phone rang again.

My one and only, Dr. Sue Abilene, she of the sweetness and light tones, had been living in our nation's capital for the better part of the last six months in order to participate on the President's Task Force on Emergency Room Medicine.

It was designed to find ways to cut costs in this managed care world without cutting the quality of care or pandering to the AMA. Plus, it would no doubt help get the requisite presidential library built after that final journey on Air Force One.

The telephone banks in this city storefront that made up the crisis hotline, 4HOPE stood silent sentry duty, ready to serve at a moment's notice. Of the fifteen black desk model phones, only four were manned. But it was early in the morning. As the day turned into night, more people would be on more phones looking for a friend in the darkness. I rented offices in the rear of the storefront for my business as a private detective. Dana Glenn, director of 4HOPE and my landlord, said it was a status symbol to be in the only business in the neighborhood with a real private eye on site. I agreed. Still, she wouldn't lower the rent, even though my presence probably raised all of the property values in the area.

Just as my bags landed in the back of the Cherokee, the cell phone in my pocket rang.

"Please tell me you are at the airport in Washington," said the voice I loved waking up to.

"Sue, the plane can't land until it takes off. My flight doesn't leave until ten. Patience is a virtue."

"I love you."

"I love you as well." For some reason I refrained from saying, "I love you too." It always seemed so dismissive. "Now I'm going to hang up, check the office one last time then step on the gas to Hancock International Airport. Put your dancing shoes on, kiddo. We've got a lot of catching up to do. Bye."

A flicker of movement in my Cherokee's sideview mirror caught my attention. I turned to face the intruder, just in case I needed to maneuver.

"May I help you?" I said.

In his middle sixties, white hair cropped close enough to resemble chalk dust, the man who stood before me topped off at about 5'7", 5'8" on a good day with his weight evenly distributed, though there wasn't much to distribute. Only the black and blue skin puffed up and around his left eye stood out from this grandfatherly person you might have seen on a Hallmark greeting card designed by Norman Rockwell. His hands shook intermittently, and were sandpaper brown and tattooed with age spots. It didn't seem like nerves, perhaps a medical condition.

"Are you Ross Malone?"

"Yes. And you are?"

He extended an unsteady hand. I didn't let it linger. "Trask, George Trask. And I am here because I need your help."

"Does it have anything to do with that black eye?"

Shame clouded his features in the form of a deeper hue to his already ruddy complexion. "Yes." His voice, not exactly booming to begin with, shrank even further. His eyes were downcast, and focused on the asphalt of the parking lot. "Someone wants to drive me out of business. I need you to find out who is doing this and stop them."

"Mr. Trask, I must tell you that I am preparing to go out of town for a few days. I couldn't possibly take your case."

"Don't say no until you hear me out. Please Mr. Malone, I have nowhere else to turn."

A slight nod of my head, followed by a folding of my arms, and leaning against the Cherokee told him he had an audience for at least another moment or two. "Okay Mr. Trask, I will at least listen."

"I don't know where to start."

In my line of work that sentence was as common as saying the check was in the mail. "Try the beginning."

"All right." He cleared his throat, then popped in a throat lozenge that appeared to be the last one in his blue and white tin. "I own a little shop down in Armory Square. My wife and I bought it right after I got out. It isn't much. We did most of our own baking, have a regular clientele and try to be good neighbors. My wife even named it, 'Home Sweet Home' because she wanted our customers to feel welcomed."

He stared off into the distance, reliving memories I could not see. "Mr. Trask, please?"

Memories of why he was there with me returned. Storm clouds altered his features. "Of course, I'm sorry." He kept his eyes downcast as he began to pace in small concentric circles. His brown windbreaker was worn over a same color sport shirt with his initials or an alligator on his pocket. The shoes were highly polished. For this time of year, it might point to a military man. Then again, that Marine Corps ring on his right hand might also be a clue. As abruptly as he had stopped, he picked up the monologue.

"Recently, the store has been the target of vandalism. First, it was spoiled milk that had been tampered with. We were told that it was done by someone using a syringe to inject drain cleaner into the wax carton. Next, the trash hauler doesn't come for weeks, says I never paid the bill. Then the Health Department threatens to close us down if we don't get the trash out of the alley. It practically wiped out the little we had been able to save."

"What pushed you over the edge?"

Instantly his fingers glided over the puffy skin around his eye. "There was a music box I gave to my wife when we were married. The police have it now because they got an anonymous tip I had narcotics in there. They came with a warrant."

"And found a little packet filled with what, milk sugar? Baby laxative?" I said.

"Something like that. Warrant or no warrant, they had no right. I tried to take the box back and got this." My eyebrows arched. "Oh, it wasn't deliberate. Just an errant elbow happened to strike my eye in the melee."

"I'm betting you are no stranger to war wounds. When were you in the service?"

"Early Vietnam. I was one of the 'advisors'. Three tours. You in the service?"

"Navy. I got in on the tail end of the latest war to end all wars."

"Pilot?"

I shook my head. "Intelligence. You're right. It doesn't sound like what you have been going through are random acts of kindness. Any reason why you are a target?" He shrugged, but his pacing came to a halt. "Mr. Trask?"

His hands slid gently into his side pants pockets, then jumped out as he folded his arms across his chest and struck a drill instructor's stance.

"I don't have an enemy in the world. Neither did Sophie."

"Was Sophie your wife?" I said.

His eyes moistened. A blink or two brought only temporary relief. He nodded. "I lost her two weeks ago. A heart attack."

"I'm sorry for your loss. I can talk to the police for you."

His white head snapped upright. Those wet eyes now aglow with fire. "I've already talked with them. At first, they were very helpful, but after the third time, they said I might want to consider relocating. Of course I refused, and then they told me that their resources were so strapped because of budget cuts that I might want to look into hiring a private security consultant. It was then that your name was brought up."

"Who brought it up? Friend or foe?" I said.

"You tell me. A Sheriff's Deputy named Otera. You know him?"

"Friend. Mr. Trask, I would really like to help you, but as I told you I'm going away. I can give you some names of other private investigators who are just as good, and available."

The color drained from his face as fast as the whirlpool of water from a newly flushed toilet. Suddenly, he started backing away. Something he was looking at had spooked him. "No, no. That's okay. I was mistaken. Sorry to have bothered you." His backing away advanced to a trot, then almost into a run.

I shot a look back over my left shoulder to see what had scared him. I caught a glimpse of the tail end of a departing dark mid-sized sedan. My eyes fixed on a decal in the rear window that appeared to be crossed sabers in stark crimson, cradling an American Flag. Trask was nowhere to be seen. It was unfortunate that I couldn't help him, but I had a plane to catch.

One last check of my office found the door I had kicked shut, ajar. Instinctively, I freed my Beretta handgun from the left side hip holster and nestled my body in the crack between the door-jamb and the door. There was a large shadow looming against the wall above my jukebox that played mostly Beatles. That shadow had not been there when I had left a moment ago. I had no secretary and it was too big to be Trask. I was out of guesses.

My foot slid slowly forward and nudged the door slightly more ajar. It didn't creak. Thank you WD-40. I could now see what I was up against. Back in my college anthropology textbook, this specimen attired in a three piece double breasted suit that didn't fit all that snug around his redwood sized neck would have been labeled, "Cro-Magnon Man." His well-developed bicep was hooked tightly around the slender neck of an attractive young woman with reddish hair that was currently permed. Jammed flush against her temple was this Neanderthal's .44 automatic handgun. Could have been Smith and Wesson or it could have been Mattel. He didn't look old enough to have a learner's permit for a tricycle, much less a lethal weapon. I trained my gun on the mythical bull's eye my mind was painting on his forehead that looked like a flesh-covered billboard.

The girl coughed her way into a smile. It was all she could do to breathe, much less talk. Her words came out in a rasp.

"Hi Malone," she said.

"Hi Nellie. Is this what you get for answering a personal ad?" I said.

"Shut the fuck up, Scumbag." The Neanderthal could talk, except he had the vocabulary of a snuff film.

"Tell you what Mr. Steroid, put down your gun and we'll have a double latte' and talk about your problem with anger management."

"No talk, just death. Yours."

"Western Union School of Diplomacy?" I said.

"Ma-lone," said Nellie Archer, my former PI protégé, occasional colleague and current hostage. It was a plea that wheezed out like her body was a human accordion being slowly crushed. I refocused my attention on that bull's eye now flashing red in my mind's eye.

"Let her go. I'll be your hostage," I said.

Neanderthal snorted. "Put your gun down first."

During my time in the police academy, it was drummed into our heads that we never, ever, forever surrendered our weapons to a felon holding hostages, or us, at gunpoint. Nellie's blue eyes searched mine for some help. My hands went palms up.

"Okay, but I want your word that you'll let her go, if I put down my gun."

With a grin that was wide, and about as sincere as a used car salesman trying to make his quota at the end of the month, my adversary nodded. "I promise," he said, in words that hissed out of his mouth like a leaky tire. Slowly, I flexed my knees and placed my gun at my feet.

"Okay sport, your turn. Let her go. You promised."

The grin got obscene. "I lied." The barrel of his gun left her temple and aimed straight at me as he thumbed the hammer back in one smooth motion. "Lenny Bogardus wants you dead. And I want the ten grand."

I winced. "Ten grand? I used to be worth twenty-five." The phone in my pocket rang.

"Don't answer that, Scumbag," he growled.

Keeping one hand free, I reached inside my coat pocket and extracted the ringing telephone. "Sorry, my significant only is on the line. If I don't answer it she'll kill me, and then you'd be out ten grand. Sue?" As gracefully as I could, I turned my back to the shooter.

"Hi Sweetie, sorry to bother you but I was just feeling at loose ends. Are you at the airport?"

"Not exactly."

Susan Abilene had been around me long enough to read my breathing patterns during our phone conversations. "This isn't a good time, is it?"

"You got that right, Tootie. Let me call you back in a few minutes."

The sound of Steroid Boy behind me sucking in most of the available oxygen in the room returned me to the task at hand. Survival was always high on my list of priorities. His reflection in the framed seascape, through which I was keeping an eye on him, told me he was aiming the gun at my back. Pulling the trigger would be his next order of business.

The cell phone fell from my hand as I nearly squatted on the floor. Quickly pivoting on my heels, I grabbed my gun and took aim in one continuous motion.

Nellie rammed her elbow into her captor's midsection. While it wasn't exactly the groin, hostages couldn't be choosers. He tightened his grip but was forced to lower the gun in trying to get her under control. I squeezed off one shot that burrowed into his shoulder, spinning him around like a ballerina. His meaty finger jerked back against the trigger sending a bullet into my solid cherry desk. He pirouetted off my client chair, and thudded onto the floor. At close range, the Beretta packed a wallop. Kicking his gun away, I towered over his prone figure.

"Better not bleed too much. I just had the carpet cleaned. Nellie, are you okay?" I said.

She gulped with great difficulty, but nodded anyway. "Malone, he's bleeding like a stuck pig. Got a towel?"

I overhanded one of the extra thick fluffy towels from my infrequently used gym bag across the room to her. It was a feminine shade of pink.

"Does Susan know that you're using her towels for hemorrhaging thugs?" she said.

"Only if you tell her." The large mass of crimson flesh at my feet moaned its presence. "Hey pal, I've got a good mind to let you lose a few quarts. Now, who gave you the contract?"

It was a struggle, but the words came out with venom aforethought. "Go to hell."

I knelt down beside him. Nellie grabbed my arm. "Malone, you should be talking to the police." I glared at her. She let my arm go.

My eyes looked directly into those of my attacker. "I'm only going to say this once, pal. I'm letting you go to take a message back to your master. This contract is null and void. Anybody else comes after me or any of my friends, I'll come looking for you first, Lenny second. Any questions?"

"Go to hell."

"That's not a question." Placing my hand on the blood soaked towel I leaned forward. He yelped. "That's better. Now go forth and spread the word, Paul Revere."

Grabbing handfuls of his lapels, blood soaked shirt and the towel, I jerked him to his feet and shoved him out the door.

Nellie shook her head. "Malone, this is a bad idea."

"I never said I wouldn't call the cops." I dialed 911. "Hello? I saw a man bleeding near Salina and Genesee Streets. I think you need to send the police or something. My name?" I hung up.

"That was dumb, Malone," said Nellie. "You know your number will come up on 911 caller ID." She paused as it fell into place. "But… you knew that. Now they can't say you didn't report the shooting. Malone, sometimes you amaze even me."

I smiled. "Only sometimes?" At the far end of my office, my cell phone rang. I leaned over and picked it up. "Hi Sue, I can still make my flight."

The voice on the other end was not Susan, and not good news. "Ross, your father's had a heart attack. The ambulance is taking him to Mercy Hill Hospital."

"I'll meet you there, Mom."

-2-

Normally, it was a ten to fifteen minute drive through downtown Syracuse to Mercy Hill Emergency if you paid attention to the lights, signs and DMV rules and regulations for the state of New York. Shoving my foot through the floorboards, I made it in six, which included a quick call to Susan.

Commandeering the first available parking space regardless of whether it was reserved, handicapped or metered, I bolted from my Jeep Cherokee on the dead run for the ER entrance.

The sight of the orange and yellow CITYMED ambulance, parked at the emergency room doors, triggered emptiness in the pit of my stomach. I still couldn't quite make the connection between my stereotypical view of a heart attack victim and my father. The thought of him breaking out into a cold sweat, clutching at his chest and gasping for air sickened me.

And then, I saw the gurney. His motionless figure more resembled a lifeless mound of flesh beneath the tangle of wires, the oxygen mask tethered to the green tank ever present at times like these, and at least three pairs of hands sheathed in plastic gloves working feverishly over him doing what paramedics do until it either works or it doesn't.

Still, another paramedic took the arm of an elderly woman, helping her down from the rear of the ambulance. A once proud, fiercely independent woman, her strong features were now stained with the terror of the unknown. Her hands belabored the tissues gathered between her fingers. She was passed the pneumatic doors before I could reach her.

"Mom?" I said.

She slowly turned her head to me, revealing bloodshot, puffy eyes, reddened nose and sadness, a lot of sadness.

"Rossiter? I'm so glad you're here." We tried to follow closely behind the path of the gurney, but a smiling red coated volunteer blocked our way.

"Hello, you have to check in over here. There is just a little bit of paperwork."

I growled. "Excuse me, but my father is having a heart attack. My mother and I would like to be with him. Can't this paper-work wait?"

Like a Star Trek transporter arrival, an official looking nurse materialized over the shoulder of the volunteer. I placed her as familiar from having had lunch with Susan often at Mercy Hill, but not her name. So, I cheated and read her nametag. She extended a well-scrubbed hand and that same official looking smile came along for the ride.

"I'm not sure you remember me, Mr. Malone. I'm Colleen Powers, Assistant Nurse Manager for the Emergency Department. Dr. Abilene introduced us a long while ago."

"I remember," I lied. "Look Nurse Powers, my father…"

She finished my sentence and I didn't like that. "…has had a heart attack. Yes, I know, and I am sorry. The doctors are working with your father at the moment. As soon as they know what they are dealing with, they will be out to talk with you and your mother. In the meantime, there is some necessary paperwork that needs to be addressed. For example, we'll need insurance information, whether he'll want a private room, a phone, if he'll accept a blood transfusion etc. It is a pain in the neck, but we find it's easier to get it out of the way up front."

Colleen smiled again. Actually, she never stopped smiling. She took my mother's arm and gently guided her to a nearby straight-backed wooden chair by a narrow, green Formica counter top. The volunteer sat behind the computer and plastered a smile on her face as well. I was beginning to think I was in the ER in the Merry Old Land of Oz.

"May I have the patient's full name?" she said.

"John Richard Malone," said my mother.

The ritual had now commenced where the patient's next of kin lays bare their life and finances in order to receive life saving medical treatment. I watched the sweep second hand on the wall clock slow down with every second it passed. The one on my watch was even slower. It was difficult not to squirm, the monotony breaking only briefly enough to answer a few questions that came up when Mom was temporarily overcome by the moment.

All too quickly, the questions began to drone on. Type of insurance. If retired, name of pension plan. Next of kin. I lost count at 27 inane questions. However, inane questions do make the bureaucracy go around. At least it kept Mom occupied, while they stabilized my Dad's condition. I tried to see through the frosted glass sliding doors into the ER proper.

The stack of official looking papers grew by leaps and bounds in front of my mother. A two-color pen, with the Mercy Hill Hospital logo on it, was placed atop the papers. Mom sighed, then began signing her name next to the "x" or Pop's name along with her initials where applicable. Page after page after page loomed before her.

"I'll be right back, Mom. I'm going to the restroom." Her nod was almost imperceptible, as she focused her attention instead on her current task. I counted myself lucky and headed off to find the restroom. At least, that's what I told my Mom. My real mission was to see how my Dad was doing. Unfortunately, I didn't have far to look.

Just inside the pneumatic ER doors, my father was still on his gurney with the paramedics all around him. I walked over and squeezed his hand. His tired, bloodshot eyes managed a brief smile at my touch.

"Hang on, Pop." I turned abruptly to the EMTs. "Is there a real good reason why my father is still out in the hall?"

The youngest medic, who was currently working hard, without much success, on growing a handlebar mustache spoke. "We just deliver them. The ER is probably jammed. They'll get him in as soon as possible."

"Not good enough," I said.

The ER layout was as familiar to me as the back of my hand. I had spent many an hour here chasing my true love Dr. Susan Abilene, getting patched up from being mangled in my pursuit of truth, justice and the American way, or interviewing clients who wanted the type of personal retribution I could provide for almost $400 a day plus reasonable expenses. Five minutes of maneuvering around allowed me to steal a glance at the monitor behind the nurses' station, which told the whereabouts of patients in the ER. The room numbers in red were the ones with telemetry monitors inside them. Room 14 was notated with a flashing logo that read, "VIP." "VIP" perhaps, but whoever was in that room wasn't hooked up to the monitors.

Taking the shortest distance from the nurses station to Room 14, found me confronted by a throng of media types trying to get into Room 14. Uniformed Mercy Hill security guards were standing between them and two very large bodyguard types flanking the doorway to the room. Talking to the muscle-bound bookends was Colleen Powers. Actually, it looked more like she was begging. I tugged at her arm.

"Why is my father double parked in the hallway? Didn't you remember that he just had a heart attack?"

"Mr. Malone, I am doing the best I can. Your father is in no danger. We are fully equipped to handle the situation."

A glance back over my shoulder towards my father made me grind my teeth in frustration. Pain flashed across his face in a tight grimace. The paramedics reacted by shooting a syringeful of colorless liquid into his IV line. "You've got five minutes to get him into a room and treat him, or I go to the press." I pointed. "That press. Understand?"

Her recently plucked eyebrows mended into a "V" to show her dislike for my ultimatum. Her face flushed crimson. Her hand cradled my elbow, and she guided me to a corner far away from the press. Her voice dropped.

"Mr. Malone, we have a very delicate situation here. We have a foreign diplomat in the last remaining room with a telemetry monitor. I was negotiating to get the room released to us for your father, when you came in and stopped everything cold. Believe me, I am not unsympathetic, but I am doing everything I can."

"You're talking to these two guys over here?" I gestured towards the bodyguards. Colleen looked, nodding tentatively as she wondered what was in my mind. "Let's see if I can help. I speak bodyguard."

Before she could reply, I moved past her and zigzagged my way through the crowd over to the bodyguards. I tapped the nearest one on the shoulder.

"Excuse me, my father is over there on a stretcher having a heart attack. He needs the equipment in this room. I need you to move to another room. A suitable place will be provided so that your assignment is safe and your protective integrity won't be breached."

Stereo silence greeted me as I finished my request. I could feel my Dad's life slipping away. My stomach twisted. I waved a hand in front of the nearest bodyguard. He must have thought he was standing in front of Buckingham Palace. Implacable. I wanted to put a mirror up to his mouth to see if it fogged up. No matter, my Dad needed what was in that room.

"May I speak with your boss, supervisor, owner? How about your keeper? I'm sure he, or she, would understand the gravity of the situation."

The bodyguard rotated his eyes towards me. "What makes you think, I do not?"

"Because you aren't moving, and I may have to move you." Could that be a thin sliver of a smile?

"The prince must not be disturbed," he continued. "The president will be here soon. I am sorry. I cannot help you. My duty is to protect the prince."

Just beyond him over the bodyguard's left shoulder, I caught a reflection off a very shiny stainless steel towel dispenser over the sink. Their prince couldn't have been more than 13 or 14 years old. His left arm was wrapped in a beige elastic bandage, then suspended in front of him by a cloth sling. To look at him, you'd think he'd just lost his best friend. I felt sorry for him. His governess, or per diem private duty nurse, sat in a metal folding chair opposite him with her nose buried in a Reader's Digest from the last century.

My father groaned louder. My blood pressure began to rise with determination. I looked at Colleen for help. "How long until the VIP gets here?"

She looked at me up and down with a wary eye. "Why?"

"Because if it isn't within the next few seconds, I'm going to take my father into this room myself. Any questions?"

Colleen Powers looked directly into my eyes. Was that a shudder that went through her slender body?

"Malone, I can't let you do this. Please. Give me some time to see if I can clear out another room." She didn't wait for my answer, but ran off to see what magic she could work.

I stood my ground, listening to the seconds tick off my watch. The sound of time passing and my father's deteriorating condition was becoming unbearable.

It was time to do something.

-3-

The wavy green lines traveling across the black screens on the portable heart monitors on my Dad's stretcher were less wavy than the last time I'd checked. His pallor now more resembled wet corrugated cardboard than the vital nearly 70 year old man I loved. My patience, once ebbing, was now exhausted. The void was rapidly being replaced by anger.

The horde of reporters seemed to be breeding at the moment. Actually, horde was being nice. They were little more than a civilized mob. I leaned forward and using football's tried and true straight arm method, I plowed through the sea of inhumanity. Colleen was making larger circles with her arms. Any larger and she might take flight. I grabbed her arms at the elbows and bodily moved her out of the way. Then I returned my attention to Mr. Implacable.

"Okay Sport, here's the way it is going to work. You and your twin pyramid here are going to escort the prince to the nearest room where he can be guarded safely. Then Colleen and her crack medical staff are going to save my father's life. Sound like a plan?"

His lips barely moved. The energy expended was less then the per capita income of Appalachia in its lean years. "That is unfortunate, but the prince cannot be moved. Orders are orders. You need to keep that in mind."

"And you need to understand that blood is thicker than orders. Look, I don't want to place your prince in harm's way but I cannot, check that, will not, stand by and let my father die. Nothing personal." With that, I tried to go past him but they closed ranks faster than the Red Sea after Moses moseyed on through.

I shoved harder. They stood fast. My arms were grabbed from behind. I don't have many pet peeves in this world, but being restrained without my consent was one of them. A quick shrug of my shoulders got me free. I turned and slugged the second pyramid in the jaw. He staggered, but didn't fall. Just like that, what was a friendly little fight of two against one deteriorated into a life and death confrontation.

Mr. Implacable pulled his weapon. I chopped at his wrist, just like a TV hero. The gun clattered to the floor. We were lucky it didn't go off. I kicked it aside and rammed my fist right into Mr. Implacable's stomach. He barely blinked much less doubled over. Then, I steamrolled past him like Butkus on a good day.

The boy prince looked at me as if I was the savior to free him from his temporary prison. The governess' magazine dropped to reveal a Beretta, similar to the one in my holster. It was pointed at my vital organs.

"Hold it Mary Poppins. I'm just here to move the prince to a more secure location. I need this equipment for my father."

Her reply was short and succinct. She thumbed back the safety catch on the Beretta. Two more gun barrels greeted opposite sides of my neck. The pyramids had returned with a vengeance. The frenzy of media behind us had the kid on edge. I felt bad about that. I have always tried not to terrorize kids under seventeen without a parent or guardian present.

"I don't know who you are my insistent friend, but these guns mean that you will now play by our rules," said Mr. Implacable, with a capacity for understatement.

An unfamiliar voice sliced through the air with a sharpness usually reserved for a knife that could cut tin cans and paper plates at the same time.

"Andrew! Jacob! Put your guns away. At once!"

The guns vanished. I took a chance and looked around. The VIP and his entourage had arrived and begun speaking in a language that I certainly didn't understand. The pyramids retreated to resume their stations, flanking the entrance to the room. That left the VIP and a shorter, more buttoned down man in a pinstriped three-piece suit, cut expensively, who stared at me with utter disapproval. I utterly didn't care. The short guy stepped forward.

"My name is Trevor Bradley, U.S. State Department. And you are?"

"Ross Malone. I'd like to stick around and chat about the new Tom Clancy novel, but my father is out in the hallway, still on a stretcher in need of medical attention for the heart attack from which he is suffering. This room has the last remaining available heart monitor. I need the boy, er prince, to move to another location. And I need it twenty minutes ago."

Trevor spoke quickly and said nothing of importance. "Mr. Malone, I appreciate your dilemma but, you must appreciate mine." He lowered his voice and his eyes darted back towards the distinguished man with the imposing presence in the background. "Do you know who this man is?"

"Ali Baba and is two thieves?"

Bradley gestured for me to be quiet. "Keep your voice down. That is Benjamin Walanna of the Republic of Laracone."

"And the Final Jeopardy question is, 'Where the hell is Laracone?'" I was in no mood for twenty questions. Trevor Bradley turned beet red. He made a half-hearted attempt to stop me, which I shook off like a flea and headed straight for the VIP. My offered hand was accepted. "Mr. President, my name is Malone. I have an urgent problem that needs your attention."

He raised a hand. "Please do not waste valuable time. I have been informed of this already. Andrew! Jacob! You will escort the prince to other quarters immediately." He added a word from his native tongue that lit a fire under the collective silk covered behinds of the twin pyramids. With all deliberate speed they, along with their gun-toting nanny, moved the young boy from the cardiac trauma room.

Colleen Powers guided the ambulance gurney carrying my father next to the wider ER stretcher covered with a paper sheet. Walanna and I exchanged diplomatic nods.

"I hope all goes well with you," he said, sounding like a press release rather than a person. He then, spun on his heels and almost tripped over Trevor Bradley cowering in the dignitary's six-foot plus shadow. The entourage left. The media horde followed. People in pastel colored scrub clothes swarmed into the room, each performing a definite and vital function.

"Out Malone." Colleen shoved me towards the door. "Get a second line in stat. Somebody call the OR and have anesthesia standby in case we need to intubate. Blood gases need to be drawn."

"Got it!" a voice replied.

"Anybody seen the patient's H and P?"

"It's on the chart Colleen, at the desk."

"That does me no good in here. Get it. How soon for the cardiologist?"

"ETA five minutes."

Colleen was not happy. "Five minutes? Call Coleman."

Someone else shouted a question about my father's known allergies. I glanced back over my shoulder to see the medical team lift my Dad up, on the count of three, in unison and onto the ER stretcher. Wires were disconnected from the portable telemetry units and reconnected to the deluxe wall models on the overhead shelves. Green wavy lines came back into view. They were stronger; at least I thought so. I exhaled the deep breath I had been holding, since I left my Cherokee in the parking lot, it seemed. The curtain, surrounding my Dad was pulled closed in front of my face. A nearby candystriper guided me out like I was wearing a lost child tag.

Two more people rushed into ER-14. Three came out. One more re-entered carrying an oxygen mask and a bag of amber IV fluid. A phlebotomist jogged out and down the nearest stairwell holding an ice filled plastic sandwich bag cradling a tube of blood. I shook my head clear and wandered back to the waiting room, more than thankful that the media circus had moved along.

My mother was seated in the farthest corner of a pastel hued room that was both soothing and sterile at the same time. A TV set hanging from a bolted down wall bracket was relating the antics of the current heartthrob talk show host schmoozing with her bandleader foil. Rosary beads and a well-worn St. Jude card had replaced the Kleenex brand tissues in my mother's hands. Her expectant eyes looked at me, prepared for the worst, almost as if it were inevitable.

"He's holding his own, Mom. Remember Nurse Powers? Well, she's in there. They are doing everything possible."

"I'm so scared. I don't like seeing your father like this."

Like this? A red flag waved in my head. Had she seen him like this before? I covered her hands with mine.

"Hang in there, kiddo. He's going to be okay," I said.

"Did the doctor tell you that?" She already knew the answer to that question, but she had nothing else to ask.

I pointed skyward. "HE told me that." Okay, so it was a little cheap and schmaltzy but it did make my mother smile. Mission accomplished.

"Core-Zero. Emergency Room. Core Zero. Emergency Room," bellowed the overhead speakers. I stiffened knowing that someone was probably having a heart attack. And that the odds were, I was related to that person. Mom was oblivious to the meaning of the page. I heard the rush of activity. It consumed all of my strength not to bolt back in there and be with my father. More importantly, if they didn't know what they were doing by now, I couldn't help them.

"Want some coffee, or Pepsi or something, Mom?"

"Not right now. But you go ahead. I'll just sit here and wait for the doctor. What could be taking so long?"

The pneumatic doors that cut off the ER proper from the relatives swooshed open. Each time I heard that noise I fully expected to see Jean Luc Picard chasing the Borg. Instead, Dr. Elinor Salas came in. Her white lab coat was impeccable, as always, with razor sharp ironed in creases. Silver thread in elegant curlicues proclaimed her name and specialty above her pocket. I stood. We embraced.

"Ross, how are you? I was passing through the ER and thought that I saw you. What are you doing here?"

"My Dad's had a heart attack. They are working on him now."

"I'm so sorry," said the OB-GYN specialist behind elegant Hawaiian features. Her expression told me she was just now linking the core-zero page with my father's presence. "How is he doing?"

"We don't know. They won't tell us anything," said my mother. Her eyes were hopeful as if no news was good news. In reality, no news was just that, no news.

"Elinor, this is my mother, Marilyn Malone. Mom, this is a friend of Susan's and mine. Dr. Elinor Salas."

"I'm glad to meet you Mrs. Malone, though I wish it were under better circumstances. Why don't you let me see what I can find out? I'll be right back. Try not to worry. Ross, how's Susan?"

"Still in D.C. helping the President straighten out the health care crisis."

Elinor smiled. "I'll bet she is. Give her my best. Excuse me, I'll be right back." Elinor kissed my cheek and left. My eyes shifted to the credit card commercial on the TV.

"Malone, I came as soon as I heard."

The large hulking frame of Sheriff's Deputy Tom Otera cast a long shadow, resplendent in his coal black uniform with gold shield and familiar bulletproof vest beneath his long sleeved shirt. We shook hands.

"He's with the doctors right now. Elinor Salas is checking for us."

"My wife and I want you to know if there's anything we can do…As you know, she makes a mean tuna casserole."

I smiled lightly. "Yes I do. And mean is the correct four letter word there." Tom turned to my mother.

"Mrs. Malone, I'm not sure if you remember me but I'm Tom Otera, a friend of your son. I'm sorry about your husband."

"Thank you," said Mom. Her voice was weaker, more distant with each succeeding word. She kept glancing past Tom and I towards the doors, waiting for Elinor's return. I was too.

"Ross, we need to talk," said Deputy Otera.

"Can't this wait?"

"Come on, let's go outside." He walked over and through the pneumatic doors. I followed. "Tell me about the shooting in your office."

"I thought the city cops were handling it," I said, trying to act innocent.

"They would have, but the victim staggered and collapsed in front of my patrol car. By some strange coincidence your name was stitched into the towel he had stuffed against a bullet wound in his shoulder. Care to explain?"

"Susan put it there. I was losing too many towels at the gym," I said.

"Ross, that's not what I mean, and you know it."

"All I know, Tom, is that Lenny Bogardus is still ticked off at me. There's an open contract on my head. That punk just mistook my office for the OK Corral."

"You know that punk won't be the last."

"I'm not going to hide," I said, more than a little annoyed that he might be suggesting it.

"Not suggesting that you should. What are you looking at?"

"Back over your shoulder about three o'clock. I think one of those branches has a telescopic sight."

Tom glanced over at the nearby grove of trees that surrounded the hospital parking lot. "Let's circle around the back."

I went left. He went right.

Slowly, we each made our way cautiously through the rows of parked cars onto the grassy island that a group of trees huddled upon, providing a break from the sometimes bitter wind. Luckily, it wasn't dry enough to announce our presence in advance by the brittle leaves or twigs crunching under our feet. Along the way, I unholstered my gun and placed it alongside my thigh, muzzle down.

My free hand knocked aside some branches intent on scratching my face beyond recognition except through dental records. There was our quarry, less than thirty yards before me. He was a thick figure in full beard and camouflage military style fatigues hunched behind a telescopic lens. I couldn't see to what the lens was attached.

Tom approached from the opposite side. He gestured. I nodded. Gently, but firmly, I nudged the barrel of my gun next to the ear of the man in the full beard. He froze.

"Release the trigger, nice and easy. Then step away and get down on your knees. Hands on top of your head." I waited. He complied at the last possible second. Tom handcuffed him. I examined what he had been aiming at the ER entrance.

"Tell me that's not just a fancy camera, Malone," said Tom.

"Jesus, I'm just doing my job. I'm a freelance photographer. Name's Caine, Able Caine."

I smirked. "Abel Caine? Your parents missionaries?"

"Nah, I just picked it because people would remember me. My press card's in my jacket pocket."

Tom fished around for a brief moment and pulled it out. He scanned it and handed it to me.

"Last time I saw a photo this bad it was on a milk carton," I said, underwhelmed by Caine's deer in the headlights expression.

"Hey, watch who you're slandering. I took that picture."

"What are you doing here?" said Tom.

"My job. Look Deputy, I heard there was some boy king celebrity in the ER. I thought that if I got an exclusive picture, I could cash in."

"Hate to burst your bubble," I said, a tad insincerely, "but actually he's a prince and, in case you hadn't noticed, you've got competition."

His head rotated in the direction of my finger. At the far right of the parking lot were no less than four TV remote trucks with satellite dishes poised ready to serve. His beefy shoulders slumped.

"Shit. Aw hell, you can't blame a guy for trying. Care to let me go now?"

Tom unlocked the handcuffs. We started back towards the hospital.

"Ross, you'll still have to come in later and give a statement. Bring Nellie Archer with you."

"So Nellie told you where I was when you stopped by the office," I said.

"That's why you get the big bucks, for being the city's resident Sherlock Holmes." He stopped just outside the entrance to replace his handcuffs in his black leather gun belt. "Let me know how your Dad is doing? And Malone? Watch your back."

"Will do, on both counts," I said.

No sooner had Deputy Otera left than Elinor Salas returned with a harried looking man who seemed to be half Drew Carey and half Albert Einstein. He was tall and wide in the same space but his hair looked like a transplant from an albino troll doll. His full brush-like mustache covered the movement of what I thought to be a very small mouth.

"Mrs. Malone, this is Doctor Gerald Coleman," said Dr. Salas, presenting her colleague.

Mom looked up and almost stood. He placed a comforting hand on her shoulder. She sat back down. "How is my husband, Doctor? Can we go home?"

"I'm afraid not, Mrs. Malone. Your husband suffered a heart attack. This isn't the first time, though, is it?" he said.

I spoke. "Of course it is. What kind of doctor are you?"

He glanced briefly at me before speaking. "And you are?"

"Ross Malone. That's my father in there. I don't mean to be obnoxious, but my father doesn't have a cardiac history."

"Mr. Malone, I will chalk up your bad manners to the stress of your father's condition, but, please understand that I know what I'm doing. In fact, your friend, Dr. Abilene called me from Washington and asked me specifically to look in on your father. Now Mrs. Malone, this isn't your husband's first heart attack, is it?"

Her eyes searched the carpeted floor for a way to avoid the question. She found none. "No, it isn't his first heart attack."

-4-

"Not his first heart attack?" I could feel my jaw scrape along the floor as I spoke. My mother's gaze was still glued downward on the pastel carpeting.

"No Ross, it isn't," she said.

Elinor Salas placed an unwanted hand on my arm. I shook it off. "This might not be the time to discuss this, Ross. Dr. Coleman needs to know about your father's cardiac condition."

"He's not the only one," I said.

Taking my mother's trembling hand in his, Coleman sat down next to her. He shot a backward glance at me; no doubt he wanted to put me in my place. On the other hand, I wanted to slap him for running interference, but only because I was feeling betrayed. Why hadn't she told me? No good choice remained, so, for now, I listened. Passing judgment could be done later.

"His doctor in Florida is Samuel Triest. Jack had several, oh what did he call them, cardiac episodes while we were in Florida last year. One time, we had to rush him to the emergency room. That's where we met Dr. Triest. I have his card somewhere. Here it is." She handed a business card with cockleshell finish to Coleman.

"I'll call him shortly," he said, "and have your husband's medical records transferred up here ASAP. From what your husband told me, it seems the best course of action would be to schedule a heart catheterization. That would be where we would insert a catheter into his artery and watch on a x-ray monitor to see where the blockages are. Once we know the extent of the damage, we can decide how to proceed."

"What are the options Doctor?" I said. It was a struggle not to demand answers, but this was not time for Malone the Bully Boy.

"It's far too early to tell. At best, we might be able to get away with what is called a balloon angioplasty where we insert the balloon and remove the blockage."

"And the worst case scenario?" I was a glutton for punishment.

"Ruling out a heart transplant, then some kind of bypass surgery."

My mother gasped. To my relief, no one seemed to notice that I almost did, too.

Doctor Gerald Coleman rose to his over six-foot height and stepped back to leave. "But that hasn't been decided. Hold a good thought. I'll be in touch when we know more. Mrs. Malone, I left my card with your husband. Please feel free to call the office if you have any questions or concerns. I'll go call Dr. Triest and compare notes."

"Thank you Dr. Coleman."

"I'll walk out with you, Doctor," said Elinor. "Mrs. Malone, you take care. Ross, if you or your family need anything, please let me know."

"Thanks Elinor...for everything." She wrinkled her nose again in a reply wrapped in a smile that would be called pert, regardless of her age. When she and the good doctor Coleman had departed, I sat down gently next to my mother, unsure of what to say but wanting to say something. Her gaze wandered off into the distance. She was probably thinking of better times devoid of heart monitors and terms like next of kin. Words stuck in my throat. What I wanted to say couldn't wait.

"Mom. Mom? I never knew that Dad had suffered a heart attack before?" My voice stayed low, even, soft and measured. Non-accusatory. No need to browbeat my mother especially with my blackjack at the cleaners.

Her eyes remained distant. "The first one was last spring. Heartburn, he told me it was heartburn. The doctor said it was a warning. And your father followed his instructions, at first."

"I'll bet the minute he felt better it was back to burgers and fries for breakfast."

"You know him too well." A slender, wrinkled finger was pointed back and wagged in my face. "And you are just like him. In the fall, he had the real thing. He woke me from a sound sleep and told me to call the doctor. We spent the night in the emergency room. The next morning they did what Dr. Coleman called, a heart...a heart..."

"Catheterization."

"Oh, I don't know. But they found the right side was 80% blocked. They cleaned it out. We thought he'd be good as new. Now this."

"There are no guarantees." It was time for the $64,000 Question. "Mom, why didn't you tell me Dad was having heart problems?"

"You weren't told because you had your own problems," she said.

"More important than Dad's life? I don't think so."

"It all happened during the time of Susan's 'condition'," came the words that sounded coated with spite.

Susan had suffered through a false pregnancy. Elinor had called it, pseudocyesis. It put her into therapy and almost broke us up. We decided it was better to believe in each other. We would work it out. Back then, we were all consumed by a firestorm of emotions. Perhaps there was truth to what I was hearing.

"Anthony and I thought it best not to burden you with this."

Shock dripped from my features. "Excuse me? Anthony knew?" I said.

"Yes Ross, I told your younger brother. He is a doctor."

"He is a dentist, Mom. The worst thing he's seen is a premeditated overbite. Did Chris know too?"

"Yes. I think Anthony did tell your sister."

Anger flared inside me. More logs of feeling neglected were thrown into the fireplace of my ego. I stood abruptly. "Is there anything else you, and my younger brother haven't told me?"

"Rossiter, sit down. Don't be absurd. We were only thinking of you."

"Mom, this may come as a shock to you but, I am a full grown adult capable of handling more than one emotion at a time. Hell, I can even walk and chew gum if I concentrate."

She shook her head slowly, still without looking at me. Her disapproval was evident. "I don't need your sarcasm or your profanity, Ross. And the part about you being an adult? You are well over 21 and still your job is playing cops and robbers."

"We aren't going to have that discussion again, Mom. I'm a private investigator. It's what I do and I am very good at it."

"Maybe you should work harder at being a better son. Rossiter, you need a career. You should have stayed in the Navy."

"I was done with the Navy. Once the Gulf War was over, there was nothing more for me to do except be a paper shuffler and brain."

"Paper shufflers don't get shot at," she said.

Why did I suddenly feel that I wanted to be read my rights and given my one phone call? "Private detectives may die of gunshot wounds, but they aren't so bored they get heart attacks."

I froze. The minute those words slithered out of my mouth I wanted to take them back. It was cruel, unnecessary. For whatever twisted reason, I felt I needed to win this argument that couldn't be won. I was used to a scorched earth policy of arguing. Passive was not in my nature. Heartless apparently was.

"Mom, I'm sorry, I didn't mean..." Her face was grim. Her eyes were full of tears. The excess started to slide down her cheeks. I shut my big fat mouth and sat back down. Soon I too, was staring off into that same distance.

"Mrs. Malone? Ross? Would you like to see him now?" said Colleen Powers.

Mom squeezed my hand. "How is he?"

"Right now, holding his own. We're readying a room for him in our cardiac wing. But, it will be a little while. In the meantime, you can sit with him. Now I have to warn you, we have him hooked up to the oxygen and, he is wired to our monitors. Don't be shocked by any of that. It's all a precaution."

We followed her to his room.

He looked like an astronaut ready for launch. In the same room where I had almost created an international incident, my father laid on his stretcher. Blanketed under a disturbing gray pallor, he looked weary.

I positioned a metal folding chair by his bedside so my mother could sit. She took his hand. They squeezed back and forth. Words were now non-existent. Nurses came in and out to record vital signs, take blood or just to keep an eye on him. I took up station against the back wall in a far corner trying to stay out of the way.

There was nothing I could do at the moment, and it was the safest thing I could do. When in doubt, don't, has been my motto.

"So what did the doctor tell you?" said my father, in a voice that was second cousin to a rasp. Mom pushed a paper cup of water to sip towards him. The flex straw flopped from the cup onto the table. He ignored it.

"He said you had to rest Jack. That this time you must listen or else," she said.

"Or else what Marilyn? We're all going to die sometime. Maybe this is my time."

Wrong answer was written all over my mother's face. She half turned around in her chair and spoke, still averting her eyes. "Rossiter, would you excuse us for a moment? Your father and I need to discuss."

"Stay where you are Ross. I don't want to discuss, Marilyn," said my Dad, fully realizing that discussing was inevitable.

My feet, for the time being out of my mouth, shuffled their way slowly towards the door. My hand pulled the curtain around the cubicle to give them some measure of privacy. I moved into the hallway.

"I won't forget this son. You might be out of the will, if I die."

"Calm yourself, Jack. You'll get these monitors buzzing again," said the woman who had held the bible when I was sworn into the Navy.

Out of the will? That could be a hopeful sign since, based upon recent events, I didn't even expect to be mentioned anyway. I headed for the Pepsi machine in the smoking lounge off the main floor. It wasn't the only one, just the nearest.

Demonic green flashing eyes that translated into "correct change only" greeted me. I decided not to waste a bullet on it and got change for a five-dollar bill from someone lighting what appeared to be a third unfiltered cigarette from the remnants of the second one.

The next order of business of being the eldest son was to inform the immediate family. A fleeting thought that Mom had already called Anthony before she called me today crossed through my mind, lingered briefly in my bruised ego, then moved along. I didn't have the guts to ask her. It was only a long distance phone call after all. I'd rather confront him over the phone than in person. It never occurred to me that the right thing to do might be not to go the confrontation route at all.

I used my calling card. Bell Atlantic used a recording. Then, the call rang through.

"Doctor Malone's office. This is Stephanie. How may I assist you?"

"Hello, this is Ross Malone, the good doctor's brother in Syracuse. I need to speak with him."

Sunshine glowed in her voice. "I'm sorry Mr. Malone but your brother, my boss, is in the middle of a very delicate root canal. May I take a message?"

"No, you may not. Stephanie, I wouldn't have wasted the thirty-five cents this call is costing me if it were not important. Now, would you please tell Dr. Malone that I need to speak with him, **now**? It is an emergency."

The phone receiver was slammed onto the desktop followed by the shuffling of hard wheels on a plastic ramp that protects the rugs under desks. A door opened and closed in the distance. There were muffled voices—one high pitched that I assumed was Stephanie's, a swear word, a door slam and someone picking up the receiver.

"Ross, this had better be important," said the younger Malone brother.

"I thought I'd give you the courtesy you didn't bother to give me. Dad's had a heart attack. He's in the emergency room at Mercy Hill Hospital. They're moving him to cardiac intensive care shortly."

The silence on the other end of the phone told me I had made an impression. When he did speak, my brother was obviously shaken by the halting way the words came out. "Roberta and I will be there within the hour. Ross, how bad is it?"

The words, "Don't ask me, you're the doctor" formed at my lips and stayed there. My Sunday school training kept me from turning my brother into verbal road kill.

"It's bad Tony. But he's stable for now. At least that's what they are telling us. Would you call Chris?"

"Yes. Ross?" He sucked in and let out a deep breath. "I'm sorry about before, about not telling you about Dad's condition."

"Just drive carefully. I'll see you soon. Give my love to the kids."

The phone had barely clanged shut in the metal coupler when all of the strength drained from my legs. For a moment, I felt like Frosty the Snowman sitting behind a jet engine. I hugged the phone for support. Take a deep breath, Malone.

Marble tombstones flew before my eyes. The chiseled names of Molly and Christopher Malone resembled yellow pastel, neon road signs to my past. When they had died, there was no emergency room, no final good-byes, and no chance to make amends or say I was sorry for not being on that plane with them. All I saw were angel wings on two kind souls who had passed through my life all too briefly.

Was God about to kneecap my soul again?

I moved from the lobby back towards the emergency room, hoping my parents had resolved their disagreements long enough for Dad to get some rest. Suddenly, I slammed into an immovable object.

"Excuse me, I didn't mean to bump into you," I said.

"Malone, it's me," said the rumpled man before me. He looked like he had slept in the basement of a castle in Transylvania. "Lucas Gentero, Daily Sentinel. What are you doing here?"

"My father's in the ER. He's had a heart attack."

Concern furrowed the reporter's Italian 36 year-old features. "Gee, that's tough. Is he going to be all right?"

I showed him my crossed fingers in reply. "What are you doing here? Chasing ambulances doesn't seem like your style." Lucas didn't hear me as he was digging through his pockets, searching for something that eluded him for several moments. All of the sudden, he pulled out a creased, weathered piece of thin cardboard that resembled at first glance an ace he had stuffed up his sleeve from last week's poker game. He shoved it into my hands.

"Give him this Malone. It's my favorite St. Jude card."

"Lucas, that is very nice but I'm sure my Mom has her own set of cards. In fact she has all fifty-two. Some are probably even autographed."

Gentero frowned. "Don't knock St. Jude, Malone. He got me through elementary school, when Ronnie Gilstrap tried to make my face so much compost because I mistook his sister for his twin brother. And he got me through college, when I stayed up all night before finals trying to drink enough to make Budweiser's stock go up an eighth of a point."

"That's very nice Lucas but," I said, however he continued on unabated.

"And, and, my good man, it got me an interview with Nicholas Davenport about me possibly ghostwriting his autobiography. So what I am telling you, is that it's got to be good for heart attacks."

The sincerity in his eyes was more than my resolve to say thanks, but no thanks. "I'll pass it along Lucas. Thank you. By the way, what are you doing here?"

A stubby thumb from the reporter's right hand was jerked back towards the media crowd around the boy prince's new home away from home. My new best friends, the Twin Towers were positioned there.

"Say, what's this beef you had with THE Benjamin Walanna?" asked the reporter, shoving his tape recorder into my face. I pushed it away.

"There was no beef. Just what you might call a 'territorial misunderstanding'."

"Come on Malone, what's the real scoop? I heard that there was a brawl between you and the guards," he said.

"No comment. Do you know a freelance photographer named Able Caine?"

"No comment." Lucas averted his gaze when I glared my disapproval. I continued to walk away. "Wait Malone, I know him. He did some good work in the Gulf War. He's always looking for an edge. Since then his one claim to fame is being spit at by *People* magazine's Sexiest Man Alive one year."

"A career defining moment, no doubt. Thanks." I kept walking.

"Good luck with your Dad, Malone."

"Good luck with Nick Davenport," I said. Instinct crawled up and down my spine. The hairs on my neck stood on end. I was being watched. I turned and saw Benjamin Walanna standing regally straight, less than an arm's length away.

"My son and I are preparing to leave. I wanted to see how your father was doing?"

I smiled. "Right now, he is holding his own. Thanks for your help in getting him in that room. My mom and I appreciate your concern. And how is your son?"

"Prince Gregory it seems, has suffered a bad sprain to his wrist. For now, the doctors say that a soft cast is sufficient." Jacob appeared behind Walanna. He mumbled something in the president's ear. The head of Laracone nodded ever so slightly. Jacob disappeared like The Shadow. "I must be leaving. Best of luck with your father."

"Thank you. The same to you and your family."

Walanna didn't so much leave as he glided out, an old Charleton Heston trick. I headed for Dad's room.

"Psst, Malone, psst. Over here." It was Trevor Bradley. "I just wanted to touch base with you and make sure that you understand the need to keep this little incident quiet."

"I understand Mr. Bradley," I said.

"Good, because I wouldn't want it blown out of proportion."

"Good-bye Mr. Bradley. Your bureaucracy is calling."

Sounds of life, maybe even a laugh or two emanated from behind the plastic curtain. I stepped behind it. Sounds of silence.

"Is it safe to come back?" I said smiling, unsure of how I would be received.

"You should go call Anthony. Then you should call Chris," said my mother. The distance in her voice towards me remained.

"Already done. I talked with Tony and he's going to call Chris. He and Roberta are on the way here."

"Thank you." The frost continued.

"How are you feeling, Pop?" I said, changing the subject before I was farmed out for adoption.

A nurse came in with a clipboard and a pen. Dad shifted uncomfortably on his stretcher.

"All right, I guess." Getting those few words out was an obvious struggle for him. His face contorted and his hand stroked his chest amid the red, black, and gray wires. The beeps got more insistent. The nurse looked longer and more intently at the video displays.

"Mr. Malone, how are you feeling? Any pain?"

"A little, not enough to hurt, but enough to let me know it's there."

"How much pain? Give it to me in a number between one and ten where one is feeling great and ten is the worst pain you could have," instructed the nurse. Her eyes were recording the activity on the monitors. A hand felt for my Dad's pulse at the wrist.

"About a five," he said.

"All right." She adjusted the drip into an intravenous line. A long pause ensued. "How about now?"

"A four, maybe three and a half." Her shoulders relaxed a bit. "Five...six..." He began to gasp for air. The alarms on the machines sounded with regularity. The nurse grabbed his bedside buzzer and jammed her thumb on it. A red light flashed above his bed. The level of activity jumped.

"Four...five...six." He barely wheezed the last number out. The nurse tossed her clipboard to the floor and kicked it aside. She slammed her hand against a red button on the wall marked, "emergency." No klaxons went off, but people flooded in like the dam had burst at a temp agency. Colleen Powers led the charge.

"Mr. Malone, you and your mother will have to step outside now."

Mom squeezed her rosary until her knuckles turned white. "What's happening Nurse Powers?"

I had an educated guess as to what was going on, but kept it to myself. The core zero pages on the overhead speakers confirmed it.

"Let's go outside Mom. They need some space in here." I took her elbow and guided her back to the waiting room. The stunned expression on her face didn't change.

"What's going on, Ross? What's going on?" said Mom. She kept repeating it.

I replied the same thing. "They'll take care of it, Mom. We have to let them work." My pleas were starting to soothe my mother until Dr. Coleman hustled by, shedding his lab coat along the way.

"I need to be back in there. Your father needs me," said my mother. She started to return to the treatment room. I blocked her way. She started to push against me. Tears were everywhere. I held mine back. This was not the time. "Let me go Rossiter. Your father needs me." When I didn't move, she started to pound her fists against my chest in a half-hearted effort to move me. The crying intensified. I hugged her. The impromptu beating stopped. Her knees buckled, and quickly I steered her over to a chair and sat beside her.

The waiting room was almost deserted. No media cameras, cables or reporters. The only sound in the room was the television set that now showed an infomercial with George Foreman.

"Ross, what's going on back there? What are they doing?" Her eyes, bloodshot with grief, locked squarely onto mine.

"I don't know Mom. Seriously, I don't. Dad's condition is very delicate. It's good that they aren't taking any chances."

Marilyn Malone, wife of Jack and mother of Ross, Anthony and Chris sighed. She probably didn't believe me, but then again, why should she? I'm not so sure I believed me.

The TV set then passed through Oprah and two thirds of the way through the ninety minutes of local news before Colleen Powers came out.

"I'm sorry that I didn't get out here sooner. We've been very busy. Mrs. Malone, your husband suffered a minor heart attack that we were able to minimize through medications like nitroglycerin." Mom and I both waited for the other shoe to come crashing down. "He's holding his own right now. We're moving him down to cardiac care."

Mom stood and was already on the move as she spoke. "Can we see him?"

Colleen had to hustle to keep up. "Sure, follow me. Oh Ross? There's a phone call for you at the desk. I believe its Doctor Abilene. I'll take your Mom upstairs. You can meet us there."

"Thanks."

A nurse's aide displaying a daffodil tattoo high on her left cheekbone offered the phone.

"Ross, how's your father?" said Susan.

"Holding his own, Sue. Barely, but holding his own," I said, mindful of how close we were to losing him only a few short moments ago.

"Dr. Coleman told me his treatment plan would begin tomorrow morning with a cardiac cath, then maybe an angioplasty."

"Maybe surgery?"

"There is always that possibility, Ross."

I pressed further. "Did the good doctor say it was a possibility?"

Before Sue could answer, another phone line beckoned her. She excused herself, but returned instantly. "Look Ross, if you need me I can fly back there in a few hours."

"Won't your arms be tired?" She sighed her number 12 sympathetic sigh. "Honey, there's nothing you can do here. I'll call you as soon as we know anything."

"Promise?"

"You betcha." Another call interrupted and we said quick "love yous" and see you laters. I went to intensive care. Cardiac Intensive Care was another floor up, I discovered.

Room 11; cardiac intensive care was almost an architectural afterthought. Tucked away in the farthest corner of the unit, it's only window overlooked the parking lot. When I got there, Mom was coming out of Dad's room. Colleen Powers kept her upright on legs of Jell-O.

"Ross, your Dad needs his rest now. Why don't you take your mother home? You'll both need your rest. The cardiac cath is scheduled for seven a.m."

"Can't I see my father?"

"Son," said my mother, "let him rest. Take me home. Anthony will be here soon."

I wanted to walk right by them and at least take a peek through the glass at him. Instead, the dutiful son kicked into overdrive. I took Mom home.

My mother's failing eyesight made a miraculous recovery as she spotted it first from seemingly ten blocks away. She smiled.

"He's here. I see Anthony's van." Sure enough, my younger brother's middle class mini-van was standing guard at the curb. Anthony and his wife, Roberta, bounded down the front porch stairs, reaching my Cherokee almost before I could shift into park. Hugs all around, murmurs of concern, a sniffle or two as I cut the engine and started to get out.

"That's all right Ross. You don't have to stay. I'm sure you have a busy schedule. Anthony and Roberta will stay with me. Thank you for coming to the hospital."

Dismissed like a concerned neighbor who helped out in a pinch didn't sit well with me. My sister-in-law sent a sympathetic look back my way as they escorted Mom back into the house where I had been born.

I ignited the Cherokee's engine, slammed the shift into drive and burned rubber away from the curb. I went back to the hospital to see my father.

-5-

Agentle hand from a floor nurse coming on shift shook my shoulder rushing me back from a very deep sleep. I hoped that I hadn't drooled. My father's bed was empty. And the monitors that had lulled me to sleep with their metronomic beeping were now silent. Their wires dangled impotently from the machines on the shelf like overcooked spaghetti. Fear gripped me. Had he died and I missed it?

My head cleared after a firm shake. Hands rubbed my eyes awake. They focused. I summoned a passing nurse. "Excuse me, can you tell me where Mr. Malone is? John Malone?"

She looked at me as if deciding whether to waste a can of mace on me. Deciding I wasn't an imminent threat, she pointed to the right.

"I believe he's down having his cardiac catheterization procedure. Down the hall to your left," she said swiftly departing.

Dragging the rest of me behind them with great difficulty, my feet began to run down the long, polished linoleum hallway. I burst through the double doors into the waiting room. The half dozen people in there I wasn't related to jumped about a foot into the air. I found Mom, Anthony and Roberta.

"I'm sorry I'm late. I overslept. How is he?"

"Doctor Coleman is in there now. Anthony talked with him."

"All is normal at the moment," said my brother who always looked dapper, even in one of those short white dental coats. "Pop told us not to wake you, that you'd been there all night. Ross, you didn't have to play catch up."

"I wasn't playing catch up. It seemed like the right thing to do. Sort of like telling all concerned family members about important things. Don't you agree?" It sounded sarcastic even to me.

Anthony threw up his hands after depositing yet another Tic-Tac breath mint into his mouth.

Mom glared at me. I didn't care. I scrounged through the magazines that had seen better days and settled on an old supermarket tabloid. Nixon resigned? I should read the papers more often. The clock slogged on. I started reading my horoscope for 1974.

"Mr. Malone? Remember me? George Trask?"

I looked up. "Of course Mr. Trask, how are you?" The man I had met in the parking lot outside my office was now wearing the red coat and hospital embroidered crest of a volunteer. His previously blackened eye looked better, but now fresh bruises on the opposite side of his face had joined it. I winced inside.

"I'm doing all right. I guess. I thought you were going out of town," said Trask. It hit my ears like an accusation.

"My father's had a heart attack. They're doing tests right now."

He clapped a sympathetic hand onto my shoulder, but it left after a brief stay. "I'm sorry." Trask stood there. I stood there.

"Is there something else, Mr. Trask?" I knew there would be.

"I feel awkward asking this. But you haven't reconsidered taking my case?"

"No. In fact, I won't be taking cases until I'm sure my father's out of danger."

His hands went palms up like a priest during the celebratory offering. "But you don't understand. I need your help."

"I'm sure you do, Mr. Trask. Look, the best I can do is to recommend the best private investigator I know to look into this for you. Here's her card."

"Her?" His face scrunched up as mine did at the first sight of broccoli at six years old. He read the card. "Nellie Archer?"

"Yes. She's as good as I am, almost. And her great grandfather was Miles Archer, a legend in the business from San Francisco." I purposely neglected to add that Miles' claim to fame was getting killed. "Nellie is a professional. I'll call her and tell her that you will be contacting her. Good luck, Mr. Trask."

George Trask extended a halfhearted hand for an uninspired handshake, then shuffled off out the door as if Mickey Mantle had refused to sign his autograph. Obviously disappointed, Trask was not at all sure he wanted a girl for a private investigator. I doubted he would call Nellie. I heard Tony's voice next.

"The gall of that man," said my brother. He was right behind me. He smelled of fluoride.

"Lighten up Tony," I said. I returned to my tabloid as my brother stared after Trask, throwing daggers into his back. "Can't he see that we're involved with family matters?"

"Oooohhhh, now it's **we're** involved in family matters. Nice to know I'm included now." I turned several pages without looking at a word.

Anthony Malone DDS started to reply then looked at my mother, and nodded at me to follow him. I did and felt for my Beretta through force of habit. I also felt for the extra ammunition clip, just in my case my message to Lenny Bogardus wasn't accepted in the spirit in which it was sent.

We left the small waiting room and navigated through the hustle and bustle of a cardiac lab with patients, tests, gurneys, orderlies etc. Our destination turned out to be a bank of vending machines at the far end of the hallway. Their most outstanding feature aside from the diversity of their contents that now included microwave meals and burritos that would survive a direct nuclear strike, was the money slot that now took dollar bills. Ain't capitalism wonderful?

My younger brother, with the haircut by appointment that came with a 30-minute scalp massage, planted his feet like we were playing king of the family and I had to knock him off his perch.

Dropping him with a right cross was my first inclination. I felt my fist clench into readiness. It took me a moment to get out of attack mode.

"Okay Ross, let's have it. Eversince you heard that Pop had a heart attack and nobody told you, you've been sulking. Don't you think it was time you grew up and joined the family?"

"Gee Tony, I didn't know I wasn't part of the family. Or was I voted out by you and Mom and no one bothered to tell me that either?"

"What really bothers you about not being told? Think back to then, big brother. You and Susan were having your troubles. Did I whine to you, 'Oh Ross, big brother, Daddy had a heart attack. Come save the family and me?' No. I did what you would have done. I handled it. So what bothers you, Mr. Big City Private Detective?"

The face that stared back at me was flushed with anger and confrontation. His crossed arms against his chest were straining to do something, anything to dissipate the emotion that was building to a breaking point all too soon.

"I wanted to fix it," I said calmly, almost in a whisper.

"What? Speak up, I can't hear you."

"I said I wanted to fix it. You were right, Tony. I'm feeling guilty that I wasn't told so I couldn't go down to Florida and fix it. That's what I do for a living. I fix other people's problems. And it would have been nice to fix my own family's problems."

"Ross, there was nothing you could do."

"I know Tony, I know. And I'm not used to feeling powerless. I couldn't help Susan. I can't help Pop. Hell, I not only couldn't save Molly and Christopher, I didn't have the decency to be on the plane with them when they were murdered."

"Murdered?" His eyebrows arched with a curiosity that would be hard to placate.

Silence fell between us. I had only found out recently that the circumstances surrounding their death were not accidental. A solution as to what I should do with all of that had eluded me, so far. This was not the time to hash it out.

"Let it go, Tony. I'll handle it." He started down the road anyhow, and I changed the subject. "Let's bottomline this Bro. You wounded my ego by trying to protect Mom when I've always thought that was my job. What do you say that we bury the hatchet and start fresh?"

Making sure that I unclenched my fist first, I extended my hand. Anthony Malone looked at me. Then he looked at my hand. After what seemed like an eternity, where I briefly considered retracting it, he grasped it.

I decided to go a step further. "Want a Pepsi? I'm buying."

"No thanks Ross. That stuff is bad for your teeth."

"Suit yourself. Means more for me," I said smiling. He looked at my smile as if calculating an estimate for bridgework in his head.

But he did return the smile, then slapped me on the back and headed towards the waiting room. I paused to get my Pepsi. I wondered as the dark refreshing liquid touched my lips, how long this familial truce would hold.

The overhead paging system blared my name. "Ross Malone. Mr. Ross Malone. You have a call at the nurse's station."

Ditching the rest of the Pepsi in the trash, I sprinted back down the hall to the nurse's station in fifteen strides. I tried not to gasp too much, as I took the phone from the unit secretary who was trying not to giggle.

"Malone."

"Tom Otera, Ross. How's your father?" He was calling from his car. I heard the traffic in the background.

"They're still doing tests."

"I still need that statement on the shooting in your office," he said.

"As soon as this procedure is over, I'll drop by the Justice Center. Will you be there?"

"No. They have me on special assignment."

I asked, "Should I be impressed?"

"You should always be impressed with me, Malone. But yes, this could be classified as impressive. I've been assigned to head a Sheriff's Security Detail at the airport for an arriving VIP."

"McCartney's coming to the Dome?" I chuckled.

Tom Otera laughed, slammed a hand twice on his car horn and swore like a sailor. "Sorry, some idiot with call waiting on his car phone almost rear ended me. The VIP lives in a large ivory house in the nation's capital."

"I guess that lets out Helen Hunt."

"It does, unless Helen is supposed to meet the President of Laracone. Gotta go Ross. My best to your family. You're in our prayers," said Otera.

"Thanks Tom. Give my regards to the First Tourist." The connection was broken. I was smiling inside. Tom Otera hadn't been with the local Sheriff's Department that long yet he was already garnering the plum assignments, such as security for the leader of the free world. He deserved it. Not to mention he had become one of the few close friends I could make money off of during the football season.

I slowly headed back towards the waiting room. The elevator doors opened behind me and I heard a familiar voice.

"Ross?"

My little sister Chris then ran full bore into my open arms, allowing me just enough time to turn full around, or we would have crashed to the floor. My body rocked back on impact, but we didn't fall. Her face was smeared with makeup that looked like an oatmeal mask she'd forgotten to peel off.

"Hi Sis, how are you?" I could barely get the words out as her hug threatened the sanctity of my rib cage.

Still in her embrace, I heard her say through gathering tears, "I'm okay. How's Daddy?"

"He's still inside having his heart catheterization. They told us not to ask, that they would talk to us when the tests were over. Mom, Tony and Roberta are inside."

She held me fast when I started to take a step back. "Not yet Ross. I need to compose myself. I can't let them see me like this. Where's the ladies room?"

"Let's see, the last time I used it..." I pointed down the hall to the generic international signage for restrooms. My sister slapped my shoulder and scrunched up her face like she did when I tried to divide the candy at Halloween in my favor. Then she headed for the sign.

As Ms. Christine Malone walked away from me, I took notice that she was no longer the same little sister I had taken to the drugstore for a cherry phosphate when a dime store really meant ten-cent items. Now, she was designer jeans and swoosh logos on her feet.

My creaking bones were almost audible to me, as I suffered through the bends while my mind raced fast forward back through the last three decades plus one-year since she was born. Her high school prom was just taking center stage when Anthony called to me. I was needed back in the waiting room. I hustled back and found George Trask there. His pallor was that of some-one with chalk white Liquid Paper coursing through his veins.

Trask pushed Nellie's business card back at me. His voice propelled the words out in a flood of stuttered syllables.

"Thank you Mr. Malone, for your help but…" I paused before taking the offering. "But I have decided not to pursue it." I kept silent. A look of disapproval thundered across my features like a cold front on a weather map.

"Are you sure you want to drop this?" I said. Trying to read his face was a lost cause. Trask averted his eyes downward, still keeping silent. "Mr. Trask?"

"I don't want to fight anymore." Even his voice seemed to have surrendered.

"Come with me. Tony, I'll be right back. Have the doctor wait."

Tony was not a happy camper. Censure for my pending absence crept across the features on his face. "Ross, do you really have to leave?"

"Yes Tony. I said I would be right back." Without further hesitation, I guided Trask out the waiting room door and down the hall to a bank of pay phones. My cell phone was not permitted in the cardiac unit. I found Christine deep in a conversation that came to a screeching halt in mid-sentence as Trask and I approached.

"Any word Ross?" she said, as if trying to deflect my attention to the reason for her phone call.

"Not yet, but it should be soon," I said. "You might want to get back."

Chris nodded then returned to her conversation. "I have to go. We'll discuss this more later. I **am** allowed an opinion you know."

She omitted the good-bye with malice aforethought, if the look on her face was any indication. Of course, she also slammed the phone receiver back down into its cradle for effect.

"Aren't you coming, Ross?"

"You go ahead. I'll be along in a minute or two. I need to make a quick call." Chris backed another few feet away, then turned, and headed off to go bond with the rest of the Malone clan. I dropped a quarter and a dime into the coin slot then dialed. "Hello Nellie?"

"Sorry, this is Gwen. Can I help you?"

"Gwen, Ross Malone. Can I speak with Nellie?" I said.

A moment later, Nellie Archer was in my ear. I briefly outlined the Trask scenario for her. She waited patiently, asking only the bare minimum of questions. I watched Trask through my recounting of the case. He practically hopped from one foot to another as his eyes swept the surroundings in wide arcs. For a man battle-hardened by the Marine Corps, I found this behavior odd. Sure, time changes people and I could never begin to imagine the horrors he saw first hand in Southeast Asia, but I was getting the nagging feeling that I was missing something else with George Trask. Or, that he was dreading what would happen next.

"Okay Ross. I'll speak with him," said Nellie.

I merged the phone receiver with George Trask's ear, then started backpedaling towards the waiting room. I ended my role with a two-fingered Cub Scout salute, which got no response from the worried grocery storeowner.

The waiting room had emptied out upon my return. Mom, Roberta, Tony and Chris had gathered their things and were preparing to leave.

"Aren't you going to wait for the doctor?" I said, knowing immediately from their expressions that he had already made an appearance and departed. "What did he tell you?"

Tony stepped over in front of me and spoke to the rest of the family. "Roberta, why don't you take Mom and Chris to the car? I'll fill Big Brother in."

Roberta Malone nodded and kissed Tony's offered cheek as if it were a job not an adventure. Then, she and Chris escorted Mom to the nearby elevators. Chris said something about stopping first in the cafeteria for something to eat. After another moment, they were gone.

"Well, what did Dr. Coleman say Tony?"

Tony put a finger to his lips and waited an agonizing moment for the elevator doors to close. "What the hell do you care? I swear Ross; sometimes I just don't understand where your priorities are? Your father, our father, is fighting for his life and you just walk out the door as if he is just another item on your to do list. Care to explain that to me? I'm a reasonably intelligent adult. Try to explain why you felt it necessary to let a scared little man take precedence over the health of your critically ill father?"

So much for the truce.

"Tony, either tell me what Dr. Coleman said, or get out of my way so I can find him." I counted silently to five and headed for the door. When my foot hit the hallway, Tony responded.

"Dad needs an operation. A quadruple bypass." Tony's voice cracked. "Or he's going to die."

I stopped in my tracks. Shivers went up and down my spine as if I had jammed a metal fork into a toaster. As much as you think you are ready for a time like this, when it finally comes, you find that you aren't really ready at all.

-6-

The wind beneath my wings took flight along with all of the air in my lungs. My shoulders slumped. My spirit did a stock market plunge. I stared straight ahead. "How soon?"

"A day, maybe two. The next attack might kill him. Dr. Coleman says Dad needs a minimum of four, maximum six arteries bypassed. It's bad Ross. Before you ask, an angioplasty in Dr. Coleman's opinion would be a waste of valuable time."

"No transplant?" I was searching for alternatives. It didn't matter how farfetched they were.

Tony brushed his knuckles against the wooden doorframe. "Knock wood, Coleman doesn't think he needs it. But none of this matters if Dad doesn't consent. Ross, he's scared he's going to die. Coleman's rationale is that if the bypass doesn't take, a transplant is always an option. I personally doubt Pop could take two major operations, assuming a heart could be found that soon. Dad is frightened that he won't survive even one surgery."

"Sounds like a logical fear to me," I said, only half hearing what my brother said. Open-heart surgery wasn't something I had expected. What was that line? Denial ain't just a river in Egypt.

"Yes Ross, it is normal. However, Coleman says the longer that this is delayed, the tougher it will be to get a successful outcome."

"Successful outcome? All doctors talk like that?" I said.

"Sure. Then there are the show-offs who also speak Klingon as well." He smiled as relieved as I was the tension was broken for the moment. I felt the storm pass once again. We headed to join the rest of the clan.

At the far end of the cafeteria, that was totally high tech right up to the skylight ceiling that doubled as the floor of a water fountain in the main hospital lobby, sat my immediate family minus grandchildren and grandfather. Roberta handed me Pepsi awash over a glass filled with crushed ice.

"I wasn't sure if you wanted ice or not," said my sister-in-law.

"Didn't they say that on the Titanic?" I returned her smile. Tony had made a good choice in Roberta. "I'll rough it." I added a second smile before taking a gulp while trying not to choke on an errant ice chip. "Mom, how are you holding up?"

She shrugged. It was a chore for her to do so. "Tony, you talk to your father. He'll listen to you. Tell him he needs this operation. Tell him he'll die, if he doesn't have it."

"Mom, Doctor Coleman already told Daddy all of this," said Chris. "You need to talk to Daddy."

Mom shook her head, fighting back even more tears.

"I think Ross should talk to Jack," said Roberta, not really sure she should be offering opinions on blood family matters. "He's the eldest."

Everyone looked at me. I finished the Pepsi, then stood. "This is Pop's decision. I'm not sure what I can add Doctor Coleman hasn't already told him. I'll go talk to him, but I won't browbeat him into saying yes to surgery. Mom, I'll call you later." There wasn't even a shrug this time.

I moved to kiss my Mom's cheek. She turned her head away at the last second. I settled for the back of her skull.

Dad was staring at a spot on the translucent wall of his glass-enclosed room. I walked in and squeezed his hand. He didn't squeeze back.

"How are you doing?"

"Your mother sent you." He looked at me suspiciously, as if whatever I said would be filtered through the polygraph in his mind. "She sent you to talk me into having this surgery, didn't she?"

"No, she didn't send me." It wasn't a lie. She wanted to send Anthony.

A wave dismissed my presence. "Well, save your breath son. I'm not going to have it. So you can just forget about it."

I let a moment or two pass so he would think I was actually considering his request. "Okay by me, Pop. Now, lets move on to other decisions."

"Like what?" my father asked warily.

"Mahogany okay?" He looked confused. "Is mahogany okay? I mean, if you're going to play fast and loose with the Angel of Death, the rest of us should be prepared. Now, Mahogany or, wait, maybe you want to be cremated?"

Dad was not happy. If his facial expression was any indication, my name was on the will in disappearing ink at that moment. "You've made your point." Then he fell silent for a long time. The expression didn't change. The breathing was monotone in both rate and the energy expended to exhale the shallow breaths. But his mood had taken a nosedive. I tried to let him deal with these sobering life and death decisions on his own without trying to fix it. My eyes fixed themselves on the TV and ESPN Sportscenter. The tint on the color set painted the anchors only a little bit healthier than my Dad. "I don't want to die. I've heard of people who go in for surgery and never come out."

"Pop, Tony's the doctor in the family. He could tell you the medical whys and wherefores. All I can say is this. More people probably die in household accidents than surgery."

"Is that supposed to make me feel better?" he said.

"Think of it this way. Unless you have the operation at home, in the bathtub or on a ladder while changing a light bulb, you've got a shot of making it through." I leaned over and gave him as much of a hug as the wires, tubes and such would allow. "Personally, I'd go with the Mahogany."

The gurgle I heard emanate from him was the best he could do for a laugh. I settled for it.

"I'll be back later, Pop. Get some rest. As for your decision? You do what is best for you, and I'll be behind you."

I left him to rest. Rather than brave that family gauntlet in the cafeteria again, I decided to give the police that statement about the shooting in my office. Just in case my Dad was laid up for a long time, I wanted to make sure that the decks were cleared.

Barely inside the door at 4HOPE, I was greeted by the not so dulcet tones of Chester Kensington, interim Director of the center and interim landlord.

"Malone, we need to talk."

"No, we don't, Chester," I said, walking past him as if he was a stiff breeze and I had just turned my collar up. He followed me into my office like toilet paper attached to my heel. I tried to close the door in his face. He was undaunted.

"This will only hurt a minute."

"Are you going to tell me Dana is on her way back?" Her absence made him interim.

"No. Ms. Glenn will be gone at least through the summer, though I don't know why."

"We all handle grief differently, Chester. What do you want?" He started to babble on. My thoughts drifted to Dana Glenn who was still grieving the loss of her friend Mitchell Droukas, a reporter who could have been the next Woodward or Bernstein, except that he ran smack dab into an icon that hungered to become a legend. Mitchell had been the deer in the icon's headlights.

"Aren't you listening to me, Malone?" He thrust a paper into my hand that had numbers on it.

"If I didn't know better Chester, I'd think that this was a rent increase," I said, tossing the paper aside.

"Perceptive aren't you? Would you like to write out a check now or just have me add it to your account?"

"You've raised the rent almost 50%."

"And that is still far below market value for a property in this location in a comparable city."

"Does Dana know about this?" His expression told me she didn't. "I didn't think so."

"Ms. Glenn knows that I was brought in to downsize and streamline this operation. Your rent is one of the few cash flow situations we have control over. The rest are charitable contributions. So in order to keep 4HOPE profitable, we need more money. This piece of paper says we need more of it from you."

Before I could fire off a snappy retort, Lucas Gentero ran into my office and collapsed in a heap behind my jukebox. He was gulping oxygen by the mouthful, and perspiring in what resembled his own personal downpour.

"You've got to save me, Malone. I'm being persecuted. Freedom of the press in this country is guaranteed. But you've got to help me. Got a back way out of here?"

"Don't you just want to crawl under the rug?" I said. I tried my best not to smirk, but Lucas looked funny crouched in his version of the fetal position clad in his post Jimmy Olsen uniform.

Chester turned his nose up. "I'll expect the increase effective as of your next rent check." He looked down his nose, literally and figuratively, at Lucas, then turned on his Italian made leather heels and left. Suddenly, the room smelled better.

"Care to get up and use a chair, Lucas?"

"No thank you. A jukebox will stop a bullet better than cheap imitation velour."

"I resent that, I think. It isn't cheap. So, who's after you?"

"We are." Lucas and I looked at the doorway and saw my old friends from Mercy Hill Emergency, Andrew and Jacob. Only this time, Jacob let his gun precede him. Andrew walked over with heavy steps, even on the carpeting, and dragged Lucas to his feet with one burly hand.

"You are coming with us," he said. It wasn't a suggestion.

I stepped out from behind the desk. The gun barrel followed me. "Gee, I wish I could think of something tougher to say, but let him go."

Andrew, still holding Lucas so that the reporter's toes barely touched the floor, edged closer to the door.

"Stay where you are, Malone. We have no quarrel with you. This is between this lowlife and the Republic of Laracone."

"Not when you try to take him from my office." I stepped closer to Lucas. "Lose the firepower and we'll talk. Or lose the firepower and leave. Either way, you leave alone."

I gently eased off my coat revealing my 9mm Beretta in its black leather holster hugging my left hip. They didn't seem impressed. Maybe I should have worn the shoulder holster like Mike Hammer.

"More big talk from another American whose bark is worse than his bite," said Jacob.

My response was a thin smile. "Care to find out how hard I bite?" I said.

Andrew returned the smile as if eyeing fresh meat. He shoved Lucas like a sack of day old laundry into Jacob's grasp. He then handed off his suit jacket. A gold tooth was the centerpiece of his grin.

"Shall we go into the parking lot and settle this like men?" A verbal line was drawn in the sand. I stepped over it.

"Fine with me. The winner gets Lucas. The loser lets him," I said.

Andrew nodded, and just like that I found myself ready to go to knuckle junction to preserve democracy. Thomas Jefferson would have been proud.

Lucas tried to cheer me on, sort of. "You'd better not lose, Malone."

"You'd better be worth it, Lucas," I said. I looked back at Andrew just in time to see a right cross rocketing towards my cheek. It whizzed by after first glancing off the bone. I felt my skin split. Papercut sized pain. The follow-up came from left field allowing me to duck it more easily. Andrew was in good shape. I, on the other hand, was finding it harder and harder to keep in fighting form as the pages of my calendar flew by.

His knuckles dug deep into my ribcage as if he were drilling for oil, or my spinal cord. So far, he had hit me twice, and missed once. I had yet to respond.

"Jesus, Malone, fight back. Don't let them take me."

The next time my face met Andrew's fist, my knees buckled. Why couldn't I get ready to defend Lucas? It dawned on me that saving Lucas, as honorable as that was, didn't require that I hurt someone else. I changed my focus to my father laying on the

stretcher in the ER and Andrew standing in my way. More plutonium rods were pulled from my internal reactor.

Resisting the urge to paw the ground with my foot like a bull
seeing red, my first response was an uppercut, up and under, tar-
geted for his ribcage. I double-teamed that with some jabbing by
my right hand. The third jab preceded a left hook that crumbled
Andrew to his knees. He fell forward onto all fours. A guttural
cough came from his lungs which must have been working overtime if he was feeling as winded as I was rapidly becoming.

I bounced back and forth trying to give the appearance of
Rocky Balboa when my insides felt like Rocky the Flying Squirrel.
He stayed down a long time. I sucked in as much air as I could, as
fast as I could.

"Well?" I said. Bouncing back and forth for image sake was
becoming tedious.

Without so much as bobbing his head, Andrew spoke. He
coughed to clear his dry throat. "Let the reporter go, Jacob."

""No Andrew, I can beat this Malone," he said. There was
fire in his eyes and no doubt, assault with a deadly weapon in
his heart.

"I said, 'Let him go.' I gave my word. I lost."

Jacob started to whine. "But President Walanna...."

This got Andrew upset to the point where he catapulted himself
to his feet and jerked Lucas away from Jacob. Lucas rushed back
behind me. Andrew put his hand on Jacob's gun and lowered it.
He then looked back over his shoulder at Lucas.

"You are lucky to have such a good friend. But the next time,
we will not leave this to chance. Do not let there be a next time."

They left. My knuckles throbbed in earnest. I went back inside
to my office and submerged them in a sink filled with cold water.
Lucas tossed me a ready-made ice pack from the little fridge I had

just to keep ice packs available. Whipping off a two-finger salute, Lucas headed for the door now, that the coast was clear.

"Hold it," I said in almost a bellow. "Want to tell me why the Twin Towers were chasing you?"

"It's not my fault, Malone. They were just steamed about a series of articles I wrote about their country."

"Laracone."

"Right, well, um," said Lucas, at a loss for words for the first time since I had known him. "Well, I also included some analysis, as is my wont to do on occasion." He started pacing the room while pontificating. "Anyway, I went to try to get an interview with their President Walanna when these guys take me into a room and tell me that they didn't like the tone of the articles I wrote, and that I should leave before I get hurt."

"But you didn't take the hint, did you?" I said.

Lucas balled up his fists and planted them on his hips. "Damn right, I didn't. I stand on the freedom of the press, and that's when they started smacking me around. I escaped and came right here."

"I'm impressed. You said all of that on one breath of air."

"This is serious, Malone." He pulled up his sweat soaked shirt-tail revealing an ugly bruise the size of Rhode Island. I removed another ice pack from the freezer and gave it to him. Even I had to wince at the enormity of the wound. "Yeouch, this is cold. Now, do you believe me?"

"Yeah, I believe you. Grab a couple of bottles of Pepsi and let's take a ride."

"Do I look like a waiter to you or something, Malone? Oh all right, I guess you did just save my life. I'll swallow my pride just this once."

There was something about the proprietary way that Andrew and Jacob had just decided in their arbitrary fashion that it was their place to flog Lucas within an inch of his ethics just because they disagreed with his writing that bothered me. I found it hard to believe that Benjamin Walanna would be a party to, or condone, that kind of mischief on his behalf by the hired help. Getting ridiculed came with the territory for a head of state or a major league baseball owner. On the other hand, my nose spent more time in *BASEBALL WEEKLY* than *NATIONAL GEOGRAPHIC.*

I wasn't sure how the press was treated in Laracone, but if Andrew and Jacob were any barometer of their regard for the First Amendment, the press was no doubt on the government's endangered species list.

Lucas kept tugging at his shoulder harness as it rubbed against his tender ribs. Then he squirmed in his passenger seat in the Cherokee. "Where are you taking me, Malone?"

"I believe the term is 'into the valley of death rode the six hundred'." An additional smile always made them wonder what you were up to.

"And when they did ride in, they were slaughtered!" His voice rose with every syllable. "Did you remember that too? Oh my God, it's the Laracone consulate."

"Your powers of observation are keen, Watson."

"Malone, on a scale of one to ten, this idea of yours ranks right down there with believing that sleeping upside down will keep you from getting bald." Lucas Gentero started to sweat as I slowed to a stop at the six-foot high wrought iron gate imbedded with the regal crest of Laracone. "Are you nuts? There's probably a contract out on me."

I wondered if the contract on his life would be for more than the measly $25,000 that was out for me. The uniformed security guard at the gate asked me to state my business.

"I'm here to see President Walanna. No need to look on your clipboard, I don't have an appointment."

He slowly shook his head as if genuinely sorry. "Then I am afraid to tell you that it will be impossible for you to see President Walanna, sir," he said.

"Just tell him that Ross Malone is here."

"One moment, sir." The guard stepped back and dug out a cell phone from a holster on his belt. He didn't appear to be armed. But I'd been in the business long enough not to take anything for granted. I studied the guard who appeared to be a college kid supplementing his income. A pro might have just blown me off, and told me to hit the road. The guard stepped back to my driver's side window and handed me his cell phone. "It's President Walanna, sir."

"Thanks. Hello, Mr. President, this is Ross Malone. We met at the hospital emergency room earlier."

His tone was friendly except that he seemed a little put out. It bordered on annoyance. "I remember, Malone. I trust your father is well. What is it you want?"

"Same as before, to save you the embarrassment of an international incident," I said.

"How thoughtful," he said, without emotion. "Call my chief of staff and set up an appointment."

"Could you possibly squeeze me in now? It will only take a moment. I have a reporter from the Sentinel with me. Andrew and Jacob, the bookends you pay to protect you, tried to revoke his license to breathe. He'd like to make his case to you rather than the New York Times. Sort of like the Salman Rushdie defense, you might say."

The silence was brief. Benjamin Walanna told me where he was. "And Malone, we are merely acquaintances. Please do not presume on my good graces again."

Walanna had the good sense to hang up. I had thought I could just drop Lucas off then head to the hospital to see how my Dad was. However my gut instinct was, if I did that, Lucas would be so much human mulch by nightfall.

-7-

The expansive courtesy suite at the airport that was a study in techno-warmth with its tubular steel furniture; its politically correct neutral carpeting and fluorescent illumination boasted more three-piece suits than a Wall Street unemployment office. More than a few had those little earpieces that the well-dressed security expert was wearing these days. The tallest, Italian made suit adorned Benjamin Walanna. The cut of his designer shirt was ruined by the body armor he was forced to wear beneath it.

He frowned when our Ross and Lucas show rolled into the room.

"Malone, once our business has concluded, our relationship will have come full circle."

"Fair enough. Tell me why you sent Andrew and Jacob to rough up this reporter?" I said, not bothering to mince words.

A dismissive wave of his hand preceded his remarks. "I do not send my people to deal with the insignificant." He drew in a large breath through his nose and let it exit the same way. "His articles were inaccurate to say the least, and inflammatory at worst. They gave aid and comfort to my political enemies back home. Andrew and Jacob were merely attempting to set the record straight, of that I am sure."

"So they set the record straight by breaking his ribs?"

Walanna eyed me as if this was the first he had heard of it. His eyes wandered down to where Lucas was still clutching his ice pack. "Perhaps a miscalculation. Their methods sometimes lack the tact of a diplomat. Though they do garner results."

"In my country, the one you are currently standing in," I said, "sometimes, they garner jail time."

"Diplomatic immunity would not allow that," said Walanna.

I turned to Lucas. "Come on, we'll go talk to MSNBC. They don't hide behind diplomatic immunity." A tug at Gentero's sleeve brought a quizzical look from the reporter's face to mine. I jerked my head towards the exit. "Let's go. He's not even going to apologize."

Lucas backed away from me until he was free from my grip. "Wait a minute, Malone. I'm sure the president is a fair man. After all, he hasn't beheaded you yet." I scowled at Lucas who continued on in his babbling. "I don't necessarily need a formal apology."

His motive was now clear. I joined in the plan. "Then perhaps, something along the lines of an exclusive interview might soothe your ruffled feathers?" I proposed.

Walanna bought into it. "Yes, an exclusive interview. I would be willing. As long as the facts are reported as I have said them," he said.

"I am nothing if not honest, Mr. President," said Lucas Gentero, with a click of his heels and a curt nod of his head.

"Tonto, our work here is done," I said, with a brief clap of my hands.

I shook hands for what I assumed would be the last time with my first world leader. The meaty hand of a nearby security guard stopped me from leaving. It was Tom Otera.

"Stay put Malone. Air Force One has just touched down," he said.

Quickly, he fell into lock step with President Walanna and his security entourage as they headed out of the VIP suite. My fingers parted the nearby mini-blinds coated with a thin layer of dust to view the proceedings.

No doubt by the flood of press people pouring into the terminal, their plane had landed first. Confined behind a cordon of velvet ropes strung together with brass stanchions, they strained to get that first picture or that headline making quote for their next deadline. Uniformed officers kept them contained and scanned their numbers for the next Lee Harvey Oswald or John Hinckley.

Next in the food chain came the requisite aides, hangers on and press reps ready to spin every word, gesture or facial tic under the most favorable light possible. VIP badges hung by chains around their necks. I also noticed a system of lapel pins denoting who was important and who wasn't in case the enemy struck. They were unobtrusive except to the trained observer.

Benjamin Walanna was then guided to his spot on stage in this photo op. Flanked by security, then national flags, then more security, he stood ramrod straight as the rest of this tableau unfolded. The hand carved presidential seal was hung on the front of the podium; a blue binder embossed with that same seal was stationed on the top. No Teleprompters today. From seeing his face on the Sunday morning interview shows, I recognized the press secretary looking up and down press row waiting for them to get ready before he cued the star's entrance. He was okay, but my favorite was still Dee Dee Myers.

Air Force One stood majestically in the background. To me, it had always represented the majesty of the United States of America. It seemed omnipotent and graceful, lethal and necessary.

Like dominoes falling in succession, White House personnel stationed around the terminal began nodding sequentially. Ruffles and Flourishes emanated from the airport's public address system. It sounded tinny, yet, nonetheless brought a goosebump or two to my flesh. With the sea of humanity before me, I had a hard time seeing anyone important exiting the plane so I contented myself with watching the inner terminal like everyone else.

There he was. Dressed in a dark blue suit, which sported a thin pinstripe, the President of the United States walked into the room. Immediately, all of the available air was absorbed by his presence. The suit, which must have cost as much as Walanna's didn't seem to be accessorized with body armor. I wondered what that said about our country. My conclusion was that it said more about the efficiency of the Secret Service.

Even Nixon, Ford and Carter as president evoked the same emotion in me. It wasn't the man; it was the office. The closest I'd been to celebrity in the past were those performers on the USO tours during my time in the Gulf.

Kate Smith singing "God Bless America" rang in my ears alone as Walanna and the President shook hands. They turned obligingly and dutifully to the phalanx of cameras, both still and video, which exploded in a barrage of flashbars that, would have blinded any normal human being. Of course, not only didn't they shy away from this onslaught, they didn't even blink.

Standing at the President's left shoulder and looking attentive, but totally focused was the First Lady. I liked her a lot. She reminded me of Air Force One, graceful and only lethal when necessary. What I saw next took my breath away.

I had to blink twice to make sure it wasn't a mirage. It wasn't. Among the last group of persons entering the backside of the terminal away from the festivities was Susan, wearing the New York Yankees warm-up jacket I got her during our last trip to the House that Ruth Built during the last World Series.

She looked radiant. My hand went to the polished doorknob of the courtesy suite. A security guard blocked my exit. I wanted to resist back but realized that this certainly wasn't the time or place.

In his trademark southern drawl, the President voiced the usual platitudes of peace, mutually beneficial trade agreements and the importance of them hitching their wagon to our rising star in the world community. Walanna followed with the same. A sign language interpreter almost got cramps in both hands when Walanna decided to speak a few words in his native tongue. The cameras then shifted into a higher gear. It seemed to go on for hours, while I champed at the bit waiting to get to Susan.

The security guard/doorstop spoke into his wrist then stepped aside. He even opened the door for me.

"Susan?" I said, as I ran over to the luggage carousel. She threw her arms around me and squeezed me like a used accordion. It had been far too long. Every time I saw her, life gave me a reality check of the spirit. We kissed once, then deeper, then enough to get flogged in some backward countries. Then we came up for air, so to speak.

"How are you Tootie? I figured that if you wouldn't come to me, I'd come to you. Miss me? How's your Dad?" she said as I hung on her every word. Lovesick when Susan was around was not just a high school affliction for me.

"Pop's hanging in there. Now he's facing bypass surgery and is none too happy about it. In fact, he's seriously considering not having it," I said.

"I'm sure Dr. Coleman told him of the risks of such a surgery, but why is your father refusing it, if it will save his life?" asked Sue.

"Because there are no guarantees. He's not sure the surgery will save him and he's heard too many horror stories or seen them on the newsmagazine shows of things that go wrong. He's afraid he won't make it through the surgery."

"Not uncommon for any surgical patient, whether its tonsils or open heart. How do you plan to convince him to have it? Maybe if your brother, the doctor talks with him?" she said.

"Tony is a dentist, not a real doctor. But actually, I was thinking of having a real doctor talk with Dad."

She walked right into this trap. "Oh really? Who? Elinor Salas?" When I didn't respond, she began to realize that the only other doctor in my life I would trust with my father's life was standing next to me at the moment. "No Ross. It's got to be his decision. Doctors can't work miracles, contrary to what you see on the soaps. All we can do is give the patient the options to the best of our ability. The rest is up to them to decide the quality of life they wish to have."

My beloved then pointed to the next pair of overly large suitcases that rounded our way from the luggage carousel. I collected them and emitted a grunt of effort as I lifted them.

"Sue, did you clean out the Treasury while you were there?"

"Oh, I just picked up a few things." I knew that smile. I also knew from past experience that a few things to Susan were enough to keep a small mall in operation for a year. "I did bring you a couple of souvenirs from D.C."

"And one of them is the Washington Monument?"

"Don't be silly. They're renovating that. But don't you think the Pentagon would look better over the fireplace?" she said. Her mature adult smile covered her face. "I'll show you when we get home."

Her suitcases plopped onto the ground as I stopped just prior to unlocking my Cherokee for her. "Still no, on talking with Dad?"

"I'll compromise."

"I love it when you talk in double word scores," I said, more than a little relieved she was going to help.

"Steady big fella. I'll go see your Dad, but I will not try to convince him. I will answer his questions. Okay?"

"Fair enough," I said. I smiled. We kissed again. Sparks flew. We were lucky there were no smoke detectors in sight.

Pop was sitting up in bed when we arrived, as much as he could be while looking like he was mugged by Radio Shack with wires and transmitters everywhere.

"Susan, meet Jack Malone, the newest Pokemon toy." Dad smiled when Sue entered and kissed him on the cheek.

"Hello again Mr. Malone. How are you feeling?" she said. They had met a few times and seemed to get along.

"I've told you, please call me Jack," he said, as he mustered up a wan smile. I tapped Sue on the shoulder.

"I'm off to find Mom and see how she is," I said, then hightailed it for the door ASAP.

My Mom was heading back to Intensive Care after a foray into the gift shop with Roberta and Tony. All three were laden down with packages and bags. I offered to lighten their load by taking a few. My attempts were rebuffed.

"No thanks Big Brother, we're okay for the moment. The tractor trailer with the other purchases is on the way," said Tony.

"Anthony, I didn't buy that much. Besides, we do not know how long your father is going to be in the hospital," said Mom.

Tony pushed what I'm sure he thought was a good-natured needle in just a little deeper. "Mom, there is enough stuff here for a manned mission to mars." He laughed. Roberta laughed. Even I chuckled. Mom was a tougher audience.

"Guess who showed up?" I said, beaming from ear to ear.

Mom wanted no part of this chitchat unless she started it. Roberta took the bait.

"By that look of a Cheshire Cat on your face, I'd say Susan flew back into town."

"You win the Kewpie doll. Yes, Susan is back. She flew in on Air Force One no less. She's in with Dad now."

This got Mom's attention. Her reply was snapped off like an order. "Doing what?"

I did my best to keep my response breezy. "Not sure Mom, but a wild guess would be, maybe, talking?"

"Don't disrespect your mother," she said. I felt like I had just been stuck with the check at The Last Supper.

"I'm not," I began, "I am just trying to understand what you have against Susan."

Half turning her back to me, my mother spoke in stern tones that reminded me of not so fond times in my youth. It was as if my opinion didn't matter. "This is not a subject I wish to discuss. But in the future, please check with me before you bring non-family members into family business."

My blood, already simmering started to bubble. I hoped it wouldn't show in my face. "Look Mom, I know that you're already under a lot of stress and I have no wish to add to it. But…"

"Then don't Ross," said Sue, once again arriving in the nick of time. "Hello Mrs. Malone, Roberta, Tony. Let me say how sorry I am that we have to meet again under these less than favorable circumstances. And if there is anything I can do to help, please don't hesitate to ask. Dr. Coleman is a good man. I recommend him highly."

Mom was polite, but the frost was already on the pumpkin so to speak. "Thank you Susan. Your offer is noted. Now if you'll excuse me, I wish to go see my husband."

"Certainly," said the love of my life sweetly. She seemed unaffected by my mother's slights. I, on the other hand, was affected enough for the both of us. "Your husband has been asking for you."

My mother moved past Susan with a brief nod and a paper-thin smile. Roberta smiled and touched Susan's arm as she followed. Tony plastered a smile across his face as only a dentist itemizing your bill could do, and brought up the rear of the procession back to Dad's room. I took Susan in my arms.

"So, what did he say?"

Susan hugged me back and rested her head against my cheek as she spoke. Whenever she did that, I knew it was something I might not want to hear.

"Your father told me that he has decided to have the surgery. He mentioned something or other about not liking mahogany just yet. I have no clue what that was all about, do you?"

I nodded and caught another deep whiff of her perfume. The memories it recalled were Hallmark moments in the finest sense and a few you wouldn't dare see in a Hallmark store. "I'll explain about the mahogany later. So, is he ready for surgery?"

"Would you be ready for open heart surgery, ever?"

"Good point."

Her cheek nuzzled in closer to my neck. Her satin voice was now softer than before. I strained to hear what I knew I didn't want to hear.

"Truthfully Ross, he's scared to death of surgery. Dying wasn't part of his game plan for the future, at least the near future. For now, he's going to try to be positive but I didn't talk him into it."

"I understand and still feel helpless about it all, but thanks anyhow. It's just another reason I love you so much."

"Care to come home and show me how much?" she said.

"How much or how long?"

Sue Abilene giggled. "Can't I have both?"

"You betcha."

About halfway going through "how much" before we even got to "how long", Tony called from the hospital and said Mom asked me to come back. When I walked into the conference room hand in hand with Susan, Mom rolled her eyes upward. Tony, Roberta and Chris sat like granite gargoyles outside the university library.

She turned to my brother. Her tone started out sharp but she took note of Susan's presence and adjusted. "Anthony, didn't you explain to your brother that this was to be a family conference?"

My ever-helpful brother shrugged. "I told him, Mom."

Susan squeezed my hand and kissed my lips, then took a step back towards the door. "I'll wait outside, Ross."

I tightened my grip on her hand. "No Sue. As far as I am concerned, you are family. If Susan leaves, I go with her."

Even a Ginsu Knife couldn't cut the tension in that room. If Ginsu made a chain saw, you might have had a shot at it.

"Mom," said Roberta, ever the peacemaker, "we're here for Dad. Shouldn't everything else wait?"

Mom was quiet for a long time. It was then that I understood how Custer felt the night before the events at Little Big Horn. My mental wagons were circled. I braced for the onslaught about my loyalty to the family.

Mom said simply. "All right, she can stay."

I felt Susan's fingernails dig into the palm of my hand briefly as we sat down on the far side of the conference table. Tony explained that the ICU staff had allowed us to use the room to have this "family" conference. He then cleared his throat.

"Mom has asked me to sort of lead this meeting."

There's a surprise, I thought to myself. Discretion at this moment was the better part of testosterone.

He continued. "Mom wanted this conference so that we would all be on the same page tomorrow."

"Tomorrow? What's going on tomorrow?" asked Chris, looking very stressed, if her red and puffy eyes were any windows to her soul.

"I think Sis, what Tony is trying to tell us is that Dad's decided to have the surgery, and that its been scheduled for tomorrow."

The look on my brother's face said I had burst his bubble pre-empting his chance to make the announcement.

His voice dropped into monotone. "He's right. Dad's on the schedule for 7:30 am. They had a cancellation."

My pager vibrated silently against my right hipbone and displayed the number for Nellie Archer's cell phone. I excused myself, though no one but Susan seemed to care. Thirty-five cents later, I got my former protégé on the phone.

"I'll make it quick, Malone. Update time. I looked into Georgie Pordgie's little problem. It's a bit more complicated than I thought."

"Complicated how? Like as in dangerous?"

She ignored my remark as she always did when it smacked of me being overprotective of her.

"Buzz through the CI's is that the store is in for a major hit tonight. Ye olde camcorder and I will be there. Care to join us?"

"Sorry Nell, my Dad's headed for open heart surgery tomorrow morning."

"No biggie. I'll call you sometime later tomorrow to see how your Dad's doing and bring you up to speed. You hang in there, Ross. I'll be praying for you both. Talk to you soon."

With that, Nellie Archer was off to work. I went back to the conference room. The eerie silence of the Intensive Care unit brought the aroma of death to my thoughts. I had to concentrate on the present not to let them overtake me.

My arrival back inside was again unnoticed or chalked up to insignificant. Mom was speaking.

"...And because of Anthony's position as a respected medical man, your father and I have designated him as the executor of the health care proxy should that be necessary. Is there a problem with that?"

Susan knew me well enough to know that I was biting my tongue as I shook my head for Mom's benefit. She patted my knee beneath the table. I patted hers as well, then left my hand there. She smiled.

Tony was back at the helm, as they say in Congress, by unanimous consent. "Something we need to consider and prepare ourselves for, just in case the procedure is unsuccessful, is the subject of organ donation."

Chris gasped and shrieked at the same time. "Isn't that a bit premature?"

"Not at all," said Tony. "In fact, there is nothing to discuss. Dad has told us that the organ donor card he signed should be honored in the event he dies."

My mother's face remained blank. I knew this was painful for her. I wanted to walk over and hug her and take her pain away. However, she might decide to donate my organs instead. Chris' face was streaked with tears and flushed with the reddish reality of Dad not surviving. Roberta handed her some tissues. Susan put her arm around my sister's shaking shoulders. Chris leaned into her embrace.

"Anything else we **need** to know Tony?" I said.

Dr. Anthony Malone wasn't used to a non-medical person questioning his judgement in that tone of voice.

"No, not at this moment. And I'd like you all to understand that Dad's surgery having a successful outcome is as important to me as it is to each of you."

Words spilled out of my mouth before I could stop them. "Then just maybe, you ought to look at him as your father and not just another patient using up his deductible."

Even Roberta was taken aback by the sharpness of my tone. "Ross, I don't think that's being quite fair to your brother."

Chris' beeper sounded. She excused herself. Tony waited until the door was closed before he replied.

"What the hell gives you the right to say that you hurt more than any of us because Dad might die?" he said.

"I may not hurt the most little brother, but at least I show it. You're so detached you could do an infomercial for cold bloodedness."

Mom slammed her hands onto the wooden tabletop as she rose to her feet. "That's enough, both of you. Your father is in there on what might very well be his deathbed and you are acting like two very little, very bitter children. This isn't about you, in case you haven't noticed. It's about that man and his needing to know that his family is solidly behind him and praying for his recovery. If either of you can't do that, then let me strongly suggest that you stay away from your father until he recovers. And I mean it. Roberta, would you take me back to Dad's room?"

"Sure Mom," said my dutiful sister-in-law. Roberta glared at both Tony and I as she guided our mother to the door. Mom sent one more volley at us before her departure.

"Tony, you and Ross had better talk," she said, then continued on out of the conference room.

"Not right now. I need to get some air." Tony practically bowled his wife and our mother out of the way as he hustled out. Susan and I were alone. I stood, turned and leaned my back against the conference table. Susan stayed seated.

"Well?" I said.

"Well what, Ross?"

I wasn't in the mood to play twenty questions. "What do you think?"

"About?" she replied with no emotion.

"Sue, you know very well what I'm talking about. Was I out of line?"

Susan stood. "Yes. You said things that may very well be true, but you had no right to say them.

Why was it necessary to hurt your brother's feelings? I thought you had patched things up between you two."

"Guess not," I said.

"And I also think that I don't deserve to be treated like your personal whipping post. Ross had a bad day so all those who love him will suffer. Not happening Tootie, not today, not ever. I'm going to see some colleagues. In the meantime Ross, I suggest that you do what is necessary to get a grip. You're no good to anyone this way, not to me and certainly, not to your father."

Before I could apologize Sue left. The room felt colder. I slumped back down into the nearest chair. If Oliver Hardy were standing next to me, he'd be saying what he often said to Stan Laurel, "Well, this is another fine mess you've gotten me into."

A medical resident burst into the room and turned on the TV set in the far corner.

"Somebody tried to kill Benjamin Walanna!" she said, as she clicked the dial upward to MSNBC.

I sat up and took notice.

-8-

Images of talking heads, wearing trench coats and heavily shellacked hairdos that resembled helmets, displayed their practiced looks of sincere concern when they splashed forth onto the TV screen. People were running every which way in the background. The shoulder mounted camera panned to the right in a herky-jerky motion and caught a CITYMED ambulance just pulling away, lights and sirens ablaze. Walkie-talkies crackled their presence intermittently. Assault rifles and body armor were now the uniform of the moment and denoted SWAT personnel who swarmed into view and blanketed the area. The guys and two girls in three piece suits and business attire were Secret Service agents. The lapel pins were a dead giveaway.

Ad-libbing in a crisis was a practiced art, one this poor street reporter had yet to master. He appeared shaken. There usually wasn't time to write cue cards for assassination attempts.

"Let's again go over what we know, and what we don't know. According to sources within the police department, witnesses have said about an hour ago, a black or dark blue Lincoln Town car rounded this corner." He pointed once and waited for the camera to take a closer shot. He felt it was necessary to point a second time to get the message across to his cameraman. "At that point, two men wearing bandannas that were said to cover the lower halves of their faces opened up with automatic weapons' fire at this entrance behind me. The barrage of gunfire wounded a uniformed city police officer stationed there for security. You just saw the CITYMED ambulance taking him to Mercy Hill Emergency for treatment. We'll pass along more information when we have it."

The director in the remote truck then cut to a pan shot of the stone façade of the old mansion I had been at only a few hours earlier with Lucas. Beyond the wrought iron perimeter, the house was currently being used as a surrogate embassy during Walanna's visit for his base of operations. The national flag of Laracone hung majestically above the double oaken doors. A zig zag pattern of bullet holes in the green fabric told me it had made an excellent target. It was also a reminder to put world peace back at the top of my Christmas list. I listened again to the sound from the TV set.

"...Fortunately, Benjamin Walanna wasn't in the consulate at the time of the attack. He was meeting across town with the President of the United States..." Sirens washed away the correspondent's remaining words but he valiantly carried on. "No one wants to go on record, however unofficial, but reliable sources tell us that they are considering the possibility that a hit squad has been sent by Benjamin Walanna's political enemies in Laracone to assassinate him during his stay in the United States. That's what we know up to this moment."

Looking more than a bit relieved, he threw it back to the anchor desk. I went into the hall looking for Susan. First, I heard my sister reading someone the riot act. When I came around the corner, I saw she was on the phone. Standing slightly out of her sight line, I leaned a little closer to listen, an occupational habit.

"I am sick and tired of being quiet every time you decide something. It's not you who must put up with these things. Yes, I knew what I was getting into. Don't yell at me. Look, I didn't think it would go this far..."

Chris began pacing back and forth, gesturing as if she had a cigarette in her hand, rather than a ballpoint pen. Out of the corner of her eye, she spotted my Nike running shoes.

"Look, we'll talk later. Good-bye." She ended the conversation then screwed on a smile that was supposed to tell me every thing was okay and put it to the test. "Um, hi Ross. How long have you been standing there?"

"Long enough. Want to talk about it?"

"No."

"You sounded angry," I said.

"I am, er, was. Oh, I don't know. It's just a roommate problem."

I pressed a little further. "A male roommate?"

"Ross, you are my brother, not my keeper," said Chris, while rummaging through her purse.

"Agreed Sis, but that doesn't mean I can't eavesdrop on your phone calls or kneecap somebody for you."

She rubbed my shoulders with both hands and put away the barbed wire in her voice. "Thanks Big Brother, but if I need your testosterone, rest assured I'll ask for it." I put my arm around her and we headed for Dad's room.

When we got there, Mom, Tony and Roberta surrounded the bed. It looked like a deathwatch. I decided to lighten the moment.

"Now that we're all together Pop, can I have your fishing rod?"

My mother shot me a look that could have melted plutonium at twenty paces. However, Dad laughed.

"I promised it to your sister," he said. He coughed, hard, and it hurt, a lot. "Besides, you never liked fishing."

"That's true, but you've had that pole ever since I was small enough to be carried around in your bait basket. It's got to be an antique. I could sell it on the Internet and retire on the money it would bring," I smiled.

"Hate to burst your bubble son, but you being in the bait basket was only because we were too poor to afford real bait. I just didn't have the heart to put you on the hook."

Chris laughed but seemed put off by the idea of me dangling on the end of a fishing pole. "That's disgusting." Roberta seemed amused by it all, yet her husband kept his face a blank mask of concern, as if we were all philistines for joking on the eve of surgery.

Another deep laugh convulsed my father creating an even deeper cough. The displays on the heart monitors spiked. Dad caught his breath. Mom's look got sharper akin to a surface to air glare but I didn't care. A nurse came in and gave him a sedative to help him sleep. We all said our good nights. Each of us silently praying it wouldn't be good-bye.

One by one we filed out. My sister-in-law, my sister, my brother all left after paying tribute to the man we all had loved for three score plus years. Before I could get out the door, Dad raised his hand for me to stop.

"Son? Please tell your Susan I very much appreciated her coming to see me."

"I will Pop. You hang in there." Once again, I kissed the dry skin on his forehead. Me looking up at him back when I was a child flashed through my head. I went into the hallway. Roberta came over to Chris and I. Tony was a half step behind.

"You three shouldn't worry. Your Dad is going to be all right," said Roberta. She had always been the eternal optimist and I thought a good counterbalance for Anthony who was more buttoned down than a Brooks Brothers' collar.

"That's right. We all need to pray for Daddy's speedy recovery. Right Tony?" said Chris. She needed his shoulder as well as mine.

"Right Chris." My younger brother was also fighting back tears. We all were. "We'll see you tomorrow morning. Come on honey, let's wait in the car for Mom."

They left. Chris looked at me. I could tell she was envisioning how the world would look if things didn't go well. "He is going to be all right, Ross. I know he is."

We hugged. "I know Chris. He is going to be all right." Mom came out of Dad's room last. Her eyes were damp, her handkerchief woefully inadequate. Chris handed her some tissues. Mom's cheeks were flushed a deep shade of amber. Chris embraced her. Mom kept her daughter at a small distance, as if any closer and she would breakdown completely. I draped my arm around my mother, seeking to protect her. She accepted it, but didn't let it linger more than a few seconds. I felt cheated. Was it unreasonable for me to want to give aid and comfort to my mother in this time of crisis? I guess she thought it was.

"Let's go Chris. I'll walk you to your car then Tony and Roberta will take me home. Ross, will you be here tomorrow morning?"

"Yes," I said. "I promise."

Even that wasn't good enough. "You shouldn't promise me, but that lovely man in there."

I bit my tongue almost in two. "I will be here, Mom. And things will work out."

An absent nod of her head and my mother started to leave with Chris leading the way. Before they were out of sight, Chris looked back at me and silently mouthed the words, "I love you." Then they were around the corner and gone.

"Hey little boy, are you lost?" said Susan Abilene.

"Not anymore pretty lady. Sue, I'm very sorry for how I acted before. You were right. You don't need to or deserve to be treated like that. Forgive me?" I was genuinely contrite and hoped it came through in my words.

Susan leaned into me a half step and kissed me. After a long lingering smooch, she smiled. I looked down.

"What are you doing, Ross?"

"Looking to see if I can still curl your toes with a kiss?" I said.

"It's not my toes you need to be concerned about, Tootie."

"That's good to know. Since I am a trained detective, I can tell there is a clue in the fact that you are now wearing hospital scrubs rather than that expensive Yankee jersey I bought for you last season."

Her head slowly moved from side to side, swirling her blonde hair like she had stuck her head outside the passenger side window as we traveled the superhighway. "My my, you are a detective. The ER is jammed and they asked me to help with the police officer who was shot earlier." Her beeper sounded. "Got to run Sweetie. I'll see you at home."

Before I could reply, Susan Abilene went back to doctoring. Nothing else for me to do at Mercy Hill except go home and get some rest. Since I had parked the Cherokee in the ER lot upon my return this evening, I had to fight through the commotion attendant with the arrival of the gunshot victim from the consulate. A glimpse of the figure on the gurney was a blast from the past. It was my old patrol partner Deke Riley swathed in blood soaked bandages, sucking oxygen as if it were being rationed by OPEC, being rushed into the trauma room where they would do their best to save his life. Later, I would make it a point to call his wife and offer my sympathies.

Call it fate or the fact my stomach was grumbling as the neon lights heralding the Paradise Sports Bar delivered their siren song to my appetite. It was still well before my bedtime so I decided to stop in and feed my face. The Paradise Sports Bar occupied the basement of CUTTER'S super club on North Salina Street just past the Sentinel Newspaper building that only looked to be miss-ing a giant gorilla swatting at helicopters.

My mouth began to water as I thought of those boneless chicken tenders with a side order of country mashed potatoes which was simply baked potatoes mashed in their skins with gen-erous doses of butter and salt. I needed the diversion of 24 televi-sion sets all tuned to one sport or another to distract me from over thinking about my Dad's surgery.

People died. Even people I knew have died. It was a sad fact of life. No matter how much you rationalized it as the population renewing itself, in that for everyone who dies there is another born to take his or her place, it was still sad. Yes, friends of mine had died. I had even killed a few of those I was told were my enemies during war. Up to now though, those deaths had not included either of my parents. As much as I accused Tony of being detached, I felt the masons working overtime inside me to build enough walls to protect me from the unthinkable. Chris had needed the reassurance that I thought Dad was going to pull through. So, I gave it to her.

Did I lie? No. I wanted Dad to get better, to survive the surgery and get back on the golf course as soon as he could. However, I dealt with realities every day and the realities of this operation were tenuous at best. He was 70 years old, had a history of cardiac trouble and wasn't going into the operation with the greatest frame of mind. It was almost as if he had resigned himself that it was over. His acceptance of the inevitable was clearly to be found in his eyes that were almost always looking at some far distant point on the wall during our conversations since his hospitalization.

A strong, puffy hand was clamped down onto my shoulder. The diamond-encrusted guitar shaped ring identified the owner of that hand.

"Hello Joe," I said, shaking that same hand.

Joseph Reneau, a.k.a. Joe Rhino plopped his bulk into the booth opposite me. He smoothed back his freshly greased ebony pompadour replete with temple to jowl sideburns then snapped his fingers. One of the waitresses, this one sporting a Yankees' home pinstriped jersey, slid over and deposited a large glass of mineral water in front of her boss. A thick lemon wedge was doing the dead man's float on the surface of the liquid.

Joe spoke with a Graceland drawl. "Why so glum, buddy boy?"

I ignored his question and asked my own. "Joe, let me ask you a question instead. You've got 24 TV sets and not a darn one has a game on it or even Russian Roulette. All I can see is replay after replay of this business at the consulate." I swallowed the next bit of chicken tender whole and almost choked. My eyes quickly refreshed my memory by rereading the nearby wall poster of the Heimlich maneuver. My throat complied, and I was relieved that I wasn't going to meet my maker with a chicken bone in my windpipe.

"Everybody wants to see who shot whom," he said reverting to a lower eastside of New York dialect. "Besides, everybody thinks the target was this Walanna guy." He lowered his voice, shifted his eyes right and left and continued. "Suppose the target was our guy from Pennsylvania Avenue?"

I frowned. "Then why hit the Laracone consulate?"

"Maybe these guys were new to the assassination business. Not every psycho is hooked up with a militia and sniper training."

"And maybe Eddie Six Pack up the street who just lost his job to foreign competition can't afford a Lincoln Town car for a get-away much less an assault rifle."

"Point taken," said Joe, who then paused to sign a few tabs for the waitress in the Rangers' hockey jersey. "I saw your partner in here earlier. Nellie Archer?"

"Yeah?" I replied, stuffing another forkful of potatoes into my mouth.

"She was stocking up on sandwiches and coffee. Said she had an all night stakeout to get through."

"How did she look, Joe?"

"Okay. Why?"

"Oh nothing," I said. "I'm just too busy minding everybody else's business."

"Ain't that the truth. That was a real stupid move letting that fuzz faced hit man get away. You should have put him in the ground, because you know if he gets a second chance he'll do it to you."

I shook my head. "Can't do it, Joe. Too many notches in my gun already. I used him to send a message to Lenny about keeping his goons away from me...and alive." Another chicken tender bit the dust.

"Lenny Bogardus didn't get to where he is by being intimidated."

"Me either. Is there a recipe for this honey mustard stuff?"

"I'll get you a case of it for Christmas," said Joe.

"What happens if I get hungry before then?"

Joe smiled. "I'll Fed Ex some to your house. How is your father doing? Don't look surprised Malone, I'm nothing, if not well connected."

He gulped his water down to the first red ring enameled onto the outside of his drinking glass, then set it down. And he was right about being connected. For a long time, Joe had sat at the right hand of Lenny Bogardus, the crime lord who was pound for pound bigger than John Gotti was in his heyday. Lenny had his hand in everything and his portfolio ran the gamut from white-collar fraud to extortion to prostitution to drugs and even murder for hire. He was currently becoming known as the Gentleman Don. Yet make no mistake; this gentleman would stop at nothing to achieve his criminalistic goals. Lenny would have been a bust as a villain in a Bond movie since his only nod to flamboyance was tinting what little hair he had left red at the beginning of every summer.

Joe Rhino had left Lenny's employ and had been running the Paradise Sports Bar eversince. Finding out about my Dad was nickel and dime stuff except for Joe's insatiable need to know. Knowledge is power, he liked to say, especially the knowledge of how to load a 9mm handgun in a split second on the dead run. We'd been occasional colleagues.

"Dad's going to have bypass surgery tomorrow and our fingers are crossed." Suddenly, I lost my appetite and signaled for the check. Joe shook his head and the pompadour remained unmoved. He snapped his fingers and took the check from the waitress and pocketed it. "Joe, you don't have to do this."

"Malone, I want to do it for you." He fell silent, staring deep into the water glass. "I never knew my Dad except that he was the guy who slapped my mother around if dinner wasn't exactly ready at 7:30 at night. Said it was important for us kids to eat proper before we went to bed. He left before I got out of short pants."

"Ever try to find him?" I asked, desperate for something to take my mind off of tomorrow.

"No reason to try. But I told you this story to remind you how lucky you are to have had a father all of these years. And if all I can do is pick up a lousy dinner check, then you'll damn well let me do it!"

With that, Joe hurled his bulk from the booth and out of the room.

I stared at the other side of the now half empty booth. "Okay."

The County Justice Center, in the middle of the city around the corner from the War Memorial looked like an anthill during picnic season. I snuck in through a back entrance and reported to the detective squad. One of the few rookie detectives not assigned to the consulate shooting halfheartedly took my statement about being assaulted in my office the other day. He was typing with two fingers at the rate of one syllable a millenium.

"And this Nellie Archer was a witness? She'll back up your story?"

"Absolutely. I take it she hasn't come in yet?"

"If she had, I wouldn't have asked if she would back up your story," said the detective, obviously upset that he was doing mundane paperwork and everyone else was chasing political assassins. "We have been unsuccessful in our attempts to reach her and then all hell broke loose." He gestured at the pandemonium just beyond the glass walls of his office.

"I can see. Ticked off you aren't allowed to play with the adults?" I said.

"Damn straight. I've been a detective for two years and the closest I've gotten to action is I got to ticket the governor's car for speeding past a nursing home," he said. With a firm tug on the top of the paper, he jerked the statement from the computer printer. It smeared the end because he had caused premature departure before it finished printing the document. "Holy Christ, I can't get a break. Hang on a few more minutes."

"Sure. Anybody know how Riley's doing?"

This got the boy detective's attention. I almost thought he was going to reach for his gun. "Who told you about Riley?"

"I happened to be at Mercy Hill Emergency when he was brought in." I could see that wasn't good enough for the new millennium's version of Officer Friendly. "He and I rode patrol together back when I was in blues."

"Sorry, I didn't know you were one of us. Rumor has it he got hit three times. None appear life threatening is what we are being told. Life threatening or not, we still want the bastards. You like saying prayers?"

"Only when the Jets are on the four yard line in overtime." He didn't smile. "I've been known to send a missive skyward when I thought it might help." I thought of Molly, Christopher and now, my father.

"Then put Riley at the head of your list." He shoved the newly minted page before me. "Sign here and we're done."

Six times. From my departure from the Justice Center until I walked into the townhouse I more often than not shared with Sue, I had tried and failed to reach Nellie Archer on the phone. No matter. I told myself that Nellie was a big girl. Besides, I had trained her and she was all professional.

I was more successful in getting through to Ann Riley.

"Hello Stranger. So it takes a few bullet holes to get you to call?"

"Guilty as charged Ann. Time just seems to slip by. How is Deke doing?"

"Your Doctor Abilene was nice enough to explain everything to me. She said that surgery will be needed to extract two of the bullets still in Deke, but he's a tough old bird. Knowing him, I'll take money he kept the bullets inside for evidence or souvenirs."

I chuckled but had little else to say. Time had slipped away more than I had thought.

"Anything I can do, Ann?"

"Come visit him when you get not so busy. And bring your lady friend along. By the way, when are you two going to get married?"

I laughed. "Good night Ann. Give my best to Deke and if you need anything…"

The hot spray from the shower nozzle felt good and relaxing. The tension I felt swirled around and down the drain. Getting some sleep before I headed back to the hospital was a more difficult task.

The window I had for sleep was a mere few hours wide. I did the best I could.

A bad feeling settled in my stomach. Sometimes, I made my living by paying attention to those hunches. I hoped I was wrong.

-9-

No matter what hospital I was in, a generic sameness permeated all of the waiting rooms. They were probably franchised like McDonald's. Mercy Hill's Surgical Waiting Room was separate from its cardiac counterpart and two floors down. It was wheelchair accessible, paneled in knotty pine veneer and smelled of anxiety. The lone window overlooked a new parking garage. It used to look out over a nearby wooded area. I bet they thought it was progress.

The Malone family, of which I still considered myself a part, was huddled in the far left hand corner much like a riverboat gambler sitting with his back to the wall so no one could ambush him from behind. It also gave us a bird's eye view of the entrance so we could see Dr. Coleman when he arrived after surgery.

A large screen color TV was bolted to the ceiling, angled downward for better viewing and locked onto what appeared to be the all infomercial channel. How can that one blond woman be so perky about a mop, cookware, and a refillable paint roller? And how many people ever paint ceilings in evening gowns anyhow?

Whatever attention I was able to muster returned to the colorful pages of USA TODAY. It was enough news to whet my appetite but not enough to make me write a letter to my Congressperson. A

sideward glance told me that my sister Chris was passing the agonizing moments by thumbing through tabloid after tabloid. Then
she paced. Then she thumbed. Roberta was reading FAMILY
HONOR by Robert B. Parker, which was making its way up the
bestseller list. Her fingernails were taking a beating.

Two electronic beeps signaled from Anthony's onramp to the
Internet. His dark eyes focused laser like intensity on the screen. It
had been over two hours since they had taken my father to surgery. We were told that the entire process from what they called
"skin to skin" would take approximately four to six hours at a
minimum. Bottomline they said, don't call us. We'll call you.

Snatching her purse and tossing the latest tabloid aside, Chris
stood and moved quickly towards the door. "I'm going out for
some fresh air."

"Me too," I said, not more than a step or two behind. I wasn't
sure if she really wanted company, but I wanted to be nearby in
case she needed to make a 911 call for a shoulder to cry on.

Outside of Mercy Hill Hospital's main entrance, Christine
Malone pulled out a cigarette after her third try from the thoroughly crushed soft pack of Winstons. A grape disposable butane
lighter appeared from her purse and the flame shot out of the top
like a blowtorch. It singed the tobacco in what had to be record
time. Chris then moved into her best Bette Davis imitation using
the cigarette to punctuate her words.

"What could be taking so long?" she said, as if oxygen was at
a premium.

I smiled. "Maybe they're finished, but have some parts left
over. Could be they aren't supposed to," I said.

"That's disgusting Ross," she said.

"When did you take up smoking?"

"A while ago. I worked my way up from the patch." Chris rolled her eyes upward to show her disgust with my question. "I don't need a lecture. Smoking, well, it helps to calm my nerves."

"And they need calming because?" I asked.

"Duh. Because our father is having open-heart surgery. Jesus, Ross, why the interrogation?"

Her eyes blinked once, twice then in rapid succession as if windshield wipers getting up to speed. The smoke irritated her eyes even beyond what her emotions were doing to her. The back of her hand swiped at an errant drop of moisture. I gave her my handkerchief.

"I'm sorry Sis. I was just trying to show a little brotherly concern. Didn't mean to cross any boundaries. We're all on edge." I said.

Chris sucked in a final drag on her cancer stick, then crushed the remainder under her leather heel. Looping her arm inside mine, we made our way back into the hospital and up to the surgical waiting room.

"Apology accepted. Ross, your concern is touching but believe me when I tell you I'm not into anything I can't handle."

For more than a few years now, I had made my living being a private investigator. These days, whenever anyone started a sentence with "believe me", I usually didn't." The pneumatic hospital doors whooshed open on cue.

Hour three came and went with the speed of a centipede suffering from gout. No word. We were well into hour four when the red coat covering George Trask flashed into view as he passed the waiting room entrance. Bolting from my seat, I caught up with him six doors down. He seemed a bit startled, flustered to see me. Also, a whole lot ornery.

"Go away Malone," he said in words that were whispered but forged in contempt. "I don't need you anymore. I'll handle things from here on out on my own."

"You didn't have to Mr. Trask. I sent you Nellie Archer. Didn't she help you?"

He laughed an unpleasant haughty snicker. "Help? She called me once and I haven't talked with her since. Help like that I don't need." Disparaging Nellie Archer to me was not George's smoothest move. Yet before I could continue, I saw Dr. Coleman heading for the waiting room. In the instant I looked away, George Trask was beamed up. It was the only explanation I could come up with, as George was nowhere in sight. I sprinted back to the waiting room just in time to hear the post-op briefing.

Coleman's white hair was barely restrained beneath a cloth scrub cap and his glasses bounced against his chest since they were tethered around his neck by a fashionable elastic cord with a New York Mets logo. He perched them upon his nose. Tired eyes looked at us each in turn over his half glasses.

"Mrs. Malone, everyone. The surgery went well. We did a triple bypass only. Everything went very well. There is good reason to be optimistic."

"Doctor Coleman, he's going to be all right then? My Jack is going to be all right?" My mother spoke and we each hung our hopes and fears on the reply. Coleman must have known this because he took a long moment before answering.

"As I said Mrs. Malone, the surgery went well. There's a cautionary period of 24-48 hours where he'll be in cardiac intensive care. And as I also said, there is reason to be optimistic." He checked his beeper that no one but him had heard. Then he shook the offered hands and bowed while backing away and accepting our collective gratitude.

Colleen Powers showed up in a starched white lab coat over scrub clothes that looked like they needed a good ironing. A darkened ring of perspiration surrounded her neck at the collar of her shirt.

"I just saw Dr. Coleman leave, but I wanted to come by myself. I was in the OR during the procedure. It went well. All of the I's are dotted and the T's are crossed. Mrs. Malone, your husband had good veins that made the procedure go that much smoother. He'll be going to Cardiac Intensive Care in about a half an hour. I'll be back to take you down there once he's settled. Any questions I can answer for you?"

Nurse Powers patiently recounted the events from Dad's pre-op shot to the final stitch, keeping her descriptions black and white rather than Technicolor graphic.

"...So if there is nothing else, I'll be back shortly," she said, while listening for a dissenting voice.

"Thank you Nurse Powers," I said.

"You're welcome. Besides, I owed him for that fiasco in the ER."

I smiled at her. "Paid in full."

Colleen Powers was weary, but she still managed enough to return the smile. The rest of the family was involved in a group hug. Relief flooded through me as well, to be sure, but not enough to do the group hug thing. Chris and sister-in-law Roberta took my mom to freshen up before she went to see Dad. Tony was on the pay phone to his three kids in Rochester relaying the good news. I was suddenly aware I didn't have anyone to hug.

I went in search of Susan.

My forever love wasn't in Radiology, the cafeteria, the parking garage or the smoking lounge. Of course, I could have called her beeper or had her paged by the operator, but I had done enough standing still. I needed to be on the move.

Next, I was on my way to try my luck in the ER when I came upon the police guard in front of Deke Riley's hospital room. I flashed my private investigator's license.

"Riley and I used to ride patrol together," I explained.

The guard smiled, wide, with too many teeth showing. "So you're the Malone who was the rookie cop who Riley said…"

I knew where he was headed with this and surrendered quickly with my hands up. "Guilty, but the statute of limitations has run out on that. Can I see him?"

"Sure, if he's awake. He kind of zones in and out, if you know what I mean." I nodded my understanding. "I'm not here on assignment. We're all taking turns taking the watch. Brother officer and all."

"That's great. I know Deke and his family appreciate it."

Now it was his turn to nod. He opened the door and I went in.

"Well, if it isn't the rookie cop who arrested the mayor's wife for loitering in front of her own house. Did you really think she was a working girl?" said Deke Riley. He wheezed the last few words out.

"For being a Swiss cheese, you look pretty good."

Deke wasn't wearing a patient gown, which I always had thought was a dress designed by a task force, and his bandages were visible. The white gauze and adhesive tape circled his barrel chest, where the thicket of gray hair had been shaved off, and continued up and over each shoulder. His color was good. His brown hair, sparse to begin with, was now matted to his skull with sweat. I'd bet he would sell his soul for a hot shower.

Deke Riley used to be kinetic energy personified. Now he was a lump, albeit breathing but a lump, surrounded by supermarket tabloids and candy bar wrappers.

"It'll take more than a few bullet holes to stop number 76, right tackle on the Westhill High State champs. Am I right Rookie, or what?"

He never got around to calling me anything other than rookie. I never got around to correcting him. I positioned a metal folding chair near his bedside and sat.

"So Deke, what the hell happened? Last I knew you were in line for a desk job to finish out your twenty then put your papers in. Now I look, and see that your new job is clay pigeon."

"Guess I don't lead by example anymore," said Deke laboring over every word. "I'm not really sure what went down. I'd just started my shift when this big black luxury car comes two wheeling it around the corner. Next thing I knew, I'm kissing the cement steps before I can pull my weapon."

"Didn't your vest protect you?" He paused; red flushed his face for a moment. It had nothing to do with his medical condition. I then knew the answer to that question. He hadn't worn the vest. He used to say real men don't need Kevlar. "Did you get a look at the shooter?"

"Shooters plural, Rook. But no, just a quickie glance as I was ducking for my life. I did notice that it wasn't the usual burrheads from the hood in a drive by."

I bristled at the slur. His insensitivity to minorities had led me to seek a job as a plainclothes officer with the D.A.'s office. And this Rookie never told Deke Riley about that either.

"These goombas were a higher class of hitter. Upscale car, expensive firepower, and leather coats that cost at least a welfare check or two."

"How can you be so sure?" I said, hoping to change the subject.

"These were Sunday go to meetin' coats, Rook. Not a team insignia or company logo anywhere in sight."

"Would you know them if you saw them again?" I said.

He looked hard at me. "Why?" That was what he said. His tone asked if I believed his version of events. I ignored it.

"No reason. Cop habits are hard to break." He was too weak to refute it, and didn't bother to try. Instead, he smiled.

"Not sure," said Deke, wincing after too deep a breath. "The captain is going to bring a laptop computer in here so I can scan the mug books without going downtown. Can you believe that?"

"High tech crime fighting is everywhere. I still get surprised when my computer tells me I have mail."

I asked if there was anything I could do, anything that he needed. Deke said no, and told me when he was up and around we'd go bowling just like the old days. I smiled and told him to get better first. The truth was I had no intention whatsoever of ever going bowling with Deke Riley again, not with a man who thought every frame was a beer frame.

Filing the information about the shooting, I then continued the hunt for Susan. She found me instead.

"And put the Lidocaine in a drip, okay?" said Susan to a resident scribbling feverishly to record her words in a palm sized spiral notebook. I slid my arms around Susan's waist and brushed my lips against her neck. She turned in my arms and kissed me. "How's your father?"

"Coleman said that things went well. Twenty-four to forty-eight hours in cardiac intensive care. I'm guessing that's a precaution and it means keep our fingers crossed."

"That's why I love you, your optimism. It means both. And open-heart surgery is a serious thing, Ross. Erring on the side of caution is not a bad way to go." We hugged tighter and I blinked back tears hoping she wouldn't see. She rubbed her hands up and down my back. I tried breathing through my mouth. "We'll all hold a good thought and pray for him, Tootie. Maybe even light a candle."

"Open heart surgery might need more than a simple votive candle or a can of Sterno. I was thinking more along the lines of the eternal flame."

When Sue laughed, a glow surged within me. Something I spotted at the very far end of the highly polished hospital hallway seized my attention. I squinted to get a better look, then said to hell with vanity and was forced to put my glasses on. George Trask, red coat and all, seemed to be the center of a thug sandwich. The two guys were college age, probably not Lenny Bogardus' minions. Out of town talent maybe. One guy shoved Trask back against the wall. The other got in his face. I started towards them.

My body went on full alert. Each step closer allowed me to catch snippets of their conversation.

"We own you, little man. Now and forever," said one thug.

"I paid you," protested George. "That's not fair." He was trying to stand up to these guys, but they sure didn't look convinced.

Consciously, I unsnapped my Yankees jacket to provide easier access to my gun. I was about fifteen feet away, readying my all purpose charming smile, when from seemingly out of nowhere Trask whipped out his military .45 and shoved it into the belly of the thug directly in front of him.

"Little man? How about this, you asshole. Little man has a gun. Now get the hell away from me and don't come back," he barked as if reliving *APOCALYPSE NOW*. Each thug in turned looked at the gun but didn't move. They were either very brave or not very deep thinkers. My guess was the latter.

"Hi George. Need a tail gunner?" I said.

Slowly, I brushed my left hand back against my jacket and showed them my gun holster and its inhabitant. I snapped off the safety strap. They began to back away.

"You're gonna regret this, old man," said one of the thugs. They went into the stairwell. Gently, I took the gun from George Trask, snapped the safety back on, removed the ammunition clip and ejected the live round that was already waiting in the firing chamber.

"I'll be right back," I said. Then I made for the stairwell like Olympic sprinter Michael Johnson, getting to the parking lot just in time to see the thugs disappear into the same type car that had no doubt tailed Trask to my office originally. It was the same car right down to the crossed sabers' decal in the rear window.

This was getting annoying.

-10-

Even though I fancied myself the last American tough guy, Susan had warned me it wouldn't be pretty. My stoic image took a major hit broadside with the new realities when I entered my Dad's cubicle in Cardiac Intensive Care. Yes, I'd seen intensive care before, yet not with a family member.

The initial shock that struck me was that it was as stark as the lethal injection chamber downstate. No more than two visitors were permitted at any one time, and only 15 minutes of each hour total. Oxygen tubes looking more and more like standard equipment, each time I saw him, assisted his breathing. Chest tubes drained off excess fluid. A catheter, well, a catheter did what catheters do. By the looks of everything, if I didn't know better I'd have thought they were building another Robo-cop. His evening nurse was poised in the corner, busying herself completing paperwork, ready to spring into action like a fireman.

I searched far beneath the cocoon of medical technology to squeeze my father's limp hand. His eyelids fluttered, then retracted. Ever so slowly, his puffy eyes rotated towards my direction. He did his best to try to focus there, on my form. It took a minute or two.

"Son?" he said softly, almost making it into two syllables.

"Hey Pop, how are you doing?"

"Ask her?" A very long breath came and went in between the words. Then with a great deal of effort, he shifted his gaze over to where his nurse was talking to Susan. "Thinks I'm alive." The last word had no sound. A thin smile was the best he could do. I lingered beside the bedside until Susan was done. She moved over and touched my father's hand as well.

There was nothing more for me to say, at the moment, except, "Hang in there, Pop. We love you. I'll be back later." I kissed him on the forehead.

During our walk to our cars, Susan recounted her conversation with the ICU nurse.

"Barbara says that your Dad is doing well. They extubated him, and for the moment, all is fine. But Ross, at the first sign of trouble, they'll stick that breathing tube right back in there. His drainage is clearing. Pulse and respiration are normal, and in keeping with the fact he's only a few hours away from having survived major surgery."

"That sounds like so much politically correct lingo," I said.

My beloved looked directly into my eyes. "You got shook, didn't you?" she said.

"Yes." Susan held the glass door open for me. I knew better than to be chivalrous at times like these.

"You need to know Ross, that it is going to get a lot worse, before it gets better. He needs to get as much rest as possible." We arrived at her new Taurus. The key chain controls beeped the locks open. I held the door for her. "The Surgeon General called today to ask me when I'd be back in Washington. I need to return the call."

"Truth is Sue, I don't **want** you to go, but do I **need** you to stay because I can't get through this? No. Besides, I'm sure our

Commander In Chief will put Air Force One at your disposal if you bat your eyelashes at him."

"Don't believe everything you read in the papers, Lover. That was then, this is now." The light that always danced in her eyes focused directly on me. "Ross, I can stay as long as you need...or want."

"I'm okay, Sue. And I always will be as long as you are in my life."

"And if I'm not?" she said.

"Bite your tongue. Better yet, let me do it."

She laughed. "You're incorrigible."

Dad needed to rest. I needed to work.

From the moment I got the first call what seemed like an eternity ago, my entire being had been centered on my father's illness, save for a few side trips into the world of George Trask. I had sent Nellie Archer into that world because I didn't want to be distracted. No, it was actually because I didn't want to be bothered. She was an excellent investigator, had a good head on her shoulders, could think on her feet in a crisis and was a good friend to boot. In fact, I had recommended her to Delilah James, a former protégé who had jumped to the big time with a security conglomerate in D.C.

But Nellie had been out of touch for a while. That wasn't like her. I collected my messages from a nearby payphone and frowned when she wasn't among them. Trask was having a hissy fit and telling me he hadn't seen Nellie at all. She had told me different. Let me see, who should I believe? Should I believe a scared little man who is carrying a gun for protection, or my close friend and former protégé to whom I have taught almost everything I know about the detective biz?

The next question was why would George Trask lie to me? I was willing to bet that since he was scared enough to start packing a gun, lying to me was a no brainer.

The last remaining Arby's in the city proper was my next stop. I decided to treat myself to a milkshake to soothe the savage beast, that and a Big Montana and Homestyle fries.

Eventually, I parked my Jeep Cherokee across the street from the little Mom and Pop grocery store owned and operated by George Trask and his late wife. My hope was that Nellie would show. The sign above the storefront sported raised gold lettering on a green background. The phone in my car rang. It was Trask.

"Malone, I'll make this really simple for you. Stay away from me. Not only did you fail to take me seriously; you pawned me off onto one of your incompetent subordinates. If you dare to send me a bill, either of you, I will sue your asses off and ruin both of you. Is that understood?"

"Trask, you said it would be simple. I guess it being stupid as well was an added bonus."

His answer was to hang up. I glanced back at the storefront. The space where the front plate glass window had once resided was now the home of several wooden planks. Still yellow from being freshly cut, there were no rainwater stains or graffiti messages spray painted across the newly installed façade. I tried to call Nellie's office, had to settle for the machine and left yet another message. Then I called her cell phone and got zip. My cellphone fit snugly into the inside pocket of my jacket. I walked over to the store.

Traffic was sparse. Pedestrian travel was nonexistent. The rumbling sounds of a garbage truck thundered in the distance. They were headed this way.

"You from the insurance company?" said a voice that came forth from a frail looking man wearing an ill-buttoned, orange cardigan sweater with a monogrammed pocket over what looked to be a flannel pajama shirt. His lower half was clad in what I assumed was the other half of the pajama ensemble. Standing in the doorway of the adjoining business, a bookstore, the man was not a slave to fashion.

"Hello. My name is Malone. I'm a private investigator." Flashing my credentials for his eyes that tried to follow but were sluggish at best, I continued on. He ignored my offered hand. "And you are?"

"Randall Warden," he said, then stopped abruptly, wondering if he were wise to give out his real identity to a stranger.

"It seems Mr. Trask who owns the store next to yours is having a run of bad luck."

Warden laughed angrily. "You could call it that," he said. "You could if you were a total simpleton."

"What would you call it?" I said.

"Trouble, nothing but trouble. That's what I call it. The police were here almost every day. Look around Malone, see anybody rushing into the stores around here?" The bitterness in his voice was further indication of the animosity he felt for George Trask.

"How long has it been this way?"

A disgusted snort mixed with laughter and then a wad of spit directed off into the corner near the curb spoke volumes. "Long enough Malone. Four other stores have already been chased out and relocated to the mall. Hell, I'll even buy him out, if that'll help. Can't expect to give top dollar, but then again, beggars can't be choosers. I'll buy him out. You pass that along."

Randall Warden started to shiver and jerked the edges of the sweater closer around his neck. He didn't waste time on formal good-byes. He just turned and walked away. I noticed he was wearing bedroom slippers.

Trying to sneak a peek between the wooden planks, the best I could discern was that the inside of the store was dark. The front was boarded up. So, I decided to see what was around back. Down the adjoining alley and around to the back of Trask's store,

I started searching for what we, in the detective biz, called a clue. It was frustrating only to find two parked cars with current registrations and plates. I wrote them down. The back door, unlike the front entrance, was locked **and** chained. No signs of forced entry. But more importantly...

No Nellie Archer.

Using my keen detective skills, and making sure I wasn't being observed, I picked the lock and them jimmied the deadbolt out of the way and went inside. The pencil thin beam from my pocket flashlight led the way. Nothing else struck me immediately as being out of the ordinary. All appeared hunky dory as I walked between the aisles that framed the blue and white checked linoleum flooring. The scent of chlorine based detergent assaulted my nose. They had been mopped very recently.

Passing the cat food displays then the Huggies, bread and batteries' aisle, I was hoping for something to stand out and say, "Look at me Malone, I'm a clue." Nothing did. In a backlit warmer the pretzels spinning slowly on the spit inside seemed a little pricey. I took a cold bottle of Pepsi from the cooler, noted the price and left a dollar on the counter beneath a display collecting quarters for Jerry's Kids.

Replaying our last conversation, I heard Nellie say that she was preparing to pull stakeout duty. Since this store was ground zero, it seemed logical that her stakeout would be here. I needed to find out for sure. Turning slowly 360°, I tried to think like Nellie Archer might. Where would she think the best place for a stakeout to spend the night would be?

The backroom off the front checkout counter didn't provide a view of the store. The inside of the back door was padlocked and chained as well. Trask must have seen a buy one, get one free sale. The only other doorway off the main grocery store was the one that led to the rear of the wall of walk-in coolers.

Upon entering that frostbitten world, I snapped my coat just a little bit tighter. I didn't mind living in the snowiest city of its size in North America but why feel the winter five months sooner than I absolutely had to?

The cement walls were adorned with instructions on which beer cases went where, and the minimum number of cases to be there at all times. Again, nothing even Sam Spade would jump on. Nothing that said Nellie Archer was here except maybe a three-legged wooden stool in the far corner. I walked over and sat down.

From this newfound vantage point, I could see most of the store from the checkout counter back to the coolers and from this spot, which used to be the front window, all of the way back to the rear wall where the snack foods were arrayed. At my feet was a crumpled paper wrapper. Unraveling it, I discovered the Paradise Sports Bar logo. Not a clue in and of itself, but buried within the wrapper was a used napkin bearing a familiar shade of lipstick and the checkout receipt upon which the date and time of the pick-up was stamped. The name Archer was scribbled upon it with a hurried flourish. To me, it all said, Nellie was here last night.

Pocketing this new "evidence," I left the store. Back into the alley, I wanted a closer look at those cars. I walked about 25 feet behind the garbage truck crawling down the alley. Neither car yielded much except the hint that jumbo furry dice on the rear view mirror were making a comeback. I moved aside to let the garbage truck shove it metal arms into the slots alongside the blue Dumpster. I had to wait.

Standing still had never been my favorite way to pass the time. Just to be doing something, I dialed Nellie's home/office number. Four rings, and then I heard the answering machine. Plan B went into effect as I then dialed her cell phone number.

It rang. I heard the high pitched ringing tone. I listened for three rings. It was coming from the inside of the Dumpster that had been jerked up into the air by the garbage truck's forklift.

"Hold it! Hold it!" I screamed, running around to the front of the truck. The driver screamed at me. I screamed back.

The tenor of the language that flew back and forth wasn't much above the tenor of what was in the back of this garbage truck. But they did lower the Dumpster back to the ground. I climbed on top of it fully expecting to have to get really dirty to find the cell phone.

I found it all right. It was right there, still in Nellie Archer's pocket.

Surgical Intensive Care was two floors away from my father, but the scenes were practically identical. Once again, I couldn't protect the innocent. The neurosurgeon's diagnosis echoed in my head.

"Severe blunt force trauma to the head, cerebral hematoma which had been drained and held in check by surgery. Patient is comatose, negative reaction to all external stimuli. She is currently aided by a ventilator in respiration."

There was no thought, not even an educated guess, as to when she would regain consciousness. I didn't even want to think about the "if" word here.

I stared at her from outside the glass wall. It wasn't until he was standing next to me that I felt another presence. He showed me a badge.

"Mr. Malone, I'm Sergeant Willard of the police. I'd like to talk with you about the circumstances of your finding Ms. Archer in the Dumpster."

"She was working on a case I sent her. A George Trask, he owns the boarded up grocery store down there. He hired her to look into some vandalism at his store."

"Funny. We interviewed all of the shop owners who use that Dumpster. He didn't mention it."

"Maybe you didn't ask the right questions," I said, weary of his tone and its intrusion into my life.

His back stiffened. "Look Malone, I've heard about you. Jude Meyers talked my ear off more than once about the 'Legend of Ross Malone.' But this is a police matter so let the police handle it," Willard said.

"It's my fault she is in there," I said.

"Then my advice is to say three Hail Marys and leave this to the professionals. I'm sorry for your friend."

Luckily, Sergeant Willard left before I could slap him silly. The elevator doors opened revealing a 26-year-old brunette with John Lennon glasses. A beat up Army fatigue jacket and a V-Neck sweater over tan Dockers slacks came into view. She'd been crying, a lot.

"Ross, I came as soon as I got your message." Her gaze ran past me and fixated on Nellie. She started crying again. "What happened?"

"She was working a case I gave her. Apparently, she got in over her head. Someone, or more probably someones, beat her within an inch of her life, then left her for dead in a Dumpster in an alley."

"Who?" asked the girl.

"I don't know Gwen. But that's not going to last for long." Nellie's significant other melted within my embrace. At that moment, it was the best I could do.

-11-

Gwen Brolin stayed glued to my shoulder as I guided her through the minefield of red tape that led to the neurosurgeon, and eventually to a nearby empty bed so she could stay close to Nellie. She had all the numbers to reach me.

Asking the right questions of George Trask was the next pressing order of business throbbing at my temples. A quick stop to check on my Dad first. The nurse was out in the hallway standing guard like a starched white Doberman. Opposite her was a well-dressed man holding a massive floral arrangement. He pushed it forward. She pushed it back.

"Mr. Malone," she said, sighing relief that the cavalry had arrived, "I'm so glad you're here. This man is trying to deliver these flowers to your father, but I keep telling him that flowers are not allowed in CICU."

"I'm the son of the man these flowers are intended for, may I ask who sent them?" A small card on creme colored stock was produced. The ornate handwriting resembled calligraphy. They were from Benjamin Walanna. The flowers were accepted with appropriate gratitude. The card disappeared into my pocket. I gave the flowers to Dad's nurse.

"Would you please see that they get to your geriatric floor? Please thank President Walanna for his consideration."

A curt nod followed by a brief click of genuine leather heels and he was history.

Because of my profession, I had gotten into the habit of checking the rearview mirror and now the side view mirrors, to make sure that no one was following me trying to unearth the secrets that made me a great detective. Of course, there were also those who were trying to collect on that chintzy Bogardus contract, too.

Three intersections, two stoplights and a U-turn on a one way street went by before the minivan glued to my bumper registered more than a mild annoyance. Obviously, he couldn't read my "Honk, if you're trying to kill me" bumpersticker. I slowed to let them catch up so I could at least get a license number. They slipped away down a side street. I, then, proceeded to my destination.

Palace Gardens was an upper middle class housing development that was a franchise deal across the country. Identical homes down to the pool table lawns and white trellises up the side of the porch, looking like the Barbie Dream home factory. Uniformed gardeners watering the Astro-Turf directed me to the brown two-story at the end of a cul-de-sac called, "Pleasantview." Trask was lettered in white on the black mailbox.

My heart raced as I knocked on the door. I wanted to kick it in, hoping that Trask would be behind it. The door opened presenting a man, middle to late twenties, slicked back hair, wire rimmed designer frames and a grin God had only issued to Jack Nicholson and self important smart asses. And this breathing mannequin didn't look like Jack.

"Can I help you?" said the Grin.

"I'm here to see George Trask."

"Mr. Trask is not receiving visitors at this time," came the reply. It came in a tone that was supposed to make me accept it as the truth from Mount Sinai.

"I'm not a visitor, but I could be his worst nightmare." I moved ahead to walk past the Grin. He shoved his hand against my chest trying to stop me. It was a foolish move. Instinctively, I grabbed his wrist and bent it back. His knees buckled. I released him and kept walking.

"Stop, or I'll call the police," he said to my back.

"Ask for Sergeant Willard when you do."

My face flushed with anticipation as I searched through the house looking for George Trask. Living room. Clear. Kitchen. Clear. Bedroom. Clear. Up the carpeted stairs two at a time to the second floor and I caught Trask descending the retractable ladder from the attic.

"We need to talk," I said. Trask froze for a brief instant at the sound of my voice. Startled, he missed the next to bottom rung of the ladder and tumbled to the floor. I let him.

"Jesus Christ, Malone. You scared the hell out of me," he said.

"Tell me exactly what occurred between you and Nellie Archer?" I asked, in a not so nice way.

"Nothing. Exactly nothing, and that is what I told the police. She came by the store to talk with me. After that, I never saw her again. She acted like she thought I was a crackpot or something."

"Nellie always was a shrewd judge of character," I said.

"I was as surprised as anyone when the police came to talk with me about her death."

My internal radar went off the scope. "They told you she was dead?"

He hesitated. "Um, well, I just assumed. They did find her in a Dumpster."

"I wonder if Nellie being dead is wishful thinking on your part, George? Besides, some of my best friends shop in Dumpsters. You need her dead, George? Dead PIs don't make good witnesses," I said, wanting desperately to slam him against the wall until his back broke. Of course, that would be wrong, even if he did have a spine.

George Trask, now standing and trying to recapture his composure, glared at me. "I stand by what I told the police."

"You do that George. You do that." I started down the stairs. "Sorry I had to rough up the butler."

"Butler? Christ, that was Gardner Meadows. You don't want to mess with him," said George, who seemed to be totally jelly kneed at the mere mention of this Meadows' name.

"And I wouldn't want to mess with him because?" I asked.

"You just don't. Trust me," said Trask.

"Trust you? Hardly. Is that what you told Nellie Archer, to trust you?" I said.

"Back off Malone. You stay away from me or like I said, I'll sue you." He shook his fist at me once or twice, then thought better of it and stuck to yelling.

I slammed the front door on my way out so hard that the lock didn't catch and it swung back open. I left it that way. Parked right behind my Cherokee was the minivan that had been following me earlier. In the front passenger seat was the infamous Gardner Meadows. He still looked like a butler to me. He grinned at me with that smiley button grin tinged with a foreboding evil. He probably didn't gargle with Holy Water. The power window slid up effortlessly and they pulled away. Crossed sabers were decaled in the back window.

My cell phone rang. "Malone."

"Ross, this is Shelly Hutton. I just heard about Nellie Archer. I'm so sorry."

"Thanks Shell. I'm kind of busy right now. Can whatever this is about wait?" I asked.

"I wish it could, Ross. Can you come by my office? We need to talk," she said. I trusted Shelly Hutton enough to know that she wouldn't have pressed the issue unless it was important.

"I'll be right along."

"Thanks for coming by, Ross. How is Nellie?" said Michelle Hutton, my attorney-at-law and my friend, affectionately known around the courthouse as *Rolling Thunder*, more for her demeanor in court than the wheelchair to which she was confined.

"No change," I said. Keeping my emotions at bay so I could function was a trait I had learned a very long time ago, the hard way.

"And Susan?"

"Okay. Shelly, I don't mean to be rude, but I need to be other places. Whoever hurt Nellie is still out there."

She nodded, then made a tent of her fingers and leaned her face forward to rest upon them. "I understand. You know, I am Nellie's attorney, as well." I nodded. My attorney then sucked in a very deep breath and took her sweet time exhaling. "Do you remember signing any papers for Nellie a couple of years ago?"

"Just some insurance things, I thought," I said.

"Yes Ross, but it also included a health care proxy meaning..." began Shelly.

"I know what it means. Don't you think this is a bit premature?" I jumped to my feet. Shelly appeared startled. "And to answer your next question, I am not ready to pull the plug on my friend."

"If that's what you think I am asking, then you can go to hell, Ross Malone. No one says you have to pull the plug, but it is my responsibility as her attorney to remind you that if and when that time comes, it is your decision and yours alone. That is, unless you refuse to do it and leave it up to the state to decide."

"Not yet Shell, not yet."

"Fine, but if or when that moment arrives, Nellie recorded a video you'll have to see first."

"Fine, but not today," I said and left. Not today and I was praying, not ever.

Too many clicks followed by a low whir of a machine starting up, before I heard the subsequent beeps that hooked me into Lucas Gentero's voice mail.

"Lucas, Malone here. Remember me? Patron saint and bodyguard to local journalists? I need a favor, anything you can dig up on a Gardner Meadows, especially in connection to a George Trask. Sooner than later, Lucas. Much obliged."

Nellie Archer's office where she met clients and conducted her business was located downtown in the Davenport Tower. I stopped in the fourth floor office to just pick up her mail. She had another office at home, like me. I'd have to go there later. Eight of the ten messages on her answering machine were from me. The other two were from Gwen Brolin. They were nothing, if not affectionate.

Next, I thumbed through the mail looking for anything that required immediate attention. I separated out a couple of depositions, credit card bills and what appeared to be greeting cards. My heart sank. Tomorrow was Nellie's birthday. The phone rang.

"Nellie Archer's office."

"This is Pam from Photo-Cam in Westvale. We were calling to make sure that Ms. Archer's recent purchases were satisfactory."

"I'm sure they were," I said, still distracted by the pile of papers before me.

"And I also wanted to remind Ms. Archer of our extended warranty protection for the video cameras, recorder and portable monitors she bought."

I sat up straighter. "Could you please tell me exactly what Ms. Archer purchased and how recently?"

She did. The last thing that Pam from Westvale told me was that the date of the purchases was the morning of the stakeout that George Trask said she never did.

The hospital yielded no new information on either my father's condition, or Nellie's. He was sleeping. She remained in a coma. I went home. Sue was there, wearing the New York Yankees' jersey I had bought for her. Number 2. Derek Jeter's number. She knew the way to my heart. I found her at the computer in the spare bedroom that doubled as my office. Still the room spoke Ross. Sports pennants, my softball trophy from last year's Salt City tournament —MVP, a cooler sometimes filled with Pepsi, and a stereo dual cassette CD player tuned to the 24 hour sports station were all little mementos I had placed in there to personalize my place.

Plus, next to my computer was an 8x10 photo of Susan and I by a mountain upstate called Poco Moonshine. It was lovely regardless of the time of year. At the right angle, you could see the profile of a horse. I thought Secretariat. Sue thought National Velvet. She had the same photo at her place, but she kept it by her bedside.

I made a mental note to take her there again the first chance we could get away.

"Hi Lover." We kissed. We lingered. We kissed deeper. Her arms looped around my neck as she rose from the chair into my full eager embrace. She was only wearing the jersey and the lower half of her Hanes Her Way set in my favorite color. "Tell me how things are in your world, Tootie?"

Without releasing the tension of my embrace, I told her of my Dad sitting up in a chair for 15 minutes at a time then segued into Nellie's condition. Susan tightened her arms around me with each word I uttered. I needed her to crawl into my soul. My pounding heart was in sync with hers.

"And on top of everything else, Shelly tells me I'm Nellie's health care proxy designee."

"It's a difficult responsibility." We were quiet for a long while. We were close. I liked it. I needed it. "Have the police made any progress on finding out who hurt her?"

"If they are, they are keeping me out of the loop. Would you like company for dinner tomorrow night?"

"Mel Gibson for dinner? I'll have to get my hair done..." she said.

"Cute, but Mel's off filming the next *Lethal Weapon*. I was thinking of inviting Gwen Brolin. She needs to take a break from the hospital. We could order a pizza."

"Or I could cook. But if you order pizza, I'll whip up a dessert. How does 'Death By Chocolate' sound?"

"Sounds like 'Death by Sit-ups'. Okay. Deal," I said.

We kissed to seal it, when the computer chimed in with the arrival of incoming mail. It was from Lucas Gentero. I sat down at the terminal and opened the missive.

"Dear Malone," it began, with its black lettering on a white background, "Ain't technology wonderful? Here's the first layer of what you wanted to know about Gardner Meadows. Late 20's, runs the City Security Association which is sort of a chamber of commerce militia. He is also the chief benefactor and director of the WARRIORS OF THE NIGHT, a Guardian Angels type group which patrols the businesses which belong to the CSA." The address was upscale mid-town.

The single spaced letter went on.

"Hope this helps and yes, Trask is a member of the association. So far, no other connection but I'll keep digging. Give my best to your father and Susan. I'll light a candle for Nellie. If you need anything, just call."

The email ended. I printed it out on my laser printer, then closed out the online server. Susan entered with that classic stoic look she was famous for. I knew duty called.

"When?" I said.

"I've booked a flight for tomorrow midnight. Will you be okay?" she asked.

"Forever and then some," I said. A smile went with it.

Susan and I didn't bother to take the time to go to the bedroom.

Early next morning, I walked into Trask's grocery store. He was behind the counter. I stood in the middle of the store and looked for any place and every place that Nellie Archer might have tried to conceal a video camera. There were none, at least none that were obvious.

Trask watched me like a hawk. Still, he kept his mouth shut as I strolled among the aisles looking for wires, unexplained holes in the wall, ceilings or coolers. Nothing. Then I spotted it, an empty video camera bracket above and to the right of the Rice Krispies. Bare wires were twisted around the metal stanchion; maybe the camera was ripped off during one of the many acts of vandalism. Or maybe, Nellie had put it up and the punks who attacked her were smart enough to conceal their tracks. No telling how long it had been gone and I didn't trust Trask to give me an honest answer. I would know he was lying because his lips were moving.

I left the store, lingering outside long enough to see Trask dial the phone. My own call found Gwen Brolin at home. She allowed me to stop over.

"We kept our office in the den. That desk is Nellie's. I'll be in the living room if you need anything."

"Actually, I do. Susan and I would like to invite you to dinner later tonight. About eight? Pizza, and Susan has promised to make a special dessert that will even satisfy Bigfoot's sweet tooth."

Gwen lowered her head and slowly shook it. "I don't really want..."

"Gwen, Susan and I really want you to come."

"All right, thank you." After I told her there was nothing for her to bring for dinner except an appetite, Gwen left closing the door to the office after her.

The minimal time I had spent in Nellie's office downtown was more so to keep her business going while she was recovering. I'd have to make a return trip for investigative purposes. Here, I was looking for her notes, reports —anything that would point me in a direction to find her assailant. There was no telling when Nellie Archer would be able to answer questions, or even breathe by herself.

Nellie's filing system bespoke of her obsessive-compulsive self. Alphabetical, color coded, and chronological beyond that. What color would vandalism come under? Ten minutes later, I found it nestled within the confines of the mauve folder. Then nineteen letters later, I found Trask.

There were no formal reports, just random notes, merely more than legible doodles. There were block letters sketched out and filled in with ink to call me. The word "stakeout" was circled. However, the page was dominated by one term that was boxed, block lettered, circled and ringed with a perimeter of arrows. It said simply, "Warriors of the Night."

Warriors of the Night. Gardner Meadows.

-12-

"Ross, I think Gwen's at the door," said Sue.

"I didn't hear a knock," I said.

"Female intuition. Trust me." She kissed me and dutifully, I went to look.

I checked the peephole to make sure that it wasn't some no neck with an Uzi calling card, then, I let Gwen Brolin in.

"Sue, why don't you ever use this famous intuition when we're picking lottery numbers?" I asked.

"That activity requires a different set of muscles, Dearest. Hello Gwen. I'm glad you could come over. The pizza will be here soon."

"What's that delicious smell?" said Gwen. I took her coat.

"Hopefully, it'll be dessert," said Susan. "It's an old recipe from Grandma Abilene. Would you like something to drink?"

Gwen requested white wine. I requested another Pepsi. Sue settled upon bottled water with a French name. Sue went to play hostess. Our guest and I sat in the living room. It was apparent that Gwen had made a half-hearted attempt to doll herself up. Her brown eyes were still puffy and road mapped with stressed veins. Her blouse appeared to be satin in a contrasting color. A calf length skirt of a complementary blue over shoes that had square heels, probably dress pumps, adorned the rest of her. Gwen's only nod to accessories was a gold ankle bracelet sporting a heart shaped charm. Then, I also took note of the gold wedding band on her left hand, fourth finger.

"Have you talked to the hospital lately?" I asked. Susan served the drinks and sat next to me. She interlaced her fingers with mine.

"I stopped by there before I came over. My boss, Mr. D'Amico says I can set my own hours while my 'friend' is in the hospital. That's how he says it, 'my friend.' And it's not nasty or mean spirited, but well, it is insignificant. You both know that I don't consider Nellie insignificant."

Susan touched Gwen's arm briefly. "You don't need to explain to us, Gwen."

Our guest took a heavy hit on her wineglass, while I did the same to my Pepsi. Sue excused herself to go check on the dessert.

I said as softly and gently as I could, "Any change?"

Gwen Brolin's lower lip, now devoid of lipstick from being chewed upon by her overly white teeth, disappeared again. She shook her head.

"Hang in there, Gwen." The doorbell rang. Susan got the pizza then followed in close order with the plates and napkins. I resliced the pepperoni delight and handed Gwen the first serving. "Do you feel up to answering a few questions?"

"I'll try," said Gwen. She was currently held together with a lick and a promise. I needed to tread lightly, but I also needed answers.

"Did Nellie ever talk about her work with you?" I said.

"Let me ask you," said Nellie's significant other, "do you discuss your cases with Dr. Abilene?"

"Not enough," said Susan, finishing a goodly piece of stuffed crust. "I guess the ending of *Murder, She Wrote* every time."

"True, but actually I am afraid of the competition. Did she ever mention a group called Warriors of the Night? Or maybe the name Gardner Meadows?"

Gwen stalled for time, too long a time for my tastes. "No. At least not that I remember. Are they who hurt her?"

"I don't know yet. How about the name George Trask?"

"No. I'm sorry. I feel like I should be helping more," she said.

"You aren't alone, Gwen. If I hadn't pushed this case off on Nellie, she might not be in the hospital now."

Gwen and Susan were quiet. I took the opportunity to finish off the surviving two slices of pepperoni pizza from my grease soaked, soggy plate. Gwen folded her used napkin into a very small package. Dinnertime origami.

"Ross, Shelly Hutton called and told me that you had been designated Nellie's health care proxy." She struggled for words. Her eyes darted to the left, then right, searching for, but not satisfied with, those that came out. The emotion built in her like a tidal wave, straining at her composure. "I know I don't have a right to ask, but please don't take her away from me."

Gwen Brolin dissolved into her grief. She was crying at breakneck speed, hyperventilating, doing her best to curl up into the fetal position. Susan held her, silently, genuinely. I could do nothing more than sit there. Whoever did this to Nellie, to Gwen, to me would have to pay, and pay dearly. The sooner, the better would suit me just fine.

The hands on the clock circled half way around before Gwen had calmed down enough to excuse herself to fix her face. Sounds from the kitchen told me Susan was doing the domestic thing. She was trying not to get in the way. I cleared away the last half slice of pizza she had left, a favorite habit of mine.

"Honey, do you know the number of the automobile club?" said Sue.

"Not off the top of my head. Why? Are you out of wiper fluid again?" I giggled.

"No," said Sue, "but it appears that your Cherokee has given birth to four flat tires."

From the window over the double wide kitchen sink I could see my four brand new tires were deflated. I resisted the urge to say they were only flat on the bottom.

My Beretta accompanied me to the parking lot. Yep, they were flat. A single sharp object, one swift stroke, four separate times. Something flashed into my eyes from the glow of the halogen street lamp. It was a lapel pin or tie tack. Might even have been a cufflink in its previous life but now it was a clue. Crossed sabers carved into the onyx surface stared up at me.

When I walked Gwen to her car, I made sure that she didn't see my debilitated Cherokee. No need to file a police report. There was nothing they could do. My car insurance had long ago stopped covering me for little things like slashed tires.

For lack of something else to say, I told Gwen Brolin that there would be no quick decisions about Nellie Archer. I wanted to tell her, no, I wanted to promise her that there would never be the need for such decisions...but I knew better.

Susan took pity on me and let me drive her Taurus to take her to the airport.

I hit the horn to accentuate my dislike of my fellow drivers on the road as I turned onto the access road for the airport. "You know Sue, a caring significant other would replace those tires as a holiday gift." I didn't bother to hide my smirk.

Neither did she. "Let me know when they start exchanging gifts on Labor Day, Tootie." One by one the passing streetlights flashed on her face. It felt like a Yoko Ono performance art exhibit at the Everson Museum. Only I was gazing at the Mona Lisa. "They're coming after you, aren't they? And this won't be the last time, will it?"

I knew better than to lie. "Yes, they are probably coming after me, and this will only be the last time they make such a statement if I heed their wishes."

"And you won't do that?" She already knew the answer, but felt better when she said it out loud.

"I can't, Sue. But they're at a disadvantage. I have right on my side."

"Don't be an ass, Ross. It doesn't become you," she said.

"What do you want me to say? If I push, I have to expect that they'll push back."

"But you don't even know who 'they' are?"

"They're scared, or they wouldn't have taken a run at me," I said.

"Scared the hell out of your tires, at least," she said. Silence fell between us as we headed into the airport garage. They had the last call for her red eye flight to Newark, then on to Washington D.C. She ran for the jet way as I checked her lone suitcase through.

All too quickly she was one hundred feet from take-off. Susan Abilene paused. I caught up with her. Her arms ringed my neck. Her perfume saturated my libido, not really a surprise. Hugging between us, no matter how brief, was as always, a sensual experience. At the airport it was also melancholy.

"Be safe Tootie," she said.

"I will, if you will. Be back soon Bubba."

"Soon as I can. Let me know how your Dad and Nellie are doing. You know Ross, Nellie isn't your fault."

Before I could argue, the flight attendant at the far end of the jet way, whose jaw was too square and his teeth too white enameled for my taste, hollered down a final, "All Aboard." Susan kissed me hard than ran down the carpeted corridor without a backward glance. I felt her tear on my cheek.

As always, I made my way to the nearest window to watch the Big Silver Bird hoist itself into the sky. The nearest vantagepoint was in the VIP Lounge. Air Force One had already taken its leave hours ago. The lounge would be unguarded and unoccupied. Or, so I thought.

The minute I opened the door it was déjà vu all over again. Two suits, one skirt, three guns. None of them being mine.

"Malone, what are you doing here?" said Andrew, replacing his all new shiny weapon of mass destruction back in the leather rig underneath his designer suit.

"Seeing a friend off. And you?"

The bodyguard from Laracone stepped to the side and gestured towards the small-framed person gazing out the window. Jacob was next to him, poised to swing into action. Eventually, the nanny's gun disappeared.

"Young Prince Gregory is waiting for his grandmother to arrive from Florida."

I nodded. "How is President Walanna doing?"

"Resting, tending to affairs of state. Why?" He started gathering steam. "Did you think he'd be cowering in the corner? President Walanna is truly a man of the people. That pathetically lame attempt to silence him, only served to spur him on."

"May I talk to the Prince?" I asked.

"To what purpose?"

"I'd like to explain about the other day, in the emergency room."

Andrew blinked both eyes, then canted his head towards the heir to the throne of Laracone. Jacob's jaw tightened as I approached.

"Hi," I said. "My name is Ross. And your name is Gregory?"

"Prince Gregory," said the boy, who had royal disdain down pat.

"Forgive me, I stand corrected," I said.

The boy prince looked at me from the corner of his eyes, up and down. I extended my hand. He let it hang in the air. I toughed it out until he took it.

"I'm waiting for my grandmother. She's flying in from Florida."

"My best friend just flew back to Washington D.C." He seemed uninterested. I'd bet he'd be interested if he knew Sue. "How's your arm?"

"It's just a mild sprain," he said, without enthusiasm. "The doctor says it should be okay in ten days or so."

"How'd you hurt it?" He ignored me. I repeated the question. More dead air. Jacob placed a hand on my shoulder. It seemed to serve no purpose if I broke his hand off at the wrist and handed it back to him, other than to brighten my day, of course. "Gregory, do you remember me?"

"Yes, you're the man from the hospital. The one who needed my room and got into a fight with my bodyguards."

"It was more of a difference of opinion," I said, feeling defensive.

"I saw it. It was a fight. I may be thirteen years old, but I am not naïve," he said, equally defensive.

"Gotcha." I loved being lectured by kids.

"How is your father? President Walanna said he had to have heart surgery. I trust he is doing well."

The kid had memorized the lingo of royalty to a tee. "It was bypass surgery, several actually, and yes, he is resting comfortably. Thank you for asking." The kid called his Dad, President Walanna?

Gregory moved closer to the plate glass window which started to rattle in its casing as Susan's flight took off and soared above an incoming 747 outlined in a rainbow of landing lights which was gliding down towards its final approach. His attention was rapt. He placed his hands against the glass as if he wanted to reach out and catch this life-sized model of a jet plane.

"You like planes?" He nodded. "Maybe someday you'll get to fly one of those metal fortresses."

His brown head snapped in my direction. His eyes blazed with thoughts of the future, igniting them. "No, my quest would be the space shuttle. I would like to pilot Atlantis or Discovery or..." He rattled off the remaining shuttle names. At least, I thought they were. There didn't seem to be a Pinto or a Hyundai among them. Suddenly, his voice trailed off.

"What's wrong?" I asked.

"My destiny is not among the stars. It is to my country as its leader." He made it sound like a burden rather than a future of public service.

"I certainly understand that, but I believe Prince Andrew of England is a helicopter pilot." Could that be a smile streaking across his young features?

Andrew moved over. "It is time Prince Gregory. Are you done, Malone?"

"Yes. Thank you. Good luck Your Highness. I'll be looking for you...up there." This time he extended his hand first. I took it and he seemed to rise in stature as he moved past me, like Clark Kent taking off the horned rimmed glasses and becoming the Man of Steel.

Flanked by Andrew and Jacob, with their nanny as their tail gunner, they walked towards the jet way. I headed for the snack bar.

Walking through the terminal, I quickly decided not to wait until I got to the snack bar. The first bank of vending machines sounded their siren call. My taste buds answered. Even though I hadn't met a vending machine I didn't like, the fact that they had been modified to accept dollar bills was an unwanted improvement. A metal sign said they also accepted Canadian money too. A commotion of sorts rumbled behind me.

I turned to see about a dozen individuals almost marching in lockstep through the lobby of the airport. Dressed alike in black and tan outfits of sharply creased, long sleeved shirts and blowzy pants gathered at the ankles, they were fashion plates of style. Add to that, rounded Chinese type collars, and balloon sleeves which were equally snug at the wrist, and they moved through the terminal like a crowd of male models searching for that next magazine cover shoot or a 24 hour tanning salon.

A picket sign was thrust into the air. The words were foreign to me, though I could make out the picture of President Walanna. They were probably going to welcome the grandmother. Okay, so even I wasn't that stupid to swallow that load of broccoli. The investigator in me took a good look at their faces as they rushed past me.

Determination tinged with the potential for violent confrontation was what I read in each pair of eyes. They moved quickly like bacteria through the bloodstream, trying to evade the white blood cells. Their voices were talking above a mumble, but not much. Yet, even if they had been shouting, I doubt I would have understood them. They weren't speaking English. A gun flashed into view. The slide was jerked back, cocking the hammer, and jacking the next round into the firing chamber.

I ditched the remainder of my roast beef sandwich and Pepsi on the dead run.

-13-

Using the sporadically spaced cement columns, some sporting the picture of our illustrious mayor in some self serving photo op, for cover, I followed the crowd. They turned right and accelerated. I knew where they were going, and I knew a short cut.

The crowd, which displayed all of the characteristics of a well oiled mob, was now heading for the jet way with all deliberate speed. Where there was one gun there was usually more. I started moving at what, for me, was warp factor six. Suddenly, a row of molded plastic seats, with TV sets bolted to the arms eagerly waiting to be fed quarter after quarter, appeared before me. I lunged over the top. My back foot nicked the chairs and I went down hard. Bruises would be appearing tomorrow morning.

Back to my feet, I hobbled a bit before I could get back up to speed. First, a trot then a canter, as the kinks slowly worked themselves out. The color-coordinated mob had already arrived. Andrew and Jacob had locked arms to form a human barricade between the protestors and Prince Gregory. I pushed my way through, throwing elbows right and left, and then hip checks worthy of Mark Messier. Where was the guy with the gun? I had to get to the guy with the gun.

The muzzle quickly came up to shoulder height, ready to fire. Could I really leap ten feet in a single bound? Only one way to find out.

"Gun!" I said. Screams filled the air. Everybody ducked for cover. Everybody, but the gunman. His mistake. My shoulder hit his dead on. We crashed to the ground. Grabbing his gun hand at the wrist, I slammed it against the floor. Once, twice, three times before he released the weapon. I slugged him hard with my fist, then, slammed his head against the floor as well. I liked to be thorough. Pausing to look up, I saw that Andrew and Jacob were caught up in a human Rubik's cube of bodies, arms and legs. Airport security was just arriving in force.

Gregory was about twenty-five feet further up the corridor. Next to him were the nanny who went rushing to aid her colleagues and an older woman that my money said was the grandmother.

The pseudo mob surged forward. Andrew, Jacob and the nanny weren't enough. This was where someone should have sent Lassie for help. I scrambled to my feet, thrust the gun in my pocket and ran towards the boy prince.

"I'll call you when he's safe." I yelled to Andrew who was crunching his fist against the nearest unfriendly face.

"Go, go, go! Protect the prince!" was his reply. I really wanted to say that his wish was my command.

"Come on Gregory. Let's blow this Popsicle stand." I scooped up the Prince on the dead run, while grabbing Grandma's hand as well. I almost pulled her arm from the socket. "It's not safe here. Follow me."

Immediately, I kicked open the first emergency exit we came to along the jet way. It was a ten-foot drop. I didn't think twice, stepping out into space, praying that I wouldn't shatter both of my ankles on impact. Luckily, my parachute training came in handy. Upon impact, I tucked and rolled, not once releasing my grip on

Prince Gregory. However, Grandma was less bold. I looked up and saw her hanging from the exit doorway by her fingertips. She fell into my arms.

Once in Susan's Taurus sedan, I slammed my foot to the floorboards and headed for route 81 south. No one followed. I handed my cell phone to Prince Gregory.

"Look, I know you didn't want to leave Andrew and Jacob or the nanny, but we had to make sure that you were safe. Do you know their number?"

"Yes," said Gregory. He was no-nonsense.

"Okay, Call them, Your Highness. Tell them that you and your grandmother are all right. Then tell them that I'm taking you both to the consulate. Think you can handle that?" He looked at me as if I was an infidel. I ignored it. "Then call the consulate, and tell them we're on the way."

Benjamin Walanna met us in the foyer of the consulate, causally dressed in a designer sweatsuit, striding forward towards us in a hurry.

"Prince Gregory, are you all right? Mother, are you safe as well?"

"We are both fine, Mr. President," said the woman who had turned stuntwoman just a half an hour ago. "Thanks to this young man. He saved your son."

Walanna sent Gregory and the mother, surrounded by a phalanx of aides, off to rest. He walked over to me.

"It seems that I am indebted to you."

"No, you're not. The boy doesn't deserve to be a political football. Just for the record, Andrew, Jacob and the nanny did good work. They deserve two things, a raise and some help. If your son is going to be a target, then it is best to keep him out of harm's way as much as possible.

"Quite so. Please accept my sincere thanks for your efforts, and tell me what I can do for you to show my appreciation."

My beeper sounded. It was the hospital, CICU.

In the time it took for the trembling elevator to grunt, groan and grind its way from the hospital lobby to the third floor, I was able to remember every song on the "Meet The Beatles" album on Capitol Records. Perhaps I should be calling Alex Trebek.

Dad's CICU cubicle was deserted, reeking of the disinfectant cleaner that nine out of ten hospitals used. The monitors were now merely silent sentries gathering dust until called upon again. The muscles in my chest tightened. A nurse directed me to Dad's regular hospital room that was located twelve stair steps down and a very long corridor away. When I got there, my mother and sister were outside in the hallway arguing with a full figured red-haired woman in a full figured pantsuit, crème colored, with a full figured silk rose stapled to the overly wide lapel. Even her hair was full figured. Mom was not a happy camper.

"I'm afraid I don't understand, Ms. Reardon. Anyone can plainly see that my husband is in no shape to come home yet. I don't care what your rules say."

"Mercy Hill understands, Mrs. Malone, that each patient recovers at his or her own rate. However, due to the curse of DRGs and the limitations of your husband's catastrophic insurance coverage, barring an unexpected downturn in his condition which we all certainly hope doesn't happen, he'll be discharged within 48 hours." Ms. Reardon added a smile for punctuation and to soften the blow of her remarks.

My sister gasped. "Forty-eight hours?" she said.

"Hi Mom, Sis. Ms. Reardon, is it? I'm Ross Malone, the prodigal son. Surely, there is some wiggle room within these massive rules and regulations of yours."

"I'm afraid not. You see the face of health care is changing."

"But is it standard operating procedure to discharge heart patients with all deliberate speed?"

"Well..." said the bureaucrat, searching for a politically correct answer. It was nowhere to be found.

"And especially in light of the changing face of the legal system which, goshdarnitall, seems to file lawsuits for the silliest things. Imagine the cost of such litigation not only in legal fees, but bad publicity."

Ms. Reardon stiffened her resolve. "Thank you for your cooperation in this matter. As Mr. Malone gets closer to discharge, we'll talk again. Good day."

She turned on her full figured heel and toddled off.

"Your father's not ready to go home yet," said Mom starting to cry. "How will I care for him? They can't be serious that he'll go home the day after tomorrow. They can't make him, can they?"

"Relax Mom," said Chris, draping an arm around the nearest shoulder. "They won't rush Dad out of here any sooner than necessary."

"She's right. We won't let them," I said.

"But how can we stop them?" said my mother, now searching for a new package of tissues.

"We'll just have to insist," I said, just to be saying something reassuring.

"Insist about what?" said Anthony, arriving with Roberta hand in hand. He kissed Mom's forehead while conveniently inserting himself between yours truly and his female parental unit.

"Oh Anthony, I'm so glad you're here. The hospital says that they're going to kick your father out of here the day after tomorrow." I saw her hands grip his, until her knuckles lost color.

"Not going to happen, Mom. Hospitals are just trying to scare you."

"I think it's working, Tony," I said.

"Ross, please, let me handle this. It doesn't require brute force."

"Maybe soon though, do you think?" I punched one hand into the other and started pacing around the circle of family members, doing my minimal best to keep quiet.

"Mom, hospital rooms are like tables at Spago. The more customers you sit at that table, the higher the profits. It's still all about money."

"You should have been there, Tony. This mushroom cloud of a social worker almost scared Mom to death with all of this talk about DRGs," said Chris.

"Sis, traffic was bumper to bumper on 81. The point is I'm here now."

My hands almost broke out into applause.

"As far as DRGs are concerned, DRG stands for Diagnostic Related Groups. Now the AMA..." Roberta touched my younger brother's forearm, and without skipping a beat he transformed into action man. "Give me the name of that bureaucrat again?"

"Ms. Reardon," I said.

"I'll be back. Try not to worry." With that, off went young Anthony Malone to slay dragons. We went in to see my father.

"Hi Pop. How are you feeling?"

"Okay, better than I expected actually." Jack Malone measured each word as if he thought it was going to be his last. He was quiet, waiting to marshal his strength for another sentence. I averted my eyes. It was tough to see my father with a zipper stitched up the middle of his chest. Most of the incision was bandaged but the very top of the cut was exposed. My DVD sized imagination did the rest. In fact, I went down the line from incision to cracking his chest to changing the traffic patterns of his arteries.

"Anything you want or need?" My eyes played tag with everything in the room, classic avoidance.

"I could use some sports. I haven't seen a game in almost a week. Maybe the Yankees?"

"Can do," I smiled. "I think Martinez and the Red Sox are at the stadium tonight. Maybe against Cone?"

He smiled. I used the bedside phone to get his TV set hooked up. He'd be smelling the new mown grass at Yankee Stadium by nightfall. I envied him.

"Thanks." It was all he could manage. His eyelids descended. For him, the conversation was over. The headline in the *SENTINEL* newspaper at his bedside foretold of yet another call for an independent prosecutor aimed at the Executive branch of government. Now there was a cottage industry. Nothing about the gunplay at the airport. Trevor Bradley's State Department Spin Patrol must have burned up the phone lines all night long.

"Jack, how are you feeling?" Mom had returned after yet another foray into the wilds of the hospital gift shop. I was at a loss to guess what Pop didn't yet have, that he still needed with the Mercy Hill hospital logo emblazoned on it. I moved into the hallway with Chris to allow my parents some time alone, for parent things.

"How is he, Ross?" asked Chris.

"Holding his own. I got his TV hooked up. He wants to watch the Yankees tonight."

"But Ross, you know how excited he gets. Couldn't he just listen on the radio?"

"No. Besides, he'll probably be asleep before they finish the National Anthem. Chris, he just had open-heart surgery not an organ donation. There's no need to treat him like a man whose days are numbered."

Roberta and Anthony returned from their mission.

"How'd it go?" said Chris. Tony's already ruddy complexion flushed red. My brother now looked very much like a human thermometer.

"Damn bureaucrat. She knows very well that DRGs sometimes make allowances for catastrophic illnesses. And Dad's insurance should pick up the difference."

"I'll check on it tomorrow," I offered. Always willing to do my part for family unity.

Tony shook his head, but with a smile. At least, I think it was a smile. Or it could have been a smirk. "Thanks Ross, but I'll handle it. Honey, remind me to get the insurance particulars from Mom. Sorry Big Bro, but I deal with medical insurances all of the time. It's just easier if I take care of this."

"Easier for whom?" I caught a glimpse of Tony's missus out of the corner of my eye. This was not the time for another mano e mano with my brother said everything about her but the words coming out of her mouth. Her hint was well taken. "Not a problem. Anybody want some Pepsi?"

"I think we have more important matters to discuss," said Anthony.

"Such as?" I asked.

Anthony stole a glance back to see what Mom was doing. He told us to regroup in the visitor's waiting room. A moment later, he joined us. He took his position in the wingback chair located between two genuine leather couches that were overstuffed, sort of like Ms. Reardon. Chris, Tony, Roberta and I sat there. Probably not as imposing as John, Paul, George and Ringo.

"Where's Mom, Tony?" asked my sister, trying to get her small frame comfortable within the embrace of the humungous furniture.

"Sitting with Dad. She's settled in for a while. I think we should use this time to make some decisions," said Anthony, obviously warming up his chairman of the board act.

"What decisions?"

"Assuming that we can squeeze a few extra days out of Ms. Reardon..."

I shivered outwardly. "Now there's a frightening prospect," I said.

Anthony stiffened his spine and disapproval. His look narrowed into a glare. "Even if we get those days, Dad's eventually going home. Bobbie and I aren't sure Mom's up to taking care of him."

"That's why they have visiting nurses," I said.

"Short term answer at best, Ross. But there is a long term solution," announced my brother.

"Which is?"

"Bobbie and I think that it's best that Mom and Dad sell the house and move up to Rochester with us. There's a townhouse in an assisted living-housing complex that would be perfect for them. Colonial Pines."

"I don't care if it's Fort Knox. I vote no," I said. Looking quickly to Roberta Malone's face I searched for even a flicker of opposition. There was none. "Tony, that can't be what they want. They've lived in that house for over 30 years. Hell, it would take them 30 years just to pack."

"I see. Ross, your position is quite clear. Chris?" My sister had kept quiet. I half expected her to start twirling her hair. "Does her silence and your opposition mean that you are both going to move in with Mom and Dad, and help take care of them? Bypass patients take up to a full year for a complete recovery. Which one of you is going to move in with them for the next 365 days? Hm?"

Chris squirmed like she was eleven and had seen her first garter snake up close. "Don't look at me, Tony. You know I'd love to move back east, but my career is on the upswing. Besides, Mom will be fine. They've been married almost 50 years and raised three kids. They'll be okay."

"You can deny this all you want Chris, but the fact of the matter is, that Mom and Dad aren't as young as they used to be. One down, one to go. So Ross, what'll it be? Are you ready to leave Dr. Susan and stay with Mom and Dad?" Anthony was pressing all of the wrong buttons, on purpose.

"I'm sorry, I was just wondering if this performance will be considered for this year's Oscars, or next." I stood to stretch my legs and looked out the window for some answers. I saw the reflection of someone who didn't look a bit like me staring back. "Look, no one says that its going to be easy when Pop comes home."

Chris jumped in. "I can't leave my job for a year. It would be professional suicide. I can stay for a few weeks then come back in a few months. But I can't stay a whole year." She turned to me and placed her hands on my chest, pleading for understanding. "Ross, maybe Tony's right for a change," she said.

"Hold off on the relocation, Chris. Tony, Bobbie, Chris and I know you mean well, but this isn't our decision to make. You're right when you say we don't know what Dad will be capable of when he gets home. All I'm saying is that let's wait and see. Colonial Pines won't go belly up if Mom and Dad stay put."

The image in the window moved. I focused on it. My hand inched towards my hip. The eyes in the window stared back at me. Slowly, I turned to see the face dead on, in person. It was a kid. The goatee was, barely enough stray strands of hair to qualify, strewn randomly about his upper lip and where his chin was supposed to have been situated. Yet those eyes were riveted upon me. Cobalt Blue and as empty as last year's Christmas club account, he was in his Clint Eastwood mode.

Cobalt Blue held the stare a moment longer, than turned and walked away. Chris tugged at my sleeve.

"Ross, what is it?" she asked, angling her head to look at what had held my attention.

"Just someone I thought I recognized. Where were we?"

"You and your sister were going to enlighten us as to how you intend to care for our parents," said Tony, with a generous helping of smug.

"Okay Tony, here's the plan. 'Since you deal with insurance all the time', find out exactly what Dad's coverage is, including any home care options that'll be available. Decisions, regardless of who makes them, shouldn't be made without all of the facts, don't you agree?" I smiled.

"Come on Roberta, this is getting us nowhere. You two let us know when you want to talk seriously about our parents' future." My younger brother Anthony and his wife promptly left in a huff that brought to mind that old Groucho Marx line about leaving in a minute and a huff.

"Ross, were we wrong?" said Chris, suddenly worried about the future and her responsibilities in it.

"No Sister dear, we aren't. We are all scared out of our wits. But the bottom line is that we have 48 hours to figure it out."

Chris sighed and leaned up and kissed my cheek.

"I'm going back to Dad's room. Coming?"

I shook my head gently. "You go ahead. I'll be along soon," I said.

My sister moved out and past Cobalt Blue. He made no move to stop her but his eyes did follow her down the hall. I used the diversion to sidle over next to him.

"You wouldn't by any chance be looking for me, would you?" I said in a monotone.

Cobalt Eyes looked up and into my eyes. He didn't break a sweat. He'd had onions for lunch, probably whole and raw. Up close, I could see in his right earlobe, the crossed sabers that seemed to me to be everywhere these days like the happy faces of the nineties.

He opened his mouth to speak, then, thought better of it and shook his head no to my inquiry and walked away, backing up all of the fifteen steps to the elevator. Those cobalt blue eyes never left me. I think I was supposed to be afraid. I wasn't, even though my hand never left the handle of my gun.

An Express Mail Courier exited the next arriving elevator car. I followed him down the hall to my father's room. Chris jumped up and accepted the parcel with a signature. The courier tipped his cap, just like in the commercials then vanished like Mercury.

"Business is business, Ross," said Chris, who beamed then went back into Dad's room. It looked overcrowded and I needed some space. I'd come back later. I went to see Nellie, still hoping for a miracle.

"He's been here all day. Once her friend left, this morning, that is," said the day nurse who was just heading off to give report to the next shift before leaving for the day.

I walked into Nellie's room. Her condition was unchanged. On the nightstand was a chocolate Hostess cupcake, with a trademark white curlicue, and an unlit candle stuck in it. Happy Birthday, Nellie.

"Hello Joe," I said. He started to rise, but I placed a hand on his shoulder so he'd stay seated.

"Malone, do you know who did this?"

"Not yet," I said.

"When you do know, I want to know as well. Do we understand each other?" said Joe Rhino.

"Yes."

Joe Rhino turned his head to me and I saw eyes reddened with sadness and anger that I knew would soon build to violence unless I could stop it.

"Tell me what you need, it's there. Tell me what I can do, it's done."

"You're doing it now, Joe," I said. "I'm not sure why she was beaten, but on the off chance someone tries to come back to keep her quiet then she needs to be looked after." He nodded, but didn't move his gaze from her.

"Malone?" he said.

"Yes?"

"Get out of here. You're wasting time."

-14-

J oe Rhino had made his point.

From Mercy Hill Hospital, which was rapidly becoming my home away from home, so much so that I could probably get dual citizenship, I negotiated through noontime traffic. My destination was the offices of the City Security Association and Gardner Meadows.

A left turn looking for a short cut found me facing several streets surrounding the temporary Laracone consulate, all blocked off as an extra security precaution. I would have done the same thing. Sheet metal plating was propped up all along behind the wrought iron fencing circling the compound that covered the gaps obstructing both the view and ill-intended gunfire.

The network satellite trucks had dispersed as soon as the hustle and bustle of breaking news was no longer urgent. On the other hand, it would only have taken one strategically placed explosive device to knock the current special prosecutor back off the front page and bring the talking heads back to town en masse.

Just beyond the wooden sawhorse security perimeter, marched the true believers in two lines, each single file. The line going clockwise was for Benjamin Walanna, while those in the counterclockwise parade weren't so enamored with him. Surely, it took all kinds to make this gigantic globe go round, but in recent years, violence had become the weapon of choice of those seeking to effect change in a heartbeat. Sort of like number one with a bullet. The ballot box or economic boycott each ran a distant second.

The World Trade Center, the Alfred P. Murrah Federal Building in Oklahoma City and almost any one of a dozen abortion clinics throughout the country had all been turned into ground zero to advance someone's twisted political agenda. I maneuvered the Jeep Cherokee with its four new tires, through the marchers, looking for familiar faces from the airport. A picket sign thudded against the top of my luggage rack.

The already slow going got markedly slower. Voices that had been chanting at the start now were screaming, more vehement than ever. The banging, at first sporadic, was now a steady drumbeat knocking the hell out of my paint job. I leaned on the horn. It fell on deaf ears. Some of the uniformed police detail came over and tried to part some of the teeming masses. Billy clubs came out, only now they were referred to as politically correct batons. Either way, in the hands of an expert, they packed a mean wallop. My vehicle inched ahead and eventually out of the crowd that was building momentum into becoming a poor man's riot.

I hit the accelerator to escape while watching the mob close ranks quickly behind me. The cops were now the focus of the protestors' ire. I felt responsible.

My keycard allowed me entrance into the subterranean garage across the street from my destination on the fourteenth floor of the Davenport Tower. Using the underground tunnel always made me feel like I was Steve McQueen in *The Great Escape*.

The first time I had entered the tunnel was when Nicholas "The building was named after me" Davenport hired me to help clear him of the murder of environmental thorn in his side, Angela

Curtiss. It turned out Nicky's lawyer killed her to frame the millionaire and run to daylight in a takeover bid which was about as hostile as you can get. All he had to do was extinguish a human life. For him, it was a cost benefit thing.

Fourteen floors went by fast. The doors opened and it took only a few minutes on plush seagreen carpeting, checking on frosted glass windows in doors to find the right one. Seven offices down and on the left, I was there.

City Security Association
Suite 1408
Gardner Meadows
Executive Director.

The receptionist was perky, dressed in a power suit in power colors probably suggested by last month's Cosmo cover story. Her champagne hair was pulled back and fashioned in a long braid that descended, I guessed, almost to her hourglass waist. She was probably packing heat, though her attire was so form fitting I had a delicious time wondering where she might be concealing her weapons.

Power color lip-gloss parted and I heard in a telephone operator's tone. "May I help you, sir?"

"I, certainly hope so, Miss, um, Miss?" Sure, I could have read her nameplate, but I wanted to hear that voice which I could have sworn had once told me the number I was seeking was not in service at that time.

"Palmer, Jessica Palmer. And you are?"

Business cards came in handy at times like these because I always felt self-conscious saying I was a private eye. And in New York State, statute or regulation prohibited me from identifying myself as a private detective, so as not to confuse John and Mary Q. Public. So, I had cards printed up that read, "Ross Malone,

Confidential Inquiries." Susan said they were classy. It took class to know class.

"What inquiry are you making here, Mr. Malone?" she asked, in a voice that angels must have envied.

"I'm here to see Gardner Meadows. No, I do not have an appointment. If you tell him I'm here, I'll just bet he'll see me."

Jessica Palmer looked at me, sizing me up. I tried acting nonchalant. Above her coifed head was a carved wooden emblem of a group calling itself, "The Warriors of the Night." Their logo?

Crossed sabers.

A clue, a clue, my kingdom for a clue.

She turned my card over in her hand three times, looked at the intercom, and then smiled sweetly. "Please have a seat. I'll be right back."

"I'll be right here." I could do saccharin smiles with the best of them, but she had me beat hands down.

The outer office walls were covered with framed newspaper headlines of the City Security Association, it's founder and mentor —Gardner Meadows, and their very likely, more militant subsidiary, the Warriors of the Night. The display spoke of courage, standing up for one's beliefs, the right to bear and use those arms, and of course, the overall theme of self-protection. "The ends justifies the means" was the unspoken message I saw in the faces of the Warriors of the Night. A closer look at the photos saw familiar bulges under their thin shirts and jackets. Very few looked old enough to have a legal gun permit unless the term, "B.B." was in front of it. Even my friend from the ICU waiting room was among the mug shots on the wall. If it was true that a person's eyes were the mirrors of the soul, his needed some serious Windex action.

I saw the Governor, the Mayor, the former governor, a U.S. Senator, a congressperson who wanted to be governor and a someone whom I didn't recognize, all with their arms locked with Gardner Meadows.

"Ross, my man. How are you?" said my multi-millionaire friend.

"Fine Nicky. And you?" Miss Palmer was back at her desk preserving her vocal chords, as the inner office door swung wide enough to allow me to see the new John Wayne of Wall Street, Nicholas Davenport. From the Italian cut of his hand-made suit, no doubt sewn by a gaggle of cornfed seamstresses, to his smile you could set a GPS satellite by, my former client and current friend, strutted towards me, a meticulously mani-cured hand extended.

In Davenport's shadow stood Gardner Meadows. He still looked like a drop out from a correspondence school for butlers. But that smirk on that clean shaven Howdy Dowdy face made my skin crawl, as if I needed yet another reminder as to why I was there.

"You two know each other, Mr. Davenport?" Meadows was in full ooze.

"Yes. Malone is the best private detective in the business," said Nicky.

"Shucks Nicky, you're only saying that because I saved your assets from a murder frame up."

"True, at first, but over the years I've come to admire your temerity, your rugged bulldog nature that…"

I raised my hands. "Nicky, stop before I get diabetic."

"All right," said the local multi-millionaire. His ever-present bodyguard appeared out of the woodwork to perch an overcoat on Nicky's shoulders. Davenport shot his cuffs like Legs Diamond, probably had running boards installed on the limo, too. "Gardner? I'm not sure what your business is with Malone, but I guarantee you, he'll get results."

"I'll keep that in mind, Mr. Davenport. Thank you for coming," said Meadows, practically genuflecting for Nicholas Davenport.

"Keep up the good work. Call Laura if you have any further concerns about your finances. She'll see to it personally. Malone, about time we took in a Sky Chiefs game soon?"

"Sure Nicky."

With that, Nicholas Davenport clapped a hand on my shoulder and exited like Lamont Cranston. That left Gardner Meadows, the too elegant for secretarial work, Miss Palmer and me.

"Come in Malone," said Gardner, adding an aside to Miss Palmer to hold his calls for now. I followed him inside and heard the door close behind me.

"Can I get you a drink?" said Gardner Meadows.

"Not unless you have the milk of human kindness on the rocks," I said.

"We're both busy men. Let's bottomline this. What do you want from me?" He started tapping his fingers on the desktop.

My eyes scanned the office. The furnishings were serviceable but not plush, save for the high backed leather chair Meadows balanced himself in as if it were his personal throne. I sat on the edge of a wooden straight-backed chair from Stickley facing the desk.

"Let's start with a simple one. Who the hell are you?" I said.

His laugh was from the bemused public figure act he'd no doubt perfected.

"I'm Gardner Meadows, and I am the executive director of the City Security Association." His thin lips glistened. A pink tongue pointed at the tip, or was it forked, swiped at the excess moisture like a snake getting ready for dinner. I waited for him to continue. He didn't.

"Since we are both 'busy men', think we could dispense with the steely eyed stare portion of this meeting?" I said.

Gardner Meadows considered this for a moment, moved to the wet bar, fashioned himself what looked like vodka on the rocks, and then went back to his throne.

"Ask your questions, I'll answer what I can."

"What does your association do?" I said.

"We foster the security of the local business community. Be it a shop in the mall, a restaurant in Armory Square or a hot dog cart across from City Hall, they all fall within the charter of our responsibilities. Malone, Syracuse is the hub of Central New York. Our best days are still ahead of us." He rose and began pacing as his speech moved into passing gear.

"Is this where I stand and salute?" He smiled. "So tell me what kind of security did you give George Trask?"

"I'm not at liberty to discuss that. I'm afraid that Association business is confidential."

"Understood, but convenient," I said. I was drawn to the oversized picture window framed by two hanging plants of the fern variety. My back was to Meadows, probably a dubious action at best, and now I was staring fourteen floors straight down.

The demonstrators could now legally be defined as a riot. Crowd control moved in, paddy wagons at the ready with batons and little plastic wrist restraints rounding out their ensemble. Suddenly, I was aware that Gardner Meadows had joined me at the window.

"Tsk, tsk. No doubt a portent of what our society is headed for," he said.

"Tell me about George Trask," I said, trying to keep the twerp in the dry clean only clothes focused on what I wanted.

"I told you Malone," he started. I interrupted.

"Tell me about Trask, or tell the police. While you're playing hard to get, I'll be doing an in studio interview at Channel 9. Then, on to the Internet."

Meadows sighed in disgust. "Trask is a member in good standing in the Association. He came to us about a continuing pattern of vandalism, in the store he's owned all his life after the military. The police refused him help, refused him protection. That's when he sought you out."

"You knew about that before he contacted me?" My eyebrows arched.

"I make it my business to be in the know."

"What did the City Security Association do to protect Trask from the vandalism?" I said.

"We've yet to complete our investigation." I'll bet he thought that would satisfy me. It didn't.

"Since I'm taking over the case," I said, "is there any information that you might wish to share that might shed some light on all of this?"

His answer was a smirk. Most of his answers were smirks. I was getting annoyed. Two small clouds of smoke puffed into existence down below, possibly tear gas. What had been a scuffle, was turning into a serious civil disturbance. Yellow school buses commandeered by the police were now parked nearby at the ready to cart away the miscreants. It seemed to me, fourteen floors above the fray, that the cops were badly outnumbered and suffering for it. I also knew from experience that they wouldn't just sit still and let it happen. Visions of water cannons flashed in my head.

"It seems that the good guys are losing," said Meadows, pulling a cell phone from his inside jacket pocket. Speed dialing two numbers, when connected he spoke one word, "Deploy."

From out of the asphalt streets came three Hum Vees, vehicle of choice for today's urban vigilante force. A couple of dozen men rushed from the vehicles into battle. Each black jumpsuit carried a fluorescent crossed sabers logo on the back and topped with a similarly branded baseball cap turned backwards.

"Your guys?" I said.

"Yes, they are the best of the best. They have been rigorously trained by several former Special Forces experts on the tactics of urban guerilla warfare."

"Armed?"

"Silly question. A true general would never send his men to meet the enemy without the proper firepower."

"They aren't the enemy, Meadows. They're people." I said. He was getting further under my skin. That was not a good sign.

"Each of **my** people has a valid pistol permit, and has survived a thorough background check by the Association."

"Sounds a little incestuous, you clearing your own people on background checks."

His back stiffened at the accusation. "On the contrary, the Association would bear the liability if any of our employees screw up. We were just doing the police a favor," he said, satisfied with his own logic. That made one of us.

It turned my stomach, but I had to admit that "his people" were efficient. Down below, the last of the buses was pulling away. The phone in his hand rang. Meadows listened then gave another order to clear out. Retreat was not in his vocabulary.

"Let's get back to George Trask," I said. "Did you know I sent an associate of mine to help Trask with his problem? And that said associate is taking up space in the coma ward at Mercy Hill Hospital?"

"Mr. Trask did say he spoke with someone, a woman I believe, and decided not to engage her services."

"Where does all of the money come from to finance your 'Association'?"

"I am relatively successful in the stock market. Online trading is apparently made just for me. Other than that, we get dues from our members and wealthy benefactors who want a clean, safe city and aren't afraid to pay for it."

"They pay for the hired muscle as well?" I said. "Or don't they know about it?"

"The Warriors of the Night are the future of urban law enforcement. I like to think of them as techno-militia, modern day minute men ready to take up arms on a moment's notice to defend their families, their homes, their ways of life."

"Where do I sign up?" I said, with more than a little sarcasm.

"An interesting thought, and not as farfetched as you might think. We could use a man like you. Military background, police experience, private business man—all distinguished to one degree or another."

"I have a flaw, Gardner, a fatal flaw," I said.

"Which is?"

"I have a conscience. And I know how to use it."

"Let me reach out to you, Malone. The Association is not without influence. We could devote considerable resources to finding out who assaulted your Miss Archer."

"How did you know her name was Archer? I didn't mention it."

"Why, um, George Trask must have told me," he said struggling for an answer. "Or perhaps I read it in the paper."

"Perhaps. Or maybe you could have found out because your minutemen have been following me around ever since Trask showed up on my doorstep. Care to tell me what two of your well trained force tried to get from Trask in the hospital when he pulled a gun on them?"

"A gun? Really? I wasn't aware of this."

"I'll bet. As for the offer, thanks, but no thanks. I work solo, conscience and all."

He shrugged in a non-committal fashion. He had determined I was not a threat to them. He had determined wrong.

"Suit yourself. But we could be an asset to each other. Our business is now over."

"Don't count on it. One last thing," I said, rapidly closing the distance between us from feet to inches in two quick strides. "If you had anything to do with what happened to Nellie Archer, your Warriors of the Night will be the Pall Bearers of the Morning. Capice?"

"You can't threaten me," he said.

"I just did."

Back in my Cherokee, I picked up my messages by cell phone and found one from the younger Malone brother asking me to meet him at the Paradise Sports Bar. When I arrived he was in the lobby, pacing and highly agitated.

"Is there some place private where we can talk?" he said. The words were shot out towards me in machine gun style.

"Follow me." I took him through Joe Rhino's office and then to a private entrance to a back room, where there was a pool table and occasionally the private high stakes poker game. Tony preceded me in. I closed the door and turned back around just in time to see a fist making the short trip to my face. I ducked and spun my younger brother around and slammed him face down onto the south end of the green felt pool table that covered the hand carved slate underneath. For effect, I chickenwinged his arm up behind his back. A trick I had learned from Deke, my first day on road patrol.

"What do you think you're doing?" I said.

"Fighting you on your own turf," he said, squirming back and forth to be released.

"Because?" There was no answer. We were both breathing hard. "If I let you up Tony, will you take another swing at me?"

"Probably. Violence is what you understand."

"Violence is my second language. I still rely on English first; it's easier on the knuckles. Now I'm going to let you up, but if you come at me again, I'll drop you." I moved back, but stayed ready.

"You don't respect me, Ross. You never have. You don't think I'm capable of knowing what's best for Mom and Dad. You ridicule me in front of my wife, our sister, Susan. Only Ross, the savior, has all of the answers. I thought if I punched your lights out at least you'd have respect for me after beating me to a pulp."

"Punch my lights out? Tony, I apologize if I've done the 500-pound gorilla bit. You have skills that I don't have, but believe me; we are all in this together. The best we can do at the moment is to make sure that Mom and Dad have options, that they aren't just pushed aside into a nursing home or somebody's spare bedroom."

"That's all very well and good Ross, but what if they can't take care of themselves?" It sounded more like an accusation than a question, but I decided to treat it as the latter.

"Tony, have you ever considered that maybe they can? Let's wait and see if there is a problem before we rush in to fix it. But Mom and Sue are right. We've got to stop fighting amongst ourselves. That's means you and me Bucco, unless you still want to duke it out. I'll make peace, if you'll let me."

"Ross, I won't just stand by if our parents need a managed care set-up. I can't, and I won't."

"Neither will I. So, let's put our energy towards helping Dad get better, agreed?" We didn't shake hands but I felt the tension leave the room. I opened the door and turned back to Tony. "Almost getting my lights punched out works up my appetite. Want to get something to eat?"

Benjamin Walanna's bodyguard, Andrew, filled the doorway.

"Make it to go," he said in a rich, threatening baritone. "President Walanna needs to see you. It is of the utmost urgency."

-15-

The words, "How long has he been gone?" pricked up my ears as I walked into the Laracone consulate. I almost tripped over the spaghetti tangle of wires all over the floor. There were three piece suits, walkie-talkies and cell phones everywhere. Firepower of the automatic weapons variety was being brandished as if they expected a direct hit. It looked like a command post from Desert Storm.

Trevor Bradley was barking commands into a cell phone, while checking his vibrating pager which he promptly dropped, and emailing somebody at Foggy Bottom. After spotting me, he beckoned me over with a wave of his pager.

"Glad you're here Malone. Let's get you up to speed ASAP. Time is of the essence."

"Let me cut to the chase, Bradley. How long has the Prince been gone?" I smiled to show him that the needle I had just thrust into him was benign.

"Longer than he was supposed to be gone." Bradley stopped. He paused to suck in a deep breath then let it out in a slow, energetic hiss. "Sorry. He slipped away from his guards in a McDonald's on University Heights. He's been gone since noon. We've canvassed the immediate area and come up empty-handed."

"And the cops are too high profile? It's only been a few hours. Trust me, the kid will show up." Having met him, Prince Gregory impressed me as responsible enough to return on his own, if he could. "Besides, I have another case right now."

"Malone, you were at the airport. The kid's a target. These wackos can't get to President Walanna, so they are going after the heir to the throne. I've asked around about you. You aren't the type to throw the kid to the wolves. Help me out here, Malone. I'm begging."

"If it will secure your services, then I will beg you as well." Benjamin Walanna had drifted into the room that was buzzing with activity and urgency. His feet were shoulder width apart and his fists were balled up and rested on his hips. His Bruno Magli shoes sported a spit polish allowing him to resemble Peter O'Toole surveying the Sahara atop his personal camel. "Malone, I am appealing to you as one father to another."

Bradley whispered into Walanna's ear now decorated with a diamond stud.

"I am sorry. I am told you have no children." He seemed cha-grinned he had made a mistake. I was seething inside that my hav-ing children or not would make a difference in my character.

My late wife's face and that of my deceased son, Christopher, salved my cresting irritation. "You've been misinformed, Mr. President." I could always count on *CASABLANCA* for a snappy retort. "I'll do what I can. I'll need to see the boy's room."

The President of Laracone snapped his powerful fingers adorned with a ring the size of Rhode Island. Andrew appeared, his coat a memory, the nine-millimeter Glock hanging like the Gun of Damocles beneath his arm. I followed him up the car-peted stairway to the second floor, passing several paintings by artists whose names usually appeared in the New York Times crossword puzzle.

"This is the Prince's room. I'll wait outside, if there is anything you need. And Malone?"

"Yes?"

"Thank you." The words barely seeped out. I appreciated the gesture.

"Call it professional courtesy. Stay close."

With that, I disappeared into the world of Prince Gregory, first born of Benjamin Walanna and heir to the throne of Laracone.

Granted, he'd only been unaccounted for since lunch, but that little coup de'tat that had fizzled big time out at the airport kicked this up a notch or two on the seriousness level.

The walnut closet ran the full length of the southwest wall of the room with a compartment for each genre of clothing, from blue jeans with designer labels and ripped out knees, then alligator shirts, blazers in several muted colors, a couple of three piece suits—one sporting a thin diplomatic pinstripe, the other—a solid charcoal, and dress shirts, all long sleeved with no buttons on the cuffs, just slits for cufflinks. Each and every hanger was filled. If he'd packed a bag, it didn't come from his GQ Jr. wardrobe.

Then again, why raid the closet when he probably had a Gold Card embossed in his name at birth? Still, that would be traceable and the boy genius would be aware of that. If he was planning upon running away because the pressure of royal succession was too much of a burden, there were other things that I needed to know. For example, who were his friends at school? Who were his enemies? Real or imagined on both counts would be important. Where would he be likely to go? And probably more importantly, why?

One more spin around the room to see if there was anything I had missed. Overall, it appeared a normal kind of room for a genuine adolescent thrown into the college experience long before he was old enough to shave. No gushy love letters were strewn around that I could stumble over, which would lead me to conclude that he was off pursuing his first true love. My guess was, he wouldn't settle for less than Melissa Joan Hart. I would also bet even money that with Prince Gregory being royalty and all, that he was kept on a very short leash. Human contact would therefore be restricted to a minimum to keep the potential threats minimal was well.

What does a prince do for recreation? A SONY PLAYSTA-TION hooked up to a big screen TV in the corner might have kept him occupied for a while. No baseball gloves, no bats or balls, autographed or even scuffed, plus no football, no basketball, no bow and arrow, no street hockey equipment and not even a soccer ball was around. The bookshelf had history books ranging from Barbara Tuchman's *GUNS OF AUTUMN* to Tom Brokaw's *THE GREATEST GENERATION*. Somehow I felt a little concerned that his reading didn't include Calvin and Hobbes, R.L. Stein or Dave Barry. However, the problem before me wasn't whether Prince Gregory was literate, but whether he was still living.

For the moment, I had exhausted whatever use his room could be. I needed to talk to the guards who were last with him. Walking past a window, the sun, descending in the late afternoon hours told me to hustle, time was slipping away.

Jacob and the nanny had been with Prince Gregory when he had disappeared. Andrew brought them into a sitting room off the main living room where the activity had been ratcheted up a few more notches. More bodies were moving back and forth reporting to everyone, and no one.

"Please have a seat," I said.

Jacob brought his attitude. "We should not be sitting and talking here when Prince Gregory is out there, in the hands of our enemies."

"Do you have proof of that?" I asked.

He slammed a fist against his chest, where my anatomy lessons told me his heart should be located. "I know in here Malone, better than you or any other..."

"Perhaps Jacob, but then again, I didn't lose him, did I?"

Jacob saw red, just like I would have, and lunged at me. We collapsed in a heap onto the plush antique rugs that Aladdin might have flown upon. Powerful fists jackhammered my kidneys in a very painful rendition of the Anvil Chorus. I punched his salivating beet red face flush with my forearms, first left, then right. He blinked and continued harder.

My third roundhouse elbow snapped his no neck, thumb like head like a Rock 'em, sock 'em Robot. I kept pressing hard against his jaw focusing all of my diminishing energy into making his neck a huge Slinky toy. A quick assessment of the situation found me losing. Abruptly, I slammed my other elbow into his face, three sharp, successive blows. His eyeballs started to spin like a slot machine. A strange hand followed by a lumberjack sized arm circled Jacob's neck then jerked him back. I pushed, someone pulled. It was Andrew who had come to my aid. I was at once grateful, and a little curious as to why it took him so long.

"Enough Jacob! Our mission is to find the Prince, not settle old scores."

Jacob glared at Andrew in between the times he was gasping for air. The nanny was still seated in her chair, nary a hair out of place. I righted my own chair, sheepishly.

"It was a cheap shot," I said. "I'm sorry. We're all looking for Prince Gregory but before I can help you, you have to help me. Now, I need to know what happened when you lost sight of the boy?"

That seemed fair enough to me. I sat back, willing my pulse rate back to normal, and then I crossed my legs and waited. Finally, Jacob stopped pacing and plopped his bulk into a nearby overstuffed wingback chair with brocade sleeves covering the chair arms. I looked at the nanny, then quite obviously at my watch. Enough was enough. I stood.

"Andrew, if you can get these mimes to talk, I'd suggest you do so. I can't help the prince if they stonewall me because of pride or stupidity." I headed for the door.

The nanny cleared her throat. I kept walking. She spoke as my hand reached the doorknob. "Prince Gregory disappeared at the McDonald's on University Heights. I went to the restroom. Jacob was with him when someone smashed into our car in the parking lot. When I came back to the booth, Jacob was just returning from the parking lot. Gregory was no where to be found."

"Tell me about the accident."

Jacob now spoke without looking, without moving, without emotion. "It was an old Volkswagen bus, a very old one, rust spots everywhere. He crumpled the sedan's back fender, all of the way across the back end."

"He? Did the driver stick around?" I said, trying to do some detecting.

"No, he was driving away when I got out there."

"Then how do you know it was a he? Never mind. Take me through what happened next?"

"Jacob and I did a quick search then canvassed the people sitting around us. No one saw anything. Then we called the consulate and searched the immediate area on foot. We didn't find him, or even any trace of him," said the nanny.

I considered all of this, tried to appear thoughtful, then continued to the door. "Nanny, you come with me. Andrew, Jacob, you stay here. Hold the fort. If the prince is in the hands of unfriendlies, there might be a ransom note or some sort of contact. And if they can't use Prince Gregory, they might take another run at your president."

The aroma from the French fry oil hit me two blocks before I was able to put my Cherokee into park. That's why French Fries were my favorite stakeout food. I didn't tell Andrew, Jacob, the nanny, Walanna and especially, Trevor Bradley that each moment that ticked away lessened the odds of finding Prince Gregory among the living.

"What now Malone?" said my companion.

"Why don't you show me where it all happened?"

The nanny, whose name I learned on the way over, was Grace, led me through the paces of the accident first. Whoever smacked the car did it deliberately. There were skid marks away from the scene, but none anywhere near the point of impact. A lookout was probably waiting for a time when the prince was most vulnerable. When the nanny left Jacob and the prince at the booth, the driver of the VW bus got a signal. It barreled into the only car in the parking lot with diplomatic plates, staying long enough to draw Jacob's presence. Someone inside grabbed the prince. Maybe he was coerced to come along at gunpoint.

I knelt down to check out some debris from the accident. Piles of red plastic and clear glass shards from the taillight, and paint chips from both vehicles were all that remained from the collision. Using a spare business card, I scooped up some of the wreckage, then poured it into a ziploc bag. Getting it analyzed would give Trevor Bradley something to do. How many VW buses could still be registered in the area? Even if it was stolen, we were one step closer if we could rule the others out.

Walking around inside the Golden Arches only confirmed my scenario. They'd been seated in a booth next to a picture window, so Jacob and Grace could see danger coming from the proverbial mile away. I would have done the same thing. There was enough added cover from the outdoor play area and still enough gaps to see a sniper sighting a scope on the prince's forehead.

If their prince had been abducted, he'd probably be kept alive for leverage against the father, financially or politically. Yet, that didn't mean he'd be kept in factory mint condition. I'd always considered kids to be the innocents of the world I lived in. Now, if the bad guys would only play by the same rules, I'd be a step ahead. If they were political fanatics with an agenda to get headlines, I'd still be a step behind, way behind.

I asked to see the manager which sent a small breasted woman, wearing the requisite uniform and plastered on smile complete with lived in face, and several gold rings grouped around a serious engagement ring, off on a mission. When she returned, part of my past walked in behind her.

"Ross?" said the manager. His countenance was light years from the last time I'd seen him when we both wore pocket protectors and were co-captains of the high school chess club.

"Frank?" We shook hands. A graying walrus mustache sprawled across his florid cheeks. He was working on connecting it with muttonchop sideburns. "You the manager?"

"Yes. Cheryl and I bought this place last year. What have you been up to?"

I took note of the military insignia tattoo on his forearm, Army Air Cavalry. "Same as you." Grace nudged me. "Frank, I'm looking for a kid, around 13-14, brown hair, blue eyes—Sky Chiefs windbreaker, blue jeans."

"Got a picture?" It had taken some doing to find a photo at the consulate of Gregory Walanna that looked like a normal kid. Frank studied the picture. "Nope, I haven't seen him."

"He disappeared in here around lunchtime. You might have seen him. He was at that table by the window." I gestured towards the booth to see if it would help to jog his memory. He looked, then shook his head.

"I didn't get here until four, but come back into my office. I might be able to help."

Even though those dual deep fryers caressing another load of French Fries were calling my name, I moved past them, along the shelves where the microwaves were heating up specialty sandwiches, down beyond a combination of employees from high school seniors saving for college or that first car payment to senior citizens saving for that next gas and electric bill, into Frank's cubbyhole of an office next to the walk-in freezer.

"Look at this." Frank opened a metal cabinet over his desk exposing a video tape recorder and monitor. "I put this in myself. It's trained on the counter and the cash drawers. I wanted to make sure that all of the money got to where it was supposed to go. Plus, I can also see if food is just being given away to friends or family."

"Fascinating, but what does this have to do with us?" I said.

"See how the camera swings in an arc? Right there is dead on to your table where you say this kid was. You're welcome to look at it. I've got to get back out there."

It only took a few minutes of rewinding, fast forwarding and pausing to find Gregory. The overhang only obstructed the top part of the booth in the non-smoking section.

"That's him," said Grace.

We rolled it forward and watched as the three entered the booth. Jacob left and returned with a tray full of food. Then, a few minutes later, Grace left the table; a stranger ran into the frame and then ran off with Jacob in hot p ursuit. I was guessing about all of this because the only part visible of the participants was from the shoulders down. Then, a new player walked into view. All I could see was that he was well dressed with a short corduroy jacket, contrasting slacks, and polished shoes. There was no sound, but Gregory slid out of the booth and left with the well-dressed man.

I took the tape and thanked Frank on the way out. We waited long enough for Trevor Bradley to send a courier to pick up the accident evidence and the store videotape.

Grace and I got back into the Cherokee. I started the engine. "Let's start with Gregory's favorite hangouts. I'm hoping he has some, places that he goes more than others?"

"Yes. I'll show you."

I'd never seen so many computer terminals at once in one place that wasn't either an insurance company or ground control at Cape Canaveral. It was a restaurant set up like microchip heaven called, "Hackers Inc." Each table had a terminal, a mouse and/or a connection so that you could hook up your own laptop. Grace told me it was the prince's one vice, surfing the web. Sometime, I'd have to ask her exactly what her definition of vice was. We found the manager who was missing a few gigabytes on the hard drive between his ears.

"Yeah, Greggy came in here a lot. What's you point?" said the bespectacled man who had middle class burnout written all over his scraggly goateed face.

"What sites does he usually access?" I asked.

"I don't know. We don't allow Big Brother to look over anybody's shoulders here."

"Was he close to anyone here? Anybody who might have seen him recently?"

The manager rolled his eyes in boredom and crossed his arms in front of his chest. "It wasn't my turn to watch him."

This retro angry young man act was tiring to watch. "I'll bet if the FBI infiltrated your terminals here they'd find more than a few users trying their luck at computer roulette with the Pentagon computers or NASA hardware? Federal offenses, I believe, which would make you a co-conspirator. Might put a dent or two in your hard drive, do you think?"

The Anti-Yuppie paused, shrugged, then leaned against the simulated wood grain paneling. "Gregory was a history buff. Always brought along his personal laptop. He spent a lot of time surfing the net, not really sure what he looked up. That's all I know."

"And you haven't seen the kid today, at all?" He shook his head. "Here's my card, if you remember anything."

The library, P&C Stadium, as well as his special spot by the lake where he liked to read, all came up empty and by then it was dark, and I was exhausted. While Grace used my cell phone to report to the consulate, I used a pay phone to check in at the hospital. I got Tony.

"He's sleeping right now, but they tell us he is still holding his own. He's been asking about you," said Anthony.

"I can't make it any time soon. I'm looking for a missing child."

"Good luck. Oh, I also checked on your friend, Nellie Archer." My heart paused for a long moment. "There's no change, Ross. I'm sorry."

"Thanks anyway. I'll be in touch." I walked slowly back to the Cherokee and Grace. "Okay, you know the prince better than I do. Now where to?"

"Over the river and through the woods to grandmother's house we go."

-16-

Grandmother Hughes, on the maternal side, responded with anger. "What do you mean my grandson is missing? He was abducted, wasn't he?" It was more of a statement than a question.

Grace placed her bone China teacup down. "Mrs. Hughes, we just aren't sure where Prince Gregory is at the moment. For all we know, he could just have wandered off to be with friends, or by himself. Mr. Malone is a local private investigator who knows this area quite well. What we need from you is anything about Gregory's likes and dislikes, any friends you might know about."

Emily Hughes' tan from her winter sojourns to Florida would last, sans maintenance from tanning salons till the end of the millenium with only infrequent tune-ups. Grace, the diplomatic nanny, and I were trying not to alarm the woman before us in Calvin Klein splendor, but we needed her cooperation.

"Ma'am, we're doing everything we can to find your grandson, from the State Department on down," I said. "If, and I stress if, he's been taken, we don't want to panic them. And if the prince went off on his own, we don't want to rattle him either."

This was beyond her comprehension. "Why would he do that? No. My grandson, Gregory, would never do that."

"Had he ever walked away from his protection before?" I said.

"Not that I am aware, but the boy liked to keep to himself, especially after all he's been through."

"Can you think of any reason, no matter how extreme or insignificant it might seem to you, as to why Gregory might want to run away?" I was a persistent cuss.

The eyes of our host closed like the curtain at the Metropolitan Opera then opened just as gradually, and took a sidelong glance at Grace.

"No, Mr. Malone, I...can't." Did she really think I was that stupid?

I handed my cell phone to Grace. "Why don't you go into the kitchen and check in with the consulate?" She left. "Now Mrs. Hughes, do you want to answer that question again?"

While she again pondered the answer, and whether it would help or hurt for me to know, I took in my surroundings. The house was in the upper middle class section of the city and she had lived here all of her life. Her daughter had met Benjamin Walanna at college and the rest was history. She was a widow through lung cancer but the estate had kept her comfortable. I had lost a child, though not an adult child. I knew the pain would never go away.

The furnishings weren't the kind with which you used paper coasters, nor were there little monthly payment books hanging around anywhere, unlike my place, of course. Emily Hughes had worked her fingers into what looked like a sailor's half hitch. She was waiting for guidance from above.

"Gregory doesn't want to be king. He doesn't like the protection, doesn't like the expectations. He wants to be a little boy. My daughter would never have allowed this. For Godsakes Mr. Malone, he's not like Diana's boys, William or Harry."

"When did your daughter die?" She wanted to talk about it. I just opened the door.

"Two years ago, she contracted some kind of jungle malaria. By the time she got the proper medical attention, it was of no use."

Enough of the trip down maudlin lane. "Do you know how Gregory hurt his arm?"

"I only know what he told me," she said.

"Which was?" I asked.

"He said his father was angry that he turned down a chance to speak at some convention of businessmen looking to do business in Laracone. He said his father started to shake him, but he broke free. Unfortunately, he tumbled down a short stairway spraining his wrist severely."

"Where were the guards during this?" I said. My thought was it was see no evil, hear no evil protection.

"When the family is in the residence, the guards are to allow them their privacy, just like the Secret Service at the White House."

"If you know this," I said, "why didn't you tell the police?"

"I had no proof. And I didn't think the boy would tell the police. Why should I put him in a position to lie? Besides, Benjamin could claim diplomatic immunity."

Grace returned. "The FBI has been called in, as a precaution."

"Mrs. Hughes, I've been told that Gregory stayed here on occasion. May we see his room?"

"I guess so," she said. She rose and glared at Grace believing that she was the one that was spilling family secrets. The difference between this room and the one at the consulate was negligible. This one was less cluttered, more utilitarian, and the next word that popped into my head was, sterile. Still, not my idea of a kid's room. The only anomaly was a stack of computer diskettes several inches tall next to a terminal. No laptop was in sight. A quick looksee through the titles told me that most were notes from classes on papers that he'd written. Two caught my attention. One was marked, "Miscellaneous" and the other was titled, "Laracone—The Future." I pocketed them and returned to the living room to collect Grace.

"Mrs. Hughes, here's my card with my cell phone number. Could you please compile a list of Gregory's friends, class-mates? Anybody he might be in semi-regular contact with, who might know where he is, would be extremely helpful. You can reach me at that number or leave a message at the consulate when it's done."

"I'll do everything I can. But please find my grandson. I don't want to lose him too."

I'd been in the business long enough to know I shouldn't make such promises. That didn't mean, I didn't make them anyhow.

When we returned to the consulate, they were gathering their forces. Thankfully, the only fortunate thing was that the news media hadn't caught on yet. Trevor Bradley called this war council to order.

"I think everyone knows everybody here. The two new faces belong to Ross Malone, a private investigator and Special Agent of the FBI, Felicity Charles. Malone, you want to tell us of the fruits of your labors?"

The floor was mine. I told them what I knew, explained about the McDonald's videotape, the scrapings from the car accident and, what the Grandmother told me sans her suspicions of how the prince's royal limb ended up in a sling. Grace stiffened slightly as I omitted the side trip into personal family business. She kept silent. Her body language told me that she knew more about that incident than she had told me. Was she keeping secrets? And if so, why?

Then, it was a round robin around the room with everyone spelling out their contingency plans. Consulate security had been beefed up, both uniformed and plainclothes. Phone surveillance was put in just in case the prince, or those who had him, wanted to contact his father. Walanna had refused to be evacuated, or to even wear body armor within the consulate. I heard the dulcet tones of sentry dogs during the sporadic lulls in the conversation. No helicopters or searchlights yet, something to be thankful for, at least. They would be in the offing if things went sour quickly.

"Okay people, let's have some suggestions. What do we do next?" asked Trevor, clearly feeling the heat from his bosses. The collar of his shirt was dark with perspiration.

Suggestions were few and far between. Some of the highlights centered around hauling in all of the protestors and shoving bamboo shoots beneath their fingernails, calling the people at Unsolved Mysteries and staking out the McDonald's where the prince was taken. I almost volunteered for that one. Finally, Trevor Bradley looked at me.

"What about you, Malone? Suggestions?"

"I think he's been taken. It's a gut feeling. But I do think it's time to spread the word. Let's act, and not react. It's dark out. We're coming upon twelve hours since anyone has seen the prince. I say President Walanna holds a press conference and splatters this all over the evening news, wire services, and the Internet. Go the road block route."

The Syracuse Police liaison said, "Been there, done that. So far we've drawn a blank."

I continued. "Maybe even a reward. How much will the State Department cough up?"

Before a quickly flustered Trevor Bradley could stammer that he'd have to check with Washington, Benjamin Walanna thumped a personal check down onto the top of the conference table for $250,000.

"I will put up the reward for the return of my heir, for the future of my country. Trevor, schedule the press conference for within the hour."

"But Mr. President..." He stammered. "We don't negotiate with terrorists."

"Mr. Bradley, I do not like to repeat myself. Malone, if you would come with me please."

Benjamin Walanna shifted his entire well over six-foot stature into presidential form, much like the bad guy in *TERMINATOR 2*. I hustled to keep up. Our destination turned out to be his upstairs living quarters directly over the living room and complete with a sitting room.

"We are alone now. You are free to say what you could not say in front of the others, Malone," he said. It sounded like a command.

"There really isn't anything else, sir."

"You may call me Benjamin," he said. He clearly thought I was holding back.

"I do have questions, but they may be awkward. However, they are important, Mr. President," I said.

"I am a politician, Malone. Awkward questions roll off me like water off of a duck's back."

"For your son's sake, I hope not, Mr. President."

"Benjamin, please."

I nodded and plowed ahead. "I need to know more about your son. What are his hobbies? Who is his best friend?"

Walanna considered my query, and sat on the edge of the sofa I'm sure Susan had shown me in *FAMILY CIRCLE* magazine. "You will need the truth to find my son. And the truth is, I don't know these answers.

"Eversince Gregory was accepted at your University here in the gifted children's program, my thoughts were more on his potential as a leader than on his present as a child. I sent him here with

Jacob, Andrew and Grace. His maternal grandmother was already here. Everything was provided for his comfort and growth."

"Everything except a father," I said. Having been denied the full shot at fatherhood, I did not suffer gladly those who shirked their duties, not realizing they were privileges.

"Malone, I am a head of state. It is not a nine to five job," said Walanna, stiffening his resolve and denying inside his culpability even further.

"Neither is being a parent. I am not here to throw stones. Could Gregory have run away because of your relationship with him?"

The answer was swift, no wiggle room at all. "Certainly not. And I resent that inference."

"Well, if you resented that, you sure as hell aren't going to like this. Did your struggle with Gregory cause him to fall downstairs and sprain his arm?"

He was quiet. Bull's Eye.

"We were arguing, over nothing. I don't even remember what," he said. "It was yet another battle of wills. Then he tried to run out of the room but I grabbed his arm so he'd hear what I had to say. Gregory was stronger than I remembered. He broke free of my grip and tumbled down the stairs onto the second floor landing. I had the guards take him to the hospital so the media wouldn't find out what really happened."

"But they did anyhow."

"Yes, but it was an accident, Malone. You must believe me." Presidents of countries shouldn't grovel. Right now, Benjamin Walanna was more father than leader.

"It doesn't matter if I believe you. It matters if your son does."

"Tell me what I can do." Yet another seeking miracles I didn't have.

"We're all doing everything we can. Do you have enemies who hate you enough to kidnap Gregory?"

"Idealistically, I would hope not, but we live in the real world. My main opposition comes from a group calling itself, 'Royalists of Laracone.' They were involved in the brawl outside the consulate. And the airport."

"Death threats?"

"Name a world leader worth his reputation who doesn't get them." There was almost a smirk.

"Touché. Have there been any threats against the prince?"

"What kind of enemies could a thirteen year old boy have?"

"A boy to me, a son to you, perhaps a symbol of the throne of Laracone to others. Tell me about these 'Royalists'."

Both hands rubbed over his face roughly. "Simply put, they wish to return to the monarchy of old Laracone. Democracy is their enemy."

"Let me get this straight. They want you in power. And they have you in power. What's the problem?"

"My duly elected term as the President of Laracone ends next year. Our constitution decrees only one six-year term for a president. They want me to continue. It goes beyond that, much beyond. A monarchy doesn't have bureaucratic red tape or parliaments who answer to the people rather than the narrow interests of the privileged few."

"Are they looking to take over the government?"

"So far no, but perhaps their patience has worn thin," he said. There was a firm knock on the door, then Trevor Bradley entered.

"I'm sorry to interrupt Mr. President, but the press conference is set for twenty minutes. It'll be in the conference room and MSNBC, CNN, and CBS among others will carry it live."

"Excellent. Thank you."

The State Department officer lingered in the doorway waiting to be invited to join in the guy talk. Walanna took the hint.

"Come in Trevor. Malone and I were going to go over what I should say at the press conference."

Shrill feedback from the bank of microphones was loud enough to crack contact lenses on an ant, and much too frequent. The press conference stopped, and started three times as technicians worked their magic. And it was magic to someone like me whose VCR flashed, "12:00" more often than not.

Trevor Bradley stepped up and introduced Benjamin Walanna. The forces of good were arrayed behind him like the Justice League of America in the person of the chief of police, the FBI, the Secret Service, the Sheriff and little old me. We were all lined up like little toy soldiers all ready to go to war for the cause. All we lacked was Buzz Lightyear.

"Thank you all for coming. Here are the facts, as we know them. My son, Prince Gregory, heir to the throne of Laracone has been missing since noon today. There are legitimate concerns that the prince may have been taken against his will.

"I have personally put up a reward of $250,000 for information leading to the safe return of my son. A hotline directly to police headquarters has been set up. Make no mistake. The money is for the **safe** return of Prince Gregory."

Monitors set up to the side displayed the photo of Gregory I'd shown around with the hotline number superimposed over it.

"Gregory, please hear me, my son. I will do everything in my power to get you back safely. Be strong, my son. You are of royal blood. Your destiny is greatness. I would ask that your captors return you unharmed, whether their quest is greed, or the lust for political power.

"And if your cause is personal," said the anguished father, "then have the guts to face me and not hide behind a 13 year old child." His strong hands crumpled the index cards Trevor Bradley had sketched out for him, in a single gesture. "Do not visit whatever you consider my sins to be, upon my son. Please."

A ripple moved through the crowd of reporters et al. Suddenly, the group parted and stepping to the microphones was none other than Gardner Meadows. He wasn't shy. Flanking him were two Warriors of the Night bodyguards.

"My name is Gardner Meadows. I am Executive Director of The City Security Association, and I am here to publicly condemn the abduction of Gregory Walanna by person or persons unknown. Accordingly, I am adding another $100,000 to the reward money for the safe return of Prince Gregory as well as for information leading to the arrest and conviction of those responsible."

The mention of another hundred grand sucked the collective air out of the room. Meadows rose to the occasion.

"Furthermore, I am publicly offering the assistance of my civilian enforcement group, The Warriors of the Night, to join the search for the prince. Now I will entertain questions."

During the onslaught of questions, my pager quaked its presence on my right hip. I slipped away. The number got me Emily Hughes. The list was ready. I got out my trusty Paper Mate pen and started writing. It was a short list. Then I found Grace.

"Want to take a moonlight ride with me?"

-17-

Dressed in a wrinkled Mets' baseball T-shirt with orange satin shorts, equally wrinkled, Naomi Sinclair's mother was not real happy that her 18-year-old daughter was receiving visitors after midnight, though she did let us in.

"I trust you know what time it is?" she said with a yawn. She led us to the living room where we met her daughter.

An explosion of red hair surrounded the highly freckled cheeks, which were round, but not yet chipmunk like. Her eyes were at half-mast. She was perched upon the edge of her chair, obviously taking a shine to being the focus of attention. I hoped she could help because, at the moment, the leads were dwindling. The list Gregory's grandmother had given us contained only two names. Naomi Sinclair was the first.

"Do you understand who we are, Naomi?" I liked to start slow and build to a crescendo.

"I think so," she said, and pointed to Grace. "She is the one who follows Gregory around. I think he said that you were his bodyguard. She turned her eyes, still semi-clouded with no clearing in sight, towards me. "I don't know you though. You her husband?"

"No. I'm a private investigator. When was the last time you saw Gregory Walanna?"

"Last week at school. We share Economics class," she said. Slurred words seemed to be her specialty.

"Do you consider him a friend?" I said.

"I guess."

"Any idea where he would go if he wanted not to be found?"

"Is he missing?" Naomi asked.

Grace clasped, then unclasped and then rejoined her hands; soon her knuckles went white. Then she joined the conversation, straining to keep her annoyance under wraps.

"Miss, I appreciate that members of your generation have attention spans geared towards MTV videos and Jeopardy questions, but could you please stretch a little here? Prince Gregory has been missing for most of the day. We...need...your...help." She was severely tested, trying not to scream at the college freshman. Naomi wasn't rattled, neither was she very interested.

"I don't know where he goes. He is 13 years old, you know. It's not like we're glued at the hip or anything like that. He is real sweet, very thoughtful, but I have friends my own age. About the only time I saw him outside of class was occasionally at HACKERS."

"Can you remember anybody who is close to Gregory? Or any place, any place at all he might be?"

Naomi thought for a moment. "I don't know where he might go, but the only name that comes to mind is Roger Willoughby. When we were at HACKERS, he was always helping Gregory surf the web. And Gregory would get him into secret websites, I think, with his father's secret code word. I guess he wanted to impress Roger. Gregory's father is the President of Laracone, you know."

"Yes, I do. I think it is where Carmen San Diego is."

Her eyes went saucer-size at that prospect. "Really?"

"Really." I gave her my business card and told her to call if she remembered anything useful. I added the caveat, that it meant anything useful about the case. "One more thing, you know anybody who owns a VW bus?" She smiled, almost laughed.

"Not unless they live in Jurassic Park."

Conan O'Brien was welcoming his first guest when we knocked on the dormitory room door of Roger Willoughby. A barefoot female in a beige camisole, matching tap pants and daffodil tattoo on her right shoulder opened the door. She was closer to Gregory's age than Roger's, much closer. I flashed my ID and stepped into the room.

"May we come in?" Not waiting for a reply, I grabbed Grace's hand and jerked it towards me, bringing her into the apartment as well. "We're looking for Roger Willoughby. Is he here?"

The female turned towards the bathroom. "Roger?"

"Yeah? Did you get rid of who was at the door?" Roger Willoughby entered the living room from the bathroom, fully naked from head to toe. Not a mole, pimple or dimple in view. He was my height, though I had a good 20 years on him, shoulder length curly hair that might have been permmed and not an ounce of fat on his slender frame that I could see at a quick glance. Grace, however, was taking a more thorough inventory, and enjoying every minute of it. When he saw there was company, he stopped dead in his tracks, but didn't bother to cover himself. I smiled.

"I guess the answer to your question is a big N-O. She didn't get rid of who was at the door. You Roger Willoughby?"

"Maybe. Who are you?" he said.

I flashed my ID with photo license again. "I'm Malone and this is Miss..." I'd forgotten to ask Grace what her last name was. She jumped in, no longer transfixed by Anatomy and Physiology 101.

"I'm Grace Rusinko. I think I've seen you before on campus. I'm one of Gregory Walanna's bodyguards."

"Oh yeah, the Ice Maiden," he smiled, then realized what he had said, and suddenly got very self-conscious. He dressed slowly, but methodically. His playmate went over to help. "That's okay Roxanne, I can do it. You go wait in the bedroom."

I stepped between them. "Actually, our business might take a little time. Grace, would you please help Roxanne get dressed, then see that she gets a cab home to her parents?" I peeled off two twenty-dollar bills. I was upset that the anti-counterfeiting measures instituted by the Treasury Department now extended to the $20 note. The new denominations may have been more difficult to replicate but now they resembled Monopoly money.

Grace merely nodded, then herded Roxanne into the bedroom and closed the door after them.

"What the hell did you do that for? We weren't done," protested Roger, my reluctant host.

"Yes, you were, Besides, you don't want Roxy breaking her curfew. And, we need privacy."

"I need my lawyer." My hand covered the receiver before he could pick it up.

"If I check your date's birth certificate, you probably will need a lawyer, and a psychiatrist before they are supplied by the court. I have questions. I need your answers. I need them now."

When the girls returned, Roxanne was fully dressed and if possible, looked younger than when I had first met her. Ankle socks will do that for a girl of any age. She kissed Roger good-bye.

"I'll call you, baby," she said.

Roger snuck a sideward glance at me. "No, better let me call you, Roxanne."

Roxanne wasn't happy, but offered no more protest than sticking her lower lip out to pout. Grace led her to the door. To my surprise, Roxy didn't kick or scream. The door closed after them.

"Tell me about Gregory Walanna," I said, wasting no more time.

"He's missing." Roger was pleased with his answer, and the smile he added revealed two dimples.

I crawled up into those dimples. "I know smart guy. We're trying to find him. Any idea where he is? Where he might go? Who he might be with?"

He craned his neck back and removed his head from my space. "I haven't seen him since yesterday at HACKERS. It's a computer meeting place. I saw him there a lot."

"How did he seem? Happy? Sad?" For now, I moved back to give Roger some breathing room. If he started jerking me around again, I'd make breathing a problem for him.

"He was a hurting turkey with his arm in a sling," said Roger Willoughby, cradle robber.

"Did he tell you how he hurt it?"

"No, so I helped him do the keyboard, but a lot of what he wanted to do only required the mouse. He used his other hand."

"Did he ever say anything about running away?" I said.

"Not to me. He really enjoyed being a VIP, having the bodyguards and all. He got me into some sensitive government mainframes in Laracone by using his father's code words and clearance. I mean, it was something, to see him hack into the military software like it was his personal playground."

"Anything else you can tell me about Gregory?"

"Nope," he said, relishing another four-letter word.

"Do you think he'll contact you?"

"Don't know."

I left my card on the table. "If he does call you, you call me. One more thing, your late night tutoring of Roxanne, or anybody remotely within acne distance of her age group is over, finished. Try to corrupt someone your own age. And if I find that you're back to tutoring between the sheets again, I will not be pleased and trust me Roger, that would not be a pretty sight."

I left the dorm room door open upon my departure.

Roger jumped into the doorway and yelled after me. "That's rich. You're dogging me for chasing kids when all this time Gregory was a little horn dog himself."

This stopped me in my tracks. I executed a pivot with military precision then marched back to Roger who probably thought I was going to smack him. It did cross my mind.

"Explain."

"Gregory wasn't the sheltered little pocket protector genius everybody thought he was," said Roger. He made it sound cheap and dirty.

"And?"

"And...he had the hots for his English professor, Katharine Greco."

"Hots? How?" I said, wanting him to spell it out for me.

"You aren't really that old, are you? Go ask her. Ruin somebody else's night."

He then slammed the door in my face. I felt honored.

It was time to reconnoiter, and I always did that better with two glazed doughnuts and chocolate milk. Grace passed on the food, settling instead for a large mocha vanilla special. We ate in the Cherokee. A gentle rain pockmarked the windshield with droplets that acted as prisms when the glare of the streetlights danced within them.

"You know, they were celebrating her birthday," said Grace.

"Pardon me?"

"Roxanne and Roger. They were celebrating her fifteenth birthday, Ross. The Pervert." She sipped her coffee to stifle a stronger assessment of Mr. Willoughby.

"May I ask a personal question?" I said.

"I suppose," she said.

"Could you tell me your impressions of the relationship between Gregory and his father?"

"Oh, that kind of personal." She seemed disappointed. "I've only been with them since the middle of last summer, barely a year. The father has definite expectations about the son following in his political footsteps. Last Christmas, he gave Gregory a book."

"Not unusual." Doughnut two was just as tasty as doughnut one. I liked quality control.

"It was some sort of first edition of Machiavelli's 'The Prince'. Did you read it?"

"The ends justifies the means," I said from memory.

"My oh my. You aren't just another pretty face."

"Actually, I am just another pretty face with an extensive collection of *CLIFF NOTES*."

Grace smiled. "They aren't close like a Dad and son going out to toss the football around. It could be the pressures of public life. Or it could be that after losing his wife, he doesn't want to get too attached to the boy who is a constant reminder of that wife. I'd say the resemblance was remarkable."

My last doughnut disappeared completely. I decided not to return to the store for reinforcements.

"Do you know how Gregory's arm got hurt?"

Grace Rusinko was quiet for a long time. "Off the record?" I nodded. She then reiterated the same story that the grandmother and father did. "Malone, I hope you aren't thinking Benjamin Walanna had anything to do with the disappearance of his son."

"Not unless I have proof. It doesn't mean the boy didn't take the opportunity to escape what he perceived as abuse." Grace was quiet again. I wondered what she wasn't telling me. I moved along. "Do you know one of Gregory's professors, a Katharine Greco?"

"Yes. She had him last semester for English, freshman composition. He aced it, though she did need to tutor him extensively at one point."

"His interest in class limited to the course curriculum?" I said.

"Meaning?"

"Did he have a crush on Miss Greco?"

"No. I would have known. And it is Mrs. Greco. Where did you get a silly idea like that?"

"CLIFF NOTES. I'm going to go talk with her," I said, while I ignited the engine.

"This late?"

I ignored her protest. "I'll drop you off at the consulate, if it'll make you uncomfortable."

"Get real Malone. Too much Raisin Bran makes me uncomfortable. Step on it."

I did.

After a minimum of detecting and a handy phone book, I located Katharine Greco's home phone number. Even at this late hour and short notice, she agreed to see us when I explained that we were looking for Gregory.

Her tract home with attached two-car garage resided in Marcellus, a suburb about 12 miles west of Syracuse. The porch light was on when we arrived. She answered the door in a Davenport University sweatshirt and sweatpants. I could feel my mouth hanging open. She was a dead ringer for Donna Reed. The

TV theme played in my head. I looked for Shelley Fabares and Paul Petersen.

The inside of her home was immaculate; Katharine Greco led us into the living room. She even sat like a TV goddess.

"Now, please tell me what I can do to help find Gregory," she said, with impeccable diction.

"First of all, thank you for seeing us in the middle of the night. I hope your husband wasn't too upset."

"He wasn't, Mr. Malone. As I told you over the phone, he's currently out of town on a business trip." She had told me that over the phone, but I liked to check in person to see if the subject sweats.

"Yes, you did. We understand that you were very close to Gregory."

"He's a special young man." I knew parent-teacher demeanor when I saw it.

"How involved did you get?" I asked.

"Excuse me? I'm not sure exactly what you mean by that?"

"Since we're all adults here, I'm asking if Gregory Walanna had an adolescent crush on you. If he did, I certainly could understand why."

Katharine Greco started chewing on her lower lip. Her breathing picked up. No tears. No blush of crimson to her freshly powdered cheeks. I noted that from the time I had called until we arrived, she had unquestionably put on a fresh layer of cosmetics. There was no way she was cover girl perfect at this time of the morning, not without some premeditation.

"Mrs. Greco? Katharine? How serious was this crush?"

She stood abruptly. "Excuse me, I will be back in a moment."

I stood as she left. It turned out to be a very long moment. She returned to the living room just before I was ready to go and find her. A medium sized cardboard box that was previously used to house jars of baby food was cradled in her hands.

"Can I trust your discretion?" she said. She seemed resigned to share what was in the box regardless of our answer.

"Of course," I said. Grace nodded her agreement. Katharine placed the box in front of me, then started removing its contents.

"This is the sum total of my 'relationship' outside the classroom with Gregory Walanna. My husband doesn't know about any of this. Needless to say, I would prefer that he not ever know. And, I certainly have no wish to embarrass Gregory. I believe that he believes his feelings are heartfelt and true. His mother is gone, and I'm sure he's using his 'feelings' for me to fill the tremendous void she left in his life."

"How intimate were you with the prince?" said my partner. I looked at Grace who was glaring at Katharine Greco. The glare said take no prisoners.

"Are you asking if we were physically intimate? The answer is no in the most emphatic sense I can make it. Grace, it was a schoolboy crush. Nothing more. If Gregory weren't missing, I'd take the time to be offended by the insinuation."

I tuned out the catfight that was brewing right before me. My money was on Grace, though. Instead, I concentrated on the stated 'sum total' before me.

There were a lot of stuffed animals, a couple of dozen Hallmark cards, some of them of the Shoebox variety, dried rose petals perhaps for an imagined anniversary or as far back as Valentine's Day, and the last material thing was a miniature jewelry box. It looked to me like a ring box, felt like a ring box and had the new felt smell of a ring box. It even bore the same raised logo of the jewelry store where I purchased gifts for Susan. I hesitated opening it. It seemed a violation of the boy's privacy, but so was holding him hostage. I opened it.

The box was empty.

"Excuse me, Mrs. Greco, what was in the box?"

She hesitated.

"There was what Gregory called, a 'friendship ring' in that box. I told him it was inappropriate and returned it to him."

"Without the box?" I was a stickler for detail, sometimes.

"It was an emotional scene as you can imagine, I'm sure, Mr. Malone. He left without taking it."

Her hands were bare; save for the telltale signs of the tan lines around where her wedding rings would be. Then I took note of a faint mark on the middle finger of her other hand. It looked too wide for an engagement ring and it was the wrong finger for another matrimonial accessory. I filed it for future reference.

All that remained in the box was a stack of rubber banded, hand written letters.

"Do you have any idea where the boy might be? Any idea at all, where we might look for him?"

She shook her head. The hair remained intact. The Jane Jetson look. "I wish I did."

"So do we. Do you think he'll contact you?"

"He might. If he does, I'll certainly call you."

I parted with my last remaining business card on my person. "Thanks. We'll have to take the letters with us. They will be returned. The rest you can keep."

Her eyes darted between Grace and I. "And you won't tell my husband?"

"I don't see any need to. Do you, Grace?"

"Not at the moment," she said. My temporary partner liked the fact that Katharine Greco was twisting in the wind. "Shall we go, Malone?"

"Sure, but may I use the bathroom first, Mrs. Greco?"

The consummate host gestured. "Of course, down that corridor to the left, two doors. The blue towels are the guest ones."

"Thank you. I'll be right back."

We left a few minutes later. In the Cherokee, I told Grace what I had found on my brief sojourn to the bathroom.

"She said her husband's on a business trip? Then he's going for a very long time. There were no men's toiletries in the bathroom cabinet or closet. None, nada, zip. Not even a hint of aftershave, deodorant or anything remotely smelling like a man."

"There could be a second bathroom."

"Not off the master bedroom like this one was, not in a house like this, it's too small." I let her stew on that for a bit, then added another thought. "On my way back, I happened to go through the master bedroom and the second dresser is barren. It isn't just dusted or super cleaned, it was emptied out, Grace. Hubby is not a current resident at this address. At least, not in that bedroom."

"Why did she lie? Maybe he saw the ring?"

"Could be," I said. "Do you wonder why she kept all of the cards, letters, stuffed animals etc.? I mean, if she really thought it was inappropriate, then why not nip it in the bud?"

"What's a few love notes and trinkets if you're going to keep a ring that must have had a four figure price tag?" she said.

"Good point." I let the silence linger. I was good at that. "Grace, did you miss this, or didn't you feel it was important enough to mention?"

"I'll assume that is an innocent question, and not at all impugning my professional judgment. I knew the prince was developing feelings for someone. I just assumed that when he said older woman, he meant an 18-year-old classmate, not a 30-year-old English professor. I'll talk with Andrew and Jacob to see if there's anything else that I missed.

"Thanks. I don't want to invade Mrs. Greco's privacy but we might consider tapping her phone at some point just in case the prince contacts his true love."

My pager sounded. I dialed the number on my cell phone.

"Ross Malone here."

"Ross? This is Gwen. I'm at the hospital. Could you please come right over?"

"Hang on Gwen, I'll be right there."

The hospital corridors were dim. The only exceptions to the dark were the baseboard night lights, spaced every three rooms. At the far end of the hallway was Nellie's room. The problem was in plain view. Gwen came over to me, distraught and teetering on the outer edge of sanity.

"They got here a few hours ago. They won't leave. Who are they, Ross? What are they doing here?" said Gwen.

"They are called, Warriors of the Night, self appointed centurions of the righteous. I'll talk to them. Gwen, this is my friend, Grace Rusinko. Why don't you go with her and get some coffee? I'll catch up to you in a few minutes."

"Come with me, Gwen. I could use a cup of tea actually."

The two women walked off with Grace casting back one last glance. I nodded that I would be all right. Once they were out of sight, I approached the guards, on either side of Nellie's door.

"Morning gents. You can go now. I'm here to protect her."

They exchanged bemused looks between them. Smirks followed. The one on the left with a mole next to his nose spoke, beginning with a condescending snort. "You protect her? Isn't that how she got here?"

Some people just had the knack for saying the wrong thing at the wrong time. This guy had it. I stepped up into his face.

"I know you've been practicing that steely-eyed stare in the mirror when your mom was banging on the bathroom door and you were saying, 'Just till I need glasses, Mom,' but I don't frighten so easily. Now take a walk, while you still can walk."

"We have our orders."

"Yes, and I just gave them to you," I said.

Guard dog two shuffled his feet. My internal radar sounded the klaxon. His hand disappeared into his windbreaker. As it came back, I saw the butt handle of what might have been a gun or a blackjack. My brain went to Def Con Four.

I grabbed the wrist before he could clear the jacket and back-handed him hard across the face. His knees buckled as he headed for the floor. I held his wrist revealing a tazer earmarked, no doubt, for the middle of my back. A quick turn of his arm and it bounced off the gray linoleum floor.

Guard dog one however, got his gun out. My old Navy Special Forces training kicked in, literally, and my foot slammed his hand knocking the gun to the floor next to the tazer. Now my gun was out, and quickly thrust deep into the ribs of this Warrior of the Night, who was damn sure not going to make his bones on me.

"Unless you both want to see the Emergency Room up close and personal...or the morgue, makes no difference to me, get your asses out of here."

"Is there a problem here?" Gardner Meadows was getting to be a human hemorrhoid.

I stepped back carefully and shoved guard one into Gardner and his entourage of muscle shirts and shoulder holsters. Then I kicked guard dog two flush in the butt as he scurried away to the protection of the safety in numbers. My gun was lowered, but not holstered.

"Did you order the bookend delinquents?" I asked, knowing full well the answer.

"Yes. I had read up on Ms. Archer's plight after our talk and wanted to make sure that those who hurt her did not get a second chance."

"If you're looking for a character reference for sainthood, this won't help. Now you listen to me, Meadows, stay away from Nellie Archer."

"I believe this is a free country," he said.

"True, which lets me be free to spread that Aryan nose of yours all across your facial landscape."

"Do you always have to resort to violence?"

"Every chance I get," I said.

"Neanderthal."

"Species who live in glass houses, shouldn't throw Molotov cocktails. Get out of here and take your storm troopers with you."

I set my jaw and balled up a fist with my free hand. My gun felt comfortable in my left hand. I was ready to go to war, almost champing at the bit for some action.

The standoff grew more tense. It would be bad, if they wanted to start something. I was in the mood to do some major damage, regardless of how many more of them there were than me. Obviously, Gardner Meadows sensed this.

"You win, for now." Without another word, he turned and left. The posse followed. Only guard dog two had the bad taste to look back and sneer at me. I would remember him.

I looked in on Nellie. She hadn't changed position, except when the nurses bodily moved her. The ventilator was still wheezing each of her breaths.

My Dad was still awake when I walked by his room. Colleen was present giving his regular nurse a break on her 12 hour shift.

"How are you doing?" I asked.

He seemed genuinely touched by my presence. His smile was stronger and lit up my world. His color was much better as well.

"I'm better. They say I can go home later today, maybe." He winced. "Just a little pain. I know she forgot my pain pill."

"Why didn't you ask for it, Pop?"

"I don't want to be a bother. Would you ask her for me?" he said.

"No. Dad, you are old enough, smart enough, and gosh darn-it all, you are paying for the privilege to be a bother, even though asking for pain medication doesn't qualify for that. I have to go, but I'll send Colleen back in and you ask her. I love you, Dad."

I kissed his forehead and left, asking Colleen to step in because Pop had something to ask her. Then, I ran smack dab into Grace and Gwen. My partner seemed agitated.

"We have to go, Malone. The consulate has received a ransom note."

Never a dull moment.

-18-

The ransom communication, while in traditional form, cut out and pasted words from the print media, was faxed to the consulate through a pirate piggyback line at a local MAILBOXES ETC. It was being given the fine tooth comb treatment when Grace and I arrived.

"Tell me the truth, Malone. Would you really have taken on all of them back at the hospital?"

I stood still as if contemplating my answer. "I might have, but it wouldn't have been one of my smartest moves. Actually, it would have been pretty stupid."

Thick leather heels transporting Trevor Bradley past us summoned our presence. We followed. Felicity Charles handed me a photocopy of the note. I read it, then passed it along to Grace. It read:

"Benjamin Walanna, we have your son. He will not be harmed, if you comply with our demands. First, we want the following political prisoners released from your dungeons and given safe passage to a non-extradition country." The list, which was alphabetical, numbered forty names. "Next, you will immediately dissolve the current constitutional government of Laracone, returning its people to the royal monarchy they desire again. You will assume the throne and

Laracone will prosper under you. Be warned. If you do not comply, your son, Gregory will suffer the consequences. After all, if there is no monarchy, there need be no heir."

It was signed, "The Royalists of Laracone."

Felicity Charles weighed in with the analytical consensus. "We're trying to backtrack the transmission from the MAIL-BOXES ETC. fax line. So far no dice. Next thing is to start rounding up these 'royalist' characters, and sweat them," she said. "I'll start the ball rolling on that with surveillance at least." Before anyone else could offer his or her two cents, Agent Charles was off to follow the only trail she had stumbled across so far.

Grace Rusinko moved over in front of me. "Shall we join the surveillance teams?"

"Maybe, but this isn't the typical ransom note."

"Seems pretty straightforward to me. Unrealistic demands that can't possibly be met, thereby forcing the kidnapers to kill the prince to prove their point. What isn't typical?"

"First, why go to all of the trouble to cut and paste these words when you can use a computer to generate something equally untraceable. Second, look at the punctuation." She did, and shrugged her confusion. "That's the point. The punctuation is excellent. How many ransom notes have you seen this meticulous?"

"You think the boy was taken by William Shakespeare?" said Grace, still not grasping what I was pointing out.

"No, but someone who knows who the Bard is. And there's no mention of money at all. No mention of not bringing the cops in or, there would be dire consequences. I can't put my finger on it Grace, but there is something here that I should be seeing."

"Care to let the rest of us in on it, Malone?" said Trevor Bradley, rejoining us along with Felicity Charles.

"Soon as I figure out what it is. What's the plan, Trevor?" I said.

"We've given copies of the note to our best FBI profilers. They seem to believe it is genuine, regardless of your misgivings. They think that the people who wrote this are wedded to strictly a political agenda and won't hurt the boy," said Trevor, as Felicity nodded faster with each succeeding sentence.

"And they base this on what?" I asked. "It says right here that they will kill the prince, if they don't get their way."

Felicity Charles took exception to my swipe at her profilers. "They base it on years of field experience. You have proof to the contrary?"

"Not yet." I said, trying to smile and failing miserably at it. My edge came from sleep deprivation. I regretted it, but did nothing more about it.

"Let's all play nice now," said Trevor, verbally rapping the knuckles of those present. His stock in trade was peacemaker. "The decision on all of this rests with President Walanna.

Our policy is zero tolerance with terrorists."

"Can he release the prisoners?"

"He could easily. Each name on the list represents a headline, though not necessarily a political one. Some are common criminals and others are true believers. The trouble will come in finding countries willing to take them. The upside to this is once the prince is safe, we should have little trouble rounding them all up again."

"Is abdication an option?"

"Malone, that would make the boy, king. If it were your son, what would you do?"

"I'd say, tell me where to sign. What if he resigned, then after the prince was in good hands, he called for new elections?" It was naïve, and I knew it the minute I said it.

"What's to stop them from taking the boy again, or worse?" said Felicity.

I nodded. "If he knuckles under, the boy won't ever be safe," I managed to say during a lengthy yawn. It was just past six a.m. "I need some rest. I'm going home for a few hours. Call me if you learn anything else."

Trevor flashed some fingers before my face. I didn't bother to count them. "Four hours max, okay?"

"I'll set my biological clock. Later." Yet another yawn came and went. I told Grace where to reach me, then left.

In times of severe stress, it was my belief that people revert to comfortable patterns, safe sanctuaries, islands of their inner self devoid of everything but their own emotional DNA.

My island had stone monuments, pint sized American flags at Memorial Day, Veteran's Day and the Fourth of July, and no cover charge. What it also had were Molly and Christopher Malone. The cemetery caretaker was Gus. He and I were on a first name basis now. Business hours at this eternal home away from home were normally from eight to eight. It paid to bring doughnuts, if you had lost track of time. According to Gus, it paid to bring doughnuts no matter what time it was. This time he counted them.

"Aren't there supposed to be twelve doughnuts in a dozen?" he said.

"This is a metric dozen," I said, then walked in as he opened the wrought iron gate.

The gravesite was manicured enough to be the 18th green at Augusta. Molly would have laughed out loud if I'd told her, during a moment in the afterglow, that her afterlife would have been spent in a sand trap. I missed that laugh and longed for the occasional tousle of my hair as I was filling out police road patrol logs back when I rode with Deke.

Truth was, I missed her each and every day and consciously made the effort to think of one of the good times, there were so many to choose from. Each was a ray of sunshine unto itself and after the sunshine came the torrent of tears. I'd waded through those tears lately, more than I'd admitted even to myself.

Sometimes, I wondered if this ritualistic celebration of the past, inhabited solely with memories and so many missed opportunities, did a disservice to Susan. It had driven my second wife, Margaret away. Luckily, there had been no children to experience that depth of loss a second time, as the marriage circled the proverbial drain.

A year ago, I had discovered by accident that Molly and Christopher had been murdered. I knew how. I even knew who had made the bomb, and who gave the order to place it on the plane. I even thought I knew why.

What I didn't know, was what I was going to do about it. I knelt next to the granite headstone and started speed praying Hail Marys off the rosary. Finishing in record time, I sat on the grass and popped a Chiclet into my mouth.

"Hi guys," I began in a low voice, "You know Dad came through the operation okay. It'll be a little while before he gets up there. Uncle Tony and I are butting heads like The Rock and Bret Hart. I think we've got it worked out for the moment. Then, there's Nellie Archer. She trusted me. I let her down, and now she's in the hospital, letting mechanical lungs keep her alive.

"I can't let her down a second time. If you have any spare prayers, send them Express Mail, her way. While you're at it, can you send me a clue as to where Gregory Walanna is? Miracles 'R Us isn't returning my phone calls. I have to go for now. I'll talk to you later."

As with Susan, I never said good-bye to Molly and Christopher. Not now, not ever. The last part of the ritual was to say good-bye to Gus. I spotted the turned up soles of his Timberland work boots first. He was face down in the wooden caretaker's shack; an ugly welt arriving with all deliberate speed at the base of his skull. A large wrench with a bloodied end lay still next to him. Its work was apparently done. A touch of his carotid told me he was still alive. I dialed 911.

The metal on metal sound of a bullet being loaded into the firing chamber of a gun alerted me just in time. I dove left over the body, jerking my gun from its hip holster along the way and sprung up into a kneeling position ready to fire. Three shots in rapid succession flew past me, burrowing new homes into the shack wall.

With a coolness I'd learned in the military, and perfected on the police force, I sighted in the target and pumped two shots into the center of the shooter's chest. All of a few milliseconds had elapsed during that brief exchange. The pops of gunfire echoed in my ears.

I walked slowly over letting the muzzle of my Beretta lead the way to where the gunman laid face down on the grass. I kicked him over with my foot. I was then staring down into the face of the gunman from the office a few days ago, still trying to collect on the contract out on me. Nellie Archer had been right. He, who fights and runs away, lives to die another day. He chose this to be his day.

The police and homicide detectives allowed me to leave once they had recorded my life story in triplicate. A caring soul had produced a tape recorder for my statement. Then I was back on the road.

The number I had dialed only rang once before it was answered. "Dr. Abilene speaking."

"Hey cutie, got a few minutes for a lonely soul?"

"Sure," she said, "I'll even waive my usual $4.99 per minute fee. How's your Dad coming along?"

"Doing well, last I heard. He'll probably go home later today, or tomorrow. I think Tony and I are finally on the same page. In any case, I'm up to my neck in work. He'll do fine making the decisions that need to be made without me."

"Ross, what's wrong?"

"What makes you think anything is wrong?" I said.

"Oh I'm not sure, really…Maybe it's the 7 a.m. phone call out of the blue. Come on, Ross, we've been together long enough that I can read you like a Braille *PLAYBOY* magazine."

"I like the imagery."

"Ross, I won't beg you to tell me," said Susan.

"Susan, I killed a man a short time ago. Actually, he was more of a kid trying to play with the pros. He was way out of his league."

"Was it his life or yours?"

"Yes. He also had bludgeoned Gus, the cemetery caretaker. If I were toast, Gus would then have been the only witness alive."

"I remember what you once told me about witnessing a crime being hazardous to one's health."

"You betcha. I just called for a friendly voice. Events are moving so fast, I'm barely keeping my head above water," I said.

"Not like you, Sweetie. Need me to relocate back home?"

"No, I just needed you to know. It helps me to feel less alone sometimes."

"Nellie isn't any better, is she?" said Sue.

"No."

"Ross, the decision to withdraw life support can lay low even the strongest of souls. There is no hurry, Ross. When the time comes, you'll know in your heart what to do."

"I love you, Susan."

"Forever, and then some, Tootie," she laughed.

The four hours I'd been promised by Trevor Bradley had stretched into six, because I was exhausted. I tumbled off the couch and onto the floor, trying to escape a nightmare and woke myself up. *THIS WEEK IN BASEBALL* was on the television set. It just wasn't the same without Mel Allen. The clock read just after 12 noon. My breakfast of champions was limited to orange juice and two microwave cheeseburgers. After a long, hot shower, clean clothes and fresh bullets in my gun, I called the consulate. Trevor answered. It was quickly apparent that he needed sleep as well.

"Any word on the prince?" I asked.

"Not beyond the ransom note. Our agents went to talk to those fanatics of the group claiming responsibility for the prince's abduction. They all deny involvement and feel that they are being persecuted. We'll slap surveillance on them anyway."

"Mind if I go try to talk with them? I can get away with persecuting them a lot easier than you can."

"Be my guest."

"Any word on what President Walanna is going to do?"

"Officially," said Bradley, " he won't negotiate with terrorists. Unofficially, he'll hold out as long as he can, but we'd better find the boy quick. What are you going to do?"

"Go look for him after I talk with 'the Royalists'. You can reach me on my cell phone. Let me talk with Grace Rusinko." She came on the line. "I'm going somewhere that I might need an interpreter. Care to tag along?"

"Give me the address," she said.

The headquarters of the political throwback group, "The Royalists of Laracone" was located on a second floor walk up on a side street in one of the less opulent sections of my city. Grace was already waiting for me when I got there.

"We're going up there to rattle some cages. They already have talked with the police. We are going to be a little more firm in our questioning. If they have the boy, I doubt they'd be stupid enough to keep him here. My guess is that they didn't take him, but might know where he is being held, or which splinter group of radicals took him."

"What do you want from me?" said Grace.

"Watch my back, translate if they don't speak English."

"That it?" she said, somewhat disappointed.

I nodded. "Ready?" She nodded. We took one step towards the doorway when directly above us, a metal folding chair crashed through a window dragging the weather beaten wooden frame and all onto the sidewalk beside us. We looked at it, exchanged shrugs then ascended into the lion's den.

Loud voices were screaming back and forth. A lot of words were being shouted that I understood. When I was a kid, they all would have required gargling with a bar of soap. The wooden door's bottom panel was missing. The group's name was spray painted in wide cursive letters on the surviving upper half of the door, no doubt urban calligraphy. I didn't bother to knock.

"Who the fuck are you?" said one of the warring voices.

"Be thankful I'm not the language police, or you'd be doing a nickel at Attica. I'm looking for Prince Gregory."

"You and half the free world. Who is she?" said the mouth behind a full beard, stumpy legs, horn-rimmed glasses and a shirt with an alligator on it.

"She's none of your business. But, I am making you my business. Haven't I seen you somewhere before?" I already knew he was one of the airport marchers. Unfortunately, it didn't automatically make him a kidnaper. He backed away, then turned away from me.

"I have never seen you before," he said, mumbling near the now vacant windowsill.

"Know where the prince is, Mister?" I said.

"No." He ignored the second of my inquiries. "We do not take children as prisoners of war."

"Is this a war?"

"Yes," he said defiantly. "To those of us who care about the future of Laracone, it is a war. Are we happy the prince is missing? No. We welcome the world's spotlight on the need to return the monarchy to the people of Laracone."

"Did Aesop tell you that one?"

"Scoff if you will, but the winds of change are blowing in my native country,"

"Maybe, but the winds of incarceration will be blowing in your adopted country, if you are connected in any way, shape or form to the taking of Gregory Walanna."

"Why do you make us a scapegoat?" said the man packing up an old oil stained leather satchel with papers. "We have done nothing."

"If you didn't take the prince, have you any idea who might have reason to do it?"

He laughed as he headed for the door. I guess he thought we were done. "You are naïve for a police officer. Who might do the prince harm? You ask that knowing that you live in a land of Jeffrey Dahmer, Andrew Cunanan, and the Menendez brothers? Look elsewhere, do not waste my time."

The man with the satchel and the vocabulary of a stevedore left. All through my discussion with him, Grace was off to the side quietly talking with the woman he had been arguing with as we entered.

Grace brought the woman over to me. "Ross Malone? Meet Deirdre Schulery. She's the second in command."

"My title is chairperson," she said, tilting her chin a little higher as she did.

"How politically correct of you. Who was that?"

"That loudmouth was Ghiamin Lora. He runs the group."

"We're looking for the boy, Ms. Schulery. We aren't here to arrest, persecute, deport or induce migraine headaches. Can you help us?"

"The police have already been here. We don't have the boy. Lora was right about that. It isn't our style."

"What about any fringe elements to your group?" I said. "The Timothy McVeighs of Laracone."

She shook her head. "I am not aware of anyone who I would consider crazy enough to do something like that." She poured herself a cup of coffee from the Joe DiMaggio model coffee maker on a nearby counter. She didn't offer us any. "Is the reward genuine?"

"As far as we know, yes. $350,000 for the boy's safe return and a couple of scalps to hang on somebody's belt. Now, do you know where the boy is?" I finally said, irritated with the politi-speak.

"No, but we aren't the only place to look." Deirdre re-knotted her paisley scarf around her crème colored neck then handed me a copy of the typewritten, photocopied, then stapled together newsletter titled, "MANIFESTO." I looked at it, then handed it to Grace. "That is the manifesto of the monarchy. Each week we get it oozing with those thrilling days of yesteryear."

"Looks pretty cheap to me," I said.

"That's our cheap, dot matrix printer. It's e-mailed to us from their website. The name of the editor and chief rabble-rouser is beneath the title."

I looked. "Anna Law. Do you know her?"

"She's just one more lone, but literate voice to our cause."

"Any idea where I can find her?" I asked.

"The only address I have for her starts with 'www.laracone.com.'"

It was a place to start.

The thought of $350,000 for just dropping a quarter and a dime into a pay phone and muttering a few words was something

a lot of people found irresistible. No doubt, the operators man-
ning the police hotline about the kidnapping had cauliflower ears
by now. Still, each lead would have to be evaluated and checked
out. It had been my experience that rewards seldom garnered anything more fruitful than a few days' headlines.

I spent the afternoon reading the last six months of Anna Law's
rantings and ravings. It went back to last summer, but my stomach
could only take so much amateur babble. When I wanted to read
about politics, I usually read Jeff Greenfield. To be sure, Anna outlined a step by step plan to return Benjamin Walanna to the
throne, whether he wanted it or not. The reasons were obscure,
but mostly centered around tradition. It was almost as if Yul
Brynner were saying, "Etcetera, etcetera, etcetera."

"So what do you want from me, Malone?" said Lucas Gentero
at his trusty keyboard.

"Lucas, I want you to sit at this keyboard and ferret out anything you can about Ms. Anna Law."

With that, the reporter groaned and entered the World Wide
Web. "And what is in it for me?"

"An exclusive with Bonnie Prince Gregory, once he is rescued
and home safe. Besides, you owe me."

"Will you take a check?" he said. "Hey Malone, where are
you going?"

"My Dad's coming home from the hospital." I left.

-19-

Grinding gears grated against my nerves as I hurried into my parents' house on Lincoln Street. Memories covered me like hot fudge on vanilla ice cream, always did, whenever I entered. When I was a kid, the house had seemed like a huge labyrinth conceivable only in the mind of Rod Serling. Now that I was the large economy sized adult, it resembled a shoebox or two, scotch taped together with doors and shutters where windows should be cut out with children's safety scissors with the blunt tips. Following the commotion and noise coming from the narrow staircase to the second floor, I saw the man from the medical equipment company coming towards me. The passageway was wide enough only for one way traffic. He was swearing up a storm. He stopped when he saw me.

"Sorry Mister, it's just that I had a helluva time getting that hospital bed upstairs and it sounds like a cement mixer. Judas Priest, now I got to go all of the way back to the shop and bring back a bottle of lubricant."

I mentioned a nationally known spray lubricant. "Would that help?"

"Jesus, you got some of that? It would save me a trip back and forth."

"Consider it taken care of." We shook hands and he slapped my shoulder like I was an all right guy. I just hoped that Mom and Dad had some of that lubricant. Finally, up the stairs and I was in intensive care, the home version of the game. Dad was propped up in his newly installed hospital bed with the overhanging trapeze bar that Tony was moving out of the way.

"Don't use it Pop, or you'll snap the wires holding your ribcage together. Come here Big Brother, grab this sheet and help lift Dad a little higher in the bed."

"How are you feeling, Dad?" I said.

"Tired, the trip home took a lot out of me." He paused to catch his breath. "There isn't any pain other than from the surgery. I need to do a follow-up with the surgeon in six weeks." He paused waiting again for the oxygen in his system to catch up with him. "Have you found that boy yet? This Prince Gregory?"

"Not yet." I never liked my failures being brought up as a kid. As an adult, I was the same. "There are a few leads, but nothing concrete."

"And that young girl," he said, searching his cloudy memory for her name. "Nellie? That's it, Nellie. How is she?"

"Still no change, Pop." I checked my watch. "Is there anything that you need? Anything I can get you?"

"Your mother and the girls are seeing to everything. But if you have time to stop in and watch a ball game sometime..." His eyes closed and he was finished with the conversation. Tony took me aside.

"Ross, everything is covered for now. Roberta and I will stay a few days. Mom will be okay and Chris said she would stay a few weeks. I'm beginning to think that you were right, and that we shouldn't jump the gun on placing them in a managed care facility."

"There's enough time to do that later, if we decide it is necessary. Tony, thanks for getting Pop home from the hospital. I know that I haven't been around a lot but…"

"But that's who you are, Big Brother. Go find that kid. Things are under control here. If they are not okay, I won't hesitate to call. The doctors have done everything that they can. Now Dad needs to rest and heal. Here, he can do that."

Anthony and I shook hands and for the first time I realized we were more like adults than we had ever been. Sure, a little adult can go a long way, but for now, it felt good.

As I headed for the front door, I passed Chris at the dining room table with her laptop. I paused and kissed her on the forehead. "How's it going?"

"Lowly production assistants' work is never done. It is my job to update the website daily. Yes, it's scut work, but it's Hollywood scut work."

"No doubt another Sherry Lansing in the making. I have to go; if Mom or Dad need anything, you have my numbers."

"Take care Ross. I'll pray for Nellie."

I suppressed a lump in my throat and mumbled thanks.

"Lucas? Ross Malone. What's the urgent message that you have to impart to me?"

"Emily Hughes, the boy's maternal grandmother has filed for custody of Gregory in state court as of thirty minutes ago," said Lucas. If the tone of his remarks were any indication, he was exceedingly proud of himself.

"Surprise, surprise," I said.

I hit the turn signal and went to get the skinny from the grandmother's mouth. Grace Rusinko, as protective of Gregory as she is, would not be an asset there. I didn't ask her to tag along.

The door was answered after the first knock.

"Remember me, Mrs. Hughes? I'm Ross Malone, the private investigator looking for your grandson. May I come in?"

She tightened her grip on the door handle and set her jaw, obviously preparing to stand her ground. "My lawyer says I shouldn't talk to anyone."

"Ma'am, I'm not here to decide who gets to keep Gregory. I just want to find him so he can be fought over. Please?"

Slowly, she opened the door wider and I squeezed through at the earliest opportunity so she wouldn't change her mind. We settled in the living room.

"Could you please tell me what made you file for full custody now, right in the middle of this crisis?" I said. I tried to appear sympathetic.

"I want him brought up in the United States. Whatever one thinks of our country, we are not the great Satan, but the greatest democracy on the face of the earth. Why wouldn't anybody want to be raised here?"

"What does Benjamin Walanna say? After all, he is the boy's father."

She huffed before responding. "Humph, what does he know? The bottom line Malone is, that I don't want my grandson brought up in some backward tribal environment."

"Laracone does have running water." It paid to watch the DIS-COVERY channel. "He does have parental rights. There's more to being a father than providing sperm."

"My seeking custody of my grandson has nothing at all to do with you, Malone."

"Couldn't you have waited, at least waited until the prince was found? I mean, there is the remote possibility you'll be seeking custody of a gravestone." It was cruel, but I said it for effect. There was none.

"I have every faith that God will return Gregory safely in the near future." My look drilled a hole through her eyes, right past her unlined bifocals. I fired a broadside.

"They've contacted you, haven't they?"

"Excuse me? I'm afraid I don't know what you're talking about?"

Lowering my head, I searched the ground for how to proceed and elicit the answers only she could give me. "Someone contacted you. You got a tape, a phone call, or just maybe, even your very own personally autographed ransom note."

Strong-arming grandmothers was never my forte, yet she moved easily to her feet and walked over to the fireplace mantel. She caressed a photo of her grandson that looked like a newborn photo. I knew it was Gregory because his name was etched into the frame in gold script. I stood, trying to force the issue with body language. My hands were crossed in front of my chest, as if I was counting the seconds waiting for the truth to spew forth.

The maternal grandmother didn't bother to look at me. "I don't know what you are talking about."

"Phone call, tape or note?" I dug in my heels.

She rocked back on her own heels and then took a step and slumped into a nearby chair next to a doily covered end table. "Phone call. It was a phone call. It came a few hours ago. They told me that they wanted the $350,000 or Prince Gregory would be harmed."

"Nothing about a change of government? Nothing about him going free, just that they won't hurt him?"

A nod flew by, preceding the first wave of tears. "Yes, but I made sure that they let me talk to Gregory, so I could be sure he was all right, safe."

"And?" I said.

"He seemed shaken, almost helpless, but I suppose that was to be expected, given the circumstances."

I offered her my always present, clean, monogrammed hand-kerchief. Each year I bought two dozen new ones, always white, and invariably had to replenish my supply each January 1st. I took it as a business deduction.

"Can you raise that kind of money?"

"Yes, it will be difficult, but I can. They said no police," she said. Her look pleaded with me to respect that caveat.

"I'm sure they did. Don't worry, its something that they learned in kidnaper school."

She wasn't pleased with my humor. Anger flashed across her face. "That may be Malone, but if you breathe a word of this, I'll deny it."

"Listen to me, Emily. Political fanatics or not, a quarter million dollars will tarnish the best of intentions. You need the police. You need professionals."

"Aren't you a professional?" She had me there. "Malone, if you keep quiet about this with the police, I'll let you deliver the ransom. Deal?"

"Yes, but only if we do things my way." I set up a tape recorder on the phone to take all incoming calls and instructed Emily Hughes on its use. "Did they say when they wanted to make the exchange?"

"No, just to get the money ready and they'd contact me."

"Call me when you have the money and/or the instructions," I said, already second guessing myself about not at least telling someone.

When I got back into the Cherokee, I realized that in other times like these I would have told Nellie Archer to watch my back. Unfortunately, I'd promised I wouldn't tell. No, that wasn't correct. I just promised I wouldn't tell the police."

"Thanks for meeting me, Joe," I began, opening my Cherry Pepsi. "How's Nellie?"

He shook his head, slowly, looking downward. "Next question. Gwen's with her right now."

"I need someone to know some things, just in case anything happens to me."

"I'm all ears. Pass the barbecue sauce."

Two well done cheeseburgers later, his with bacon, some Pepsi, his coffee and one Nutty Buddy ice cream treat for me, I told Joe Rhino everything to date as to the whys and wherefores of the abduction of Gregory Walanna.

"And you want what, from me?" asked Joe.

"It seems kind of silly to say, I just want it on the record." He said nothing. "Thanks. I'll be in touch."

"Give my regards to your father."

I didn't look back, but waved a reply.

What nagged me at the back of my neck was the loudmouth with the Royalists of Laracone, Ghiamin Lora. I'd seen bluster like that before. It was an occupational hazard. He didn't seem the type to kidnap a child. However, that didn't mean he was above cashing in on it to the tune of three-quarters of a million dollars. And if Emily Hughes had talked to Gregory, then Ghiamin Lora, whether he took the kid or not, sure as hell knew where to get in touch with him. Being the only shred of a lead I had, at the moment, I decided to follow it.

Therefore, my next battle plan consisted of sitting outside the Royalists of Laracone's command center, then follow the little nerd when he came out. I felt guilty for not being with my Dad, guilty for getting Nellie hurt, and frustrated as hell that Gregory Walanna was being held somewhere against his well. There had to be a reason for all of this happening in my world. I tried to remember back, to the last time that I had broken a mirror.

Stakeouts were boring work in the best of times, but necessary. Since my last extended surveillance, I'd added more toys to keep me amused. The list included a Rubik's cube, three crossword puzzle books, the latest Lawrence Block novel, the latest edition of USA TODAY, and a transistor radio to have music or sports without running down the car battery.

The cube was half done on one half of one side when Ghiamin Lora arrived in a cab and disappeared upstairs. He seemed excited, hurried, and operating solely on tunnel vision. I ran across the street, zigzagging in front of a couple of cars that honked their annoyance at my jaywalking. The restroom at the self-service mini-mart was a welcome sight to those on stakeout. Coffee cans in the back seat are definitely last resorts. I hustled back, hoping that I hadn't missed Lora's departure.

One hour passed, then a second. I hadn't heard from Emily Hughes. I was tempted to go wait by the phone with her, because in her emotional state, she might deliver the money and worry about my feelings at a later date. That would be a mistake, and possibly a fatal one, for both her and Gregory. The sunlight was in its last throes for this day. Darkness was never an ideal condition for tailing someone.

Hour three of my crusade was well on its way to biting the dust when a cab pulled up, and Lora came flying out of the building on the dead run. I barely got my seatbelt/shoulder harness snapped before the black and yellow taxi was a full block and one stoplight ahead. My cell phone was tossed onto the seat besides me.

Taxi drivers, regardless of their ethnicity, are a breed unto themselves. They always drive as if each fare in the backseat had screamed, "Lose that car behind us and I'll double your fare," as they got in. This cab had a back tail light cracked and the plastic was gone but the unsheathed bulb still worked. It helped me to pick it out of the traffic jams ahead.

Their destination was a motel on the north side of the city, just off the Route 81 exit. Sixteen units linked together, resembling the product of adult Lincoln Logs. The "No Vacancy" sign was lit. The cab stopped in front of the office. Only a few cars were stationed outside the various bungalows. Lora went into the office; the cab stayed, with the motor running and the meter spiraling upward. Adrenaline was being infused into my body. It felt good to be out on the hunt again. This was my element. I felt in control.

Lora was out of sight, but I didn't want to be seen just trying to get a closer look. Five minutes later he came out, paid off the cabbie and entered Bungalow 16. I decided to wait another fifteen minutes to a half-hour before I went to peek in the window.

Suddenly, a wild card was tossed into the mix. A green Honda Civic pulled in and parked in front of Unit Sixteen. Deidre Schulery got out, knocked once, then let herself in with a key from her shoulder bag. Damn. I had the sinking feeling I had wasted an entire afternoon waiting for the Odd Couple to rumple the bedsheets that they had probably rented by the hour. The cell phone rang. I had hoped it would be Emily Hughes.

It was Colleen Powers at Mercy Hill Hospital.

"Ross, there's been a change in Nellie Archer's condition. You need to be here."

-20-

An ominous feeling shrouded me when Colleen Powers shut the double doors to the conference room after we entered. I sat on the edge of the overstuffed couches ringing the center conference table and twelve chairs, the setting for "12 Angry Men." Nurse Powers, now dressed in civvies, wore a cable knit short sleeved sweater that matched her eyes. Her glasses, still on that canvas tether around her neck, hung low. She placed a sheaf of documents between us. The lights were dim, the television off. The mood was somber. I began to dread her next words.

"Ross, in addition to my other jobs, I also occasionally function as an ombudsman of sorts, a patient advocate that conveys necessary information. I do not, and will not, make decisions concerning long term care plans vis a vis'..."

"Nurse Powers, you aren't talking with C. Everett Koop on the Surgery Channel. You'll have to break it down for me, please."

"Simply put, as the designated health care proxy, we are informing you that..."

I interrupted again. "Is she dead?"

"That determination still needs to be made. The legal definition of death these days, is that it has occurred when all cerebral function has ceased and is irreversible."

"Has her breathing stopped?" Instead of answering, she handed me a paper from the pile between us, listing the conditions that needed to be in evidence before a determination to pull mechanical life support from a patient or allow organs to be retrieved for donation. The list numbered five: bilateral dilation and fixation of pupils, absence of all reflexes, cessation of respiration without assisting (specifically ventilators), cessation of cardiac action, and completely flat lines on the brain wave monitor. "So, what are you telling me with all of this?"

"Ross, in the course of her treatment, her doctors tried to wean her off the ventilator to see if she could breathe on her own. She couldn't. It isn't my place, or that of her medical team to tell you what to do. However, it is our responsibility to tell you what the options are."

I kept silent. The enormity of the pending decision loomed before me, and was starting to crush my spirit. Colleen Powers took this as an opportunity to continue. Up on her feet, she talked, walked and lectured.

"This part of my job sucks, Ross. Ms. Archer had also shown negative brain wave capability since her arrival in the ICU."

"And that hasn't changed at all?" I was grasping at straws. "Not even a blip?"

"I'm afraid not. I'm sorry, and there's been a new development. Her physicians have determined that without the vent she couldn't breathe."

"Then, according to this paper," I said while waving it in the air, "she's legally dead. No extraordinary measures, those were her wishes. Those are my wishes as well," I said rushing the words out of my mouth as fast as possible to mute the pain.

"Ross, it just isn't that simple. Several doctors need to examine her, then, they must certify, in writing, that these facts are present.

Then, it will be your decision as to if she is moved, to a long term care facility for continued monitoring."

"Doesn't seem to be much point if she's not thinking and breathing." Colleen kept quiet. "What's next?"

"The doctors are waiting to talk with you officially to convey her situation," she said softly.

"Now?" I was not ready. This was unquestionably moving too fast for me.

"Yes. Then within 72 hours, we will need your decision on whether you plan to have her moved to a long term care facility."

"So, I pull the plug or you ship her out? Do I have that right?"

"Legally, we would have to go to court. But, believe me, we don't want to have to do that."

I repeated my question. This time she declined to answer verbally, but my crudely put and unfair query hung in the air. Her facial expression betrayed her. "Okay, bring on the doctors."

Clinically sterile was the only way to describe the meeting between Nellie's doctors and me. It consisted of her cardiologist, her neurosurgeon, her cardiac surgeon, her internist and me. All we needed was a smoke filled room and poker chips. Their answers to my questions were clipped and well-rehearsed, full of medical lingo with terms like Bibinsky, and little in the way of compassion and emotion. That was Colleen's function, no doubt, to provide the warm fuzzies while the angel of death placement squad interviewed you. I left Mercy Hill Hospital struggling with pulling the plug. I needed an ear upon which to bounce a few thoughts. Shelly Hutton got elected.

"Why are you in the office so late?" I asked, just to make conversation.

"They don't call me 'Rolling Thunder' because I come to court unprepared. Did you come directly from the hospital?"

"Yes. Does it show?"

She produced a half-filled bottle of Black Velvet whiskey from a desk drawer with two very large shot glasses. Shelly filled both glasses to the white line around the rim and placed one in front of me. "You need this."

I shook my head. "I prefer to fly solo. Mercy Hill gave me 72 hours to pull the plug or get her in a nursing home."

"They just want to make bed space available for a more worthy, read that financially viable, candidate. Cheers."

"Great," I said. "A hospital with a clearance sale."

"Is she legally dead?"

"By their definition." I recounted, in as much detail as I could, the two meetings with both Colleen Powers and the medical SWAT team attending to her. Shelly finished both drinks during it. "I've never taken a human life without that life trying to take my life or another one first."

"What about the quality of life? It's time for you to see this, Ross." Shelly Hutton steered her wheelchair away from her desk over to the bookcase and pulled a videotape out of a concealed wall safe. She handed it to me. "Watch this. I'll be back when you're done."

In an instant, I was alone. The dark screen on the TV set came alive, with Nellie Archer sitting in her own living room. A smile was painted on her face, radiating hope. Her voice, full in all its vibrancy, touched my heart.

"Hello Ross. If you are watching this tape, then Shelly gave it to you because I am in a position where I need your help, **really** need your help. Before I get to the tear jerky stuff, I want to thank you Ross Malone, for your professionalism, your friendship and for your belief in me, and occasionally, your humor. Okay, so I groaned a lot at your jokes." She gestured quotation marks around that last word.

"But you taught me a lot during the years we've known each other. You taught me when to use my head, or that it wasn't a sin to use my feminine wiles, when I needed to get some information. You taught me it was better to be accurate, than to be first. You taught me the difference between the sacrifice fly, and the hit and run." I smiled at that one and pulled the chair closer to the rest.

"Above all else Ross, you taught me that integrity wasn't a dirty word. I know it is not a pleasant task to watch this tape, and then face the decision that you do. But I chose you because I knew that, regardless of your personal feelings, you would do what was right, and follow my wishes. So, what are my wishes? Most of them are spelled out in black and white on the paper that you signed when you agreed a lifetime ago to do this.

"Ross, let me boil this down for you. If I have to be kept alive artificially, if I have to get several nurses to move me each day to keep bed sores at bay, and if I won't ever again be able to experience the beautiful sunrises during the hot air balloon festival first hand, then that's a life I do not want to live.

"Ross, thank you so very much for helping me this one last time. I will always love you. Good-bye, my friend."

Nellie Archer smiled one last time then faded out; the screen went from black to snow. I let it. My face lowered into my hands and I cried. My soul screamed in abject frustration. I swept everything off the shelf of the bookcase and crashing down onto the floor with one swing of my arm.

I didn't hear Shelly's return. She looked at the floor, then let me cry. And I would have continued to do so, except my cell phone rang it all to a stop. I sucked in two lungfuls of air, then answered it.

"Malone," I said, but my heart wasn't in it.

"Emily Hughes. They've called."

"Did you get them on tape?"

"No, it all happened so fast, I couldn't work the buttons quick enough," she said.

"I'll be right there."

But first, I cleaned up the mess I had made.

I had pulled myself together by the time I got back to the grandmother's house. She recounted the instructions.

"They want me to take the money to the Rosamond Gifford Zoo at Burnet Park, over by the new tiger enclosure. Leave it in the trash barrel marked number 23, and then leave the park. Next, I am to drive to a pay phone on Salina Street and call this number," she said, reciting the number. "The money will be here in an hour."

"Mrs. Hughes, I strongly suggest you rethink calling the police."

"No!" Her reply was sharp, almost violent. "You promised me that you wouldn't tell the police, not a word."

"And I haven't. Did you tell the kidnapers I was going to deliver the money?"

"Yes, and I must tell you, that they were not happy about it. But I told them, no Malone, no money." Had she really grown a backbone since I was last here?

"What about Gregory? Did you talk with him?" I asked.

"They wouldn't let me speak with him, this time. But they said that if Benjamin dissolves the government, my grandson would be released unharmed."

"And if he doesn't?" The crestfallen look that came over her face told me that she hadn't really considered that possibility.

"Now we wait."

-21-

So this is what it was like to drive a Brinks' Armored Car carrying a well over a quarter of a million dollars on the passenger seat? I made the final turn onto the gravel service road behind the Rosamond Gifford Zoo at Burnet Park. A chill shot through me, as I remembered the times Christopher and I would run through a spring rain, trying to catch the baby elephants one last time. I hopped the fence, tossing the satchel filled with $350,000 in unmarked, non-consecutive, used bills in various denominations over onto the ground first.

Prior to the drop, I had had enough time to change into the requisite cat burglar ensemble. Clad from head to toe in black, no labels for identification and dark colored surgical gloves, the latex free, non-powdered variety and I was ready to do battle.

Five hundred yards later, after maneuvering through park benches, tables with umbrellas growing out of their centers, and various cages where animal radar worked better than human eyes, they sounded my arrival. If I were Rex Harrison, I could have told them to shut up. Trash barrel #23 was zebra striped, under a lone light pole, and dead ahead. I did as I was told, and dropped the satchel in, then left the way I came in full view of anyone watching from afar.

Then I made a beeline for the phone booth and made the call, not from the pay phone but from my cell phone.

"I dropped the money. Release the prince."

The voice I heard had been electronically garbled. "We don't take your orders. Go home, Errand Boy." They broke the connection. I went back to work.

Hurdling the zoo fence a second time, albeit in a hurry, ripped the knee out of my ebony running pants to shreds, a casualty to such haste. Trash barrel #23 was now empty. A long shot at best, I'd hoped I'd be able to follow the money back to the prince. No such luck. It was time to play the card up my sleeve.

Back at the Cherokee, I dialed the Phone Company.

"…Now I'm not one to make trouble, but my 14 year old son just used this phone for two hours and I want to know the last number dialed. Why? Because I want to know he's not calling one of those 900 sex lines, that's why. Yes, I pushed the redial button, but I kept getting a busy signal. All I want is the number and the address. No, saying it's in the city doesn't help. I suppose I could ask the police for help or my friend at the newspaper."

Bingo. Name and number arrived on a silver platter.

A quick look at the map sent me northeast of the city past Shoppingtown Mall. The address turned out to be a vacant factory. The previous tenant had soaked the state and local officials for tax breaks, sweetheart deals on cheap power and whatever else it could extort from a state desperate to keep commerce from leaving for what the sunbelt had to offer. Then they shut down, stole away in the dead of night, and relocated where the yearly snowfall measured in the low single digits, if at all.

But if this factory were totally out of business, why were their slivers of light from various cracks in the painted over windows. I parked the Cherokee and pulled out the infrared binoculars. No guards were visible walking the perimeter. No other cars, trucks, or motorcycles in sight. I'd give it thirty minutes, then reconnoiter.

Unfortunately, the last thing I needed was down time. My mind replayed the videotape of Nellie Archer. She had trusted me. I had let her down. I couldn't let her down this time. Whatever I decided had to be right. But it would have to wait.

A crème colored VW bus, dotted with rust spots, with front-end damage, pulled up alongside the dilapidated brick building. The headlights went dark. Up went the binoculars and into my field of vision appeared the driver of the van. A good six or seven inches taller than I, this prime suspect in the kidnapping of Gregory Walanna walked directly to the door and entered. All I had to do was get a peek inside to make sure that the prince was still alive and well, then call out the cavalry.

Crouching as low as my aching back would accommodate, I made it through the darkness behind the van and let the air out of all four tires. Even if they got past me, they wouldn't be making their getaway in this. Quickly, I moved next to the building. The PI gods were smiling down upon me. The factory windows were painted on the outside. My pocketknife delicately helped me scrape a little peephole in the lower left-hand corner of the nearest window. I put my eye to the glass.

Surprise, surprise. I saw the van driver who looked familiar: could he have been the mystery man at McDonald's? There I saw Ghiamin Lora looking like a fatted calf and fondling the fondable backside of Deidre Schulery—a regular Bonnie and Clyde. The laughter rang out as they tossed ransom money into the thin air like confetti. Then Lora ordered Deidre to bring the boy out.

I never saw the prince as a blunt instrument was slammed against the base of my skull. Instead, I saw nothing, nothing at all.

A whiff of ammonia knocked me back to consciousness. I felt fingers at the back of my head. It felt like they were touching bone. Voices that started out as murmurs focused into sentences. The first one I could discern did not lighten my heart.

"At first glance, they were all shot with Malone's gun, or one just like it. I'll rush the tests through."

I groaned and sat upright. A paramedic was tending to my wound. My eyes focused and I saw Tom Otera.

"Ross? Ross? Are you back to the living?"

"I am, if you call this living." Like adjusting the tracking on a videotape player, my eyes rounded into focus all of the images before me. I then took in the whole of my surroundings.

There were three yellow blankets that the cops used to cover dead bodies with. I could smell the death.

"Tell me what happened," said Tom.

The paramedic interrupted. "Sorry Deputy, he's got to go to the hospital. He needs to have his head examined. He could have a concussion or a fractured skull. He needs a doctor."

"And I've got three dead bodies that apparently were shot with his gun, money all over the place and no kidnapped prince. I'll compromise with you. Put him in the ambulance and I'll talk with him on the way in."

I was in no position to argue. Though once inside the ambulance, I called Shelly Hutton. She would meet me at the Justice Center.

Tom told me that someone had phoned in a tip about shots being fired at the factory. Uniforms responded and found three adults who had been shot to death, and me, inside the room, out cold. My gun was in my hand and had been fired. The number of shell casings matched the number of holes in the victims.

I told Tom what I knew, including the identities of two of the corpses. The third was a mystery to me.

"And you didn't see the prince?"

"No. Lora wanted Deidre to bring him out, and that's when I got clubbed, from behind."

"Think there was a guard outside you missed, or an accomplice who got greedy, and got away?"

"I guess. I really don't know Tom. Right now, it hurts to think."

"You'd better try Malone, because if there wasn't another shooter then you're on the books for three murders. And they didn't have any weapons that we can find."

"Right. Let me get this straight. I shot three unarmed people, then clubbed myself in the back of the head and dragged myself in here so the police would find me at the crime scene. Oh, I almost forgot, I also thought it was a good idea to leave $350,000 in plain sight."

"I didn't say the theory was perfect, but if everything else has an explanation then what is left is the truth."

"Don't paraphrase Sherlock Holmes to me." The paramedic gently pushed my shoulder back down onto the stretcher.

"You want me to call Susan, and tell her that you got your head split open again?"

"No. Am I under arrest?"

"Not yet, but don't leave town," said Tom.

"Any ID on the third body?" I asked.

"The crime scene boys printed all of the victims. There wasn't any identification on him. Know who he is?"

I shook my head and found out that was a bad idea. "I thought he might have been the guy in the Mickey D's video. But I'm not sure. No sign of the prince?" Before we had boarded the ambulance, Deputy Otera had walked me, with the aid of the paramedic, into the backroom on my legs of fruited Jell-O and showed me the prince's home away from home. Magazines, books, fast food refuse and newspapers plus a single cot with rumpled sheets. I had seen enough. "Any leads?"

"Not so far. We know he was here, but we don't have a clue as to where he is now. We're canvassing the area. And if the people who took him could do this?" He gestured a hand covered by a plastic glove back at the factory building holding the three corpses. "I fear for his safety."

"Keep me informed?" I asked.

"I'll do what I can, but you are a prime suspect in a triple homicide." He seemed embarrassed about it all.

"Tell me Tom, that you really know I didn't do this, that I didn't shoot three unarmed people in cold blood."

He was quiet for a very long uncomfortable moment. "Get some rest, Ross."

The remainder of the trip to the hospital was silent and foreboding. I had the good sense to pass out.

The district attorney threw a hissy fit, but Shelly promised to keep me available whenever they wanted. She dropped me off back home. The crime scene evidence technicians had impounded my Cherokee. At least, it would get the carpets vacuumed.

I called a rental car company and they dropped off a newer model. After signing for the car, I went into my living room. My head was pounding as if i-t were hosting a duel between Ringo Starr and Mick Fleetwood. Ten stitches at the base of my skull kept the breeze from whistling through my head. I speed dialed Susan in Washington and clicked on the speakerphone. The answering service was my reward. It wasn't any different than the local ones except that when you were placed on hold you heard "God Bless America."

"Please remind Dr. Abilene that I still love her, forever and then some." The operator giggled and said that she would. The thunderclaps bouncing around in my head would soon produce showers in my soul, if I sat around and did nothing but feel sorry for myself. I left to accomplish the unthinkable.

When Gwen Brolin saw me standing in the doorway, she gasped. It was all the emotion that she could muster.

"May I talk to you for a few minutes?"

She stepped back. I entered in my new job as the Grim Reaper Welcome Wagon. We sat on the couch.

"Ms. Hutton called me. I know you saw the tape Nellie made, Ross. I know that you've talked to the doctors. I know you've made up your mind, Why are you here?"

"To clear my conscience. I've always been an optimist. If you wait long enough, say your prayers, brush your teeth and help old ladies across the street then everything will have a happy ending."

"You aren't Jimmy Stewart, Ross, and this isn't 'A Wonderful Life.'"

"I am also not God, Gwen. I have no business deciding who lives and who dies."

"Nellie thought you did. Malone, I was here when that video-tape was made. We talked long and hard and about it. She said someone in her line of work needed to cover all of the bases. Do you have a tape, Malone?"

"Pardon me?"

Gwen swallowed hard. "A tape like Nellie's, leaving your last wishes."

"No."

"Nellie said that you thought you were indestructible, that a living will on tape would seem unnecessary to you." Her mood went from lighthearted memory to the cold, serrated edge of reality. "Have you decided?"

The words stuck in my throat. I merely nodded.

"What do you want from me? It seems asinine to ask how I can help," she said.

"Do you want to be there when this occurs?"

"No, I've already said my good-byes."

"Do you need help with the funeral arrangements?"

"Mr. Reneau has already helped me navigate that minefield. He insisted on paying for everything, including the burial plot. I've never really heard of him before. Is he a partner of yours?"

I considered this for a moment. "A silent partner." I stood. Everything else I could figure out by myself. "Thank you Gwen. I'll call you when I know."

I piled the miles on the rental car while trying to get up the nerve to make that final journey to see Nellie Archer. It would be soon, but first, I needed a few hours to sleep. To my disappointment, I found some reporters camped outside of my place when I returned. Maybe suspects in multiple homicides needed a press secretary? The urge to sleep was overwhelming. I decided to brave the throngs. Starting to push my way through, the first question shouted at me, knocked the wind completely out of me.

"Malone, how do you feel about the prince being found?"

-22-

I didn't even bother to put my key in the front door.

Getting through the remaining security assets at the consulate, even as a murder suspect was easier than I would have thought. With Gregory Walanna, apparently well and back in the fold, the number of guards had been visibly reduced, no doubt replaced by an electronic web of cameras, microphones and motion detectors, and probably Dick Tracy wrist radios.

Only Andrew and Jacob blocked my entrance to the makeshift operations center that Trevor Bradley had created when the prince had turned up missing. They didn't move. Neither did I.

"Isn't this how we started out?" I said.

Jacob spoke first. "The prince is back. No thanks to you."

"Is he all right?"

"The doctors are checking him over," said Andrew.

"Go away Malone. You are no longer needed, and certainly not wanted," added his twin, obviously separated at birth with malice aforethought.

"I think the world of you too, Jacob. I want to see Trevor Bradley." It wasn't a request as much as it was a statement. My head pulsated its message of pain north and south and all points in between. "Any objections?" They didn't speak, but they also didn't move. I pushed my way through. They offered token resistance, like a well-worn blocking sled.

The law enforcement firepower once amassed to find the prince of Laracone had thinned out. Trevor Bradley was huddled in a corner with some junior Bradley wannabes. I tapped him on the shoulder.

"We need to talk, Trevor."

"Why?" he said. "The prince has been found. I don't know why you killed those people, but that is not a State Department problem." He turned his back to me and returned to his conversation. Wrong move. I grabbed a handful of gray Armani suit coat and the nearest wrist and maneuvered Bradley with all deliberate speed into a nearby anteroom kicked the door shut behind me.

"I asked nicely. For your information, I didn't kill those three people."

"I told you Malone, that wasn't my problem," he said, struggling minimally to get free of my grip. I held firm.

"Guess again, Trevor. There'll be a special prosecutor in your future, if I tell the press that you knew what I was doing all along." I heard his mind click and whir as this information was entered into his internal computer.

"Okay, suppose I buy that, what do you want?"

"To get out from under three murders I didn't commit, for starters," I said.

"If you want absolution, I've got contacts at the Vatican." I was not in the mood for his sarcasm and jerked his arm up further behind him.

"You self centered, smug sonuvabitch." The door opened and Benjamin Walanna came in.

"What's going on here?"

"Nothing Mr. President, nothing at all. I was just making it clear to Malone here that since the prince is safe, we no longer require his services."

I loosened my grip and set Trevor free.

"I see," said Walanna. It was a sight to behold. Benjamin Walanna transformed from worried father to detached head of state right before my very eyes, leaving the details to underlings in less time than it took David Cone to snap off a fastball. Without another word, he shot those starched cuffs then turned and left.

"Remember Trevor, I did ask nicely. I won't ask nicely again."

I went back to the rental car. Grace Rusinko was leaning against the midnight blue passenger side car door. She half smiled.

"You look like you could use a friend. Follow me," she said.

We drove five blocks up the street to a little out of the way bar that was dark, sported an overused dart board and the jukebox had Natalie Cole. Things were once again fine in Laracone. Grace bought the first round.

"How are you holding up?" she asked as she slid the bowl of peanuts closer to me.

"I'm not really sure what the etiquette of being a murder suspect is. How is Gregory?"

"He is disheveled to say the least. Also disoriented, but overall none the worse for wear considering he's been gone a few days. After all, you must remember that he is the once and future king."

"A toast to the once and future king," I said. We clinked glasses. "Was he released or did he escape? Were they filming an episode of COPS and needed a famous victim? How'd he get home?"

"You haven't heard? Gardner Meadows' minions found him wandering the streets. They called their boss. He called the press, and then brought the boy home in full view of a grateful nation."

"I'll bet. Have the police debriefed the boy yet?" Even chewing peanuts hurt my head.

She shook her head and finished her drink. I gulped the last of my Pepsi and chewed an ice cube. "President Walanna won't let the prince be interviewed, says he's been through enough."

I smiled. Okay, it was a smirk. "Was he talking about the prince or himself?"

"Good question. Where are you going?"

"I'm going home and straight to bed; and I'll try not to live down to my reputation and kill somebody on the way. Thanks for the drink."

"Want some company?" she said. I stopped in my tracks and looked into her face to gauge her sincerity. Not to see if I would take it, but whether I could brush it off with a wisecrack or should be more delicate. The latter won out.

"Thanks Grace, but I'm spoken for."

"Pity."

"I don't think so, and I sure as hell hope she doesn't think so," I said, and left.

All of the way home, the image burned into my mind's eye of Gardner Meadows triumphantly waltzing Prince Gregory back into the consulate, grinning for all of the 24 hour cable news cameras he could find. He would milk this into an ad for the Gardner Meadows way of life—a prescription for law and order with a side order of frontier justice. Clenching my teeth made the stitches at the back of my neck throb in earnest.

I had set my alarm clock to awaken me in time to catch Tony Kornheiser on ESPN radio. I needed to take my mind off of all of the madness around me. Worrying about game winning RBIs, point spreads and pitching match-ups seemed a good way to do that. Tony and Dan Davis, the Duke, never arrived. My ringing phone woke me up.

"Ross? It's Tony. Are you all right? Have you seen the papers this morning? What the hell is going on?"

"I'll tell you in a minute. How's Dad? Mom?"

"They'd be a lot better if their eldest son wasn't wanted for murder. But no, they don't know. Roberta and I are keeping them from the news as much as we can."

I pressed the point. "Are they okay, Tony?"

"Actually yes. The visiting nurse says he's right on schedule and Mom has settled into a routine. I just have to remember to buy some WD-40. Ross, there's something I need to ask you. I just don't know how."

"I didn't kill those people," I said, trying to anticipate his query.

"That wasn't the question, but I'll be insulted later that you might think I'd ask something like that. I want to know what we can do to help."

I took a deep breath and tried to sit up in bed. Bad move. My head started to gyroscope on me, so I gently put it back onto the pillow.

"At the moment, there's nothing anyone can do. Just take care of Mom and Dad."

"Do you need some money?"

I laughed, even that little chuckle hurt as well. "I'm not heading out of town. I'm innocent. Besides, I have other obligations."

"Nellie Archer," my brother said softly.

"Yes," I replied.

"All right Big Brother, we'll sit tight until we hear from you. And Ross? Remember that we all love you."

"Thanks. But keep your baloney grabbers off of my baseball card collections. I might need to hock it for bail money."

Luckily, he laughed at my gallows humor. "Take care, Ross."

No sooner did I hang up the phone, than an insistent banging started on my front door. That was good because at first, I thought it was just in my head. I grabbed my spare gun and went to the door partially hiding my weapon behind my hip. Peeking through the peephole, the only thing I saw was an FBI identification. Felicity Charles had come calling.

"Open up Malone. We have to talk." She started banging again. I placed the gun in a nearby drawer, then opened the door. She entered with a partner. "For chrisssakes Malone, put some pants on."

In my rush to stop the noise, I had gone to the door clad only in my red Hanes briefs and T-shirt. I acted as if I wasn't embarrassed, grace under pressure that's me. When I came back fully clothed, sneakers to glasses, Felicity had made coffee and raided my stash of Freihofer's Australian Toaster Cakes.

"Say, why don't you make yourself at home?" I said. Pouring myself some orange juice, I first placed the ice-cold glass against my forehead.

"Cut the crap, Malone. You're up to your Miranda in a triple homicide. If you cooperate, just maybe I can spare your life."

The partner was working hard on blending in, but failing. He was poised to take notes once his breakfast was gone.

"I didn't do it, Agent Charles. If you question the prince, he'll tell you I am innocent."

"He's being kept incommunicado at the moment. However, we have a report back from our firearms experts who confirm that your gun was the murder weapon. A paraffin test proved that you had fired a weapon recently, and the amount of blowback on your hand would be consistent with the number of shots you fired."

"I didn't shoot anybody."

"You know, you get a good lawyer and tell the court that you were afraid for the boy's life, you might make a case for manslaughter. Oops, I forgot one little, important point. They were all unarmed," she said, obviously pleased with herself.

"Agent Charles, please get your lovely butt out of here, before you eat me out of house and home."

"I'm trying to do a favor for you, Malone. If you don't come clean now, I won't be able to save you later. Murder is a capital offense. Murder in connection with a kidnapping is a double whammy. I was just trying to save your worthless little life."

"Don't bother. I wouldn't want to have to add you to my Christmas card list."

Felicity Charles didn't get flustered easily. She and her partner took their time and finished eating. They placed their dirty dishes in the dishwasher, collected their briefcases and things, then left. No one said another word.

Since I didn't want to keep reminding the police that I was still free and on the street by bumping into their murder investigation, I decided to turn my attention back to finding out who hurt Nellie.

To do that, it was back to square one. George Trask's store was still boarded up. It was now adorned with a shiny new padlock and chain. The latter was wrapped several times around the Iron Gate. I peeked through the slats. There were still bottles and cans on the shelves. I couldn't tell from my vantagepoint if the bread had turned to penicillin yet, but this didn't appear to be George's busiest time of year.

I pulled out my pencil style flashlight to get a better look inside the darkened store. Trask hadn't been opened for business in quite a while. The pile of mail on the floor beneath the drop slot was a good indication he was making himself scarce. Suddenly, I began to sweat, not perspire as in the TV commercials, but sweat. As I looked between the slats, the images came back with a vengeance. My brain projected pictures, ugly pictures of Nellie fighting back, screaming, but overwhelmed then savagely, maybe even methodically, beaten. Her youthful, lithe body curled up in the fetal position, waiting for the onslaught of punches and kicks to subside long enough to escape further attack.

But she couldn't get away. They wouldn't let her get away. I knew inside it had to be more than one assailant, perhaps a wild pack like the ones that were thought to roam through New York City's Central Park, in search of easy prey. My instincts were to discover who did this, hunt them down like the animals they were and deliver swift retribution in the most painful way possible, then turn them over to the police. That is, if there was anything left worth turning over.

I started down the alley looking for something that would start the hunt. When I got to the back, the yellow police crime scene tape had been trampled down to the ground. The cars that I'd gotten license numbers from were gone. All that remained was the Dumpster. I heard a noise behind me. Quickly, I lunged for the cover of the Dumpster and drew my weapon. Crouching as low as my impromptu hiding place would allow, I peeked around the corner.

About 25 yards back up the alley, I saw my quarry. She was past middle age at a gallop, her hair was striped gray as if splattered with a wide paintbrush, and a pink smock covered her middle age spread. The grunting and scraping I heard came from the overstuffed trashcan she was struggling to get closer to the Dumpster. I holstered my gun and moved leisurely out into the open. I put on my Mr. Friendly Smile.

"Hello, need some help with that?"

The middle-aged woman did two things when she saw me. First, she shrieked and then she pointed a .38 snubnose revolver directly at my forehead.

"A simple no thank you will suffice," I said.

"Who are you, Malone?"

I told her the truth. "Now, may I help you with that?"

She stepped back. "Darn nice of you."

"How did you know who I was before I told you?" I was puzzled.

"I do read the papers, even though my lips still move when I read." She laughed then snorted. "Sorry, I had to pull my piece on you. It's just that after that girl was mugged, that Nellie Archer, well, I needed to protect myself."

Once I'd hoisted the can and emptied its contents into the Dumpster, I followed her back into her small shop that she had named, "The Apothecary." It was quaint, as if from the pages of *YANKEE* magazine and full of odd shaped jars and bottles of cut or blown glass. Some were tinted and others were clear as the morning dew rolling down your bedroom window. At least, the ones still on the shelves.

Broken glass crunched under my feet. It wasn't isolated in one spot either. I counted three separate areas—one high shelf broken, a glass display case smashed in the front and a large antique wooden tub filled with herbal medicines was face down on the floor—its contents streaming into multi-colored rivulets across the floor.

"Who was your decorator? Stone Cold Steve Austin?" My words fell on deaf ears. Her back was deep into cleaning. I grabbed a nearby second broom and started to help. We worked in relative silence for about three-quarters of an hour. It wasn't finished, but it was more presentable.

"Thank you. You didn't have to help."

"Thank you for not shooting me. Let's call it even." I said.

We shook hands. She offered coffee that I renegotiated into a large glass of chocolate milk instead.

"I really am sorry about the gun, and all," she began, "but it's not safe here anymore."

"Doesn't that sign in your window say you're protected by the City Security Association? Doesn't that mean the Warriors of the Night?"

"Who do you think did this? Yes, I pay dues to the association, but this is called a personal services fee, which is a percentage of my weekly gross."

"I'll bet it is a high percentage. The cops would call it extortion."

She shook her head. "Don't even go there, Malone. I saw what happened to George Trask. You can see what happened to me just for being a few hours later. I'm no hero."

"You're in luck." I smiled. "I am."

Precisely one hour later, the two Warriors of the Night who were at Nellie's bedside in the hospital showed up. I had learned their names were Franco and Chuck. I bet they had visions of DeNiro and Pesci playing them in the movie. Adele, the store-owner, stayed behind the counter as I'd asked. I was in the back-room watching it all.

"Do you have the money now, Adele? Or do we have to remind you how valuable our personal service is?" They wasted little time threatening her. Meadows had drummed efficiency into their thick skulls.

"Um," started Adele, nervous as all get out. Her hands shook so much, that she grabbed the cash register with both hands to steady herself. "That won't be necessary. You see, I, um, I've hired a private security consultant. I won't be needing your personal services anymore."

Franco and Chuck exchanged glances. Then they looked at her and moved closer, getting their mouths next to her ears. "What? You don't understand, Adele. You do not have a choice."

"My consultant says that I do," Adele said, without skipping a beat.

"And just who is this mystery consultant?"

I stepped into the light. "Surprise. Well, if it isn't my old friends, Chuckie and Franco—trying to give Bert and Ernie a run for their money."

They seemed surprised to see me. "Malone, what the fuck are you doing here?"

"Consulting. Now you two can just cross Adele's name off of your little extortion list. And if you show your butt ugly faces in here again, I'll kick your asses all of the way to Attica."

"You're bluffing," said Franco, who was obviously the spokesperson for the twosome.

"Care to put your ass at risk to find out?" I said.

The standoff lingered, just like in cardiac intensive care. Once more they retreated. They made a lot of threats, remembered how to do a couple of obscene gestures but the bottom line was, they left without any more money.

Adele looked at me after their departure. "Okay Malone, now what?"

I told her.

-23-

The shadow I cast by my presence in the room stretched before me longer than my height. I stood, motionless, just watching, taking in the surroundings; the only sound in the room was the slight wheeze of respiration. It sounded safe. It felt secure. My Dad was asleep. The room that had once been a hideaway on rainy days where sleeping bags were arched over tall, straight backed chairs that became tents and caves where cowboys and pirates hid, now smelled of antiseptic and way too much chicken noodle soup.

The stack of old newspapers in the chair nearest to his bedside had outlived their usefulness and found their way to reincarnation in the recycle bin. The recent copies of *BASEBALL WEEKLY* and *THE SPORTING NEWS*, I brought with me, were placed within easy reach of his hand. I settled into the chair I had cleared out hoping to rest my aching head. However, it wasn't high enough to disturb the bandages protecting my ten stitches. I stifled a yelp. Having had a lot of practice in recent days with that, it was easy.

Here I was in the presence of a man who had endured open-heart surgery with nary a whimper. And at least inside, I was moaning and groaning about a few threads holding my body and soul together. I felt like a wuss.

"You okay, son?" said my father, his fluttering eyelids were now fully raised. "I'm glad you're here."

"Nowhere else I'd rather be. How's the recovery going?"

"I've had better years. Say, would you help me sit up a little higher?" He extended his arms as if the answer were a foregone conclusion.

I rose and gripped his upper body tight enough to move him but I hoped, not tight enough to do any more damage.

"How's that?" I said. He was heavier than I remembered as so much dead weight.

"Good, thank you. How long can you stay, son?"

"A few hours. Want to watch a game?" I said. There were always reruns on cable.

"Maybe a little later. Could we just talk?"

That sounded easy enough. "Sure. What would you like to talk about?"

"Not yet. First, make sure that your mother isn't listening." Going over to the entrance at the top of the stairwell, I checked and heard the bustling of the rest of the family in the kitchen, probably boiling up some more chicken soup. Signaling the all clear, I sat back down in the chair, only this time right on the edge. "I don't want your mother to hear us," he said. His voice was nearly a whisper by choice.

"If we're going to talk about what ifs should you take a turn for the worse, I think Tony and Roberta and Chris should be here."

"No, that's not necessary. I want to talk just to you." For a brief second, I was at a loss as to what he wanted to talk about. It was a very brief second. "Ross, I saw the news this morning. Your brother thought I was asleep. I let him think that. He doesn't know that I know. I'm sure he was just trying to protect me. And I know you want to protect me as well, but I'm telling you I would rather know the truth."

"What truth would you like to know?"

"Do you know what it's like to hear that your son is suspected of killing three innocent people?"

"Dad, I didn't kill them." I wasn't about to debate with a post-op heart patient whether the three decedents were actually innocent or not.

"I believe you. Can you understand that it's better for me to hear it from you?" I nodded. "How in the hell did you get caught up in all of that?"

He said he had wanted to know, so I told him—chapter and verse from the attempted mob hit in my office to the ten stitches once again throbbing at my neck. Then I chugged a 16 oz. Pepsi without taking a breath. I needed to be quiet. He needed a few moments to digest everything I'd dumped on him.

Somehow though, I felt relieved, a weight had been lifted from my shoulders then; I realized that maybe he knew that all along. Watching the Yankees do battle with Roger Clemens facing David Wells with the Blue Jays used up the rest of the afternoon. Pinstripes beat the Birds 3-2 in 10 innings. Things were beginning to look up. But it was time to go back to work.

I leaned over, squeezed my father's hand and kissed his forehead. He held my wrist with his other hand.

"Son, be careful. And remember your mother and I love you."

Even I didn't have a witty remark for that, so I just smiled.

Nighttime in a city the size of Syracuse brought the requisite darkness and in some sections of my town, it also brought quiet. It was not the quiet of a darkened upstairs room on Christmas Eve, but rather the still of a summer vacation home in the dead of winter. I shifted my three-legged wooden stool trying to find a more comfortable position. There was none.

I stretched up to my full height and took another look into the main store area of "The Apothecary" focusing in particular on the front door. I stiffened automatically, but briefly, when the flash of headlights from a pizza delivery car went by.

"You want some more fries, Malone?" said Joe Rhino, on the other three-legged stool and no more comfortable than I was.

I shook my head. "Knock yourself out."

"It's getting late. Maybe they aren't coming," said Joe.

"They'll be here. I saw it in their beady little punk eyes," I said. "They were surprised to see me this afternoon. I've faced them twice and made them back down twice. They'll want revenge. And they'll want it soon."

"You hope."

"I know," I said. Annoyance reared its ugly head. "Look, if you have someplace else to be, I can handle these guys."

"Relax Malone, where else would I be? I could be managing my highly successful supper club, be with any number of young eligible and very willing female companions, or making money at my favorite pastime picking winners at my personal sports book in the Cayman Islands. Other than that, there's no place I'd rather be."

"Sentimentality, thy name is Joe Rhino." I took a deep breath and flexed my sore knees. "Thank you for sitting with Nellie."

"It was something I wanted to do," he said.

"I know, but it was still nice. Just accept the damn compliment."

Out of the corner of my eye, I saw Joe Rhino execute a half-hearted salute. "Did you make a decision?"

"Yes," I said.

"When is it going to happen?"

"Colleen Powers says that I have to come in and sign some papers in front of witnesses, then they can proceed with what they have to do, organ donation or whatever."

Tough guy Joe Rhino shuddered. "Taking somebody's body parts and placing them in somebody else, gives me the creeps."

"Nellie's wishes were that whatever could be salvaged from her be taken and used to help those who needed it. That's the kind of person she was."

"I don't think I could have made that decision, Malone." I knew he wasn't talking about the organ donation choice, but rather my decision to withdraw artificial life support from my friend.

"Something I learned a long time ago Joe, was that the hardest thing to do is usually the right thing to do."

He started to respond, then stopped. I went to say something but he held his hand up and then pointed to his ear for me to listen. Then I heard it. Bolt cutters on the front link chain around the wrought iron gates announced the arrival of, in all probability, Franco and Chuck. I was sure they weren't high enough in the Warriors' food chain to be able to pawn off strong-arm errands on the dregs of the organization. In fact, they probably were the dregs of the organization. Nope, they had to do their own dirty work.

Joe and I moved into better positions to catch them in the act of vandalizing Adele's store. They had come prepared.

Franco and Chuck were dressed in soft-soled shoes and dark sweatsuits, sans logos—stylish and efficient. They were confident enough not to bother wearing masks. It made sense. My guess was that in the Warrior of the Night game plan, this was their sector to patrol and shakedown; so for them to be seen in this part of town, this late at night wouldn't seem out of the ordinary. Franco had his merit badge in vandalism as he was wearing a little fanny pack around his middle that he wore in the front and which probably held his accessories.

Meanwhile, Chuck was doing the heavy lifting, lugging in a five-gallon container, which reeked of gasoline.

"Where do you want me to start, Franco?"

Franco looked at him and punched him in the shoulder. "You dumb fuck. Do I have to do everything? Start behind the counter and over there by the wall. Pour a lot in that wooden tub. The cops'll think that the medicine spontaneously combusted."

It was like watching Laurel and Hardy in a Mack Sennett short called, "The Arsonists." Chuck did as he was told and started splashing the liquid accelerant where Franco had directed. As he came near the backroom where Joe and I were secreted, I had to resist the urge to stick my gun in his neck. Not yet. Pouring fuel on the floor was vandalism, but it wasn't arson. I had to catch them, in the act.

"Hey, what the hell is this?" said Franco, who had stumbled upon the camcorder I had placed in a corner to catch their act for the authorities. He flicked the off/on switch and rewound the tape for a few seconds then played it forward, watching through the viewing lens. "We've been taped Chuck. Get your stuff and let's get the hell out of here." Franco extracted the tape and smashed it under foot.

Chuck was hurriedly trying to gather everything he and Franco had come in with. Franco, on the other hand, was a cool customer. He continued to place a long white candle on the counter next to a string that he then tied around the base of the candle. The bottom part of the string was left dangling in the pool of gasoline Chuck had dumped.

The reasoning was that when the candle burned down it would ignite the string, which would then fall into the gasoline and send Ye Olde Apothecary to the insurance deductible graveyard. As Chuck moved past the backroom one last time, I stuck my foot out and tripped him. He fell forward and his flailing arms knocked over the wooden tub, its contents crashing down onto the floor and into the puddle of gasoline all around it.

Franco's head, which was shaped like an egg with a double yolk, snapped back into our direction. Joe sprung like a mousetrap and launched himself into the air ending up on Chuck's back and I made for Franco. With one foot on the bottom of the wooden tub, I flung myself like a Patriot missile out and upward towards the last standing Warrior of the Night. In mid-air, I saw him pull his 9-mm gun and cock the hammer. If he pulled the trigger, there was enough gasoline in here to make the store an impromptu Roman candle.

Luckily, I hit him with such force that the gun was knocked from his hand and hit the floor. How it failed to go off is something I would have to thank the big guy upstairs for. I was dead weight on Franco. He tried to knee me in the groin; I blocked it and delivered my own well-aimed knee. I grabbed his head in both of my hands and slammed it against the floor three times as fast as I could manage it.

It would have been four or five more times if Joe Rhino hadn't pulled me off. Franco's face was a bloody mess, what in pro wrestling they call a "crimson mask."

"That's enough Malone. We need them alive." I was operating on all cylinders with the pedal to the metal, overdrive, and automatic pilot all rolled into one. If Joe hadn't stopped me...

One last kick at Franco pushed him far enough away so I could sit up. Joe had bound Chuck with duct tape and sat him on the floor against the display case. The gasoline was soaking through the lining of his sweat suit. My blood pressure was parachuting back down to earth. I helped Joe bind Franco and place him next to his cohort. The gas splashed onto my pant leg. It was the least of my problems.

Joe tossed me a stool from the back and I placed it very close to our prisoners. As the aroma of the Molotov cocktail they were preparing buffeted my senses, I sent silent thanks heavenward that

I had the foresight not to use Adele as a guinea pig any more than I already had, instead choosing to send her to a relative in Binghamton.

"You guys know the routine. I'm not a cop. You guys don't have rights. Shall we begin?" I said.

Franco was again the group spokesman. "We don't have to tell you shit."

"Of course not. And we don't have to let you go until you do. Listen up wise guy, you're on the hook for attempted arson, which is a felony, and if you add the fact that Joe and I were here, it might get bumped to attempted murder. Ready for door number three?"

Before I could react, Joe Rhino a.k.a. Joseph Reneau stepped up and backhanded Franco across the mouth with his diamond encrusted Graceland ring. It tore the skin off his cheek but did little else. Joe moved to hit Chuck, but I stepped between them.

"Not yet. I still think Chuck here is going to be smart and tell us what we need to know." Joe let loose a low guttural sound that said he wasn't happy.

Chuck was seemingly unafraid of what might befall him. "What is this, good cop, bad cop? Like Franco said, we aren't telling you shit."

"Okay, then let me tell you what I know. I know you two yutzes have screwed up again. You were sent to collect protection money from Adele. She told you to take a hike. And if I know Gardner Meadows well at all, he doesn't take kindly to failure. So he sent you back to teach her a lesson. You dim bulbs decide to teach the whole damn neighborhood a lesson and burn her out.

"But when you get here, you not only find yourselves on tape, you are taken prisoners by two old cagey veterans."

"Watch it with the old stuff, Malone," said Joe, nervously waiting for his turn at bat if I failed. He kept punching one fist into the other open hand.

"Tell me what I want to know, then point the finger at Meadows and you'll deal from strength. Keep quiet, and you're on the hook for two felonies at least. And make no mistake about it, Gardner Meadows will cut his losses and hang your butts out to dry." I sat back down. "So what's it going to be?"

They looked at each other then down at the duct tape encircling their wrists. Franco looked back at me and spit on my shoes. His one eye was rapidly closing and I really wanted to shut the other one.

Joe stepped into the picture.

"You punks know who I am?" said Joe. His game face was on and this was definitely not good thug, bad thug to him. "I used to work for Lenny Bogardus. Maybe you've heard of me, Joe Rhino?"

Franco didn't flinch, but Chuck blinked more than once. "Can't say as we have. What makes you so important?"

In less time that it takes to spell cat if you already have the c and the a, Joe was in Franco's swelling face, less than the width of a paperclip away.

"Hear me good assholes. I've been in the joint. I've been the target of a federal sting operation. I don't have a book deal but I do have scars from bullet holes that were there before you jerk-offs were born. I was a three-time loser before the law was changed. And do you know what I learned during all that time?

"I learned that the only thing punks like you understand is power. You fear someone that you can't control. Malone here is a goody two shoes. He even puts dollar bills in the collection plate on Sunday. Me? I don't even bother going to church. I've already made my pact with the devil. Now tell us what we want or you're dead."

Franco spoke and his words dripped with disdain. From his rap sheet, I knew that he was a two-time loser before he was expelled from high school. He thought he was tough. He even had the bad sense to laugh. "Which scene from *GOODFELLAS* was that speech from?" He didn't fear Joe Rhino, another bad move.

The stout man, who didn't want to wait until the next life to be Elvis Presley, laughed in kind. Then he stood and extracted a Cuban cigar from his pocket and clipped off the end. He ran it across his tongue and under his nose. He lit it with a gold lighter. I held my breath hoping that the fumes from the gasoline weren't dense enough to go boom.

Slowly, Joe blew smoke in Chuck's face, then Franco's. "You done fucked with the wrong Goodfella." He smiled briefly then stood, and lit the candle with the burning end of the cigar. "Kiss your smartasses good-bye. Come on Malone."

Duct tape was then stretched across each of their mouths so even if they wanted to confess they couldn't. I kept a wary eye on the candle. Joe headed for the back door that led out into the alley.

"Let's go Malone, unless you're wearing asbestos under-wear." I leaned over and snuffed out the candle. "What the fuck are you doing?"

"It's my show. We call the cops."

"You call the cops. I owe you Malone, but this pays us in full. I'm out of here. Fucking pussy. You're going to get yourself killed."

I ignored him and called Tom Otera.

-24-

My plan was simple. First, I called in the cavalry in the person of Tom Otera and his law enforcement posse. It took just over two hours until I was through picking Franco and Chuck out of a line-up. The police lab was also going to try to resurrect some of the videotape that was smashed then soaked in gasoline. It didn't look promising. Joe Rhino had already exited the scene by the time the police showed up. Tom stopped me as I made my way out of the Justice Center.

"Malone, you'd better think about keeping a lower profile. While you were in giving your statement to detectives, Franco and Chuck were sprung."

I laughed, but it wasn't one that was rooted in humor. "What else is new?"

"What are we supposed to do? The only two witnesses are a murder suspect and an ex-mob contract killer," said Tom, pointing out the obvious.

"That's 'alleged' contract killer. This hasn't changed from the time I was a cop. The perps were back on the street before the paperwork was done." I uttered an expletive.

"Relax Malone. You know, all I'm saying is to watch your back."

"Thanks." I was done with the conversation whether he was or not. Watching my back had always been second nature to me in my line of work. I didn't need to be reminded I was target dujour, every dujour. Still, I looked back over my shoulder and checked the rear view mirror a few extra times. I was annoyed, but I wasn't stupid.

Jennifer, the Maitre'd at CUTTER'S, said Joe was out of the office for the day when she answered my third call in an hour. She said that she'd take a message. I didn't leave one. I needed to cool off. Part of me realized that Joe Rhino came up with violence being the first and last solution in his world. But it wasn't in mine. He might even have been right, especially if Franco and Chuck came back to kill me. But it wasn't my lot in life, I'd decided long ago, to be judge, jury and executioner.

He'd get over it eventually. I wasn't about to kill two people to keep a friendship. Besides, it was possible that they could be squeezed enough to roll over onto Gardner Meadows. It was a long shot but for the moment, all I had left were long shots.

With very little direction from me, my rental car turned down the street where Gardner Meadows lived. A very familiar car was parked out in front; in fact I'd taught Tony to drive in it a lifetime ago.

The interval between what appeared to be my parents' second car and my rental remained at two blocks. I let the motor idle, then cut it off. Why would my parents need to see Gardner Meadows? Actually Dad was laid up, so that left Mom. It wasn't Tony or Roberta unless they drove Mom over because they would have used their mini-van. Of course, I was assuming they came of their own free will.

I pulled out my gun, removed and replaced the ammunition clip to check if it was full, fifteen rounds and one in the firing chamber. Then I saw the door to the Meadows' home open. He appeared on the doorstep shaking hands with his departing guest, my sister Christine. I waited until her car was around the corner then honked my horn. Pulling up alongside her, I powered down the passenger side window. Her expression told me that I'd startled her.

"Pull over. We need to talk," I said. I gestured to a nearby parking lot.

She did as instructed, easing into the parking lot. This particular parking lot was of the new wave of what I called, chain malls. A chain drug store, chain grocery store, chain five and dime, and chain pizza shop bordered it. No mega multi-plex movie theaters here, just quick stops and back on the road again.

"Ross, what are you doing? I thought I was going to be carjacked. What's so damned important that you almost ran me off the road?" Cherry apple hued cheeks greeted me when I got out of my car.

I ignored it. "Tell me what you're doing with Gardner Meadows?"

"And I should do this because, why?" she said. "My business with him is none of your business."

"I'm not kidding Chris. I want, no, I probably need to know about you and Meadows."

A cigarette appeared in her lips. Before she could light it, I snatched it and crushed it before her eyes.

"What's going on with you, Ross? You want to talk about honesty? You tell me why your face is plastered on the front page of the *SENTINEL* as a murder suspect in a triple homicide? Let's start with that."

"I was set up. Beyond that, you'll have to trust me," I said.

"Then you trust me." She shoved me back with both hands and got behind the wheel. I reached in and yanked the keys out of the ignition slot.

"I think Gardner Meadows had something to do with Nellie's beating." There it was out in the open. My sister didn't blink an eye.

"Do you have any proof?" she said.

I stared at her. "Not yet. This is where the trust comes in. Now, your turn, Chris" I said and waited.

My sister gripped the wheel tightly, her knuckles went white, and then she pounded both fists on it and got back out of the car, slamming the door shut.

"All right Big Brother, here's your goddamn trust. I was with Gardner Meadows because I was ordered to by my boss."

"Who is?" I said, trying not to let my patience wear too thin. Inside I was embarrassed that she and I had drifted apart that I needed an answer to this question and didn't know from keeping in touch when she moved to the West Coast.

"I work as a segment producer for a syndicated tabloid news show called, 'The Driscoll Report.' Don't you remember? I sent you a press release last year. Don't you read your mail?"

"Sorry Sis. What does Driscoll want from a smug sleaze like Meadows?"

"He's news, Ross. Finding Prince Gregory was plain dumb luck, but it makes him news. The fact that I was here tending to a sick father just puts us a step ahead of the competition. We're thinking about doing a piece on him."

"Did he ask if you were my sister?" I said.

"Yes. And I told him I was. He dropped it after that," she said.

"Am I wasting my breath telling you to stay away from him?" I said. It was a revelation to me that I didn't already know the answer.

She nodded, hugged me, and kissed me on the cheek. Then she retrieved the car keys, got back behind the wheel and drove away. The moment she came out of the Meadows abode, she ceased just being my sister and became, in my eyes, a potential hostage, someone Meadows might hurt to keep me in line. I was in the business—being hurt came with the territory.

My family was off limits.

I took a moment to collect my thoughts and chugged a 16 oz. Pepsi, then let it settle in my stomach for five minutes. I went back to Gardner Meadows' house.

Parking my rental car in the driveway, I blocked his Lincoln Town car in, and left a dent in the fender as a keepsake of my visit. I wasted few steps getting from my car to his front door. I slammed my foot right next to the doorknob and splintered the doorjamb. Pushing it out of the way, I entered the house.

"Meadows! Your presence is required in the drawing room. Now!" My voice boomed through the rooms that were larger on the inside than they appeared on the outside.

There was a general commotion in the back rooms as I waited. It was no surprise to me that Meadows wasn't the first one who appeared in the drawing room. He left that task to one of his bodyguard minions. I spun on my heel and kicked the sacrificial lamb high on the upper cheekbone. Even I was amazed at that move. I hadn't used it in years, shows you what you can accomplish when you're motivated.

The search was on, room by room, more urgent and fervent with each passing moment. My anger could only adequately be measured on a seismograph.

"Meadows!"

"Yes?"

I stopped suddenly. The voice had come from behind me. If he was with guards, they would be armed and they would be pointing their weapons at me. No need for a blood bath. I turned slowly back towards where the voice had assaulted me. Two body-builders picking up walking around money flanked him. Miss Perky, with the skintight smile from the office, was just behind him. Office temps...neither rain nor sleet nor...anyway, she, as far as I knew wasn't part of this.

"Get rid of the beef. Send them out to graze or something. What I have to say is, private?" I said.

He smiled and spread his hands wide open. "I have no secrets from my inner circle."

"Your choice Meadows. Let's start with arson and extortion."

Meadows quickly dismissed his entourage with a wave of his hand. He walked over and closed the door after they left. That left just him and I, but I wasn't naïve enough to believe the room wasn't wired for sight and sound. It didn't matter. I had an agenda and he was going to listen.

"Now, what are these frivolous allegations that you're tossing about? Looking to be sued for slander and libel?"

"Ah, but you forget the truth of said allegations is a defense in such matters. You aren't going to sue me and expose the inner workings of your little protection racket to the scrutiny of the media."

"So what is your point, detective?"

"I caught your Warriors of the Night with their wicks exposed in Adele's shop next to Trask's grocery store. Your days as king of the payoff are over. Better start downsizing your lifestyle and wardrobe. I don't think that they let you have entourages in prison unless you call it a crew, and they are all of the same sex. And unless they own a piece of your butt, of course." I smiled at the image of Gardner Meadows introduced to the harsh realities of the Gray Bar Hotel.

"You're out of your league, Malone. Way out of your fucking league, you asshole. You've got problems of your own, if the papers are correct. And as far as protection? You could use some, or at least your sister." The hook was in deep and he opened his mouth to shove it deeper. I started to boil. "Then, there is your father who just survived open heart surgery. Better be careful

Malone, heart patients can have complications and you can lose them like that." He snapped his fingers for punctuation. "And how is Ms. Archer doing these days?"

He wheezed in and out, simulating the sounds of Nellie on the respirator.

"You've been warned Malone. All bets are off."

I practically ran out the door because if I hadn't, I would have beaten him to death and probably enjoyed every minute of it, at least until my morals returned from vacation.

My pulse raced around my body. My adrenaline level was a billion times my minimum daily requirement. Fingernails dug into my palms when I got into my rental car and smoked the tires leaving the driveway. Stripping the gears, I slammed the accelerator to the floorboards and headed away.

It seemed like I didn't take a breath until I stopped all of the way out in Skaneateles and grabbed a hamburger at an ice cream drive-in place. Their gravel parking area wasn't conducive to roller skating waitresses. Bummer.

A car pulled up behind me, blocking my way out. I tensed and placed my gun under the newspaper on the seat beside me. The driver got out and came to my driver's side window.

"Open the window Malone, it's hot out here," said Lucas Gentero. "Mind if I get in and share your air conditioner?" He didn't wait for me to say no. I moved the paper and put the gun away just as he plopped his bulk onto the passenger seat.

"Hello Lucas. What do you want?"

"What do I want? You asked me for a favor buddy, not the other way around." He began shuffling papers. "Anyway, you asked me to check up on an Anna Law and her website? There wasn't much biographical data on her, but there is a snail mail address where the people can write to her. I wrote it down for you since you don't seem to answer your email."

"Don't tell Bill Gates. No residential address or photo of her?"

"None. And I searched the data base even at the Library of Congress." He handed me the mailing address. It seemed that Anna Law, author of the Laracone newsletter had her mail delivered to the same mail drop from where the ransom demand had been sent.

"Thanks, Lucas. I'll be in touch."

"Ross, two things. I hope your Dad is all right and I'm really sorry about Nellie. If there's anything I can do, you need only ask, my friend." Lucas placed a comforting hand upon my shoulder.

"Thanks, but what you are doing is a big help."

"Okay," he said, getting out of the car and instantly starting to perspire. He made a show of being affected by the heat. It was a performance that was Tony award stuff. I think I almost heard him yell the name, Stella. Lucas flashed a wave, then moved his car and let me be on my way to find Anna Law.

If the bad guys were looking for me, they'd be looking for the Cherokee. Score one for my side. My sightline to the picture window showcasing the lobby, filled with post office boxes of the private mail company, was straight and unencumbered. My binoculars were trained on the box number Lucas had given me. All I had to do was wait until Anna came to pick up her mail.

People came and went all afternoon. None went near the box I was watching. I was trying not to nod off when I sat bolt upright at the unexpected appearance of a familiar face. This face went right into the mail lobby and right to the box I had under surveillance. The contents of the box were collected and were starting to depart with this courier when I took a photo of the face that I had come to know and loathe.

Roger Willoughby, up close and personal.

-25-

Roger Willoughby, the boy who would be pervert, sauntered nonchalantly to the bus stop and waited like he didn't have a care in the world. He was dressed in a white tank top T-shirt that was a size or two larger than necessary but was snug enough against his body for me to see the outline of a gun tucked in the waistband of his muslin pants in the hollow of his back.

The blue on top, white on the bottom Centro bus, sporting advertising billboards running the entire length on both sides, slid up to its appointed spot. Roger Willoughby flashed a cursory glance in every direction except for up and down. Tucking the large manila envelope into which he had stuffed the contents of the mailbox closer to his body, he boarded the bus.

I kept a greater distance than usual behind the bus. It wasn't like a car that was easily lost in heavy traffic. After I memorized the bus number, displayed in large fluorescent numerals for better visual sighting by police helicopters and passengers looking to travel in the most direct route possible, I even let a few more cars get between us. Yet each time it stopped, I made sure those departing didn't include Roger. The destination sign on the front of the bus had said that it was headed for somewhere in the University section. I settled for a lengthy journey of stop and go driving.

Since he knew me, I couldn't board the bus and see if the package had been passed off to a confederate. Of the comings and goings I could observe, Roger still had the mail and I still had him in my sights.

Ten bus stops came and went uneventfully before Roger made a move. I had almost been lulled into believing he was going back to the college campus. The envelope caught my eye. I sat up straighter and paid attention. He checked around to make sure that he wasn't being followed. Satisfied that he had eluded any surveillance, he hopped the next bus that came along going in the opposite direction.

I couldn't see the destination sign in the front of the bus this time, so I had little idea of where we were going until I decided to call the dispatcher. The answer I got was not a surprise, but it was curious. The trip would be a little over a half an hour in duration, if traffic on route 690 West was light.

The bus let him off at a four way stop. He looked around again, less interested than before, but probably out of habit. Satisfied he had eluded any surveillance; he did the homing pigeon thing and returned to the coop. To do so, Roger diagonally crossed a lawn or two to make it his shortest trip between two points.

Knocking once at the door, it opened and he entered with the door closing quickly after him. I didn't see who answered the door, but I knew who lived there, Katharine Greco.

It was time to go detect again. I brought my gun because detecting could sometimes be dangerous work.

The rental car blended in nicely with the sparse traffic in this upscale development. I felt fortunate that I'd thought to upgrade from compact, which had caused me more than a few bruises on my knees. Twice I cruised up and down the street, turning around in convenient driveways, just out of sight of the Greco household. Roger and his host were still inside.

I parked and locked the rental, then headed for the door. My finger leaned against the doorbell, then I dropped to one knee, out of range of the peephole pretending to tie my shoe in case one of the neighbors was watching, but still hiding my face. Sounds of someone approaching the door caught my ear. I hunched up into almost a three-point football lineman's stance. Once again, I hit the doorbell. The voices inside were louder, more anxious, and their profanity was audible as the door opened.

Hitting the door low and hard with my shoulder, I knocked Katharine Greco into and over a nearby table sending her, a floral arrangement and its glass vase crashing onto the floor.

"Sorry," I said. My eyes searched for Roger Willoughby and more importantly, Roger's gun. He appeared in the foyer about fifteen feet from the brick fireplace. I had shifted into full attack mode. He made a move for the gun in his back waistband; my instincts took over. I took three quick steps then wrapped him in a bear hug that lifted him off of his feet. He offered little resistance as I careened the remaining distance, ramming him against the brick fireplace with extreme prejudice.

The wind from his lungs rushed past my face. Before he could regain it, I spun him around and mashed his face against the hard, rough façade. One forearm held his shoulders tight against the wall. I kicked both of his feet back away from the wall, just as I had been taught in police academy training. My other hand lifted his shirt and pulled the gun, I'd seen earlier, full into view.

"I know you must have a permit for this." It disappeared into my jacket pocket then I finished searching him. Once done, I threw him hard, back onto the nearby overstuffed, plush couch. "Stay put, or else. And have the good sense not to ask, or else what."

Katharine Greco's mouth was opened and she was breathing through it as fast as she could, I started towards her, fully intent upon searching her for weapons. Suddenly, I realized that all that was concealing her was a see through slip, now less one strap, probably torn in her tumble when I barreled in here. The Oriental style kimono that had accompanied her ensemble was now soaking up flower water amidst the broken glass.

"Have a seat on the couch, Katharine. You, boy toy number two and I are going to have a heart to heart." She looked at Roger, then back at me. I was through playing games. "Either sit down, or I will sit you down."

Roger started to get up to protest and I kicked the coffee table into his shins and he recoiled in pain, but he did sit down. She went to his aid. That's what Donna Reed would have done; though I doubt she would have only been wearing a slip at the time.

"You get the hell out of my house, or I'll call the police," she said. It was almost hard to understand her between the tears and the sniffling.

"Don't make idle threats. You threaten the cops. I say, go ahead and call them. I give them Roger's unlicensed gun, and they cart him off for a year in a state prison because that's the law, no first offender or juvenile status for this no longer a kid. He'll have a record and he'll be in the system, but what's more important? The system will be in him. That unspoiled, almost, youth that makes you pant quicker than a Nora Roberts' novel won't come out so unspoiled. Still want to call the cops?"

She lowered her head and her eyes. I had browbeaten her into submission, a trait I had cultivated in all my years as a private investigator.

"Now, let's start at the beginning," I said. "You both better pay attention or I'll call the cops myself. Where's the envelope that Roger brought?"

Katharine produced it and I took it. Dumping the contents onto the tabletop, it consisted solely of correspondence addressed to Anna Law and her Laracone newsletter.

"Now, I may not act like I'm playing with a full deck most of the time, but I can figure out an anagram when I see one. Anna Law is Walanna spelled backwards. Whose idea was that?"

Roger looked at Katharine then back at the floor. He needed her strength, and she was more than willing to give it.

"Actually, it was Gregory's idea."

"So he thought up running a computer website espousing the return of the monarchy to Laracone." They nodded. "Why?"

"Gregory believes that his father should return to the throne of Laracone to the Walanna family, that he should never have abdicated in the first place."

"Doesn't the little prince believe in democracy?" The thud inside my head was deafening. "The Little Prince, Machievelli. Of course he doesn't believe in democracy because a king has no one to answer to, but himself. I guess that we should be glad that his father didn't give him *MEIN KAMPF*. Was the kidnapping Gregory's idea?"

"No," said Katharine. I gave her an exasperated look and started to pace. The framed pictures in the wooden, glass-enclosed hutch in the dining room were arranged, obviously by the look of the hairstyles, chronologically. I could see Katharine grow up, frame by frame. I pulled out one of the photos and showed it to her.

"This you in the photo?"

"Yes. My husband and I took a trip to the Grand Canyon that year."

"That's him in the photo with you?" I said.

"Yes."

"And that's your vehicle in the background?" A VW bus, no front-end damage in this photo, but there was the last time I saw it.

"Yes?"

Roger has searched high and low and found his nerve some-where. "Get off her back. She told you what you wanted to know. Why do you care anyhow?"

"Maybe because I am on the hook for three murders that I did not commit. Maybe because I hate being played for a fool by a kid with visions of grandeur." My mind was racing about how cruel I really wanted to be. I tossed Katharine Greco a nearby afghan and she swirled it around her shoulders and upper torso with a flour-ish. I sat back down, still staring at the photo.

Roger was gathering nerve. That might be a bad omen. "So, now you can get out."

I didn't take my eyes from the photo in my reply. "Roger, shut the hell up or I'll hurt you so your little angel...What's her name? The fifteen year old you were sleeping with?"

Katharine Greco's eyes grew wide, then narrowed into a glare. Nothing quite like a teacher scorned, unless it's a private detective scorned.

"A fifteen year old? You've been letting me...Why you sonuvabitch!" Katharine leapt over to Roger and slapped him across the face harder than I would have, but without the accuracy. I pulled her off and tried not to laugh as she got in a couple of well-aimed kicks at his genitals before I got her far enough away. Roger was screaming at her.

"You dumb ass. I was doing you a favor, letting you have me," screamed Roger. "Why in the hell do you think I'd want an old bitch like you for, when I can have all of the young sweet stuff I want?" I turned and raised my hand. Obediently, Roger shut his mouth. I held Katherine's slender wrists tightly as I imparted my new found information.

"Katharine, listen to me."

"Let me go," she said fighting to free herself. I tightened my grip.

"First, you settle down." She stopped struggling and nodded. I still didn't let go. "Katharine, there were three bodies in the abandoned factory when the police found me. Two were identified as Ghiamin Lora and Deidre Schulery. The third man was unidentified, the man in this photograph. I'm afraid your husband's dead."

"You're lying. He's not dead." I stared back at her. Slowly, she crumbled before my eyes. I pulled her wrists and her towards me and hugged her tightly. She was screaming and crying at the same time. I remembered it all too well from the time I witnessed Molly and Christopher being killed.

The time went by slowly. I let her cry herself out, then dry her tears and start the cycle of grief all over again. On the fifth time around, her tears had degenerated into dry heaves of sorrow. The floor was littered with a mountain of used tissues nearing the arm of the couch.

"Okay, now it's time to tell me all of it. I didn't kill your husband or the others, but I'll need your help to find out who did. Please. So was it Gregory's idea for the fake kidnapping?"

With all of her dreams unraveling right before her puffy, bloodshot eyes, Katharine Greco stared off into the distance. Pulling the afghan closer to her, she tried to fight off the chill of resignation, of reality.

I prodded. "Katharine."

"Yes. He set up the whole thing. He's a very bright child." I might have substituted the words conniving, despicable and in serious need of a permanent attitude adjustment. Bright just didn't make that list. "The plan was for him to get his bodyguards to take him to McDonald's on campus. When Grace left, the van arrived and mashed into their car with the diplomatic plates. When Jacob ran out, Eugene..." She sniffled and teetered again on hysteria.

"Eugene, the late lamented husband?"

She nodded, her Donna Reed do looking more like it belonged to Rex or Oliver Reed. "He collected Gregory and left by a side exit where I was waiting in my car."

"Who drove the van? Was that you, Roger? Were you the wheel man?"

"No, I didn't have anything to do with the actual kidnapping. All I did was maintain the website."

"I'll bet. Well Katharine, does Roger speak with forked tongue?"

Eventually, she shook her head. "Not this time. Ghiamin was driving the van. I took Gregory to a motel. I don't remember the name but we went to Bungalow 16. Deidre was there. We stayed there a few days until the headlines made it unsafe, that's when we moved to the factory where you found him."

"Tell me about the ransom. Was that the prince's idea as well?"

"Yes. He wanted to repay us for our help. He knew that his grandmother would go along, especially if it would make the father look bad."

I arched my eyebrows in an exaggerated fashion. "Bad blood between Grandma and the monarchy?"

"In spades," said Katharine; her voice was now taking on a harsh tone like the difference between aluminum foil—light and shiny, and a molten pot of nickel slag. "Gregory loved them both, but that wouldn't do for Emily Hughes. She poisoned the boy into believing that his father was the cause of his mother's death. Now he thinks that the best avenue to revenge is to succeed President Walanna as the ruler of Laracone."

I continued her thought. "And a 13 year old is too young to run for president, but not be appointed king if the father abdicates?" Katharine Greco nodded. The tracks down her cheeks now merely echoed dried memories. "Cute. Kill the thing that Benjamin Walanna loved more than his mother—the intoxication of absolute power. The boy learned well."

Roger spoke up. "We've told you everything. Now, let us go." His nose had mushroomed into a bulbous and hideous rainbow of muted soreness in Technicolor.

"You didn't tell me who killed those three people in the factory. As far as you both knew, Gregory was still there when the murders occurred?"

"Yes," they said in unison.

"Any ideas who the killer is? Did anybody know about the money beyond the deceased and those present in this room?"

"Emily Hughes," offered Katharine, only too willing to cast aspersions in other directions.

"Would she kill three other people to save $350,000 and put the boy at risk? Then again, the boy wouldn't be at risk if she hired the killer, to tie up loose ends while making sure the boy was unharmed. The boy wouldn't tell because he was the original mastermind. So who would she trust with such a secret? Just for the record, where were you when I was having my skull air-conditioned, Roger?"

His head almost swiveled around 360 degrees. "Me? What the fuck would I be doing killing anybody? I was with Katharine. Tell him Katharine, honey. Tell Malone we were together when those people were murdered."

"A moment ago I was 'old bitch Katharine.' Now it's 'Katharine, honey.' Jesus Christ, you've got balls Roger. It's a shame you couldn't keep them to yourself." She sighed as he silently prayed to whomever he worshipped that she would bail his good for nothing posterior out. "He's right Malone. We were together at the time of the killings. I knew Eugene would be picking up the ransom and that he was going to stay the night with the other three. I decided to have Roger spend the night."

I stood and slowly began working the feelings back into my legs by pacing one step at a time. "That's all well and good Katharine, but it does create a problem. You are his alibi, but, then again, he is yours. Convenient."

The gasp in the room was audible and all Katharine Greco's. "You can't seriously believe I could murder three people I know in cold blood?"

"Maybe not you alone, but you and the boy toy here might do a mixed doubles act."

"There's proof Malone." Katharine stole a look at Roger. "There's proof we were here, together."

"Such as?"

"A tape, a videotape of our lovemaking. I made it with a camera in the mirror over the dresser overlooking the bed. The date and time are on the tape." Roger's mouth was hanging open. It was his best side.

"It's original, I'll give you that," I said.

"You're an asshole Malone," said Roger.

"I'd be more impressed with that Roger, if I thought you could spell it. Now people, here we are. I have the mother of all headaches. Please don't interrupt me."

Roger reached out for the hand of Katharine who gave it, synergy in action.

"I'm going to call the police in the person of Deputy Tom Otera. You will each tell him exactly what you told me, word for word, adverb for adverb, dependent clause upon dependent clause. And Roger? His 'or else' is just as bad as mine."

I walked over to the phone and dialed. As I waited for the dispatcher to pick up, the throbbing at my neck was not the stitches sewn in there, but suspicion reborn.

Katharine and Eugene Greco, Roger Willoughby, Emily Hughes, Ghiamin Lora, and Deidre Schulery were all part of the plot, but something was missing, or rather someone. What better co-conspirator than a surrogate mother?

Another piece fell into place.

-26-

If you asked the American Medical Association, I'm sure that they would not recommend swallowing pain medication with the remaining contents of a bottle of warm Pepsi. However the cliché, any port in a storm applied here. I was sitting in the parking lot of Mercy Hill Hospital, trying to muster the courage to go inside. I needed God to be my co-pilot, but He was probably thinking that He helps them who help themselves. We were having a battle of wills, I was sure to lose.

After my skull session with Roger and Katharine, I needed to clear the decks before I put myself in harm's way, yet again. Unfortunately, the main task at hand gripped my soul with the ferocity of a demon. I knew why I had never gone to medical school. I never wanted the weight of being the one who made the ultimate decision on life or death. Now, to be true to my friend, I had no choice.

There were other things I needed to be doing, but what if one of them killed me in the process and Nellie had to suffer the indignity of someone who didn't honor her friendship by being with her in the final moments. No, that would not be right.

"Malone! Do you know how hard you are to catch up with?" said Lucas.

"Lucas, what is so important that you have to scare the living? Anyway, what do you want?"

"It's not what I want, pal o'mine. It's what you asked for. Remember that you asked for Gardner Meadows' money person? It's none other than Martha Dowd Patterson, of the newspaper Pattersons?"

"How much is she a benefactor?"

"Last donation list I saw, she had two commas and a high seven digits."

"That's a hefty chunk of change to restore law and order to a middle class upstate city," I said.

"Maybe Martha doesn't want him to stop there," he said.

"Good point. Stand back, I'm leaving." I kicked over the engine and put it in reverse.

"Need someone to ride shotgun, Malone?" His face was wide-eyed and genuinely concerned.

"No."

I left the hospital parking lot with unfinished business, but an excuse too good to pass up. As for getting killed? I'd be careful, of course.

The Martha Dowd Patterson estate surrounded three quarters of her own man made waterfront property and was as deep as three or four football fields, until you got to the main house. It took a good fifteen minutes to drive from the highway to the south portico. A valet met me. I gave him the keys to the rental car and followed a second valet into the house and on into a tremendous dining hall where Ringling Brothers could have placed their three rings with room to spare.

"You must be Mr. Malone," said the voice at the distant end of the grand ballroom. As the voice approached, the body took shape and I recognized her from the photos on Gardner Meadows' wall.

She extended a bejeweled hand. I accepted it and she had the good grace not to count the jewels upon its return.

"Hello Mrs. Patterson. Thank you for seeing me on such short notice."

"You're welcome. You told my assistant that you had something important to impart about Gardner Meadows and the City Security Association?"

"Yes. As their chief benefactor, I believe that you need to know what is going on there," I said.

"Follow me into the library."

Our mini-procession moved from the room that had to have been an aircraft hangar in its previous life into a more ornate, though smaller library. The room enveloped me in history. I could picture Winston Churchill sending cables to Roosevelt as Hitler moved on Paris. The door closed behind us, though neither of us did it. It served as a reminder that we were not alone.

Martha "of the three names" Patterson sat behind the oak desk that dominated this half of the room. All that the other half needed to make it complete was a Plexiglas backboard and rim ten feet above the ground.

"Please state your case, Mr. Malone. You have my undivided attention."

I felt like I should begin with, "May it please the court." Instead, I went up to the plate to get my cuts.

"Could you tell me your interest in Gardner Meadows?"

She lifted her chin to its highest point and not a wrinkle appeared. Martha had been nipped and tucked to perfection. She was a vision of ivory loveliness in an understated business suit and a combination Celeste Holm/Mona Lisa smile. Her hair was cut stylishly and pure white. On her it looked good. The magazine covers she had graced over her lifetime numbered in the triple digits. Maybe I could ask for an autograph before I left.

"Mr. Meadows and I support the same causes, same objectives—law, order, a place where decent people can thrive based on achievement, rather than skin color or quotas."

"That's a mouthful."

"You also know, or you wouldn't be here, that I am the biggest contributor to his City Security Association. Now, what is it that bothers you?" Her words came across as a challenge.

"Got a VCR?" She pointed to a wall unit where the cabinet doors retracted with the touch of a finger. On my way over to the Patterson spread, I took a chance and stopped at the police crime lab and collected a copy of Adele's surveillance tape that had been stomped and mangled. The images had been enhanced electronically via computers. In some spots even 3-D glasses couldn't have helped. I was warned that the images would be fuzzy at best and the sound would be non-existent. I brought it anyhow. My point was that you didn't need x-ray vision to see Franco and Chuck readying "The Apothecary" for a major burn. The tape ended. I ran it a second time to the same silent audience that was there from the beginning.

"What was the purpose of showing me this tape?" Her gaze focused on me, almost daring me to answer. I didn't break out into a sweat.

"To show you how your millions are being misused. Those two, upstanding citizens you saw committing felony arson and attempted murder are members of your vaunted Warriors of the Night."

Her head slowly moved from right to left, then back again. "I saw nothing on the tape that would indicate that to be true. They did not identify themselves as such or wear clothing representing their status. I'm sure that if you talked with Mr. Meadows about these people, he would say, if they are guilty, they acted totally on their own without direction or approval from the Warriors' hierarchy."

"I'm sure he would, but the fact remains that earlier that day, they tried to shake down the sweet old lady shopkeeper who owned the store. She refused and this was the result. She'll testify to that." It was a bluff and Martha Dowd Patterson called it.

"Do you think the court would really believe an old woman who wishes out of the association, pushed into lying by a two bit private eye looking for a reason his partner was beaten almost to death? It is hardly what you would call, 'bloody glove type' evidence. And if you try to associate this alleged act of violence to either Mr. Meadows or myself, I shall sic several law firms upon your license, bank account, and whatever reputation that you might have left." She paused, then added a punchline. "And then, I will go after your loved ones."

"Gee whiz, good thing you don't have any Kryptonite here, or I'd really be in trouble." She held her sweet smile dipped in brass and if she had possessed male genitalia they would be brass as well. In a fair fight, she could take Roger Willoughby and maybe even Laila Ali, daughter of the legend. "I'm sure that you have heard I'm under suspicion for three murders. What makes you think that you won't be number four if I snap?"

Martha Dowd Patterson laughed, her gaze rock steady, her posture stayed ramrod straight. "Two reasons Malone. First, there's been a high powered rifle pointed at your head eversince you entered my home. Nothing personal, of course, but you **are** wanted for murder."

"Of course."

"Secondly, I have a .357 magnum revolver, fully loaded centimeters away from my hand. You would quickly become the largest clay pigeon I've ever seen. Let me show you something."

With a flick of her finger again, two large panels, recessed into the bookcase, disappeared back into the wall around it. The process took barely more than 45 seconds. It revealed a map of the continental United States plus Alaska and Hawaii with at least a hundred little colored pushpins scattered throughout, mostly near major cities.

"Behold the future, Malone. Each pin represents another step towards bringing America back to the law and order values that made us great as a country."

"You're going to franchise the Warriors of the Night?"

"Exactly. So far, we've had interest or ongoing plans to place a Warriors group in every major city in the continental United States, Alaska, and Hawaii. Then on up into Canada."

"Didn't the founding fathers reject the idea of a national police force even though brown shirts and swastikas are always in demand as a nifty fashion statement?" I said, thoroughly unimpressed.

"Go ahead, mock us now, but you will fear us soon enough. Making those responsible for the tearing down of the moral fiber of our country pay a price for their actions is directly from the Bible."

"And those who disagree with your eye for an eye philosophy?"

She smirked as if the answer was apparent to anyone with an I.Q. "Why, they'd better get out of the way. The Warriors of the Night are no different than Ethan Allan's Green Mountain Boys hiking off to defend their freedom or the Tuskegee Airmen flying off to defend the American way of life. Do you know what the only difference is?"

"The battleground is here."

"Exactly."

"How does extortion fit into your plans?" I said.

"You have no proof. Besides, some would just say that we must employ the same tactics as our enemies to defeat them."

I retrieved the tape and shook her free hand.

"Thank you for your time. I just came by to see if you were involved in this mess and if so, how deeply?"

"And did you?"

I left without reply.

The beeps on the monitor almost lulled me to sleep like the steady beat of a metronome. I sat in a metal folding chair with a brown padded backrest, holding Nellie's hand, looking as far inward as I had to, for the strength to help her as she put it, "one last time." Upon my return to Mercy Hill Hospital, I had them page Colleen Powers. She told me she would be there directly with the proper documentation for me to sign and the proper number and type of witnesses needed for the closure Nellie had asked for.

"Hi Big Brother," said a familiar voice. I looked up and saw Chris and Anthony standing just outside the Intensive Care cubicle. "We thought you could use some moral support."

My eyes filled with tears I thought were long since shed and I moved to them. Hugging Chris as tightly as her breathing would allow, I shook Tony's hand. I didn't want to let go. I was grasping for any excuse to evade the inevitable.

"How is she?" said Tony, showing concern of one fellow human being for another.

I shook my head. "Colleen Powers will be here any moment to do the rest of the paperwork and…" The words would not come out.

Now my sister was crying and digging into her purse for the ever-present pack of tissues.

"How are you holding up?"

"I'm okay," I said, but even though they knew differently, they allowed me that lie. I pulled out a business card and wrote down Tom Otera's number. "Sis, call this deputy, mention my name and he might give you a scoop on the prince's kidnapping, but if he does, you have to hold it until I say so. Agreed?"

Chris took it. "Agreed, and thanks Ross. I know this might not be a great consolation, but try to think of the good times."

It was good advice because soon all I would have left would be those memories. "You're right Chris. I remember the first time I showed Nellie how to do videotape surveillance. She positioned the camera wrong and when she came to my office to show me the tape, we saw three hours of the back of her head. Of course, she blamed it on the videotape recorder."

I stopped. Videotape recorder. Videotape recorder. It was among the list of items that Nellie Archer had purchased prior to the Trask surveillance. If she had remembered everything I'd taught her, she would have remembered to store the recorder in a separate place away from the camera, in case it was discovered, then there was a back up. It might still be there.

"I have to go."

"Ross, we'll stay with you. You don't have to go through this alone."

"Tell Colleen I'll be back," I said as I pushed my way into the stairwell and careened down the stairs, powered by the adrenaline rush and the possibilities my mind were racing towards at the speed of justice.

-27-

Slamming down the trunk of my rental car with my free hand, I quickly directed the bolt cutters in the other hand to lay waste to the link chain, still wrapped around the wrought iron fencing blocking my entrance to the grocery store of George Trask, who had been conspicuously absent as of late. If I found what I was looking for inside, I would soon be looking for Mr. Trask in earnest.

Scratch one chain. My set of lock picks made easy work of the two dead bolts, the former marine had installed. I went straight for the camera stand where the camera had been ripped from its wires. My search began there. I followed the wire that had been tethered to the camera and was the connection to the videotape recorder down the wall, around the baseboard and back into the cooler.

Nellie had spared no expense, something else I had taught her. The client was paying for quality. Treat each dollar that you spent as if it were coming out of your own pocket, because if you screw up, it will, in the guise of future revenue that you fail to get because your reputation is shot.

Nellie Archer was a professional, just like her great grandfather, Miles. Twenty-five feet of video cable later, I found the videotape recorder inside the cooler in the bottom case of a stack of Molson Golden Ale. The false bottomed crate was reinforced with wood and carried a large battery pack in case of a power failure.

The power switch was still in the on position, but the battery had long since expired. I got the tape out and returned home.

Usually when I'd plop myself in front of a TV set, I'd do so with a small snack. Susan, in her own inimitable way, said my version of a small snack would make sure that the Farm Belt had a very plentiful Christmas that year. It occurred to me that she always was a little faint of heart when I ate.

There would be no snack today. I sauntered up the stairs, resisting the urge to take them two at a time. My hope was building as to what would be on tape. But what if I was wrong? What if it was blank? Or fuzzy or full of middle-aged women on double coupon day? I pushed it from my mind.

God owed Nellie this one.

My home office, a converted spare bedroom on the second floor, had been turned into a high tech state of the art command center with a computer, fax, laser printer, speaker phone, and at least three versions of Super Mario. I removed the tape of last night's Yankees game and replaced it with Nellie's surveillance tape.

I pressed the play button on the remote control and held my breath. The first image that came alive, on my 30" television set with picture in picture, was an extreme close-up of Nellie Archer's nose. Her voice made the heartache I felt Sensurround.

"Please little camera, Aunt Nellie needs you to be good. I need to show Uncle Ross I'm a big girl and can handle big cases all by myself." She giggled and wrinkled her lightly freckled nose. "You take care of your father, Ross. I'll hold the fort until you get back."

The next words I heard were a date, time and place surveillance ID. Then silence. I didn't fast forward the tape. I needed to see what Nellie saw, hear what she heard. My eyes were transfixed on the screen. The little amount of breathing I managed to do was shallow and infrequent. I couldn't have any distractions.

As the tape wound down, my hope for seeing what had happened faded in direct proportion. Suddenly, I heard what she had that night.

They came in the back door, no sound of a lock being picked, a crowbar being used to jimmy the door, or brute force bashing it in. In all probability, they had possessed a key. Four dark suited figures came in led by Franco and Chuck. Self confidence reigned supreme—masks or disguises of any kind were non-existent. Picking them out of a line-up or photo array would be a piece of cake. What sparse, non-literate communication passed between them, centered on how they were going to trash the store and make sure that George Trask got the message. Nobody messed with the association. One of the musclemen limbered up by smashing his naked wooden ax handle onto the countertop near the lone cash register. Sweeping it, with malice aforethought, the length of the counter, he cleared away a brass rack with monogrammed key chains, two lottery ticket dispensers of the scratch-off variety and three glass canisters of what used to be called penny candy. All went crashing to the floor.

Muffled voices surrounded a high pitch female shriek. Sounds of a struggle were clearly audible then two of the intruders dragged Nellie Archer into view. The defiant spitfire clawed and kicked at her captors but there was four of them and only one of her. For the moment, they had the upper hand.

I leaned closer to the TV set, straining to hear. Franco seemed to be in charge. Someone handed him Nellie's wallet. He rummaged through it, pocketing the cash and credit cards.

"Don't plan on using the plastic, Einstein. They are maxxed to the limit."

Franco then pulled out her PI license. "So, you're Nellie Archer."

"And you're not," said Nellie, occasionally straining against their hold, always testing. Looking for an escape route and finding none.

"Did you search her?" The lack of a quick response satisfied Franco's curiosity. "Hold her." Their grips tightened as he stepped forward. Finger by finger he took off his leather gloves. Then he started with her neck; his eyes locked onto hers. Deliberately, his hands probed and fondled, searched and violated. They lingered on her breasts and removed her belt. He handed her gun to a subordinate. They used the belt to bind her hands. His mouth went next to her ear. "Ever had a real man?"

"Since there isn't a real man here, I'll bet you think that you'll do." Franco slapped his hand against her face. My fingernails dug into the arms of my chair. I felt the covering split beneath the pressure. "What are you going to do with me?"

At first, it seemed the question had Franco stumped. He mumbled to one of his buddies who then left the view of the camera. A long nine-inch switchblade was extracted and the shiny blade was popped out, then he slit Nellie's shirt from the neck down to her waist. With a short, sharp stroke, the tip of his blade sliced through the elastic of her bra, snapping the cups apart and exposing Nellie to one and all. Nellie didn't flinch.

"I bet the last place they had you didn't let you have sharp objects," she said.

Franco grabbed her pants, jamming his fingers into the top of her waistband and jerking her forward against him.

"I'll show you a sharp object." The sound of her zipper descending was painfully clear.

"Keep it in your pants, Franco," said the barely post-pubescent voice of Gardner Meadows, who strutted in like a prison guard from COOL HAND LUKE. "Hello Ms. Archer. Do you know who I am?"

Nellie considered this for a moment. "The short answer is asshole. Want me to elaborate?" Meadows nodded, smiling all the while. "Beyond that, you are the leech bleeding these merchants dry. They pay protection money, but the only protection they get is from you and your fashionable juvenile delinquents. George Trask had had enough. He went to the cops who eventually blew him off. He went to Ross Malone. Ross gave him my name."

"How lucky for you," said Meadows. "Anything else?"

"In addition to vandalism, conspiracy and extortion, I can now add assault and battery. You aren't stupid enough to make it murder."

Gardner contemplated an answer, still smiling, and still coiled to strike.

"So, it's like the slogan from the commercials, 'No fear'."

"You are obviously what passes for brains among these Neanderthals," said Nellie, sensing the tide was turning in her favor.

"Well I have a slogan too, Ms. Archer. No witnesses."

Without warning, Gardner Meadows snatched the ax handle, wound up like Mark McGwire and swung. The wooden club hit Nellie a glancing but powerful blow to her skull, putting her lights out instantly. One better aimed swing crushed in her ribs. Skin and blood splattered all involved. They recoiled in horror, letting her crumple to the floor, nothing more than a use once and throw away human being.

"Make her look like a rape or mugging victim, strip her down and get over on her, no wait. You guys might not be able to spell DNA, but the cops can. Make them work to identify her, if you catch my drift, then dump her in the Dumpster. She'll be dead before the next pick-up. But clean up this place, just in case some-body comes to look for her. And get rid of the damn video camera and that tape in it."

Meadows wiped his hands on Chuck's back, then left. I watched them strip Nellie, then beat her until she more resembled a Muppet in a garbage disposal than a person. Then they dragged her out the back door and out of the view of the camera. The last thing that I saw was Chuck climbing up towards the video cam-era. The screen went dark.

I lost it.

I grabbed my autographed '99 World Series baseball, spun on my heel and threw my best fastball which knocked my favorite framed photo of Susan and I off the shelf, shattering the glass as it met the floor. Both hands then grabbed the edge of the desktop, ready to overturn it. I stopped. This wasn't the way to get revenge. I knew better. I slumped back into my chair, breathing as if air, and lots of it, would make the pain go away. It didn't.

Miss Perky was back at her desk when I arrived at Gardner Meadows' office. I didn't break stride as I headed straight for his door.

"Stay put pumpkin, you don't want any part of this," I said, opening the door marked, private, closing it quickly behind me to stifle curiosity.

Meadows was behind his desk looking over his computer print-outs. Franco and Chuck were his ever-present gargoyles on either side of the desk. I slammed a copy of the surveillance tape from Trask's store onto the desk top before him.

"What's this Malone?"

"Something that would make Jerry Springer blush. It's a video-tape from a surveillance camera in George Trask's store showing you and your band of merry men assaulting Nellie Archer then disposing of her body in a Dumpster waiting for her to die."

Chuck stood, ready to take offense, itching to exact retribution. "He's lying Mr. Meadows. I took the tape myself." His voice trailed off as he realized what he had just said, and even before I mentioned the word Miranda. Then again I was a private detective; I didn't have to read him his rights.

"Shut the hell up Chuck. Malone, if you had real evidence then you wouldn't be here. You'd be talking to the cops. As a murder suspect, you still have no credibility, do you? I'll bet if there really is such a tape, it's fuzzy, out of focus and certainly not admissible in court."

"What about the court of public opinion, Meadows? Or maybe just the opinion of Martha Dowd Patterson?"

"Martha told me that you came to see her. As for this?" He gestured towards the tape. "I'll bet she would say it is just the cost of doing business, protecting her investment so to speak. Is there anything else, Malone?"

I wanted to bring my Reggie Jackson model bat and imprint "Louisville Slugger" on his vital organs. I wanted to hurt him so bad that when he walked he'd sound like a bag of plastic Lego toys. I wanted him not to see it coming until the very last excruciating second in the same way Nellie did. I wanted Gardner Meadows to start looking over his shoulder.

"I take care of my own, Meadows. And Nellie Archer was…one of mine."

A side trip to a friend who made copies of videotapes for his friends for a small handling fee netted me six more copies of the surveillance tape. I mailed the original to myself at the office where from there; I'd stash it in my safety deposit box. One would go to Shelly, another to Tom Otera, another to Felicity Charles just because, one to Delilah James, a former protégé in Washington D.C., and the final videotape I'd send out would go to Jude Meyers, a former city police detective, now with the State Police in their criminal investigative division. These would all be sent the minute I could prove the rest of the story.

Adele from "The Apothecary" might testify, but I needed much more than that. I probably needed to find George Trask, but was he even still alive?

I was exhausted. I got home, made a sandwich but tossed it out without a bite. The images from the Trask videotape were sickeningly fresh in my mind. My appetite had gone south for the evening.

Pressing the button on the answering machine led me to find at least five messages from Susan of concern, support and unconditional love. When this was all over, no matter how it turned out, Susan and I would go away and she would help me find closure. Susan loved me because of who I was, not because of what I could do for her. I learned early on that relationships took work, even the successful ones.

After this, I would talk at length but for now, I had to go it alone. She would be a liability in this situation, though I doubt she would see it in the same light. Secretly, I think she harbored delusions of being my Nora Charles. Sue Abilene certainly had the legs for it.

The other message was from Gwen Brolin saying that she was going out of town for the weekend and would call me when she got back. I kicked myself for stalling on Nellie's request. My mouth decided to yawn, long, and loud. I needed to sleep.

The hot shower worked like sleeping pills for me. I pulled the covers back on the bed, lamented the fact that Susan wasn't there to hold me, slipped into my sweatpants only then tumbled face forward onto the bed. I set the CD player to Andrew Lloyd Webber's *PHANTOM OF THE OPERA* with a sleep timer engaged. It was low enough to lull me further into sleep. I didn't lull though. It was a direct free fall from consciousness.

If I had dreams during the time I was asleep, I didn't remember them when I started to return to the present dimension. An acrid smell invaded my senses. I rubbed a hand against my nose. The aroma remained. I coughed, sneezed, and started choking. I preferred the music or alarm to wake me up, not my gag reflex.

My eyes were watering, as I blinked mightily, as I opened them to a bedroom full of smoke. I could hear the roar of flames from the hallway. I fell onto the floor and, remembering my elementary school training, was fully prepared to crawl down the stairs and out the front door far below the gathering clouds of smoke crowding out the remaining oxygen.

When I got to the hallway, I saw quickly that the fire had started downstairs. I rolled over onto my back to catch whatever breath I could and saw the smoke detector cover hanging down from the ceiling at the top of the staircase. The batteries were gone.

Back into the bedroom, I kicked the door closed behind me. I heard the sirens in the distance but didn't know if I could hold out long enough for them to get a ladder to my second floor window. My mind went through the escape plans I'd had for the townhouse. The fire escape ladder had been torn off last winter and still hadn't been replaced. I needed a quicker way out.

I dragged my New York Yankees' wall hanging down onto the floor and crawled on my stomach over into the bathroom. I heard a series of small explosions on the first floor below. This was not a good omen. I soaked the cloth under the bathtub faucet. Then, I splashed as much of me as I could with water. Using the clothes hamper to steady me, I got to my feet, sucked in the last available air and opened the bathroom door.

At a dead run, I flung the dripping wet wall hanging over my head and shoulders and jumped through the plate glass windows off my master bedroom. It was only two floors down and I was in good shape.

What was the worst that could happen?

-28-

The moment my irresistible force hit the immovable object, I knew what had happened. My short-lived flight from the second floor window, intended for the nearby bushes and floral garnishes around the townhouse entrance instead wound up on the top of my rental car.

The crater I made in the roof also smashed all of the windows in one fell swoop. But I was still alive. The fire trucks and paramedics had arrived. They lowered me from the car rooftop on down to the ground to see what the hell kind of idiot uses a car roof for a trampoline.

My state of alert faded to black intermittently as I was being treated. Words like precautionary X-rays, overnight for observation and what the hell was he thinking, came into my head, leaving after the briefest of moments. They sat me on the back bumper of the rescue truck. The hubbub of making sure the fire didn't spread was way too loud. I pulled their blanket over my head. Someone walked over to where I was. I saw a pair of shoes.

"Malone, how are you doing?"

"I'd know those spit polished boots anywhere. What did you find, Tom?"

"Burn pattern, accelerant, batteries out of the smoke detectors downstairs and upstairs. Arson seems a safe bet. Any thoughts on whom?" he said.

"Alphabetically or chronologically? Not right now, Tom. I'll come in later and give you whatever I have. Just not right now."

"Okay," said my friend in a tone that I found a bit too impatient for my taste. "Don't make it too much later. Thanks for the heads up on the Greco woman and Roger Willoughby. I think they both know more than they are saying. Anyway, don't make it too much later, Malone. Do you have a place to stay?"

"He'll stay with me."

Tom Otera stared at Joe Rhino. They had been on opposite sides of the law and order question more often than not. Each thought they still were.

"Watch your back, Ross," said Deputy Otera, leaving. He brushed shoulders with Joe on his departure. Neither gave an inch.

"I hope it was something I said," said Joe. "Come on, Malone. You can stay in the spare room at the club."

"Do you have room service?"

"Don't push it."

A fire marshal came over carrying a cell phone. "Mr. Malone, there is a call for you."

"Malone," I said after a smoke-induced cough.

"I'm so sorry I can't bring the marshmallows."

"I'll bet you are Meadows. Show your face and I'll make sure that you are the first human shish-kabob."

"Feeling the heat, are we? Of course, my services or those of the Warriors of the Night are at your disposal to find whoever set fire to your home."

"No thanks."

"You might want to reconsider. We did find the prince and we could use the publicity."

"Keep your mutant Boy Scouts away from me, and out of my way, Meadows."

"No!" he shouted. "You stay out of our way."

Gardner Meadows broke the connection. I watched the last of the flames get extinguished. The firemen would board up the downstairs windows to discourage looters. I left with Joe.

The next morning I started by leaving a message with Susan's answering service because I wanted to avoid talking directly with her for now. She would hear the message and let me do what I needed to do. I would most certainly do the same for her. My next phone call set up a mid morning appointment. Once that was done I sat down to breakfast with Joe.

Several strips of crispy bacon, scrambled eggs, toast or bagels and home fries were before each of us. We ate in silence. As I finished my orange juice, Joe slid a Glock 9-mm handgun and two extra ammunition clips over to me.

"Thanks."

"You'd do the same for me."

"I'd do what I thought was best."

"Whatever," he shrugged. "When are you going to the hospital?"

"Gwen's out of town." I thought that was a good answer.

"I know. I sent her. She needed the break. When, Malone?"

I had tried to forget that glaring omission in my to do list. "Afternoon, right after lunch."

"You're thinking of lunch with everything you just ate?"

"Hey, I'm a growing boy."

Joe Rhino said he would stop by my office and retrieve the package I'd sent there. He'd keep it in his safe until I was ready for it. He gave me the keys to his car, saying that he'd use Jennifer's Subaru for a few days. I thanked him, then went for my appointment.

"Thank you for seeing me," I said as Grace Rusinko poured Pepsi over ice chips in cut crystal goblets. She handed me one. "I need to speak with Prince Gregory."

"I'm afraid that is impossible. President Walanna has forbidden any contact except for his doctor and family. I know I said that I'd help you Malone, but don't ask me to do this."

"Grace, I'm not here to negotiate this. I've talked with Katharine Greco and Roger Willoughby." She sat straighter as if hearing a strange sound and preparing for danger. "Grace, I know."

She stood, carrying the glass to the window with her, leaving her back to me. Staring outside she sipped at the drink. I waited. Answers were not forthcoming. I wasn't prepared to wait much longer.

"I could never have children," she said, her back still to me. "So I threw myself into my work. I specialize in bodyguarding children and families as opposed to corporate bigwigs and their mistresses. The job is not without many perks including traveling the world."

"What about the pitfalls? You love him, don't you?" I said as gently as I could.

Sounds of emotion emanating from Grace Rusinko were now audible. "Yes, I came aboard just after he got here. He was still reeling from his mother's death. He needed a mother figure and I needed to be one. What's the harm in that, Malone? We each had needs that got filled."

"You know the first cardinal rule of being a bodyguard is that we aren't supposed to get emotionally attached to our assignments."

"And you never have, I'll bet?" Her tone was accusatory. It would serve no purpose to answer her, but I had done exactly that back when I was guarding Susan, many years ago.

"How did you get in so deep?"

She sighed. "Mothers protect their children. We would have long talks about the future, his hopes and dreams. He wanted to rule Laracone."

"To get even with his father?"

"In part, I guess it started out like that. But I think it evolved into other reasons. He didn't feel that his father loved him. He saw how the people of his country adored Benjamin Walanna. He wanted that for himself, to get from the people of Laracone what his father couldn't, or wouldn't, give him."

"Walk me through this, Grace. How did a 13 year old boy manipulate a country to the point where three people were murdered?" I said. Slowly she turned back and looked at me with tear streaked cheeks.

We talked for another hour. She told me all she knew prodded occasionally with questions to keep her on track.

"That's all I know, Malone. What happens now?"

I smiled and stood. "Now, you take me to the prince."

When the guard outside of Prince Gregory's room changed for the lunch shift, Grace took me in to see the prince by telling the new guard that I was the boy's new psychiatrist. We found him lying on his four poster bed, on his stomach, reading a comic book.

"Gregory? I have someone here to talk with you."

Gregory sprung to his feet. He was scared I was there to take retribution. Grace ran over and encircled him with her arms.

"Don't worry darling. I won't let him hurt you."

I was the epitome of cool, or at least I tried to be. I sat in a nearby, overstuffed winged back leather chair with studded arms, crossing my legs like Sherlock Holmes, making a tent of my fingers against my closed lips.

"I don't want to talk to him. He killed those three people." Gregory didn't need cue cards for this performance.

"Give it up Greggy. I talked with Katharine and Roger and now Grace. I know it all. Drop the adolescent angst. You want to run Laracone? Start by owning up to your responsibilities. I've read Machievelli too."

The prince would really have been shaking in his boots if he knew that I read Tony Kornheiser, Robert B. Parker and Charles Schultz as well.

"Have a seat." I indicated the other wingback chair across from me. "Or aren't you man enough?"

If I didn't know better, I would have said I was dealing with multiple personalities. Gregory Walanna squared his shoulders and adopted what I'd call a regal bearing, walked over and sat in the chair. It was amazing to watch. The next thought in my head was, now what? I plowed ahead anyway.

"Do you have to read me my Miranda rights? I saw that on NYPD BLUE. They give suspects their rights," he said.

"I'm not a cop. But I'll run them by you, if you wish."

He shook his head and said that wouldn't be necessary. Gregory then accepted the offer of Grace's hand for support. She was seated on the floor next to his chair, like a lady in waiting. I found myself wondering how motherly she had gotten.

"Tell me why you concocted this plot to get yourself kidnapped. What possessed you to seek a quarter of a million dollars ransom? And what did you hope to gain by all of this?"

Gregory thought for a moment. His brow furrowed just like a king's. "You must understand the politics of my country, Malone. When we were a monarchy, the people looked up to my father. Once he transformed us into a democracy, it all began to break down.

"There might be benefits of being a democracy, but there are also pitfalls. The press runs to any extreme and prints whatever they wish about you, regardless of its veracity. No longer are decisions made and carried out. A committee or a task force studies them. Newspapers write editorials about the wisdom of your decisions and usually disagree. The people no longer believe in the sanctity or wisdom of their leader. Dissension is rampant."

It had been a very long time since I heard someone younger than the Dali Lama use the word veracity in a sentence. "I'm not registered to vote in Laracone, even by absentee ballot. Cut the rhetoric and tell me why the plot?"

Quicker than the snap of my finger, Gregory switched from idealist to pragmatist.

"The plot was my idea to force my father to return the monarchy to Laracone. Then I would succeed him eventually."

"Immortality complex?"

He snuffled a smirk. "Hardly. I prefer to believe that I would have studied and learned by watching my father and other world leaders how to, or more importantly, how not to govern. My people could only benefit from such a dedicated education."

I took note of the term, 'my people.' Then he surprised me.

"The kidnapping wasn't the first thing we tried. Oh no, Malone. There was a method to this madness. First, we started with the drive by shooting outside the consulate."

"Andrew and Jacob did that?" I said as matter of fact as I could manage.

"Yes. They are loyal subjects who want the monarchy back as much as I do." Gregory was really enjoying this give and take.

"Loyal subjects does make it simpler than hiring unknown thugs to do your shooting."

He pointed a finger directly at me. "And I know what you are thinking. That police officer getting shot was strictly an accident.

I've made sure his hospital bills and family were taken care of, though discreetly."

"Benevolent despot, no doubt."

I had struck a nerve. "Do not mock what you clearly do not understand." His tone was angry, sharp. He didn't like being trivialized. I didn't care what he didn't like.

"Let's skip to where you were at the factory. You <u>were</u> there, weren't you?"

"Yes. That was part of my plan. We thought the motel was too much in the public eye. The authorities were getting too close. We all went to the factory. I knew it was abandoned and that the police patrols in that area were few and far between."

"How did you know that?"

"Roger and I hacked into the police computer where the patrol routes are kept. We may have been amateurs, but we weren't stupid."

I moved from the chair to right in his face. "Then tell me how three people got murdered in cold blood? Explain which part of your master plan was that?"

"Of course it wasn't part of the plan. I feel quite bad about that."

"You hold it in well. Convince me Gregory," I said. Then I straightened up and started to pace in my controlled ranting mode. "Convince me that those three people weren't just expendable for the cause. You could have kept all of the money for yourself. You and Katharine Greco or Grace maybe?"

"You bastard. Hold it Malone. He is only 13 years old," said Grace, barely moving a muscle to do so. I also didn't care what she thought.

"That only means he'll be tried in juvenile court. Well Prince Gregory?"

"Whatever you may think of me, Malone, I am not a monster who thrives on bloodlust to achieve his goals."

"Some felonies are good, some bad?"

"I did not kill those people. Why would I? If I did it for the money, why wouldn't I have taken it with me?"

"Maybe you panicked. The rumor is that you're only 13 years old."

He seemed offended. "Leaders don't panic."

"Pardon my ignorance. How did you get from the factory to 'being found'?"

"I was kidnapped." I couldn't stifle a smirk. "Laugh if you will, but it was the truth. When Deidre came in to get me I heard voices. People came in, wearing hoods. I first thought it was the police. But they grabbed me, put duct tape around my wrists and mouth and a hood over my head. Then they put me in a truck, on the floor on my side in the back and drove away. Believe me, Malone, when I left those three people were still alive."

"You didn't see me or hear any gunfire?"

"No."

"Then what?"

"They drove me around for a long time, maybe a couple of hours. Finally, they took me somewhere and put me in a room and tied me to a cot. It was cold there. After a long time, someone came back in and untied me, cut the tape from my wrists and re-tied me with rope or clothesline."

"Any idea why?"

He shook his head. "No, but they didn't do a very good job. I was tired of being a hostage. I figured the worst they could do was to kill me. I got my hands untied easily then took off the hood and the tape off of my mouth.

"Next, I opened the window and climbed out. I was in the basement of a house somewhere."

"Would you remember it if I took you back there?"

"No. When I got out I didn't look back. I'm sorry."

"Any idea who the hoods were?"

"No," he said. The composure of royalty was beginning to soften. "They didn't speak during the time that they had me. After I escaped, I ran into some people calling themselves, um…"

"Warriors of the Night?"

"Yes, I think so. They called their boss, a Mr. Meadows, then took me back to the consulate."

I sat back down and finished my Pepsi that was now watered down with melted ice chips.

"Anything else, your highness?" For the moment, I put away the verbal blackjack.

"There is one thing. I'm not sure if this means anything." He walked over to his desk and opened a drawer. Then he pulled out a locked box, unlocked it with a combination and removed a piece of something. He came back over and dropped it into my hand. "Does this mean something? I found it on the floor in the room they kept me in after I was taken from the factory."

I looked down and saw a broken half of a cufflink with one saber. A defense lawyer would get it barred in a heartbeat. It did nothing more than cement suspicions of mine, but that was enough.

"Why didn't you take this to the police?"

"I'm not stupid, Malone. If I did, then they might find out that I set up the first kidnapping or the drive-by shooting. You say that you talked with Katharine?"

"Yes."

"How is she?"

"As well as can be expected considering the mess that she's in," I said.

"Can you get a message to her?"

"I can try. What's the message?"

"Tell her that I didn't lie when I asked her to be my queen. Tell her that, all right?"

"I'll see what I can do. Grace, can I talk with you?"

"Of course," she said, now standing, but the trust between us had been broken in her eyes. I wasn't sure if I blamed her for thinking that. Her sitting beside Prince Gregory like Barbie Concubine would make me look askance at anything that might come out of her mouth in the future.

"Gregory, go powder your nose." I said. The heir apparent left the room for the sanctity of the bathroom. "If I'm right, the prince is still in jeopardy. Those people who kidnapped him from the factory and killed your friends don't like to leave witnesses behind. I know that for a fact. Now, they don't know that the Prince doesn't know who they are, but they might not be willing to take that chance."

"So what do you suggest?" said Grace.

"A road trip."

Under the cover of night, in a field just beyond the county of Onondaga border, the caravan was formed including a mini-van and two security cars. The hospital was lowered on my list of priorities one more time. I knew, in this case, Nellie would have approved.

A minimum of effort was expended before it was time to send them on their journey. I gathered the principles together. A lone flashlight illuminated our faces.

"We all on the same page now?"

One by one the faces surrounding me nodded. First, Tom Otera in the lead security car, then Andrew and Jacob in the follow-up security car signaled their agreement. Grace and Gregory then each also nodded in turn. That only left my brother, Anthony.

"You ready Little Brother?" I asked.

"Yes. And while Gregory is at my house, I'll give him a full dental work up free of charge. A full series of X-rays, impressions, cleaning and maybe removal of any amalgam that he might have."

"Tony, I want to save his life, not battle gingivitis. But thanks for letting him stay at your place until I can get this squared away."

"That's what families are for. Stay well, Ross. Roberta and Chris will stay with Mom and Dad until I get back."

"Fine. Okay, let's rock and roll."

I stood back as the three-vehicle caravan rolled onto the highway and made a beeline for the nearest Thruway on ramp.

Slowly, I walked back to my car, checking my gun on my hip for readiness. I slammed the car door shut and stepped on the gas.

It was time to settle accounts.

-29-

For the next few hours, I tried to amuse myself and not think about the caravan to Rochester to get the prince out of harm's way. I seemed to be inordinately nervous about the whole thing, even though I trusted all concerned, except Grace Rusinko, as I still thought she would do anything to protect the prince. Two and a half-hours dragged on into what seemed like four hours before I started pacing while waiting for the all clear.

Nellie would understand. At least, I hoped she would. The phone rang.

"Malone."

"We've arrived and hunkered down. I'm on my way back," said Deputy Otera. "Wait for me Ross, before you do anything stupid."

"Tom, thanks for the offer, but I don't need any help being stupid. I'll talk with you later." I hung up the phone. It rang almost instantaneously.

"Malone."

"I will try to say this calmly Ross, but you had better listen." It was Susan, and I could sense that she was grinding her teeth with every word she uttered. "I don't know what's going on with you, but I really dislike hearing about things from beat reporters, when I should be hearing them from you."

"Beat reporters?"

"I've tried for the last couple of days to get a hold of you and the closest I could get was the answering machine. So I called Lucas Gentero to get a message to you, only to find out that you are now the prime suspect in a triple homicide; the boy prince who was found had nothing to do with you finding him and, that your townhouse was burned to the ground. Did he leave anything out?"

"Susan. What can I say? I'm sorry."

"I won't interfere in your work and you have given me the space to do my job, but my job doesn't involve murder or arson or kidnapping." She was losing steam which was good, because I didn't think I could stand much more of this long distance lecture, regardless of her good intentions. "However, I do expect you to tell me the big things. I've earned that Ross, dammit, I've earned that."

"Susan?" I waited for her to continue but instead of words I heard crying. "I'm sorry for not telling you. Even though I didn't want to worry you, I was wrong in keeping it from you. It's just that I'm dealing with a helluva lot right now."

"Ross, I thought we were in this together."

"We are. Sue, look, for what it's worth, I didn't kill those three people; the prince masterminded his own kidnapping, and as for the townhouse? I was thinking of asking you to move in with me anyhow."

Sue Abilene laughed loud and deep. "Now I know you've lost it. Sorry sweetie, we couldn't afford the increased insurance premiums. I've got to run. Stay safe, Bubba. Forever and then some?"

"Forever and then some," I said. "Love you."

"Bye Tootie."

When this was over, I needed to make it up to Susan, for not trusting that she would be all right with whatever I was going through. I didn't think I would have handled it as well, if our situations were reversed. It went on the back burner as I headed out to rattle some cages.

The cars were lined up in rows of two like they were about to board the good ship Noah, or take the green flag at the start/finish line at Daytona. All makes and models were represented. The one common denominator was the crossed sabers decal in a rear or side window. I was about to walk into the lion's den wearing Hamburger Helper underwear.

I didn't care.

The bulletproof valets at the door of the Patterson mansion took me back to the drawing room I'd been in earlier, that might have seated 50,000 for football, 37,500 for basketball and an even 20,000 for hockey in the dead of winter. On this occasion it held about 100 or so Warriors of the Night, give or take a skull and dagger tattoo. At the head of the room holding court were Gardner Meadows and Martha Dowd Patterson. I went by the refreshment table, but refrained. They probably used the Jeffrey Dahmer cookbook for when you had friends over for dinner.

All eyes were riveted on me as I moved through the crowd that resembled the graduating class of Depravity U. Meadows stopped in the middle of his current diatribe and waited to see what I had to say. Martha D. Patterson sat beside him. Meadows had been playing the role of Lord High Minister of Propaganda for all it was worth.

"You're not welcomed here, Malone."

"But I fit in so well." I looked back at the assembled masses. "Just a minute, I'll leave my scruples at the door so we can all be on the same page." A rumble moved through the crowd, it was guttural and meant for me.

"State your business and leave."

I ignored him and directed my comment at his female benefactor. "Did he show you the second videotape I brought him?"

"He did," she said, barely moving her lips.

"And?"

"And what Malone? For all I know, it has been staged or electronically altered. It is certainly no secret Malone that you harbor great ill will towards the City Security Association, and its Warriors of the Night, as well as personal animosity directed at Mr. Meadows."

"Damn. I thought I'd hid it so well."

Meadows came from behind the mahogany dais, stopping right in front of me. His eyes smoldered with the darkness of unadulterated anger at my intrusion in his life, his scheme.

"I think you had better leave."

"I think I don't care what you think."

A slight nod from his head with the double digit priced haircut sent two of the closest Warriors of the Night straight for my back. I was ready for them. Jerking out my Beretta handgun, I rotated my hips, while keeping my feet still and pistol-whipped their faces in succession. They went to the floor, did not pass go and did not collect $200. Not waiting to be jumped by the rest of them, I shoved the gun into Gardner Meadows' face.

"Call off the cretins Meadows, or your next stop is the crematorium."

Gardner Meadows waited as long as he thought I would stand before acquiescing to my order. He did it through clenched teeth. "Stay back...for now."

"Good boy," I said, patting his cheek with my free hand. "Now, I know you have to get back to finalizing your game plan for a Warriors of the Night Theme park, and remember to save me a seat at the nightly book burnings, so I'll get right to the point. Your days are numbered, pal. You and Pavlov's pitbulls have beaten your last victim, soaked up your last extortion payment, and intimidated your last shopkeeper. From now on, I'm going to make it my personal crusade to tear down everything..." I paused and took a final glance back at Martha Patterson. "And everyone, who is with you."

"You're making a big mistake, Malone," said Ms. Patterson.

"Willing to bet Gardner's life on it?" I stepped back; still keeping the muzzle of the Beretta aimed directly at his jugular vein. If he was going to die by my hand, I wanted it to be agonizingly slow. Backing slowly towards the door, I kept watch for any true believers looking to throw themselves onto their swords for the cause.

I continued. "Besides Gardner, I'm going to prove that you, or one of those poster children for ugly, killed those three people and kidnapped Prince Gregory."

"More wild accusations?"

"Hardly. You see the police have a witness, though they don't know it yet. Tomorrow afternoon, I'm going to take the prince down to the Justice Center so he can tell them he saw the faces of the hooded men who took him from the factory. They'll put together a photo array of felons and known scumbags. I'll tell them just to use a Warrior of the Night yearbook. But you know the cops. Anyway, once that happens, the next people knocking on your door will have arrest warrants."

"You're bluffing Malone. The prince didn't see anything."

"Only way for you to know for sure is if you were there. Oops, time's a-wasting. I have to take Benjamin Walanna to the airport. He's returning home to explain this to his people. Greggy will be joining him later. I'd like to say this has been fun. Next time, I'll bring a dish to pass. One more thing."

"What's that?" said Meadows.

"Might as well take my name off your mailing list. Bye, bye."

I slammed the door closed and propped a chair against the handles. It wasn't permanent, but if I hustled my butt as if I were running towards the Golden Arches, I might just have gained enough time to get to my car before the hordes of Gardner Meadows were unleashed. One valet tried to make a last ditch attempt to block my way. Bad move. I kicked him flush in the groin like Pele aiming for the top right corner of the goal net. He folded. I kept moving.

My engine roared to life. My foot pressed downward to renewed urgency upon the accelerator. I headed back home to Kansas, not concerned if Toto had gotten out as well.

There was no moon in the sky imparting onto the grounds of the Laracone consulate an eerie Lon Chaney in the bushes feeling. The lone sounds I heard were intermittent, with long silent pauses interspersed between the cars departing from nearby watering holes, obeying the 2 a.m. closing law though probably flaunting the DWI statutes; tractor trailers delivering their grocery produce in the dead of night so as not to slow the morning's rush of customers, and the occasional siren of a rescue vehicle or police car passing by. There was no human movement on the consulate grounds. In the eyes of the authorities, the immediate threat of the Royal family of Laracone was gone. Therefore, a show of law enforcement muscle was both unnecessary and a decidedly unexpected drain on everyone's finances.

Downsize was their watchword.

No lights were on in the prince's bedroom. I took yet another look outside from behind the drawn bedroom drapes that were the darkest color they could find, and reinforced with Kevlar for maximum protection from stray gunfire. My eyes swept the perimeter of the grounds, all the way to the street and back. I was tired from top to bottom, inside and out. I lay down on the floor next to Gregory's bed, keeping it between me and the balcony doors. Maybe they wouldn't come.

My trip to the Patterson Estate was made solely to entice Gardner Meadows to make that fatal mistake of wanting to tie up loose ends. His phrase from the tape when he beat Nellie reverberated through my head until my head hurt. "No witnesses," he had said. I was counting on him being true to his word.

My hope was that Meadows would dispatch some of his flunkies to kill the mannequin I had arranged in Prince Gregory's bed. Then I would capture them; they would talk; and Meadows would become just another number you couldn't call collect.

Time seemed to have stopped. My mind drifted, no longer able to fend off the images of Nellie Archer and what I had to do, what I must do. Sadness became my mood of choice. I promised myself that come sunrise I would go to Mercy Hill Hospital and take care of business, with no more excuses and with as little remorse as possible.

After that was over...suppose I guessed wrong and Meadows didn't take the bait? Suppose that I really was on the hook for the three murders? They might not be able to prove it, but my career as a private investigator would be shot to pieces. I wouldn't even be able to get a job as a security guard in a warehouse full of Sing and Snore Ernie dolls.

Get a grip, Malone, I told myself. I needed to be alert. It wasn't sunrise yet and the prince was safe for the moment. If I failed, the only place he might truly be safe again was in the palace in Laracone. Had I doomed him to that existence? He might have been better trading places with Leonardo DiCaprio and that iron mask, instead of entrusting his safety to me.

My breathing stopped. I thought I heard movement outside the window. I held it for as long as I could, then resumed, taking the shallow lungfuls of air, letting it exit through my mouth in slow, deliberate waves. There it was again, the faint thud of rubber soled shoes against the metal fire escape. The sound was getting closer. Not just one pair of thuds, but at least two. These bozos never did anything alone. I'd show them there wasn't safety in numbers.

They picked the lock with minimum scraping and scratching, but the noise was unmistakable. I'd done it enough myself. Hopefully, I was a little more adept than these idiots were. Slowly, the sliding bedroom door that opened onto the balcony rolled back in its metal track. I'd placed Styrofoam peanuts, spray painted black, in the tract to make a distinct noise in case I had drifted off. They crunched. I heard, and readied myself for the final act. The thought that Meadows had really lost it and decided to come himself was too delicious to entertain.

No, Meadows thought of himself as the mastermind. Masterminds don't put themselves at risk, unless they were desperate. Was he that desperate? I'd soon find out. I heard voices, footsteps of two intruders.

"Get it over with. I don't like the fact that there wasn't guards outside."

"Watch the window," said the second voice. "I'll do it with my knife."

I did a quick silent count to ten, going by twos, and raised up in time to see a knife being raised to stab the mannequin. I let it plunge in once for legal reasons, but when it was raised for a repeat performance I bolted upright and grabbed the descending wrist and jerked it towards me. Luckily, the body followed and he screamed in surprise.

His body slammed onto the carpet next to me. I rolled on top of him quickly to neutralize his threat. I pulled my gun and jammed it into his ribs.

"Let it go," I said, as my free hand struggled to keep the blade from my body. He screamed louder and thrust the knife with his last ounce of energy into my shoulder. I pulled the trigger, almost on reflex. He went slack. There was no time to dally, less time to bleed. There was still the matter of the other invader. I rolled over onto my back ready to be assaulted. Without the attack immediately forthcoming, I scrambled to my feet to see the second thug heading out the window.

I pulled the knife out of my shoulder, wincing at the serrated edge slicing through my flesh as much as on it's path of entry, then tossed it aside. I ran for the balcony and barely missed grabbing the fleeing felon as he continued down the fire escape.

I was getting good at doing things with a minimal amount of thought, so I mounted the wooden balcony and took flight downward, aiming directly for the body on the fire escape. My arm encircled his neck and ripped his body from the ladder. We crashed to the ground in a heap. The adrenaline was pumping at breakneck speed through my body. I pulled my freshly fired weapon and got on top of my prey.

"Jesus Christ! I think I broke my leg. What the fuck did you do to me?"

I pulled the mask off and reacquainted myself with my old friend Chuck.

"What the fuck did I do to you? I probably just saved your life, asshole. Your buddy's dead, and you could follow him to scumbag Valhalla if you don't start telling me what I want to know." I jacked another shell into the firing chamber for effect.

"You can't shoot me in cold blood. That's murder."

"I'm already on the hook for three I didn't commit. They can only execute me once."

"I thought I asked you to wait, Malone."

"Never said I would, Deputy Otera," I said.

Chuck's eyes looked at Tom Otera, in his deputy's uniform, as his savior. "I surrender Deputy. Get this madman off of me. He's going to kill me."

"I see no evidence of that. Besides, I'm technically off duty tonight. If I was on duty, then I might be able to restrain this citizen from making an arrest or taking your miserable life."

"You're in this with him?" said Chuck. "You're a cop. I'm surrendering to you. You've got to arrest me."

"I haven't seen you do anything wrong. I'm much better at arresting people who confess to something, or to many things."

I smiled wider. "You're out of luck, asshole. Maybe you can room with Ted Bundy when you get to hell." The cold muzzle of my weapon started to press deeply into his cheek.

Chuck lost whatever semblance of manhood or dignity he had remaining which surely wasn't much to begin with. The smell that emanated from his lower loins was proof of that.

"I'll confess. I'll confess."

"Not without hearing your Miranda rights."

"Then give me my fucking rights before he kills me," he screamed.

Tom looked at me then, after my nod, he recited the Miranda warnings. "Now you can confess. But none of this misdemeanor crap. Either confess to felonies or you're wasting my time."

"How about triple murders? That's right. Franco and I were ordered to follow Malone just in case he found the prince before we did. We followed him to the factory and found the prince. It was Meadows' idea to frame him for the murders. No witnesses, just like that broad PI at the store. Franco coldcocked Malone. We dragged him into the abandoned factory and shot all of those people by placing the gun in his hand and pulling the trigger by pressing his finger against it so the blowback would be on his hand.

"Then we took the prince to another section of town where only we patrolled. He was allowed to escape and then Meadows sent us to 'find' him so we could get the publicity."

I sat upright. "So I didn't kill those people? Damn. I guess since I didn't kill them; I can't kill you. Here Deputy, he's all yours."

I got up off of Chuck and let Tom handcuff him. I holstered my gun and started to walk away. A few feet away, I half turned my head back towards Tom.

"There's a body in the bedroom. I'll call you later."

"Malone, are you all right?"

"No."

I kept walking.

-30-

"Are you ready, Ross?" said Colleen Powers, holding a folder full of papers that I needed to read and sign.

"Yes," I said, with a very dry throat that made it into two syllables. I had gone home to Susan's, showered, shaved and put on my charcoal Grey three-piece suit with a thin pinstripe running vertically from the top down.

All in all, I put my name to close to twenty documents from insurance forms to hospital required forms to organ donation forms to releasing of the body afterward to a funeral home form. When the last signature was affixed, Colleen offered me coffee.

"No, thank you. I've put this off long enough."

Just as we were leaving the anteroom where the papers were dealt with, two of Nellie's doctors arrived and offered their condolences, shaking my hand, telling me they wished that they had been able to do more. I was polite, even though I was angry deep down inside my gut that they couldn't save her. The truth was, I was angry I couldn't save her either.

The walk back to her cubicle was far too short for my taste. The hospital chaplain entered and gave Nellie Last Rites. I stood by, waiting for the ritual to be over. I had enough guilt for a convention of mothers. The priest also shook my hand before he left.

"Do you want me to stay, my son?"

"No, Father, that won't be necessary. Thank you for coming." He exited through the pulled curtains. The entire cubicle was sealed off from view. Colleen Powers came in. "Could I have a brief moment with her before…"

"Of course. I'll be right outside. Take all the time you need."

"Thanks." What I needed would be brief, what I wanted was something I couldn't have. I wanted a chance to reverse the decision to give this case to Nellie, knowing that by doing it myself I could have saved her life for that much longer.

I placed my hands on hers. Her skin was cooler than I thought. I spoke in whispered tones.

"Well Nellie, it looks like this is it. I'm so very sorry that this happened to you. I know if you were here you'd kick my butt and say it was an occupational hazard, and that you were just grateful I thought you could handle it.

"For what it's worth, I know who hurt you, and they will pay. I promise, on my honor, that they will pay." I paused. I didn't want the moment to end quickly, but I didn't want to degenerate into gibberish. "Good-bye Nellie. I'll miss you."

Slowly, I bent down and kissed her on the lips, hoping for the slightest response, even though I knew there would be none. I undid my tie, unbuttoned my collar and removed my St. Jude medal from around my neck and placed it in her left hand, wrapping the chain around her fingers.

"Hang on to this for me until I get there." I smiled almost involuntarily. "And yes Nellie, I think we'll be going to the same place." I stepped back. "Colleen."

Nurse Powers entered. "You don't have to stay in here for this."

"Yes, I do."

One by one, the machines were shut off, first the ventilator. Bells and whistles instantly sounded the requisite alarms. One by one, they were silenced. A doctor came in and pronounced Nellie Archer expired, which was medicalese for dead. Colleen guided me back to the outside of the cubicle as others went to work doing the necessary things for organ donation.

"May I use your phone?"

"Yes," she said, and pointed to the nurses' station.

I dialed the number I had memorized. "Gwen? This is Ross Malone."

"Thank you for calling," was all Gwen Brolin said before she hung up the phone.

I felt a hand on my shoulder. It was Susan. I practically lunged into her embrace, tough guy image be damned. I needed her.

"Let's go home, Ross."

-31-

Klieg lights were arrayed in semi-circle fashion on the lawn of the Patterson estate. Gardner Meadows and Martha Dowd Patterson were seated on a TV set apparently in the middle of filming something. The moderator seated between them was the former dean of local news people long since retired. As I got closer, I could see the banner behind them proclaiming the Warriors of the Night as the pre-eminent local security force to augment the police.

I walked onto the set during the filming; my sister Chris and Deputy Tom Otera were close behind. Felicity Charles moved to a surveillance point on the opposite side of the set. Her partner, cradling an Uzi machine gun took up station diagonally across from her.

The director yelled cut at my appearance within the range of his camera lens. "We're filming here. Could you please get out of the shot?"

"I could, but I won't. Hi Gardner, Martha. What are you guys doing? I'll bet you're taping an infomercial about what it's like to go to jail for four counts of murder, extortion and, let's not forget arson."

Martha spoke first. She had tired of what she considered my snappy patter. "Malone, this isn't funny. Leave or I'll call the police."

"No need, Marty. I brought them with me." I gestured towards Tom Otera. "I brought the police with me. Think of me as a full service pain in the ass. Now, you can confess for the cameras or call your mega-money lawyers and stall this for a while. If I were you Martha, I'd dump this sleaze ASAP. Cut a deal while there is still one available, Meadows."

He smirked. I caught the image in a nearby monitor. "Why would I want to do that?"

"Because at the moment, you can help yourself. We already have a witness that will testify you ordered the murders at the factory and that you personally killed Nellie Archer. Remember that fuzzy tape? This witness isn't so fuzzy."

Gardner laughed nervously. He was searching his memory banks for what to do and coming up blank. "There is no witness." Bluff was the best he could come up with.

"I would have had two witnesses, but I had to kill one when you sent them to kill Prince Gregory."

"You sent people to kill a mere boy?" I had found Martha's Achilles heel. "I did not approve that. My God, Gardner, I have grandchildren his age."

I jumped into the fray. "And if you don't want to visit them through Plexiglas barriers Martha, you'd better talk. Otherwise, you'll be buried as an accessory and co-conspirator at the very least. They'll freeze all of your assets. And here's the really scary part, consider how you'd look in bulky prison denim with New York State in block letters on your back?"

"Shut the fuck up Malone," said Gardner, still at a loss for a plan. "You can't prove anything."

"Yes, I can. And what's more? I'm going to give you what you want. Coast to coast exposure. Chris?"

My sister stepped up and placed a video camera in front of Meadows and Patterson. "Don't thank me now. It was my pleasure to get this on the air tonight."

The lead story of "The Driscoll Report" that Chris worked for began with the tape from the grocery store. Martha and Gardner watched in horror as their plans started to smolder, and were close to going up in some very serious flames.

"I didn't condone the killing," said the benefactor, cracking first but cutting her losses like a good benefactor knew how to do. "I'll tell you what you want to know."

"The hell you will." Gardner Meadows pulled a gun and grabbed Martha as his hostage. "Let me get out of here, and I'll let her go."

"Let her go and maybe, and it's an iffy maybe, I'll let you live. Maybe." My gun was first out, but not the only one. Meadows backed further away. We matched him step for step. Threats were hurled back and forth. Tom Otera called for a chopper to be on stand by in case Meadows got to a car.

Quickly, the car was behind him. "Stay back and I'll let her go."

Martha had had enough. She swung a hand backwards and clawed at his face. It occupied him long enough for her to get away, but he ducked into the car before any of us could get a clear shot off. I ran forward and latched onto the luggage rack on the rear trunk lid. The car burned rubber as it headed for the highway and I hung on for dear life.

Meadows saw me in the rear view mirror. He jerked the wheel left and right to try to throw me off the back. I wouldn't let go. However, I still could not pull myself up as I felt the stitches in my shoulder get ripped out and the wound start to bleed again in earnest.

I was in no position to shoot out a tire. But I could shoot at Meadows. I aimed my Beretta gun hand as best I could and fired.

The back window shattered, shards flew back past my head. How they didn't get into my eyes, I'll never know. The car swerved left and right. Finally, I looked up and saw Gardner Meadows take serious aim at me. He wasn't watching the road. I was and saw that there was a tree coming up fast. I released my grip and rolled off onto the road and off to the left, as I heard the car crash headlong into that tree. Moments later it exploded in flames. I heard Meadows scream.

I ran over and dragged him out of the burning car while watching the gasoline drip onto the street knowing we had to get away now. The explosion knocked us farther from the scene of the crash.

Meadows spoke between gasps of air. "You should have let me die."

"Told you I had a character flaw."

-32-

Thick gray clouds rolled leisurely along overhead as the priest recited his sermon at the gravesite. I moved closer to Susan, clutching her bare hand more tightly. Joseph Reneau and Shelly Hutton were the other mourners. Gwen Brolin had opted to heal elsewhere, for now. When she was ready, and if she wanted, I promised her I'd return with her.

My mind drifted to the rush of activity over the intervening few days since Gardner Meadows was arrested. Martha Dowd Patterson sent Meadows to the wolves as did Chuck. Neither shed a tear. The latter also gave up the location of the shallow grave George Trask now occupied, having long since outlived his usefulness.

The police rounded up those who were in on hurting Nellie as well as extorting merchants in the city through the activities of the Warriors of the Night. I was now officially off the hook for murder. It felt as good as I thought it would.

Meanwhile, Trevor Bradley had been putting out diplomatic fires right and left as the news organizations were slowly getting wind of Prince Gregory's grab for power. It might have been big news if his father hadn't stepped in and declared that the Prince and all those concerned were covered under diplomatic immunity including Andrew, Jacob, and even Grace Rusinko. Grace was an American citizen. But I'm sure to keep this from being the latest international incident, Trevor caved in on that small point. I also suspected that his father would dole out the needed punishment when they got home to Laracone.

Still, I did wonder if Gregory was going to ask Katharine Greco to go with him. On the homefront, my Dad was still on the mend and both he and my mother had relented and allowed us to hire a live-in nurse for the short term while he recuperated.

Anthony and Roberta headed back to Rochester, for now, to resume their lives and bring up my niece and two nephews. Chris got a huge promotion and was named roving correspondent for "The Driscoll Report." Joe Rhino and I had managed to hurdle another serious abyss in our friendship, at least for now. There were still more to overcome not the least of which concerned murder. We each knew where the other was coming from and respected the other's decisions without compromising our own.

The priest was winding up. I looked down at the coffin beneath the garland of white roses I had picked out especially for Nellie. Gwen had me include a single red rose from her. The ground may have taken Nellie Archer's body, but her spirit would be all around us.

The service was over. The clouds parted and the first rays of sunshine I'd seen in a while melted down from the sky. Susan and I walked slowly back to where the cars were parked.

"When are you going back to Washington?" I said.

"I'm not. I resigned. I told them I had to be with my family," said Susan.

"Pardon me?"

"You and me are family, Bubba. And I wouldn't have it any other way."

"Damn straight."

The sunlight got brighter than it had been in a very long time.

The End

Coming Soon: Ross Malone in KILLER SMILE

An Excerpt

Chapter 1

My blue eyes, recessed behind my designer sunglasses, glared at the rear view mirror for the third time in as many blocks. I brushed my left hand reassuringly against the hard metal comfort of my Glock 9-mm handgun snug against my hip. Usually I carried a Beretta, which felt lighter and was easier to conceal. Tonight's firepower required a bulky New York Jets' jersey, a throwback to their Super Bowl glory days, over black Dockers slacks and canvas shoes, a hundred dollars less than if they had a swoosh.

Another check of the mirror. Nothing. Being a private investigator always necessitated a minimum daily requirement of caution. However, there were times like these where minimum effort could prove fatal.

Someone had been rattling my cage over the past two weeks. Maybe it had something to do with the murder contract still hanging over my head? Benefactor of said contract was local crime czar Lenny Bogardus. At last rumor, the going rate for seeing me dead was $25,000. Like most mob guys who had since moved into management, Lenny was too much of a coward to do it himself.

Out of the corner of my eye, a large yellow school bus flashed into view. I slammed onto the brakes just in time to avoid pile driving the front end of the Burgundy Taurus into the victorious Golden Warrior football team. The skid marks were twice the length of my car. I exhaled with a vengeance and wondered who got the money if I was stupid enough to kill myself.

Up ahead two stoplights, and a wicked right turn, perched the imperial looking Bradley Club. It was brownstone, upscale and the membership fee probably had to include stock options. I parked where it said members only then I threw back my shoulders, tilted up my chin and stuck my nose in the air. I always tried to fit in. The doorman was not a Jets fan.

"I'm sorry, Sir. This is a private club, strictly for dues paying members. Are you a member?" He already knew the answer and I detected the smirk in his tone.

"No, but I aspire to greatness more often than not."

"Get lost."

"Sorry. I need to get in there. You need to try to stop me."

He smirked again. "Try?"

"College boy, you are out of your league. Just tell me one thing. Is Douglas Copely currently in residence?"

"Like I said, get lost."

He spread his feet shoulder width apart and hunched a bit forward, obviously having seen too much professional wrestling in his young life.

"C'mon old man, take your best shot," he said.

Actually, my best shot was one from the gun on my hip, but college boy didn't know that, and I decided it wouldn't be in my best interest to put his scalp on my belt.

I shrugged my shoulders and left. The doorman's gaze followed me until I made the turn around the corner pausing at my car only long enough to pick up my trusty clipboard and a red, white, and blue Priority Mail envelope. Hopping a low hedge, I rang the bell on the delivery entrance to the Bradley Club. A man clad in a starched white chef's blouse and albino stovepipe hat met my insistent ringing with a wearisome look from tired eyes.

"Yeah?"

"I've got a letter for Douglas Copely."

"Take it around front. The doorman will sign for it."

I shook my head, snapping the bubblegum I had added for effect. "No can do. I need Copely's John Hancock. Besides, that bozo in the three piece suit of armor told me to get lost."

The wearisome look transformed into a knowing smile.

"Edward can be a prick when he wants, and he usually wants." The chef paused for a minute then stepped aside. "Second floor, third door on the right. Tell the guy on the door that Mr. Gourmet sent you."

A light went on in my head. "Mr. Gourmet that's right. What's a class act like you need with a society of checking accounts?"

"Cookbook signings and a personalized line of crockpots doesn't match the 50K the club puts in my pocket."

"I'm a drive-thru window kind of guy myself."

Another knowing smile showcased part of that 50k in grand style. "You aren't a delivery guy, are you?"

I shook my head.

"Second floor, third door on the left." He chuckled as he returned to the aromas and textures that had buttonholed him as the poor man's Wolfgang Puck.

The third door on the left, down the second floor hallway, was marked with a brass lion's head knocker that probably transformed into Jacob Marley's head each Christmas Eve. On the other side of the door was a large person. Only his eyes shifted in my direction.

"Letter for Douglas Copely." Meaty hands and a Super Bowl Ring reached for the clipboard. "He needs to sign. Mr. Gourmet sent me." The meaty hands returned to their original position followed by a slight nod of the head that might have been on a neck or just welded to his shoulders.

At the far end of the conference room was a large circular table covered with a black, silk cloth that contrasted against the rainbow stacks of poker chips in front of each of the six players. Some stacks were higher than others.

I glanced back and saw the guy near the door flash three fingers, which I took to mean he was seated three chairs to the left of the dealer. Actually, I had a recent photo of the retired bureaucrat in my pocket. The trail was three weeks old and twisted in my gut like a junkie's ulcer on the first day of methadone. My job had been to find him, in a hurry. I had made it clear to the family that while I would locate him; the decision to return would be his and his alone.

"Douglas Copely? Letter for you, Sir."

Douglas Copely had galloped past forty, white hair stylishly short in the current Julius Caesar mode. He tossed in another blue chip.

"I'll pay twenty to see that inside straight, Marcus." His hands were poised like a receiver. I placed pen and clipboard in them. He signed; handed me a five-dollar bill, then retrieved his cards. He had two pair, aces and jacks. He was ignoring the letter.

"The guy said it was important."

He didn't look at me, but spoke. "So is my getting even before it gets to be my bedtime, young man."

I stepped back into the shadows. The inside straight blew his getting even out of the water. He opened the cardboard container, reading its contents quickly at first.

The letter inside, which I had written, explained that I was a private investigator retained by his family to find him. It said we needed to talk.

Slowly his head rotated until he saw me. "Deal me out boys. Delivery boy, let me buy you a drink."

We moved over to the teak bar, fully stocked from Absolut to Zinfandel. I opted for Pepsi, regular. It was served over ice in a monogrammed tumbler. Douglas had a screwdriver, easy on the orange juice.

"All right Mr. Malone, you've found me. Now what?"

"Best case scenario is that we finish our drinks and I drive you home."

"I can't go back. Not now. Not ever. You don't understand." His knuckles, wrapped tightly around his drink, blanched of all color.

"Mr. Copely, I…"

"No! I can't go back. Did my family tell you exactly why they wanted me back?"

"They said your mother was very sick."

"Sick?" he said, under a sarcastic tone coating his words. "Her doctors gave her six months to live. That was two years ago. The insurance money ran out long ago. Do you know what it is like to keep a death watch?"

I nodded and remembered how Nellie Archer forced me to make that life and death choice for her.

"Didn't you get a visiting nurse or some kind of help?"

"At first, yes. Eventually, they said there was no point in their coming anymore, that there was nothing they could do. I had to bathe her, feed her and keep her as clean as possible. Her kidneys shut down; consciousness was intermittent in the best of times.

Mom had come full circle. Malone, this was a woman who had practically raised us single-handedly now reduced to a fleshcovered bag of bones. The whining got to me. She doesn't know what she's saying but it's like a little child who can't take care of itself. I just can't take it anymore."

"That's a lot for any family to handle."

"No, not family, me. This is all about me. Since all of the money had run out, save for selling the house, I've been appointed not only the primary caregiver, but the only caregiver. My two sisters and one brother live out of town. They have families, jobs, lives and responsibilities. I, on the other hand, am retired, divorced and totally available to move back into the house to take care of my mother."

"You get no relief at all?"

He shook his head and swallowed some more vodka laced orange juice. "What do the kids say? I was there 24/7. When my sisters came back for the birthday party, I went out for ice cream and never went back."

Tension made his voice shake. Suddenly, his hand crushed the tall drinking glass in two. Crimson rivulets decorated his flesh, dripping down his wrist to his watch, then down onto the polished teak surface. The bartender brought a clean towel. I checked the wound. Superficial at best, a franchise medical clinic wouldn't need to crack his deductible to fix it.

"Mr. Copely, Douglas, I cannot begin to imagine what you've gone through, but I am sure that running away isn't the answer. How would you feel if your mother passed away while you were on 'sabbatical'?"

He didn't answer. I continued.

"I'm not a social worker, but I do believe in personal responsibility. To me, that means keeping your word to everyone but especially, to people you love."

"But my family doesn't care."

"Your mother does. My advice would be to go back and face your family. Tell them exactly how you feel. If you want, I'll go with you. Douglas, you know it's the right thing to do."

I gulped the last of my Pepsi to avoid saying anymore. I had this tendency to want to be a full service private investigator.

"What the fuck are you doing here? I thought I told you to get lost." It was Edward, the doorman.

"You did. I just didn't listen. Think of me as moron challenged."

"Guess I'll have to throw you out." I glanced quickly to make sure this was a solo attack. The other guard threw his hands up and backed away. Edward took two steps and reached for my jersey.

With a fluidity of motion that surprised even me, I grabbed his wrist, dipped my shoulder and launched the doorman onto the top of the poker table. The wooden legs snapped and he came to a sliding stop near the fireplace.

The still standing guard spoke quickly. "You'd better leave. I'll clean up."

"Thanks. I owe you." I gave him my business card and led Douglas Copely down to my car.

As I pulled back into traffic, I went back to checking the rear view mirror every few seconds. Caution was my co-pilot.

Six blocks and a U-turn later I spotted the tail. Two cars behind and closing fast.

"Tighten your seatbelt, Douglas. I'm taking a shortcut."

I jerked the wheel to the left and jumped the curb. The car behind me followed suit.

Coming Soon Ross Malone in KILLER SMILE

About the Author

JEFFREY MCGRAW grew up wanting to walk in the ink stained footprints of Arthur Conan Doyle, Raymond Chandler and Dashiell Hammett whose series characters of Sherlock Holmes, Philip Marlowe and Sam Spade excited his imagination. The next wave of inspiration came from John D. MacDonald's Travis McGee, Gregory McDonald's Fletch and anything by Lawrence Block, be it Evan Tanner, Matthew Scudder or a burglar named Rhodenbarr. Then came Sue Grafton's Kinsey Milhone and Robert B. Parker's literate, tough, funny private eye Spenser. To coin a phrase, the game was afoot.

After completing college courses in Criminal Investigation, Special (Homicide) Investigation and Private Investigation, McGraw show-cased his series sleuth Ross Malone in the debut full length thriller, SHOOTING STARR. He also created and wrote the original for audio series, MACE CONNERS ON THE LONG HAUL. His psychological thriller, RELATIVE INNOCENCE was a past winner at the America's Best Screenwriting Competition.

He is currently working on the next Ross Malone thriller entitled, KILLER SMILE.